More Stories FROM THREE BROTHERS

More Stories FROM THREE BROTHERS

DAVID GEORGE,
MICHAEL ALLEN GEORGE,
BUD GEORGE

ARPress
45 Dan Road Suite 5
Canton MA 02021

Hotline: 1(888) 821-0229
Fax: 1(508) 545-7580

Ordering Information:
Quantity sales. Special discounts are available on quantity purchases by corporations, associations, and others. For details, contact the publisher at the address above.

Printed in the United States of America.

ISBN-13:	Paperback	979-8-89356-478-5
	eBook	979-8-89356-477-8
	Hardback	979-8-89356-479-2

Library of Congress Control Number: 2024904586

This Book Is Dedicated To

Sam - Bud's Daughter
Bonnie - Michael's Daughter
Alex - David's Son

These are the people who keep the three brothers going.

Books by the three Brothers

Stories From Three Brothers
More Stories From Three Brothers

Books by Michael Allen George

Horses Lemons And Pretty Girls
More Horses And Pretty Girls
Of Rain Barrels And Bridges
Finding Peri Gray

The Refuge Mystery Series

Contents

Dreams of Albuquerque

By Bud George

They gathered at the door, waiting as Frank walked the isles, turning off the lights, all pull chain fluorescents.

It was still snowing lightly - the last snowfall of the year, maybe.

He stopped to let a bus pass, then slowly crossed the street to the lot his car was parked in. He brushed off the snow on the driver's side door, sat down, choke out full, key on, light touch on the gas, clutch in, touch starter, lovely sound of V8 starting almost instantly. Pleasant slow drive home in very light traffic.

He cleaned up, dressed in the best clothes he owned and left to pick her up. This was to be their last date for a long time. Maybe forever. She told him the previous week that she was leaving soon on a trip to Italy with her mother. She'd been saving for most of a year. This was a surprise to him. At age eighteen, he had thought about a closer relationship with her. Well okay, freedom. His daydreams about a move to Alaska started looking brighter, even possible.

She met him at the door and headed for the car walking fast. "Let's go."

She was not dressed in her usual date night clothes, instead jeans and a high school jacket. Something was really wrong here; she was really pissed at him. Her mother? Some friend? He had no idea. They climbed into the car. She sat with her back to the passenger door, as far away from him as possible.

"Supper? A movie?" he asked.

"Just drive," she said.

It was a beautiful night, snow about done. Every surface, street, sidewalk, and roof were covered in white. He knew the cities well, drove gently, slow, avoiding steep hills, up or down. She rode along silent, not a word. He tried to think of a comment, something to say, a question about Italy. He came up empty. No idea, no way to break the ice or get her to speak.

Instead, he told her about the old man's dreams of Albuquerque. Sitting in his red plastic easy chair with cigarette burns from spilled ashtrays, and his quart bottle of muscatel wine. A hundred and ten in the shade, and no shade. Hitch a ride on a practice flight in a B24. At ten thousand feet, nice and cool. His WWII stories, the best time of his life, great place.

As a twelve year old kid, yeah, a great trip. Drive a jeep to New Mexico, turn around and get on a greyhound and head back north, way north.

Didn't look like there'd be any sweet goodbyes, any I'll write, I'll miss you a lot, have a great trip, see you again soon, I hope.

He parked in front of her house and got out of the car to walk her to the door. She went up one step and turned to face him.

"I am pregnant," she said.

Voyage to Chacmool

By David George

A bullet shattered the cobblestone sidewalk a few feet in front of me. Someone yelled, "*Señor Boggs, ¡agáchese!*" I dropped to the ground at the command as more shots followed. I looked around for the *soldados*. No military uniforms in sight.

No one had called my name. I was no longer in war-torn Guatemala. I was on the campus of South Texas University. The shooting, though, was not imaginary. A backward glance revealed bodies collapsing like marionettes with severed strings.

I sprang up and rushed to a hiding place behind a concrete planter bordering the mall. I scanned the area around me for the shooter's location, then poked my head above the planter. The sniper was shooting from the tower that sat atop the library. Not precisely from the tower. He must be on the observation deck. I should be safe if I stayed behind the concrete planter.

Safe like in the Guatemalan village of Chacmool where I worked as a Peace Corps volunteer in 1982?

The urge to take action was insistent, which was odd because in Chacmool rescuing villagers from the *soldados* hadn't been part of my assignment. Yet now, with bullets raining down on the campus, I left the safety of the planter and ran toward the library. Not exactly ran. Stumbled.

A policeman lay on the concrete near the library entrance. He had a nasty a leg wound. He slipped in and out of consciousness. I hunkered down next to him, trying to rescue from memory my first-aid training as a Peace Corps volunteer. Though my arms trembled, I managed to remove his belt to use as a tourniquet. Seemingly of its own volition, my right hand grabbed his pistol, pushed it into the front of my shorts, and covered it with my shirt. *Armed and ready.* Where had that thought come from? Not from my first-aid training. I dragged the policeman and deposited him inside the library's entryway. I checked to make sure the tourniquet was holding fast. His eyes fluttered open.

"Hang in there, buddy. I'll try to get you some help."

He muttered something inaudible and closed his eyes.

The crowd inside the library was so loud—screaming, crying, cursing—I couldn't make out anything intelligible. Beyond the card catalogues and book stacks a security guard wearing a blue windbreaker stood in front of an elevator.

I approached and spoke to him. "I just pulled in a cop. See? Over there by the entryway. He's got a bad leg wound. Can you call for an ambulance on your walkie-talkie?"

"There's a sniper up in the tower. He'd pick off your EMT in a second."

"But he's hurt really bad."

"Christ almighty. This is a crisis situation. Please move back. I've got to watch the elevator to keep people from going up to the tower," said the guard, "or the shooter coming down. It's turned off."

Chacmool, Guatemala. Is it my responsibility to save the people in the Mayan village? What should I do if the soldados come? Me, a Peace Corps volunteer working on an irrigation project. When the mucky mucks gave me this assignment, they told me in no uncertain terms to keep out of politics and social conflicts. At the first sign of trouble, I'm to abandon my post and return to Peace Corps headquarters in Guatemala City.

I moved back into the stacks and kept an eye on the guard, hoping he'd leave his post. My wish was granted soon enough. He picked up his walkie-talkie and placed it against his ear. He ran toward a library exit sign.

I glanced back toward the library entrance where a small group was tending to the fallen cop.

Was I really going to do what I was thinking? Me, a former Peace Corps volunteer and now a student. My legs were shaking. My facial muscles were tight. It seemed as if my face would crack and shatter like a porcelain doll. Somehow my body moved toward the elevator and entered. After several tries my trembling finger managed to flip the on switch, press the up button, then select floor 17, Observation Deck.

Chacmool. The village elder, Balam, oversees my work on an irrigation system for the maize fields. His daughter Rosalía follows me everywhere. Apparently, I have become her ichan, her honorary uncle. When she asks me, "Are the soldados coming?" she hugs the worry doll that never leaves her side. I have no answer. My assignment in Chacmool is to help with agriculture, not to get involved in politics.

The elevator door closed. I considered the options. It was hard to focus. ***Press the button for another floor. Get out and hide.*** My fists were clenched like claws. The elevator passed the 5th floor, 6th floor. ***A pistol against a high-powered rifle?*** 9th floor, 10th floor. ***No contest.*** 15th floor, 16th floor. ***All I have is the element of surprise.*** The elevator was reaching the 17th floor, which would provide access to the observation deck. I huddled in the corner of the elevator, pistol in hand.

The door slithered open. ***The shooter's waiting for me. Hit the down button. Get the fuck out of here.*** Yet I managed to steady myself with a force of will I didn't know I had.

There was no one in sight. I rushed out and found myself in the reception area, a stairway leading up to the observation deck. No dreaded shooter in view. I faced another kind of dread, a half dozen people lying on the floor, a mass of tangled limbs. Clearly the sniper had initiated his massacre here before shooting from the tower.

The copper smell of blood and the stench of evacuated bowels curdled in my nose. A scene not entirely unfamiliar to me, yet shocking because it was set not in a rainy Guatemalan village but on a university campus.

I checked most of the fallen for vital signs. It took all my willpower to place my hands on their necks to find a pulse. Beneath the body of a woman, I spotted a girl, shredded with bullet holes. I couldn't force myself to touch the child.

Chacmool. The image of a Mayan worry doll flashes before me. Pink, orange, and green strands of wire for the skirt, blue yarn for the bodice, red fibers for the headdress. The doll belongs to Balam's daughter Rosalía. It's a kind of pacifier; I never see her without it.

I had to look away from the child in the reception area. What if any of these victims were still alive and I didn't help them? Try to save someone who was probably dead? Or try to stop the sniper from massacring people below on the campus? My body felt slack, useless. How could I face a sniper with a rifle? I knew my way around a gun from shooting cans off a fence with my dad as a kid. I also knew that my chances against a well-armed sniper in a face-to-face encounter were slim to none. Could I figure out a way to trick him? ***Are you nuts? Get out of here. Guatemala wasn't your war and you made it out. This isn't your war either.***

Yet instead of getting out I sidled past the bodies and looked up the stairway. No one in sight. My heart pounding, I crept up the stairs and stepped on to the walkway between the tower wall and the parapet. I approached the edge. My head felt dizzy, my stomach churned, my legs stumbled backwards. Taking deep breaths, I slowly returned to the parapet and leaned forward just enough to take a quick glance down at the campus mall. People lay in the open. Dead or wounded. There was no way to tell. Others scrambled in search of refuge.

Chacmool. Rosalía almost never leaves my side. Now that I've become her ichan, her uncle, she has become my responsibility. She follows me into the maize fields and observes the progress on the irrigation system. She even tries to help, though only one hand is available, since the other never let go of her worry doll. I enjoy her company. She teaches me phrases in her language, Maya Quiché. Though full of glottal stops and raspy consonants, I find it pleasing to the ear.

Gunfire erupted from somewhere on the tower. Unsure of which direction to take, I moved slowly to the right, toward the north side of the tower, with my back glued to the wall. The sound of shooting decreased in volume, which propelled me in the other direction, toward the south side. As I got closer the gunfire exploded in my ears.

Chacmool. Silence pulls me out of my hut into a night as black as the bottom of a cenote. There's not a sound in the village; the nocturnal creatures are hushed, even the night monkeys. I've been here for several months, and it's never been so quiet. A voice whispers to me, half in Spanish, half in Mayan.

"Ichan Boggs. I'm scared. They took mami and papi away."

I turn on my flashlight. It's Rosalía. She's clutching her Mayan worry doll.

"What do you mean they took your parents away? Who took them?"

"The soldados. I'm so scared. Help me find them, ichan."

A figure loomed, kneeling, his rifle pointing through a gap in the parapet surrounding the walkway. His position afforded a clear view of the campus, looking south toward the Rio Grande Valley. High-powered rifles were stacked next to him. I raised my pistol and took aim, then remembered to check the safety. *Off.* I raised the pistol again. My hand shook and I almost dropped the gun. I tried to steady my right hand with my left. By the time I pulled the trigger the pistol was pointing upward. The sniper's head swiveled toward me. I pulled the trigger again. It made no difference because this time the gun jammed.

The sniper jumped to his feet and began blasting in my direction. A bullet ricocheted off the tower wall above me. I ran back to the observation deck entrance, hesitated, then continued around the tower to the north side. I dropped to all fours and crept back in the direction I had come from. The entrance to the staircase came into view. The shooter was peering down the staircase. He lifted his rifle and fired several shots. He raised his fist in a sign of victory. Did he think he had shot me? The sniper headed back toward his nest.

My mind echoed with, **You can't shoot him. Go down the stairway. Get out while you can.** Instead, I began walking north, in the opposite direction from the stairway. **Go back to the stairs. This is not your war.** I gritted my teeth and continued north, away from the stairway and the sniper.

I stopped to briefly survey the area below. My first attempt to look down brought back the dizzy spell. I took several deep breaths and leaned over the parapet. The view extended all the way to Guadalupana Street, the main drag running along the edge of campus. Shop windows were shattered. Had the sniper been shooting from this side? I held my gaze, my fear of the shooter eclipsing the fear of heights.

A flash somewhere below was followed instantly by a loud crack. A bullet gouged out a small section of the granite wall next to me. My right eye stung from the debris. Rubbing it didn't help. My hand dropped to my waist in search of the canteen I always carried in Chacmool. **Shit. Canteen? Get a hold of yourself, Allen Boggs.**

Dropping to my knees I crawled the few feet to the parapet, steering clear of the gaps in the wall. Someone was shooting from down below. They must have mistaken me for the sniper. I sat with my back against the parapet wall. More shooting came from the south side of the tower. The sniper was at it again.

I glanced down at my pistol. Why hadn't I checked it before I got into this mess? A cartridge was lodged in the chamber. Trying to remove it with my fingers was futile. There was nothing I could do but sit tight for the time being. Or get out of there.

The shooting continued on the south side of the tower. I looked down at my unruly pistol. **Unjam, for god's sake.** Frustration led to banging the gun against the wall to dislodge the cartridge. Stupid, I knew. If only I had a knife. What about the reception area? Inspect the bodies? It didn't occur to me what a ghoulish plan that was.

I crept back to the stairway, keeping a lookout for the sniper. I ran down the stairs, then checked the bodies. A cold chill washed over my body, in spite of the Texas summer heat. In the pants pocket of a young victim was a Swiss Army Knife. After looting the knife, I looked down at the young man and apologized, as if that would redeem the grave robbery.

Back up the stairs. **Stop. Save your ass. Get the fuck out of here.** My body refused to obey my mind. I rushed up and took a wary glance to the left. The sniper was still at it. I moved in the opposite direction to get as far away as possible, in the hope the shooter wouldn't stray far from his nest. I sat down, took out the knife, and pulled open the pliers. Bad choice. Next, I tried the blades one by one and finally hit on the right one. The cartridge popped out of the chamber. I pocketed it.

Chacmool. Rosalía grabs my arm with one hand and with the other holds tight to her doll. I let her lead me. Where are we going? Burning huts light up the center of the village. We stop behind a tree when we see a soldado standing in front of Rosalías's family hut.

A bullet ricocheted off the top of the parapet. The sniper had not forgotten me. A hulking figure shuffled into view reloading his rifle.

"Hey!" I yelled. Why did I warn him? Stupid.

The shooter looked up and saw my pistol pointing at him. He twirled around and darted out of my line of sight. I chambered a round and ran after him, passing the stairway that led to the newly created tomb. Around the next curve in the tower wall the sniper was facing me and in the process of raising his rifle. I took a wild shot, rushed back to the entryway, and flew down the stairs. Once again among the victims, I positioned myself so if the sniper came down, I'd have a clean shot. I crouched to make myself smaller.

Chacmool. Curled up with Rosalía in an irrigation ditch on the edge of a maize field on the outskirts of the village, we're surrounded by soldiers. Bullets buzz like deadly flies over our heads. I've been warned about the evangelical dictator Ríos Montt's campaign to exterminate the Mayan villagers because he considers them heathens, undeserving of the right to life, not to mention liberty and the pursuit of happiness. But I never thought his genocidal campaign would reach us in this remote location. This is not what I signed up for when I joined the Peace Corps, yet how can I abandon these people who have come to accept me almost as family?

Rosalía tugs at my jacket sleeve. "Ichan Boggs, mi muñeca, they're going to shoot her. I have to go get her." This is the first time I've seen Rosalía without her worry doll. It's my fault. I pulled her away from the village when the soldados began shooting. She must have dropped it during our escape.

"Rosalía, we can get your doll later. But now we have to stay here. We have to hide until the soldados go away."

She jumps up and runs back toward the village. I try to stand up and go after her, a bullet grazes my head, and my body goes limp. I remain immobile until dawn. The shooting stops. I stand unsteadily and look around, walk back to Chacmool, and approach Rosalía's family hut. Lying in the doorway is her worry doll, shredded with bullet holes.

As I now stood among the victims near the elevator, I pondered my role as a Peace Corps volunteer during the Guatemalan civil war in 1982, just over a year ago. I thought about Rosalía and her family. As far as I could ascertain, they were buried in a mass grave on the outskirts of Chacmool.

The siren call of the stairway urged me to climb back up. Once on the walkway I halted. I was calm, no dizziness. I leaned over the parapet wall and took a slow, deep breath. Should I head left toward the sniper's nest or right for a rearguard action? Left it would be. The sniper was back in his nest. I took careful aim. Could I do this? Kill another person? I slowly raised the pistol and tried to squeeze the trigger. My finger refused to obey. I closed my eyes to summon Rosalía, the doll, the victims by the staircase. Nothing. Just a blank screen. I opened my eyes. The sniper's head was turning toward me. I squeezed the trigger and fired. The shooter's body seemed to deflate, then shuddered as I emptied the gun into him. The bullets spent, I detected no movement but couldn't bring myself to approach. I was afraid I'd throw his body over the side, as if killing him once wasn't enough. Once for the sniper's innocent victims and again for Rosalía and her family. My family.

Time to go. I collected the casings ejected from my pistol, returned to the elevator, and rode it down to the third floor. I looked around and saw only book stacks. To avoid detection, I took the stairs to the first floor. I hoped to remain anonymous, to resume a normal life. No publicity, no 15-minutes-of-fame, no hero-of-the-day notoriety. Would the guard I spoke with before taking the elevator up to the reception area finger me as the executioner?

The gunfire had stopped. The sniper was dead. Medical personnel tended to the wounded, corpses were carted off, and crowds of dazed students and faculty wandered around the campus.

I washed out my eye, still stinging from the debris. The next order of business was wiping the wounded policeman's pistol clean of fingerprints and depositing it in a bush near where I had found him. The shell casings I had collected were stashed in my pants pocket. Hopefully no other incriminating evidence would place me in the tower.

What about the fact that I had killed a man? Shock began to set in. I knew it would get worse.

I set out toward home on my Vespa. The wind whisked away the final scene of my own private war that had begun on my voyage to Chacmool.

The Great Potato Pick

By Michael Allen George

I was only working for the Slaters a couple of months when they made their annual visit. The three migrant farm workers. Their visit was only annual in that every year there were three of them. Always from Mexico. And always, they were there for three weeks.

"You won't find better workers anywhere," Steve Slater told me when they arrived.

I didn't know anything about them, so I didn't answer his comment. I thought though, that they didn't look like anything special as workers. They looked like ordinary working men to me. Jose was the oldest, close to forty maybe. Miguel was a little over thirty. Carlos, the youngest, wasn't much over twenty.

The first day, whenever we were anywhere near each other, all we did was exchange stares. Even so, it didn't take me long to realize what good workers they were. Whatever the task was, they simply did it. They never made a negative comment about the work, no matter how difficult or heavy it might be.

It was about the middle of the third day that we started to get acquainted. I commented about something unpleasant they were doing. Even though they didn't speak English and I didn't speak Spanish, they picked up on what I said from my tone of voice. All three laughed and shook their heads yes.

Our ability to communicate grew from there. I found myself enjoying the time I worked with them on the rare occasions I did. They were a friendly bunch, and the day they invited me to eat lunch with them, is still a day I like to remember.

Jose was the cook. The meal he served was a bit strange, and it also was the same meal he cooked at noon everyday they were in the United States working from farm to farm.

He started with regular egg noodles, which he fried, unboiled, in a cast iron frying pan, using plenty of lard. Once it was nicely fried, he added some water, and whatever vegetables were available. In this case it was carrots, potatoes, and radishes, which were the Slater's crops.

I think Jose added some herbs and spices, because the food actually tasted pretty good. I never got tired of it. I only ate it in small portions. The bulk of my lunch was always the sandwiches I brought from home. I offered to share them a couple of times, but was always turned down. They seemed to be unsure of the food I ate.

One of the days I'd planned to eat with them, Mrs. Slater came out and invited me to eat with her, Steve, and their son, Kenny. Not sure what the right thing to do was, I accepted her invitation. I instantly saw the looks of distrust from the three. I knew their welcoming me to their table wasn't something they normally did, and eating with the Slaters instead of them, did not send them a good signal. I knew then that the smart thing to do would have been to turn down the invitation from Mrs. Slater.

I didn't say much when we sat down to eat. I just took out my sandwich and quietly chewed away. Steve and Kenny pretty much ignored me. Mrs. Slater noticed my discomfort, but didn't comment until I put my second sandwich away.

"Not much appetite?" she asked as I did.

"No. I'm just not hungry today."

"That's too bad. I was going to offer you some of our fried chicken."

"Thank you. I appreciate it," I said. But I thought, "you could have offered it before I ate my sandwich."

"Well, maybe next time," she said.

"If there is one," I thought. I nodded toward her in answer to her comment.

A short time later I excused myself and left the table, glad to escape the somewhat strained atmosphere. Outside wasn't much better. So for the rest of the day I did my best to ignore everyone and just do the work that needed doing.

Things got better as the week wore on, even if I purposely ate my lunch alone every day. Then Friday, Steve asked me to do him a favor.

"The guys," he said, "would like to go to town and do some shopping tonight. Would you mind taking them? I'm going to be busy. And if you will, I'll pay you your regular hourly wage for the time you spend with them."

"Sure, no problem," I agreed. What I didn't tell him is that he didn't have to pay me. I'd have been glad to help those guys out.

Even though they no longer seemed to have total trust in me after the lunch incident, they were pleased it was me taking them.

When we started out, I expected it to be a simple shopping trip. That wasn't to be. The area around Slater's farm had several vegetable growers. All of them used migrant farm workers, nearly all of them Mexican. For reasons no one could ever explain to me, most of the retail store owners in the local town hated and feared the Mexicans.

I didn't go in with them at their first stop. It was a western wear shop, and they wanted to buy western style hats. They'd no more than gone in there when I heard a loud, scolding voice inside. Jose answered the voice in Spanish, but he was shouted down. So I went inside.

"Is there a problem?" I asked the lady doing the shouting.

"There certainly is," she growled, sounding like a cross between the nasty old lady she was, and a sick dog.

"So, what is it?"

"These people were going to put hats on their heads."

"Isn't that what people do when they want to buy a hat? Try it on to be sure it fits."

"We don't allow their kind to handle any of the clothing. Not even the hats."

"How are they supposed to find a hat that fits then?"

"All the hats are sized. They should know their hat size." That was enough for me. There had to be a better way. So I convinced them to wait on most of their shopping. It was difficult with the language barrier, but I somehow told them we'd do the shopping on Sunday.

I knew that people in most of the shops liked to intimidate the Mexicans, just because they were different. They also had a tendency to overcharge them. Something I really didn't like. So I quickly formulated a plan to turn things around. At least for Jose, Miguel, and Carlos.

I called my two brothers. Alex, my older brother, stood six feet four, weighed around two hundred pounds, and didn't have an ounce of fat on him. He managed the produce department in a giant supermarket, and worked extremely hard everyday.

Sandy, my younger brother was only six feet tall. He was a college professor, teaching Spanish, which he spoke fluently. He didn't work hard physically, but he worked out on a regular basis. He carried the kind of body that said, "Don't even think about messing with me."

I was six feet two inches tall, worked hard, and was in decent shape. I knew that any clerk with an attitude, would likely change it when they were facing the three of us standing together.

Our first stop Sunday was the western wear shop. We let our Mexican friends go in ahead of us. We joined them with the first raised voice. It was the same old lady, barking at our friends.

"Is there a problem?" I asked.

"You know there is. They were messing with the hats again. You know we don't allow their types to do so."

I picked up a hat and put it on my head. It didn't fit, so I took it off. "That's all they want to do." I said. Then I picked up another hat, bent it several ways before putting it on my head, and rejected it because it didn't fit. "Now," I said, "my brothers and I might be interested in new hats. It might take a while to find the right ones."

Sandy picked up a hat then, did his best to reshape it, and put it on his head. It didn't fit, so he put it back. When Alex reached for a hat, she relented.

"Okay," she agreed, "they can try on the hats. But please, no bending."

We used similar tactics with other people who objected to them shopping in their stores. The fact we needed to pissed me off to no end. All the guys wanted to do, after they bought their hats, was to buy clothing and other items to send home to their wives and kids. All but Carlos, who wasn't married yet.

When they finished shopping, we stopped for a beer at one of the local bars. We got the same game there. They didn't want to serve Mexicans.

Since it was a very quiet Sunday, there were only a few customers in the bar to get involved in any dispute we might have with the bartender or waitress. When they refused service, Alex walked to the bar.

"I want six beers," he told the bartender. "You gonna refuse me service too?"

"You'll just give three of them to them damn Mexicans."

"What I do with them, is none of your concern. So serve me, or you won't like what we might do to your bar."

Sandy and I left our chairs then, and stood, staring at the bartender. He served the beer. We only drank one each, and left with the thought in mind that we'd never again go into that bar. They apparently didn't need our business, and we definitely didn't need their bullshit.

Our next stop was our father's small grocery store, to pick up a few last minute items for lunch. While Alex shopped, Sandy explained that the guy at the cash register was our father and the owner of the store. After that, all three of them were nervous around Dad.

In Mexico, people at their level in society didn't mix with anyone at a high enough level to own a store. So they were glad to be out of there when we left.

Our last stop was Alex's. His wife, Geri, prepared a beautiful Sunday dinner. Fried chicken, and a lot of it, was at the top of the list. Added to that was baked potato, fresh green salad with several dressings to choose from, and broccoli and cauliflower in cheese sauce.

We thought we were giving them a real treat, especially the mounds of fried chicken. We were wrong. They were all close to being vegetarians. At their economic level, they could afford very little meat. Since they weren't used to it, their bodies couldn't handle it beyond small portions.

Sandy asked them why they weren't eating much of it. When they explained, he told the rest of us. It made sense, so we quit staring at them for not eating the way we expected.

They did eat their fill though. Salad and baked potatoes, with just a little butter, did it. Even the vegetables in cheese sauce was too rich in any quantity.

It proved to be a nice visit anyway. And interesting in many ways; one of the more interesting things was their curiosity about us. They couldn't understand how I, a simple farm worker like them, could have such rich relatives. Alex lived in a big house, drove, to them, a fancy van, and could afford to eat like a rich man. Sandy spoke Spanish and was highly educated, and our father owned a grocery store. That kind of diversity didn't happen in their world.

So after that Sunday, even though we got along as well as ever, they tended to look at me with a lot of curiosity. That look grew even more while I picked potatoes with them, and never lessened after those two days.

It happened when Steve hit a spot when he didn't have any work for me. So he put me to work picking potatoes. "Don't try to keep up with the Mexicans," he said. "You can't and I don't expect you to. They get paid by the bag. You'll get paid by the hour, the same as always. So don't worry about how much you get done. It's just fill in work."

Almost all the potatoes were picked with a combine, which dug them out of the ground, more or less separated the potato from the plant, and dumped the potatoes onto a truck.

The problem was they needed some potatoes to fill an order and the combine operators weren't yet available. So they dug the potatoes with an old fashioned digger. It only dug the potatoes and dropped them on the top of the ground. It was our job to pick them up.

To start the process, we walked down the picked rows, and periodically dropped an empty, one hundred pound, burlap potato sack. We picked the potatoes from the ground into a wire basket, then dumped the basket into the burlap sacks as we came to them. Each sack, when filled, weighed about fifty pounds. The Mexicans were paid by the sack. I figured it would take about twenty sacks to match my hourly rate.

I didn't have anything beyond getting through the day planned when I started picking. I knew that being bent over all day was going to kick hell out of my back, and stretching muscles I rarely used was going to end up painful, no matter how slow I took it. But when all three of them moved down the first row well ahead of me, I didn't like it, even if it was what everyone expected.

I'd already decided it was okay if they picked more than I did. They were in shape for the work. I wasn't. Still, I found out I could keep up if I pushed it some. As the day wore on, it became obvious Carlos was going to pick the most, Miguel would be second, Jose third, and me dead last.

I don't like being last, so I decided to keep up with Jose. Doing so was easier than I thought it would be. So I caught up with Miguel. When he noticed I was, his look of surprise was something special. It was accompanied with a grin. And that inspired me.

I pushed some more and caught up with Carlos. His look when he saw me was more shock than surprise. But he shook his head as if to say, "This isn't going to last. Americans can't really do this kind of work."

The look he gave me bugged me some, so I hung in there with him. All day. I had the luxury of a watch, so I knew when it was close to quitting time. I was still even with Carlos so I decided the hell with it. I didn't like coming in last, so that made first feel good. Especially when everyone, me included, expected last would be the result.

Despite the pain from all day bending, I kicked myself in my highest gear, and ended up slightly ahead of Carlos. When Steve pulled into the field with his two ton flatbed truck, he had a real curious look on his face, due to the section of the field I was standing in.

"Why are you standing there?" he asked. "You didn't make one of them trade sections after picking, did you?"

"No," I answered, pretty much irritated with his question. "I'm here because this is where I picked."

"You picked that much?"

"I did."

"You gonna be able to walk tomorrow?"

"Can't see any reason why not." Other than the fact I was already in a lot of pain.

As Steve drove down the rows, each of us loaded the potatoes we picked. We counted the bags as we did, then gave Steve the total when we finished. He shook his head at me the whole time I was loading. I was in a hurry to finish up the day, so while I loaded, I picked up a sack in each hand. The Mexicans never loaded more than one at a time. But where they were in condition for picking, I was for heavy lifting.

"It was something what you did today," Steve said before I left for the day. "But I'd appreciate if if you'd back off on it some tomorrow.

You push it like that again, and you'll probably need some time off to heal. We need you to work. So take it easy."

I was plenty sore when I went home. When I woke up in the morning, I didn't have many muscles anywhere that didn't hurt. I was sure I'd be taking Steve's advice about not pushing it.

Then the picking started. It was almost an instinct that took over, and from the start I paced myself with Carlos. All day again. To say I was sore is a gross understatement. I hurt like hell everywhere, and was worse the next morning.

No one expected me to show up for work that day, and were quite surprised when I did. What got me the most is the fact that neither Jose, Miguel, nor Carlos showed the slightest effects from the work. What they did show though, was a touch of admiration toward me for showing up. I think I admired them for the fact they could do work that hard and not have to pay for it the way I was doing. In the end, it cemented the friendship we'd been building since their first day there, and definitely built a mutual respect.

I can't say the same for my American counterparts. The job they had for me to start the day was torture, as I was fairly sure it was meant to be. Steve's son, Kenny, backed a three ton box van up to the loading dock, opened the back, and said, "I've got a delivery to make today. I'll need the truck loaded by noon."

I didn't have to ask him what it needed to be loaded with. The only thing we used that truck for right then was potatoes. One hundred pound sacks of potatoes. He grinned when he said, "Have at it," as he left.

I sighed, knowing I was in for a hell of a long day. But I only questioned myself for a moment about what I'd done picking those potatoes. The look of respect I got from my new friends was worth any bullshit that could be sent my way for not following orders. That was what I really won those two days. Not a contest of who could pick the most potatoes. We all knew the answer to that from the beginning.

They could.

A First Day Fishing

By Michael Allen George

Dad always said he hated fishing. It was boring. Why would anyone want to sit in a boat and wait for some damn fish to come around and bite on a hook. And even if they did, so what?

It was our second day at the resort. All we did the first day was take a short boat ride. Mostly, mom sat in an easy chair and read a book. It was her favorite pastime, so she was happy. Dad took a nap a couple of times. That made sense for him too. He always worked his ass off, managing a grocery store, so he was tired. Especially so, since this was only our second vacation since the war.

My brothers and sisters didn't seem to care much what we did either. I was the only one who was restless. I wanted to go fishing. Why drive all those miles to a resort stationed on a chain of lakes in northern Minnesota and not go fishing.

Admittedly, I was only fourteen, but I was disgusted with the lot of them. By early afternoon of the second day, I finally demanded to be allowed out in the boat alone. I was told no. So I made enough of a fuss that mom and dad finally agreed to take me out on the lake for a couple of hours.

I'd already loaded our meager fishing gear in the boat, so we were able to start out immediately.

"Are you going to fish?" I asked dad. I knew mom never would, so I didn't bother to ask her.

"No, I'll drive the boat. That way mom can read and you can fish."

"But, Dad, you can fish while you run the boat."

"How. I've only got two hands. I don't like fishing anyway. You fish."

"If I show you how easy it is, will you try?"

"You're not going to stop pestering me until I do, are you?"

"Well, no. This kind of fishing is called trolling. So you can drive the boat and fish too."

"What are the fish supposed to do? Chase the bait on the end of the line? We're going too fast for that, aren't we?"

We were in a sixteen foot, round bottom, wood boat being pushed by a small, three horse motor, so we were definitely not moving too fast.

"No," I explained. "We aren't going too fast. But if you'll take this rod and reel I have ready, I'll show you how to make the bait look even more real to the fish."

Unbelievable as it seemed at the time, he took the rod and reel with his free hand. I'd already let the line out, so it was ready to go. I'd attached a Lazy Ike onto the end of his line so he had one of the better artificial baits on it.

As soon as I got my bait in the water I showed him what to do.

"To make the bait look more real to the fish," I told him, "move your rod back and forth."

I moved mine forward, then let it drift back as the boat continued to move. That created a start and stop movement under water, much like a minnow or some such critter would move.

Dad followed my instructions to the letter, but when we didn't attract any fish, a look of boredom quickly filled his face. But being the good dad, he was he continued with the task anyway.

The time wasn't wasted though. Even without any fish, it was a nice boat ride. Dad stayed near the shoreline as we headed toward the far, north end of the lake.

We saw a lot of shore birds whereever the shore was open enough, and lots of gulls everywhere. About a half hour into the ride, we watched a bald eagle take a large fish from the middle of the lake. That alone made the ride worth it. It was too bad mom didn't set her book down quick enough to see it.

Dad was ready to turn the boat around as we neared the end of the lake.

"Before you turn around," I asked, "will you go through the bay here? Stay as close to the lily pads as you can, without us tangling our lines in them."

"I'm sure there must be a reason for doing it," he said, "even if there aren't any fish in this lake."

We didn't get far into the bay when it happened. Dad's line snapped back hard, bending his rod close to the breaking point. It happened so fast he didn't react right away. His line was moving out fast.

"Shut off the motor," I yelled.

He quickly got his wits about him and did.

"Now try to reel it in, Dad. If it pulls the line out to the end, you'll lose it."

It took him another moment to let go of the motor so he could use both hands to deal with the fish. When he did start to reel the line in, there was no finesse involved. He simply cranked that reel as hard and fast as humanly possible.

He was holding a well used rod and reel, cheap to begin with. It was only built for fishing pan fish and other small fish, so was never meant to handle a fish the size of the one he apparently had hooked on the end of his line.

As he cranked the reel, the tension on the line grew stronger. Suddenly, the reel broke free from the rod. Dad stood and tried to grab the reel flying in midair at the same time. It rocked the boat so hard, mom lowered the book she was reading to see what was going on.

All this time, I was reeling in my line. As soon as I had the line in, I dropped my rod and reel on the bottom of the boat. Dad had his rod and reel in hand, but there was little else he could do. I stood and moved to the back of the boat. I took the reel from him. Luckily, the fish momentarily stopped fighting.

I don't know how, but even though I was doing a lot of fumbling, I managed to reattach the reel to dad's rod.

"Try reeling him in again," I said.

Again, absolutely no finesse. Just dad cranking that reel for all he was worth. Twice, he pushed so hard while reeling in the line that his hands slipped off the reel. The line then screamed as the fished pulled it off the reel. The handle on the reel was spinning out of control both times dad grabbed it to again start the reel in process. I think he got some bruised fingers in the process.

Mom, being the person she was, watched our antics with a big grin her face. The fact we were rocking the boat so hard it was close to taking on water didn't faze her a bit.

As dad got the fish near the boat, I netted it in.

"What is it?" he asked before any other questions.

"A northern," I said. "At least five or six pounds."

Mom was laughing now. "That was quite an adventure you guys had," she said, then laughed some more.

Dad just sat there for a few minutes, shaking his head. Finally, he said, "I guess fishing isn't always boring." He paused a moment, "Will you put the fish on the stringer?"

I did, and hung it on the side of the boat, down in the water. Dad started the motor and turned the boat around.

"Where are you going now?" Mom asked.

"To town," Dad told her.

And we did. As soon as we got back to the cabin dad went inside for his billfold and checkbook.

"Let's go," he said to me. He didn't bother to ask the other kids along.

In town, we went to the biggest sporting goods store. Dad bought all new fishing tackle, a new rod and reel being the featured item. He bought me one too. Not as fancy as his, but far better than I ever expected to own at that stage of my life.

As soon as we got back to the cabin, we put the equipment together. The two of us went back out on the lake. It was dark when we came back in with another northern, three bass, and two walleyes.

Mom thought we'd overdone our time out on the lake a bit, so we ate a cold, leftover supper. We, however, didn't give a damn. We were fishing.

He woke me up at four-thirty the next morning. We were quickly out on the lake. It was near nine before we went in for breakfast. We stopped around noon for lunch, then stayed on the lake until dark.

Mom never went fishing with us again, and the other kids only occasionally did. It was rare when I wasn't out on that lake with my dad. And even though we often didn't catch much there, we loved fishing those lily pads in the bay at the upper end of the lake.

Dad would never fish any other way than troll, but he loved fishing that way. For the next several years, it didn't matter who came with us on vacation. I was always out on the lake with dad more than anyone else. Especially in the early morning.

There isn't much I wouldn't give to be out there with him again. To once more get up in the small hours, walk out on that dock smelling the early morning lake air, and climbing into that big old boat.

We didn't talk much. We didn't have to. We were going fishing.

The Ballad of Shotgun Orin Lee

By Bud George

They heard the noise. Outside cattle and cowboys.

"Orin No! No! Don't go out there."

He lifted the gun off the pegs over the door. She wrapped her arms around him. "No!"

At dawn they opened the door. The family dog was dead. Shot, facing away from the door trying to chase away 200 head of half wild cattle and cowboys. The garden, the crops gone. The fences, the milk cow, the team of draft horses - gone.

They walked a half day to town with a few belongings. Orin Lee found work easily - the store was busy, the town growing.

Orin Lee was a quiet man by nature I guess, but now almost always just silent. She stayed with this silent man for about a month, then left town with a happy dry goods salesman.

It was Orin Lee's habit to stop at the saloon on Saturday evening after work at the store, for a cool glass of beer. He sat at a table alone in a corner.

The bar was crowded that evening. Lots of dusty cowboys just in after roundup and branding.

Three young local cowboys - they had heard the gossip about Orin Lee's wife. Having a great time with lots of whiskey and loud talk, offered Orin Lee a heifer to keep him warm for the coming winter. Orin Lee sipped his beer looking across the room, deaf.

Get the hell away from our table the cowboys ordered Orin. One pushed Orin back away from the table. Orin set his beer glass down gently. Then he turned and took one step toward the biggest, oldest cowboy. Orin Lee picked that cowboy up, off his feet, off the floor and threw him over the bar and onto the back bar. Busted a bunch of whiskey bottles, busted the mirror. The cowboy ended up bleeding on top of pile of broken glass in a pond of whiskey.

The other two cowboys jumped in to aid their out cold friend. One jumped on Orin Lee's back, an arm around Orin Lee's neck - choke hold the other. The boxer came at him from the front. Orin Lee twisted sideways and ran the choke hold hard into the edge of the bar. The bartender said later that he heard four ribs break. The cowboy slid down the front of the bar. Ended up on the floor - his head on the brass rail.

The boxer - fast hands - light on his feet - a dancer, faced Orin Lee throwing fast jabs and hooks. Orin Lee, not even blinking, walking slowly toward the boxer backed him into a corner and hit him once. Broke his jaw and bartender said lifted him clean off his feet.

Orin Lee turned away from the boxer out cold on the floor, looked around the room and asked, "More?"

Silence - not a word.

Orin Lee finished his beer and left.

Monday morning Orin Lee arrived at the store at his usual time. The store owner - his head down - looking at the floor - said, "Orin Lee I gotta let you go. Them three cowboys you met Saturday night all worked for the Circle Three. Probably my best customers."

"Thought so," Orin Lee said, and walked out the back door to the stables.

He gathered his personal gear and as he was leaving met the stagecoach driver, on his way in to ready his team for the days run.

"I was in the saloon Saturday evening and I noticed you was in there too."

"I was," Orin said.

"Well," the driver said, "I got a hell of a problem. My shotgun guard up and quit and I'm hauling a load of silver today. You be interested in a nice stagecoach ride today?"

"What time do we leave?" Orin asked.

Orin, wearing a long canvas coat, with a bulging pocket, for the dust - a wide brim hat for the sun, and a ten gage double barrel shotgun, climbed up beside the driver.

"The company will furnish you with a twelve gauge shotgun if you want it."

"Nope," Orin Lee answered.

"The load of silver was no secrete I guess."

About five hours out on a narrow trail the coach was stopped by four masked, armed bandits. One on each side of the coach, two others holding the lead team horses. No one spoke a word. Orin Lee blew both bandits off their horses with that ten gauge goddamn cannon. The driver said later he reloaded faster than the blink of an eye and shot one of the other bandits in the back as he turned to run.

The fourth bandit had a faster horse.

"That one shot in the back is still alive," the driver said. "Should we pick him up?"

"Nope," Orin answered. "He needs time to contemplate a new line of work. He ain't much good at this one."

Seems like shotgun Orin Lee found the right line of work. No bandit ever took a strongbox off a coach that shotgun Orin Lee rode. And quite a few did not live to try again.

Oh yes, Orin Lee did take a couple of bullets once from a sniper on a hill. But by then, Orin Lee carried an old 50 caliber Sharps along with his ten gauge. As far as I know that rifleman is still up on that hill.

The west was changing - calming down - I guess. For about ten years Orin Lee worked stagecoaches, but about the end of that time he also sometimes worked as a farm hand - no guns needed. By that time I was foreman of the Circle Three Ranch.

Early one spring one of my cowboys reported to me that the old Lee place was occupied. It was kind of a surprise to me so I rode over to have a look.

The place looked a bit rough, maybe because we drove a couple hundred cattle straight thru the place to our winter range every fall.

The new occupant was a woman. I told her my name and that I ran the Circle Three. She was a too tall, slim, stern looking woman with long gray hair. She said she trained harness horses. Mary Maloni she said. Well - a long hot summer with plenty of work.

In the fall we were moving a couple hundred young stock to our winter range, moving along nicely, then as we got near the old Lee place they slowed - almost stopped. Bunched up. I hurried to the front of the herd. A brand new four wire fence straight as an arrow - still shiny.

I heard a familiar voice. "Son, you cut that wire and I'll kill you and your partner and maybe your boss too."

About then two of my riders arrived. I heard a Winchester cock. It was Mary smiling. "Hell, Orin Lee," she said, "I believe we can do more than that."

"Boys," I yelled, "Turn this goddamn herd around. We're taking the long way home. We're out gunned and outnumbered. That is Shotgun Orin Lee. He's known to keep his word."

Well, we got the herd turned and about a half a day's extra time to our winter range.

That incident happened about 5 or 6 years ago. There's a pretty good trail around what we now call Mary's place.

Yes, Shotgun Orin Lee and Mary are still there. She's gained a couple of pounds, looks better I think. Kind of took the sharp edges off.

Mary's known for first rate horses. The place looks really good now. They painted it even.

I guess I better tell you the rest of the story now. That cowboy with four busted ribs. That was me.

What Am I Doing Here?

By David George

What am I doing here? How did I let myself get talked into coming to this insane place?

The clattering drums are driving me crazy. And these weird chants they keep repeating over and over.

The woman in the huge white dress and the veil hiding her face. Her body is shaking. It's like she's having a seizure. Except she's also dancing around the room. It's more like staggering.

Wait a minute! Somebody's handing her a sword. And two men are laying a small boy in the center of the room. Cryptic symbols written in chalk on the dirt floor surround the child.

The dancing woman is waving the sword back and forth over the child's body. Holy shit! Is this human sacrifice?

Somebody punches my shoulder. I jump a mile. It's Caroline.

"Hey, dude. What's going on? Why are you muttering to yourself?"

"I can't believe you brought me to a… to a… ceremony where… human sacrifice. Let's get the fuck outa here."

She laughs. "Didn't you hear a word of my explanation? This is Umbanda. It's a curing ceremony. To heal the child. The woman is possessed by, you know, a god or a spirit."

"Oh, like voodoo," I say.

"Voodoo is Haiti. This is Brazil. So no pins in dolls, no zombies. And for sure no human sacrifice." Caroline laughs again.

I notice the drums have stopped, the woman with the sword is seated with a group of women dressed in similar costumes, and the boy has been taken away.

I've calmed down. I think about how I got here. Caroline, who like me is an exchange student here in Rio de Janeiro, is into what she calls the "nitty gritty' of the local culture. She invited me to this ceremony in a favela, a shanty town, where you can check out the real deal, the authentic culture. She said it would be in a temple, but it's more like a shack.

"Don't freak out on me again, but we're gonna see something really cool." Then Caroline says something like "Hey shoo."

"Hey what?" I ask.

She laughs again. "You're so thick-headed sometimes. It's spelled EXU. He's what they call the trickster. It's the next possession. Exu is the god of the underworld. Some people associate him with the devil."

My jaw drops. "The devil? You didn't say anything about a satanic ritual."

"Stop being a douche," Caroline says. "I didn't say Exu was the devil. I said some people associate the two… Now shush. The priest is about to be possessed by Exu."

The man she calls the priest is dancing around like the woman with the sword. Now his body is shaking. Like an epileptic fit. His face is twisted into a fright mask. He guzzles a whole bottle of rum, douses candles on his tongue, lights gun powder in his hand, and staggers around the so-called temple insulting people. He staggers over to me. I'm freaked. He asks me if I'm an American. I stutter, "yes… s-s-s sir." "*Não*," he growls like the creature from the friggin' exorcist, "*você é um filho da puta.*"

He staggers away and I ask Caroline, "Did he just call me a son of a whore?"

She giggles. "Yes. Isn't it cool to be called an S.O.B. by a god?"

"Very funny. Let's get out of here," I tell Caroline.

"Don't be a party pooper. There's lots of righteous stuff gonna happen."

I stand up. "I'm outa here." I walk through the door and immediately stop. I'm not willing myself to stop. I just stop. There's a voice in my head. "Nobody walks out on Exu." I can't move, no matter how hard I try. Flames shoot up all around me. There's a bitter taste in my mouth.

I hear another, different voice. "Exu is gone down. I have sent him away. I am Beelzebub. You are under my command." My body moves back into the temple, though I have no sensation of movement. I see my hand picking up the sword from the curing ceremony, though I can't feel anything. My eyes move back and forth, picking up images from around the room, and lock on Caroline. My body slithers toward her.

Anthony

By Michael Allen George

This was his third delivery, and the largest. She let him in when he rang the bell and directed him to the kitchen. She pointed at the kitchen counter, and he set the box of groceries on it.

"I'll get the other two," he told her.

"Two more? Really? I didn't know I ordered that much."

"I guess you did. I'll get them."

He tried not to, but he looked at her stomach before he turned to get the next box. She frowned at him for doing it.

"Yeah," she said, "it's getting bigger. It'll keep on getting bigger until the day comes."

"I'm sorry. I didn't mean to stare. I try not to."

"You bet. You and everybody else."

He went out for the second box. He noticed she hadn't started to put the food away yet when he returned. She still hadn't when he brought in the third box. It bothered him that she hadn't.

"I can help you put the groceries away," he told her.

"No thank you. I'll get it done."

"I know, I just wanted to help."

"Sure you did. The question is, what is it you want for helping?" she said, making it clear what she suspected him of wanting.

He knew from the tone of her voice that offering to help was a mistake. So he apologized again. "I'm sorry if I made you think that. I wish you wouldn't. I'm not that way."

"Not what way? A typical male. Even you, still a kid, want the same thing. I'm sure you think I'll be easy. Here I am. Pregnant and living alone, just ready to spread 'em if you make the right moves. Ain't gonna happen. Even if I was interested, which I am not, you are too young for me."

"I'm not looking for something like that from you. I only wanted to help you. I still do, if I can."

"Why the hell would you want to help me. I can't pay you. I won't do sex. And I'm getting fat and ugly."

"Because you're a nice person, and you might need some help. And you for sure aren't getting fat and ugly. What you really are, is the prettiest girl I know."

"For a kid, you already have a pretty good line. Prettiest *girl* you know? Compared to you, I'm an old woman."

"You're not that much older than me."

"You seriously don't think so? I'm twenty-five. What are you? Fifteen, sixteen?"

"I'm nineteen. Not that much younger than you."

"Too much younger for us to ever have any kind of relationship."

"I'm not too young for us to be friends."

"I guess not. If you can leave it at that. I'll never be anything more than that with you. And that will only last until the baby's father comes back."

"That's all okay. We'll just be friends. I'm Anthony. I only know you by Mz Carlson."

"I'm Liz. Everyone thinks my given name is Elizabeth, but it's not. It's just plain Liz."

She let him help her put away the groceries, and found that he was decent company. He was polite to the extreme, and when he accidentally ran his hand across her back, he apologized profusely for it.

When they finished with the groceries, he was reluctant to leave. His crush on her started with his first delivery there, and continued to grow with every visit.

He soon began going there to do various chores for her. The first was mowing her lawn. The second was to rehang a sticky door. As his visits became more frequent, his excuses for them became flimsier.

He knew he was pushing it with her, but for him, life was the best when he was close to her.

For her, she liked him well enough, but felt she needed to keep a certain distance between them. He was, she was sure, way too young for her. When he didn't take the hint, she finally told him to stay away.

He was heartbroken but did stay away. Most of the time. The exceptions were grocery deliveries and lawn care, including a very regular lawn mowing. She normally would bring him a glass of water when he was about half done with it.

But that was the extent of the visit. Until one evening a few weeks before she was due, she waddled out with his water, and was hit with a heavy contraction. It doubled her over, as much as she could be doubled over, given the size of her stomach at this state of her pregnancy.

He immediately ran to her and held on to her as a second contraction hit her.

"I think it's time," she said.

"Do you want me to take you to the hospital?"

"I think you better."

He didn't ask if she could walk. He simply picked her up and carried her to his car. Neither one of them thought to bring the bag she had packed for this expected visit, or to call her doctor. He just drove her to the emergency room.

It proved to be a false alarm, and she was sent home that night. When they got there, she said, "I really appreciate all your help, Anthony, but this doesn't change anything between us."

"Actually," he told her, his tone of voice letting he know he was serious, "for now, it changes everything. When the real time comes, I'm going to be here. When you were having contractions, your pain was so strong you couldn't even think."

"I don't think that'd be a good idea. We have to keep our distance."

"You keep saying that, even though it isn't true. But because you believe it, I'll make you a deal."

"I don't know if I like the sound of that. What kind of deal?"

"A simple one. Let me stay and take care of you until his father comes back or he's born. Either thing happens, and I'll leave. I won't bother you any longer. Not even to deliver groceries. I just want you to be safe and okay. When I know you are, I'll get out of your life, and stay out."

"You mean like, not ever see me again? I thought we were friends."

"No, we aren't. Not really. I care very much about you anyway. So let me stay until I know it's okay. Then I'll tell you goodbye, and not be a bother to you."

"Just like that, Anthony? Goodbye?"

"It's what you want, isn't it?"

"I just don't want us to get into a tangled mess."

"We're already in a tangled mess, Liz. So please, just let me be here when you need me, then I'll untangle it for you."

"I guess that'll be okay."

Anthony moved in with her and slept on the couch. She was obviously physically uncomfortable all the time, and had a difficult time doing much of anything. He helped her as much as possible, and simply ignored it when she grew frustrated and snapped at him.

He was sure she was anxious to be rid of him as soon as it was possible for him to be gone. And that would be right after the baby was born. He wouldn't even stay around to find out what she named him. That was a task she'd already told him she didn't want his advice on.

When her time came, they were ready. Everything went smooth to start, but it was a difficult birth. By the time the baby arrived, she'd called him every name she could come up with, and claimed several times that it was all his fault.

He knew it was only her reaction to the severe pain of childbirth, and stayed with her, holding her hand until it was over. When he went to the waiting room as she and the baby were cleaned up and they moved her to her room, he thought of what to say before he left her. In the end he decided a simple goodbye would be best. It was the last thing in the world he wanted. He loved her. But that was why he was willing to do it. He loved her enough to do what she wanted, what was best for her.

When he finally went to her room, she gave him a big smile. "I'm sorry," she said, "for being so nasty to you. I didn't mean it, I was just reacting to the pain."

"I know. And it's okay. I won't be staying now. I just came to tell you…"

"Before you say anything more, I want to tell you what I decided about the baby. I decided to name him after the kindest, the strongest, the best man I've ever known."

"That must be his father. I'm sure that when he comes back, he'll be happy you named the baby after him. But now it's time for me to tell you…"

"I'd like for the baby and his father to have the same name." She surprised Anthony by taking his hand. "That's why I'm naming him Anthony."

Matriarch

By Michael Allen George

As always, she was the first to rise. She stretched, drank some water, then woke her pups. Her mate could wait for whatever his needs were. She groomed the pups, starting with the largest male and finishing with the single, small female.

She woke her mate, telling him to get ready for a hunt. All the meat was gone from the last one, and she knew the pups were getting hungry. The mate was curious about the hunt. Where, and for what?

They worked the area across the river. There was still plenty to catch and eat there. They didn't even think about the nearby chickens. They weren't for them. They were only for the two leggeds. They didn't need that kind of trouble. Her mate didn't like her rules, but knew she was right.

Before they left for the hunt, they took the pups out for their relief call, telling them to do it quietly. They didn't want to attract the neighbor's attention. The neighbor's were, she knew, the kind who loved their fire-sticks. Especially the one with the chickens that were such easy pickings if she'd wanted to take them.

She was right. They were nearly all that kind. Trace Killburn, who kept the chickens, liked nothing better than to go out in the woods and shoot something with his AR-15 loaded with its forty bullet capacity magazine. He knew he was safe, even hunting wolves, deadly and dangerous as they were, with that gun. And hunt those evil creatures he would, if he could ever find them.

But they were careful at all times. They knew the danger from two legged was constantly increasing. More and more of them were out hunting, and she knew she and her family were the primary targets. That's why she and her mate were meticulous about avoiding them, and even more, the animals they kept caged. Instead, they always hunted the much more elusive wild and free creatures.

But they, too, were more and more often murdered by those with the fire-sticks, so this would be the last day in their current den, even if it provided a perfect place to raise the pups. Its entrance was small enough to make it difficult for the fire-stick carriers to enter. It even had, way in the back, a small, spring-fed pool of water for drinking.

Good a place as it was, she knew they had to move on. If they stayed, because of the constant killing of all the game by the fire-sticks, and worse, the fire-sticks hunting them, they simply needed to move on.

And she was right about it. Trace Killburn was more determined than ever to find and kill the wolves. All of them if he could, but even just one would be satisfying. Especially if he could kill their leader, who he was sure was a big male.

It never would have occurred to Trace that their leader would ever be a female. After all, everyone knew that females were always inferior, no matter what the species.

Of course, he was wrong, about all females, no matter the species. And he was especially wrong about her and her small family pack. She'd been their leader since they'd gone out on their own two years previous. Something they'd done because she believed they'd be safest as a small pack. The larger packs were bound to leave more traces out and about. Traces which always attracted those seemingly powerful creatures with the fire-sticks. Fire-sticks often called AR-15s.

For her, she only wanted safety for her pups, and the chance to hunt when hungry. Also, maybe when times were better, the chance to stay longer in a warm, dry den, preferably far away from those so determined to kill her.

That however, was a wish far away from what Trace Killburn wanted. His wish was to kill all of them. He hated wolves. To him, they were dirty, thieving things that had no business anywhere. All they did was invade his place in the world.

So it was a fateful day for the small family pack and Trace Killburn. She and her mate had just caught and killed the second creature for their daily bread, and were headed back to the den when Trace spotted them. He only had an instant to decide. He chose the biggest of them and fired. He only wounded his target.

They both dropped their food and took off at a run. Trace opened up with his forty bullet magazine in his AR-15 semi-automatic rifle. He kicked up a lot of dirt and raised hell with some tree branches, but he totally failed in his quest to kill the wolves.

He had to give up after he emptied the gun's magazine. He was so sure that forty bullets would be enough, that he failed to bring any more along. Dejected, he went home, hoping tomorrow would be a better day.

She didn't expect that. She just hoped she could nurse her mate through the difficult time of healing from his wound. She would do all she could to care for him, even while she did what she needed to do to feed her pups.

They would have to wait for dark now, but then she would once again go out to provide for them. The only question was, what would she hunt?

When the darkness came, she'd made her decision. Hunting alone was far more difficult than it was with her mate, so she decided to take a different path from any she had ever taken before.

When she went out to hunt that night, she went straight to Trace Killburn's house, and the pen where his chickens lived. It wasn't much of a pen. Enough, maybe, to keep the chickens in. Nowhere enough to keep an intelligent wolf, with a few years experience as Matriarch of her pack, out and away from the chickens. She was inside the pen in minutes, picked out one of the choicest morsels, and brought it home.

It was enough to fill the pups, and the second one she brought home was more than enough for her and her mate. After they'd all eaten, she went outside the den. There she lifted her head and howled.

Anyone listening close to the statement she was making, would have heard these words, "I've only just started with you, Trace Killburn."

Leaving Behind

By Michael Allen George

I stood there in the big empty room. The living room of the home that was ours for the past forty years. It was hard to leave. Even harder to leave was the old friend, Sarah, sitting by my side. She was thirteen now, actually fairly old for a Nufie.

She knew something was going on, she just didn't know what. I hoped that she, as she'd always done, could accept what was happening. Always before when we went anywhere, be it for a couple of hours or a couple of weeks, she would patiently wait for us to return. She was always confident we would.

I hoped this time would be the same for her. She would simply wait for us, even though this time, we wouldn't be coming back.

We sold the house, with its five acres, to our oldest son. He loved Sarah, so was more than willing to take her along with the house. I was very hopeful that Sarah would adjust to the changes, and that her last years would be happy.

Martha, my wife, was not waiting patiently. Everything we were taking with, to our two-bedroom apartment in town, was already delivered. We'd just finished loading the car with the last of a few odds and ends, and she was understandably in a hurry to get to our new home and start putting things away.

I wasn't in a hurry. It was my fault we were leaving this old house. With over sixty years of hard physical labor to make a living, my body was giving up. I couldn't take care of the place the way it needed taking care of anymore. So, I had let it go.

But I needed one last look around. Sarah was right there, next to me, as we moved from room to room. All the time, her eyes were on me. Time ran out, and I knew we had to go. Sarah came out with us. We didn't worry about her being out when we left. She was trained to wait outside on the deck when we went anywhere.

The training left her this time though. She followed the car to the road. Then, as we drove up the hill, leaving her behind, she stood in the middle of the road watching us go. Her head was hanging low, and the rest of her body seemed to sag. Her eyes stayed with us.

I slowed down and watched her through the rearview mirror. She knew. Somehow, she knew that this time we weren't coming back. I knew then that we had quit too soon. A couple of years more taking care of the place wouldn't have been that difficult.

We could have done it. Martha, always the willing one, would have been okay with staying those few more years. If I would have said it was best to stay longer, she would have said yes. Actually, she probably would have preferred it that way.

I suddenly wondered what it was that I was thinking when I made those decisions. We were leaving so much behind. So many memories of so many years. So much of what we always were.

They were important, but what was most important I now realized, was what I was watching behind us. She looked so sad, even from that distance.

Of all the things in life that are supposed to be important, we were leaving one behind that was as important as anything could ever be.

A broken heart.

A Trip to the Cabin

By Bud George

An out of town job. A new lake home west of the cities. Ken left on Monday morning. Bill and I finished some roofing and siding on a new garage in the city and went west on Tuesday morning.

Kind of a bad start I guess. No lumber load. It was due Tuesday AM. Dark sky, probably rain. Ken had done some necessary demo work on the flat rock basement that had been used as a lake getaway for a couple of years.

Ken decided to go look for the lumber truck. It was coming from a mill about forty miles north of our site. Bill and I finished the demo work and sat down to watch the darker sky moving toward us.

Ken found the driver in a roadside bar and strongly suggested to him that it was quite important to us that we receive his load quickly. Ken was six foot six inches tall and around two hundred forty pounds. When he had something to say, people usually noticed.

It started to rain, one of those light, steamy all day things. We heard the lumber truck, a big diesel, coming on the gravel road with Ken behind him. The driver made the right turn into our driveway. Or rather, tried to make the turn. The back end of the flatbed slid sideways into the ditch.

Nothing to do but sit inside that badly leaking basement and wait. We knew we'd have to hand unload and hand carry that lumber down the slippery, muddy driveway. The rain eased and we went to work.

The driver felt that since he had arrived on our job site, the lumber was ours and we did not need his assistance. Ken suggested to the driver that he would need our help to get his truck out of the ditch. Ken also suggested that the driver probably needed a bath and that he would be happy to provide him with one in the lake, if that was what he wished for, instead of helping us move the lumber.

The driver went to work with us. Ken pushed hard. Bill and I were used to this. We picked up our pace accordingly. The driver wasn't used to it. He looked pretty beat by the time we got him out of the ditch. It was pitch dark.

"I think he's a better man now," Ken said.

It was a bad start, but we made good time framing. It was Thursday night. We had an almost complete shell. We settled in for a good night's sleep. Both gable ends were still open. No sheathing, so I picked a spot on the upper level on the theory that mosquitos could not fly that high. I was wrong.

Bill was on the opposite gable, sleeping on a piece of foam insulation. Ken was under the new stairway on top of some plastic bags of fiberglass insulation, with a roll of sill seal for a pillow.

The rain hit about two or three AM. Bill said he woke up when his mattress started to float. The rain was blowing horizontal between those gale ends. I was soaked.

Ken said he woke up because we made so much noise stomping down the new stairway.

Our plan had been to work through Friday and head back home for the weekend. Did not work. It took all day Friday to clean up the outside and the neighbor's yards. It took Saturday to close in both gables.

We decided to load my pickup with some planks, scaffold, and braces that we no longer needed. We left about dark on Saturday. I was very tired and my truck, and older, steady Ford F150, was a little too heavy.

I think it was close to two hours into the drive that I passed a semi coming out of some small town. He was probably overloaded. You could see the clutch chatter when he took off from a stoplight.

A short time later I awoke to the blast of and air horn and bright lights blinking in both rearview mirrors. I was well off the road and aimed at a culvert. I barely got the pickup where it belonged and me awake.

The semi hauled ass around me and kept on rolling. He saved my backside. Sort of raised my view of truck drivers.

Letters to my son: What Was the Neighborhood You Grew Up in Like?

By David George

L ike all such questions, dear son, the interpretations and answers vary significantly. In today's story, I focus on life on the farm. I jot down whatever comes to my mind.

Though I was born at the University of Minnesota Hospital in Minneapolis, I spent my early years on my grandparents' farm in southern Minnesota. The reason: my father fought in WWII and my mother had to move in with her parents. There was no way she could take care of five kids by herself.

My memories of those early years are sketchy and some are second-hand, stories told to me by my mother and older siblings. I was apparently a wild child and there were ample opportunities to get into trouble on the farm. For example, at age two or three I climbed to the top of the windmill and sat just below the rotating blades. The adults and older siblings had a fit. My mother was frantic. But since I'm still around after all these years, obviously the windmill blades didn't chop me up. I don't know how I got back down. Probably my grandpa George Alexander—whose name you carry—climbed up and fetched me.

Another tale, perhaps apocryphal, is that my brothers raided the hen house, stole the eggs, threw them down the well, and blamed it mischief on the wild child, me.

In yet another dramatic story, it was my want to stand between the horses' legs. My grandpa didn't have a tractor. He used gigantic work horses for all the farm work.

I do remember a few things. In my mind's eye I can see myself wandering through a cornfield, lost. Another part of my routine was to disappear. My uncle Paul, who would later take over the farm, found me.

I also remember an old lady in white, my great grandmother, who was abed, awaiting death, the whole time we lived on the farm.

I do not remember my baptism in the local church. Baptized in Swedish, the language of the community.

I do remember a few words in Swedish, which my grandparents spoke with each other and with my mother.

I mentioned above that my uncle Paul eventually took over the farm. The memories from the "neighborhood" during that period are quite clear. While still a child and later adolescent, I learned to perform myriad tasks on the farm. I drove my uncle's Ferguson tractor to plow, rake hay, and pull the wagon where the hay bales were piled. I also did the physical labor, lifting the hay bales on to the wagon if I wasn't driving the tractor, stacking the bales in the hayloft in the barn.

I have some bizarre memories. The lady on the farm next door had breast cancer. Since I was a child, I wasn't sure what that was. But I remember visiting her farm – I was friends with her boys – and seeing her chest when she bent over. It looked like a massive wound, the scars I now presume left over from breast removal.

To continue on the happy subject of cancer, living on the farm was my favorite person in the whole world, Bonnie. She was a waif, the closest thing to being an orphan. Her mother, my aunt Ruby's sister, gave birth to Bonnie at a very young age and was unable to take care of her. Somehow, she ended up on the farm. Though I wasn't living on the farm, I spent a lot of time there. Bonnie and I were inseparable. At around age nine—Bonnie and I were, I think, the same age—I had a dream: something was wrong with Bonnie's blood or heart (my memory is not clear on that point). The dream was very upsetting. Two weeks after that my mother sat us kids down because she had something important to tell us. Bonnie, she said, had leukemia. The kids didn't know what leukemia was and mother explained. I associated it with my dream and was very frightened for Bonnie. Two weeks later our mother told us that Bonnie had died (in those days the mortality rate for victims of leukemia was very high). We were required to go to the funeral. The casket was open. Bonnie was unrecognizable, her body swollen grotesquely. I ran out of the church screaming.

But let us end with a positive note. Spending parts of my childhood and adolescence provided experiences I never could have had if I'd been an urban kid exclusively and gave me a physical strength that lasted into old age.

The Old Man and the Rose

By David George

Every night the old man slept on the side of the bed closest to the window. The first light of dawn always awakened him. Even on dark cloudy mornings the palest of rays pulled him out of his slumber, like a child flailing beneath the surface of a lake in a desperate search for rescue. His first act was to embrace the pillow like a lifebuoy. When he felt safe, he fluffed the pillow, straightened the covers, and reached for the derringer he kept in the nightstand drawer.

The kitchen soon filled with the smell of coffee mixed with an equal portion of cream, which the night before he had skimmed from the small pail of milk Bessie the cow still produced. At the end of the day the old man would empty and wash Bonnie's mug.

The farm was a tiny fraction of its former self. When he and Bonnie had it up and running, he drove the old Ferguson tractor that pulled the wagon where the bales were piled, then stacked in the barn. He and Bonnie loved the smell of the hayloft, the haze that filtered sunlight and created dust streams of pale gold.

Waking up at five in the morning, walking hand-in-hand into the newly born day was always a moment of transport. Time would stop. They could not distinguish themselves from the air, the frail light, the damp grass beneath their bare feet.

Once upon a time they celebrated harvest with the farmers' co-op. Shared machinery let out a roar to signal the reaping of autumn's bounty: tractors, combines, threshing machines, mowers, balers. It was as if the farm's heart had begun to beat, a thrilling race was about to begin: rake and bale the hay before rain could spoil it, cut and thresh the wheat, pick the corn before the crows finished it off, dig out the potatoes before the gophers got them, keep the cows out of the alfalfa fields before they ate themselves to death.

Bonnie picked pails-full of black raspberries in the woods while warding off dark clouds of mosquitoes and avoiding the thorns which tore at clothing and skin.

Over the years, to keep food on the table, the old man had sold off parcels of land to Big Agriculture. All that remained was the house, its small yard, Bessie's shed, and the thin strip of forest traversed by a muddy brook. Years ago—he couldn't count them all—he could reach the churchyard and cemetery riding the last of his ponies along the narrow dirt road. Now it was a four-lane blacktop with mammoth shrouded tractors speeding to some unknown destination far beyond the churchyard.

His path to the cemetery took him along the narrow swath of trees and through the muddy brook. In his pocket the old man kept his two-shot derringer, always cleaned and oiled, though he no longer remembered why. At intervals along the path he maintained wildflower beds. At a bend in the stream, he nurtured a rose bush concealed inside a briar patch. By the time he reached the cemetery the flowerbeds had provided a bouquet of dead-nettles, purple archangels, and bleeding hearts.

He lived to commemorate the anniversary of Bonnie's child. Though the creature was stillborn and took her mother's life with her, he was certain Bonnie would have begged forgiveness for the child. Never had an anniversary passed when he failed to adhere to her silent plea, not even the year when he had spent a week stricken with the plague, with barely enough strength to drag himself to the well and painfully crank up the bucket. The anniversary had not been forgotten. The old man crawled through the muddy stream, reaching into the briar patch to crown the special bouquet with a white rose from the bush that produced but one blossom a year.

Today was special… but why? The old man searched deep into his fading memory and retrieved the day: fiftieth anniversary. The first ray of dawn had not summoned him into a silent morning sprinkled with bird whistles. In their place he heard the ululation of machines, wood breaking, brick crumbling, and stone cracking through the strip of forest. The cemetery. He was certain the matter had been settled in court. Hadn't Big Agriculture agreed to leave the church and the cemetery untouched? Had he somehow forgotten to appear at the last court hearing?

He plunged into the muddy stream and slogged toward Bonnie's grave. He stopped to retrieve the white rose. When he reached the churchyard, a backhoe was lacerating the grave. Splinters of wood and bone fragments extruded from piles of dirt. He tore the derringer from his pocket.

"He's got a gun!" shouted a security guard standing in front of the tomb. The backhoe shut down and silence gripped the cemetery. The old man dropped the pistol, replaced it with the rose, pointed it at the grave, and stumbled toward Bonnie and the child.

Summers for Bonnie Kay

By Michael Allen George

Plates of pineapple, crushed
As her blood and life, must

It be empty, neither love nor hate
For others yes, much too late

Gowns of fear, one long week
Her mother's arms, no chance to speak

Barns, a kiss and vicious kick, the stare
Of blue eyes cold, mouth black, blond hair

White silk, long box so sprightly gray
Her home sings of terror, so far away

A lone geranium, no stone, a plaque
Lilacs, remember soft, to bring her back

Father drunk, he sheds no tears
But drinks of death, and wasted years

Beneath the trees and hardpan clay
Were lost the summers for Bonnie Kay

A Fall Walk

By Michael Allen George

It was a beautiful fall day. Full sun and in the seventies. The maples were about done but the oaks still held some color. We were out for a ride in the country, traveling aimlessly from one place to another. Then we realized we were close, so we decided to stop.

It was physically comfortable to walk there. Trees for shade and new mown grass to walk on. No rocks, but lots of stones. Stones that told stories of sorts, at the head of each grave.

She walked close, and it made me want to hold her hand. I didn't. She might think I was trying to be too intimate. Still, it was nice when occasionally her shoulder rubbed mine.

We read the stones as we meandered along, until we came to the two that were those belonging to the grandparents we shared. Grandparents I'd been fortunate to spend a lot of time with. She hung her head, sadly, as she read them. She looked up at me, the shadows of tears in her eyes.

"Were they happy?" she cocked her head and asked. "Were they really happy?"

"As much as any of us, I think," I answered.

"I hope so. They were good people. They should have been."

Then she took my hand and led me away, as if it were too painful to linger in that spot too long. To my surprise, she continued to hold my hand. It was the first time she'd ever shown me any of that kind of affection, even though we'd often spent time together. Always though, there was an invisible wall, telling me not to get too close. Close was something we shouldn't have.

We walked nearly all the graveyard before we reached the one stone that grabbed my heart. She was so young when she died. I never knew her as well as I wanted to, but it was a huge loss in my own young life.

As always happened when I visited this spot in this place, I dropped to my knees. Tears welled in my eyes. I rested my hand on her stone.

"I'm so sorry," I said. "So damn sorry. You shouldn't have been taken from us so soon. I should have been nicer to you."

I felt a hand on my shoulder, then a light squeeze. I looked up and stared at the church in front of my blurry eyes. I remembered all the Sunday mornings I spent there. It was part of the price I had to pay for being allowed to spend a large part of the summers of my youth on the farm less than a half mile away.

The farm I always remembered with affection. The church as a place of torture. For me, it was never a place of kindness. Only a place to endure. The time on the farm was worth the price.

She finally spoke when I stood up. "I never knew you felt so strongly about her. You must have been awful close to her."

"Not close enough."

"Do you always react like that when you visit here."

"I don't have to be here. Just remember."

What I saw when our eyes met was new. Softer. It reached into my soul. I couldn't help myself. I kissed her. Her response was a bit cold.

She pulled her head back and cocked it to one side as she stared into my eyes. Finally, she said, a slight smile on her lips, "Well, okay."

She pulled me to her. Our next kiss was lot warmer.

A Fourth of July Weekend

By Bud George

Thirty-two miles. A gravel road, the river just off to his right. Now an exit, an old rusty steel truss bridge leading to a town across the river. The bridge had a sign that said nine thousand maximum weight. The road he was on had its own sign - road closed ahead.

"Let's see just how closed it is," the man said to the dog dozing on the floor. The dog knew this was an important question, so she hopped up on the seat next to the man.

They passed a gravel pit (an open pit sand and gravel mine) dug well into the hillside on the left. There was a short, very heavily built wood bridge across a ditch at the entry to the gravel mine, probably there to keep the mine dry. The road was closed a short distance beyond and down the hill from the mine. Telephone poles with heavy planks spiked across them, and lots of reflective paint used for the words, road closed.

The road beyond the sign was completely gone. Likely washed out years ago. He turned the pickup and drove back to the mine entrance. Time to take a piss and get a drink of water. He crossed the short timber bridge and parked next to a small cement block building. The weigh station and office when the mine was open.

The man pulled a metal pan from the truck seat and filled it with water for the dog who had just finished leaving a liquid message on a shade tree being the building. He then opened a bottled water for himself.

A sixty-mile round trip just to get to the town a mile across the river. An empty gravel truck was too heavy for the steel bridge. The man looked around a bit. There was a pole building with a large sliding door. An old single axle Mack truck was inside. Still a few piles of sorted rock and graded sand.

This might be a good place to camp for a few days. "What do you think?" he asked. The dog's tail wagged. "I could leave you here in the shade. It's gonna be a hot afternoon. I'll be gone a couple hours, get us some food and more water. That sound okay to you?" The dog's tail wagged again.

The man refilled the dog's water and added another pan with food. He wrapped a piece of steel cable around the tree and clipped it to the dog's collar. When he left, he bent down to pet the dog and received a wet kiss in exchange.

When he returned the dog was gone. Part of the cable was still around the tree, but broken or cut. Lots of new tire tracks around the tree and the building. Off road motorcycles and four wheelers. He followed the trail cut into the mine. He found the dog. Dead. Tire tracks around a bloody two by four on the ground next to the dog. Who could do a thing like this? No reason, no sense.

He called 911 to report this senseless act, He talked to the local town cop who said, "Probably teenagers. They party in that mine. I'd rather have them raising hell up there than in my town. Sorry, but you're on your own."

He dug a grave and marked it well with the heaviest stones he could carry. He rested for a while, then walked the gravel pit. Many empty wine and beer bottles. Evidence of bonfires. Some discarded clothing and a cell phone with a functional battery.

At dusk the party began. It lasted until early morning. Loud teens mostly. Some pretty nice cars and trucks. In the morning he went to work. The pole building was well boarded up, so he removed a metal siding panel. The building was a shop. Some older hand tools, a small generator, and a portable air compressor. A green 260 gallon storage container about a third full of diesel fuel, and a red fifty gallon barrel with some gasoline.

Working days, he got the Mack to run. He borrowed a battery from one of nice new pickups. He loaded the Mack over a few days with sand.

A full load. He collected bottles, filled them with fuel, and plugged the necks with shop rags.

He climbed the steep grassy edge of the pit and placed the full bottles along the top edge of the excavated cliff. He located some empty five gallon buckets and filled them with fuel. He moved his pickup onto a field across the road.

He soaked the short access bridge with gasoline, and placed the five gallon buckets in the weeds next to the ditch. He used his newfound cell phone to call every number stored in it. Big fourth party - free beer.

Nice big crowd, lots of noise. He waited until full dark, then drove the old overloaded Mack onto the rusty steel truss bridge. It was way over the posted limit. He wedged the Mack against both the right and left railings. The bridge was swaying a little and he could hear the rivets popping. He climbed to the top of the mine cliff and threw molotov cocktails over the edge. It set the cliff on fire. The crowd cheered.

He climbed down and found a car with the keys in it. He parked it on the short, gas soaked wood bridge and set the bridge on fire. He dumped the five gallon buckets of diesel fuel in the ditch and threw a burning bottle of gasoline in it.

The party goers stopped cheering. They were surrounded by fire. He stepped back into a dark area opposite the pit. He rested. Sixty-four mile trip from the town. Long string of flashing lights, sirens. The nice shiny Crown Victoria cop car in the lead. He tapped on the cop's window and it rolled down.

"I called you about my dog."

"I don't have time for that bullshit now," the cop said. He rolled the window back up.

The man began walking away. As he did, he rolled a molotov cocktail under the cop car gas tank. It blew when the man was less than a hundred feet down the road.

Letters to My Son:
Pyramids and Sharks

By David George

There have been adventures galore in my life, the principal adventure fathering a child, you. But that, dear son, is not the tale you're awaiting. So I'll tell you a Mexico story.

I spent the summer of my 23rd year visiting archeological sites throughout Mexico. At the time I was fascinated by the ancient native civilizations, not just the Aztecs and the Maya but many others. I wanted to see close up what those great civilizations had left behind. It meant driving from Minneapolis to Mexico City, and then into the great unknown (a bit of hyperbole there). My companion was my wife, Mary.

The first site was Teotihuacán, located about an hour's drive outside Mexico City. It is a vast archeological site, with many structures still intact. It was inhabited for some 700 years, from around 100 BCE (Before the Common Era) to 700 CE (the Common Era). It should be noted that these dates are approximations and archeologists are not all in agreement. Teotihuacán was apparently the center of a great civilization whose influence extended all the way down to the Mayan zones of southern Mexico and Central America. Who were the inhabitants? No one knows. Even the name, Teotihuacán, is an Aztec word. The Aztec civilization came to prominence nearly a thousand years after Teotihuacán. The site itself contains rows of temples and great pyramids. The largest, the Pyramid of the Sun, is comparable in size to the ancient Egyptian pyramids.

The adventure part was climbing to the top of the Pyramid of the Sun. There are steps—huge ones—the intrepid voyager can climb. The climb is steep and precarious. I had to go up by myself; Mary was terrified. But I was young and bold (or just plain careless) and up I went. When I got to the top—where a temple once stood, apparently something to do with human sacrifice (woohoohoo)—the view was spectacular. I was awestruck, on top of the world, and a bit dizzy. I thought, how am I going to climb back down the damn thing? There were a lot of people at the ground level looking up, but I was the only climber, so I didn't have any would-be instructors or guides to clue me in. I tried backing down, but the distance between steps was too wide to navigate backwards. So I did it frontwards. Each step was like tottering into the abyss. But I made it. If you doubt it, well, I'm still here all these years later, telling you all about it.

Mary was pissed. Watching me was apparently as frightening as doing the actual climbing. How can they allow people to do that? She asked indignantly. Well, in those days, there weren't a lot of rules in Mexico. And I'm sure many adventurers fell rather than climbed down.

From Teotihuacán we headed to the Gulf Coast near Vera Cruz, where another pyramid-building civilization was located. These were the Totonacs, the first native peoples in Mexico to encounter Hernán Cortés and his band of Spanish *conquistadores* (conquerors)—the unwoke would say "explorers," "discoverers." The Totonacs provided food and acted as guides for the Spaniards, who had heard tales of a great city to the west filled with gold and other treasures. It was no myth—that great city was Tenochtitlan, the Aztec capital, such a wonder that when the *conquistadores* first saw it they thought it was something out of a fairy tale. Of course, that didn't stop them from totally destroying the "fairy tale" city. But that's a story for another time. Suffice to say that the Totonacs pointed the way to Tenochtitlan.

Back to my adventure. I wanted to visit an ancient Totonac city, El Tajín, that had a monumental structure called the Pyramid of the Niches (La Pirámide de los Nichos), so named because it had 365 indentations or niches corresponding to the days of the year.

An aside here: the ancient ruins in Mexico reveal how advanced the pre-Hispanic civilizations were in mathematics and astronomy, in many ways far more advanced that the Spanish conquerors. So much for "primitive" Indians.

My goal was to see the niches with my own eyes and, of course, climb to the top of the pyramid. Not as large as the Pyramid of the Sun, but at some 60 feet in height, not a straw hut. I climbed to the top without incident, took in the view, and climbed back down. The adventure come a bit later.

I'm driving on a dirt road out of the site. On the side of the road is an old man on a burro. Suddenly, the burro bolts to the left, right in front of the car. I swerve sharply and miss burro and rider by inches. Thank goodness for the quick reflexes of youth.

From El Tajín we drove to other lesser—but no less wondrous—sites. On the way to Vera Cruz, we found huge stretches of beautiful beach with not a soul in sight. Yup, you guessed it, perfect for skinny dipping. Only later did we discover that the beaches around Vera Cruz were full of sharks and that there had been many shark attacks that summer. More about sharks later.

Vera Cruz, a port city, was great. Seafood to die for. A fabulous square in the middle of town surrounded by great restaurants and perfect for people watching. Roaming bands played Caribbean style music.

We then headed south to visit the site of another fascinating civilization, The Olmecs (Los Olmecas). Driving at night in search of a hotel or even a hut to sleep, the road was suddenly covered with thousands of crabs, migrating I supposed. It was unavoidable. You either pulled over and stopped or you ran over them. I can still hear the crunching sounds in my mind. We finally found a place that rented huts. We didn't get much sleep because, guess what, there were crabs climbing over—around?—the hut. Were these the souls, I wondered, of the crabs I had pulverized with my car? I didn't really think that, but it sounds good for an adventure story, don't you agree?

The next few days we headed toward the Olmec site of La Venta. Who were the Olmecs? The first advanced civilization of the Americas.

Archeologists estimate the dates 1200-400 BCE for the civilization. Why advanced? They built monumental structures like pyramids, had a sophisticated mathematical system based on 20 (ours is decimal, based on 10), and they invented the first writing system. Who were they, what language did they speak? No one knows. The name Olmec (Olmeca) is an Aztec word. There were no pyramids to climb. In fact, the "ruins" were in ruin because the site had been taken over the PEMEX, the Mexican national oil company. The PEMEX folks weren't in the business of preserving ancient sites.

But all was not lost. There was an Olmec museum in the city of Villahermosa, capital of the state of Tabasco. Many artifacts from La Venta had thankfully been moved to the museum. The most notable Olmec artifact were giant stone heads (check 'em out on Google). But there were other wonders, such as very modern looking sculptures and a palace floor covered with tiles in the shape of a giant jaguar (the sacred animal of the Olmecs).

From Villahermosa we headed into Mayan territory. We drove to the neighboring state of Chiapas, which borders on Guatemala. The roads were very primitive. We had to cross rivers on ferries—rafts really—that were powered by hand. The boat folks moved the ferries across the rivers by pulling on ropes. Was I ever concerned about what would happen should the ropes break? What, me worry?

We were headed to a Mayan site known as Palenque (226 BCE to 799 CE). The maps we were using weren't very helpful, so we asked the locals for directions. The problem with that was that the locals, the Mayan peoples (yes, they're still there), didn't speak much Spanish. We drove around on barely passable dirt roads, got stuck several times, got caught—at night!—in tropical rain storms the likes I've never seen before or since, but finally reached our destination.

Palenque was the most amazing site of any we visited. Impressive buildings surrounded a huge courtyard. A pyramid was topped by a temple (very few of the latter still exist—the Spaniards destroyed the "heathen" temples). If you climbed up the pyramid and entered the temple, you discovered a stairway leading down into the center of the pyramid. At the very bottom was a gigantic, perfectly preserved stone slab covered with inscriptions, hieroglyphs (the Mayans had the most advanced writing system in the pre-Hispanic Americas). As it turns out, the stone slab was a tombstone for a king name Pacal (yes, archeologists have figured out how to read the Mayan hieroglyphs).

At night we witnessed another wonder. It just so happened that a dance troupe called El Ballet de Bonampac was in Palenque for a performance. Their dances were based on murals located in the Mayan site of Banampac depicting scenes from everyday life, warfare, gods etc. The performance was at night, in the courtyard mentioned above. Watching the dancers and listening to the flutes and drums was like being transported back to the time of the ancient the Mayans. What enhanced this feeling was the fact that most of the spectators sitting on temple steps were the local Mayan people. Unforgettable.

Post-performance, where to sleep? We were far from any towns, so we'd probably sleep in the car. However, a local guide took pity on us and led us to a hut, the home of a local farmer. He agreed to let us string up our hammocks on the porch outside his hut. We settled in, nearly asleep, when suddenly we were attacked by some animal snorting loudly and bumping against the hammocks. I looked and it was… a jaguar! Just kidding. It was a pig. He snuggled up against my hammock and wouldn't move. I guess for the warmth. I decided, no worries, we now have a WATCH PIG!

From Palenque we drove across to the Pacific Coast, where we stayed in a Zapotec fishing village (the Zapotecs also once had a great civilization in Oaxaca). We slept in the car, used a shower belonging to one of the local families, bought freshly caught fish, and even learned a few words in Zapotec (which I no longer recall).

There were a few other Americans in the village. Apparently it was a hippie destination. I met a fellow from Florida who asked if I wouldn't like to join him for body surfing on the big waves. I had been catching waves in the bay where the village was located, but hadn't gone to the open ocean beaches where you could catch big waves in the "gnarly" surf. I declined at first; I was a neophyte when it came to surfing. My new Florida friend assured me there was no problem. He had grown up surfing in Florida and would guide me safely. Groovy. So I went, like a lamb to slaughter as the saying goes.

Off we walked a mile or two to the open ocean beach. The waves were huge and breaking far from shore. And beyond the waves giant manta rays were cavorting (we had seen them previously in the bay). I swallowed my trepidation and out we swam to where the waves were breaking. The body surfing was fantastic. Though seeing those giant rays just beyond the breaking waves was not exactly visual valium. Suddenly, cutting parallel through the surf I spotted a large fin. Was it a manta ray? No, not the way it was moving. A dolphin? No, it was NOT moving up and down through the water like a dolphin. A shark?! I tapped my "guide" on the shoulder and pointed. He looked and… swam like an eel out of hell toward the beach. My surf guru abandoned me! The fear surged through my body as I watched the greyish-white fin slide along the bottom of the wave. I was suddenly as weak as baby Moses, with no basket to carry me. Fear was replaced by panic and my strength returned. I swam, caught waves to accelerate my flight, and after what seemed like an eternity collapsed on the beach. I looked at my guide and we both laughed like a couple of donkeys. Why wasn't I angry with him? To this day, I don't know. Perhaps the feeling that I had survived the biggest scare of my life was more powerful than anger.

There were more adventures on that trip. We'll save them for another occasion. Ciao ciao for now.

Boat Ride

By Michael Allen George

The lake was choppy as they moved out of the river and onto it. It made for a rough ride, but not enough to worry Jamie, the sixteen year old boy driving the boat. It was stable enough, even if it was fairly old. It was built from wood, with a round bottom and nearly big enough to carry all people in it safely.

Up in the front of the boat were four children, running in ages from eight to twelve. In the middle, sat his father, Frank, alongside his new step-daughter, Malissa.

Normally, Frank drove the boat, but Malissa had asked him to teach her how to fish. So Frank let Jamie drive it this time. He wanted his new family to be as satisfied and compatible as he could make them. Teaching Malissa was simply another way of doing it.

They were on the last leg of this time out fishing, and were still trolling for northerns. It had been a better than average day of fishing. The kids up front were using light tackle and had only caught a few pan fish. Malissa caught a three pound northern. The first catch of the day, and with Frank's help, she had a great time landing it.

After her successful landing, she stuck her tongue out at Jamie. Her way of claiming she was right when she made sarcastic comments about the funny looking, antique lure he was using. Her lure looked like a real minnow. His was a Lazy Ike. Frank gave it to him when he was six, one of the first lures in his first tackle box.

The tongue incident didn't surprise Jamie. There was no hiding the fact that Malissa didn't like him. She was a cheerleader at the high school they went to. He not only didn't participate in any sports, he didn't much care for them. To him, all sports taught anyone was that in order to be successful, someone else had to lose.

He didn't participate in any activities at school. His afternoons were spent working in Frank's hardware store. It was the place he preferred to spend his time. He not only made a decent amount of money there, it was also a constant learning process. This was especially true, because Frank's store was growing constantly, rather than dying as most family type hardware stores were doing. He'd even added new departments, like the equivalent of a complete hobby store, and the most complete kitchenware department in the entire city they were located in.

But Malissa didn't see it that way. She was very popular in school, and had little to do with the people like Jamie. People she considered part of the lower class. She also wasn't fond of the fact her mother married Frank. All he did was own and operate a hardware store. Her own father, who she rarely saw anymore, was an accountant. He worked for a big corporation. He did important work.

Even so, she did her best to butter up Frank while at the same time did what she could to snub Jamie. She told him, when they were forced to be together at the wedding, "Don't get the idea you and I could ever be any kind of friends. There's no way I'd ever so much as hold your hand. So don't get any funny ideas about me"

That bothered him some, but not enough to let it ruin his fishing vacation with his father. He also wasn't vindictive, so when he landed an eight pound northern he hooked with his *stupid*, antique Laze Ike, he didn't sneer at Malissa. Instead, he simply smiled as he silently put the fish on the stringer.

He hadn't smiled since though, and now his face was filled with a serious frown. The wind came up suddenly, changing the waves from choppy, to large enough to swamp the boat. They were about a hundred yards out from shore, and running broadside to the waves. As soon as the wind started, he turned the boat into the waves.

He knew from the size of the waves that they were in a bit of trouble. They were still nearly a mile from the cabin, and to get there in a straight line, it would be broadside to the waves all the way. He was sure they'd capsize and drown if he tried to make it back that way.

The only chance they had, he was sure, was head into the waves at an angle, and turn the boat when they were about half the distance to the cabin. Then angle the boat home with their backs to the waves.

Taking that route had two problems. First, the outboard motor pushing the boat had barely enough power to move them against the waves. Second, the boat was overloaded. Added to that, the farther out into the lake they got, the less chance any of them would survive if something went wrong.

And it wouldn't take much for something to go wrong. So he told them, his voice loud and clear, "Don't anyone move until we get to shore. Not so much as an inch. And reel in your lines. I don't want anyone trying to land a fish in this crap."

"Who do you think you are?" Malissa asked, obviously insulted by him giving orders. "You can't tell me what to do!"

He sighed heavily. "I guess," he answered, "because I'm the one driving the boat, and I don't want all of us, or even any of us, to drown. So please, don't move. It's going to be tough enough, keeping this boat from going over. Your moving will make it just that much worse."

"I think you're just trying to act important."

Frank broke in. "I think, Malissa," he said. "We should do what he says. It won't take much, and we'll all be in the water. I doubt any of us swim good enough to make it to shore. And most of all, Jamie's been driving this boat since he was a small child. He knows what he's doing."

She didn't like it, but Malissa sat still and quiet. As she did, she started watching Jamie. His look was grim as he put his full concentration on keeping the boat as steady as possible. What she couldn't see, was his concern about turning the boat at the halfway point. Too sharp could take it over, even without help from the waves. Too broad a turn, and the waves would take them over. Even now, the motor didn't have the power to push through the waves. Instead, the boat rode over the top, then slammed down, jarring all of them and soaking them with the spray, only to do it again with the next wave.

When the time came for the turn, he wisely told everyone to lean into the waves, in the hope their weight would help counter the fierce push of the very high waves in their attempt to turn the boat over. They did as he asked, and he made the perfect turn. Not too tight and not too broad. He smiled as the boat started its move toward shore.

"Hot damn," Frank said, "no one could have made that turn better than that, Jamie. You did yourself proud."

The kids up front gave him a few small cheers. Malissa stayed silent, which was about the best Jamie would have expected from her, so he shrugged it off. As much as he wished they could get along, or maybe even be friends, he was sure that would never be possible.

He also didn't really expect any praise for his boat driving. He'd been on the lake with Frank often enough to know that if Frank were the one driving, he for sure would have gotten them safely back to the cabin. So from his own perspective, he hadn't done anything special, only what he needed to do.

The last of the ride was uneventful, and everyone was rather quiet when they docked and left the boat. Even the kids now realized how dangerous it had been for them out on that angry lake.

Jamie helped Frank unload the boat, then after everyone else went inside the cabin to get dry clothes on, he stood alone on the dock, watching the constant waves stir the lake's water. There was knot in his stomach now, as he thought about how easily it could have turned to disaster.

He wasn't there long before Malissa joined him. "What brings you out here?" he asked, when she stood so close her shoulder brushed his.

"I want to tell you how sorry I am for arguing with you when you told us all to sit still. I was wrong."

"Don't worry about it. The ride is over and we're all home safe."

"Thanks to you. What you did out there on that lake was a lot more than brave or strong. It was smart. How did you get so smart?"

"If I'm smart at all, it's because of my dad. Most of what I know, it's because he taught me."

"He is a good person. I guess that's why my mom married him. When she divorced Dad, she said she'd never get married again."

"Dad said the same thing when Mom died."

"Well, anyway, I am sorry for giving you a hard time."

He just shrugged, turned away, and walked off the dock. It wasn't that he didn't believe she was sorry so much as he was sure things like that would happen again. No matter what he did, she'd never like or much approve of him. And her anger over the turn life had taken for everyone in their new family, would be directed at him. At least until one of them grew up and moved out on their own. Given he wasn't good enough in her eyes to so much as ever hold her hand, his expectations about their relationship ran from extremely low to nonexistent.

Off the dock, he started to walk down the beach. The waves out on the lake had been his dire enemy. Here, their crashing hard on the beach, their sound and their smell, gave him a sense of peace. Something he was sure he'd never get from any of the additions to his family.

He'd walked a fair distance from the dock when she suddenly was again by his side. Neither of them said anything. They just walked together, her much closer than he'd ever expected her to walk.

He kept his eyes focused on the landscape in front of him, but he could sense her watching him closely. He missed her eyes though. He didn't see the change there. He could feel her wish they could talk, but he didn't have anything to say to her. It was what it was. He couldn't see how anything could ever change that.

Then she took his hand and held it.

What's in a Name

By Michael Allen George

He always got a lot of crap about his name. Billy was a kid's name they told him. You should call yourself Bill now. He took it well. He'd just smile and say, "Billy's the name Ma gave me, so I guess I'll stay with it. It'd break her poor heart if I threw it away. Besides, what's in a name anyway?"

That's the way he was. You couldn't rattle him. Whatever kidding or grief he got from the other cowboys, he just shrugged it off. Which was good. There wasn't much they could give him their usual nonsense about. He could do anything there was to do in rodeo about as well as anyone. Everything but bull riding. When it came to bull riding, he was the best.

He rode his first bull when he was twelve. In competition with full grown cowboys. He didn't come close to winning that first ride. He just rode better than anyone ever would have thought he could. He stayed on the full eight seconds.

He rode regular after that, getting better with every ride. By the time he was seventeen, he was winning more than he lost. Often as not, he competed in other events too. He was doing well enough so that shortly before he turned eighteen, he'd made enough to buy himself a brand new Ford F150 and a twenty-two foot travel trailer to pull behind it.

It wasn't that the pickup or the trailer were the most powerful or the largest, it was just that they had everything on them any cowboy could ever want.

The season after his eighteenth birthday started great for him. He won every bull riding and bareback riding event he entered. It was beginning to look like he was going to be unbeatable. Especially the bull riding. It seemed as though no one could ride a bull the way he could.

Then came the night he drew the biggest, meanest, most difficult bull on the circuit. This would be Billy's first time on the bull, so there was a lot of speculation as to how well he'd do. He was a great bull rider, but was even he good enough to ride a bull that the few who stayed on never made a good ride of it?

We were all holding our breaths when Billy and that bull came charging out of the chute. That bull immediately threw his ass so high in the air he looked like he was going to flip over on his back. He came down with a twist so hard any other cowboy would've been thrown right there. Not Billy. He seemed to be glued to that critter. And all the time he held his hat high in the air, constantly raked that bull with his spurs, and best of all, he did it with a goddamn smile on his face.

The rest of the ride was more of the same. Every move the bull made, Billy countered. If ever there was a person made to do what they were doing, it was Billy on that raging bull. It was the most brilliant ride I've ever witnessed. Billy couldn't have been better. He even stayed on a couple of extra seconds before making a spectacular dismount.

The roar of the crowd was deafening as Billy raised his hat and bowed to them. He knew what he'd done, and he was damn well justified in taking a few extra bows. And the crowd loved him for it. Even when the bull charged him.

Billy was ready for him, and with the help of the clowns, easily dodged it. That's when he made his mistake. He turned back toward the crowd for one more bow.

He'd forgotten something he'd said so many times. "What's in a name."

"There can be a lot in one," I'd sometimes answered.

But Billy being Billy just shrugged it off.

I wish now I could have explained better why, even if it didn't matter in his case, sometimes a name did matter. Because this was one of those times. As Billy happily waved at the crowd, the bull stayed true to his name.

Twiceback. His name was Twiceback because it was a rare time that bull didn't come after the rider at least twice. And this time, he came twice back at Billy about as hard as a bull could. He hit an unsuspecting Billy in the small of his back, breaking it. The blow was so hard it snapped back his head hard enough to also break his neck.

Billy didn't suffer. He died right away. He didn't have to. It only happened because he forgot to pay attention to what's in a name.

To Save A Few

By Bud George

They were born days apart on small neighboring farms in Sweden. Big families - Olaf was number eight - Lars was number seven in both order. First cousins. Pretty good boys most of the time. Looked more alike than most brothers and always together - a pair.

At the beginning of school, the cousins were five years old. Early on, their fellow students found that you could not fight just one of them. It was always two. No one was foolish to try. They sailed through school nicely, until they turned sixteen. A two family meeting was called.

A decision had to be made. It was a dry year. The farms - both of them too small anyway, could not support all these people. Someone had to go. The cousins Olaf and Lars, big strong and always hungry, understood and were ready for adventure anyway.

They left the farms. Olaf had a big hunk of ham. Lars had a loaf of bread and some cheese. It got them to the ocean - the waterfront. They signed on a rough looking cargo ship as deck hands. They knew nothing about sailing or ships or the ocean. They thought it would be easy to learn. They did learn, but it was not easy.

The ship left them in Liverpool, England. They had a few coins from their sailing adventures, but no real skills. And, of course, little skill in the English language.

They found work shoveling coal on the waterfront. Hard, heavy work. The dust would kill you. The cousins left work after a long day - bent over like old men, covered in coal dust and looking like hopeless bums. With a few copper coins in hand, a voice rang out, "Your money or your life!"

A big man with a pistol in one hand and a short sword in the other, blocked the cousin's route off the dock. The cousins, now almost eighteen years old - hard and fast - surprised the bandit. Lars grabbed the gun hand, pushed it down. The pistol went off and removed two of the robbers toes. Olaf at the same time grabbed the sword arm and dropped it hard on the robbers other arm, slicing it to the bone. The cousins each took one of the robber's arms and dropped him off the dock. He hit the water and something hungry pulled him under.

A voice behind them said, "I see you can fight. Can you sail also?"

The cousins turned to face the voice - ready for another fight. They saw a well-dressed man wearing a pistol and a sword, but with his hands turned up. Not a threat. "I am captain John Steal. My ship is the Hasta La Vista. If you think you can sail, join me in the morning."

The cousins found the ship in the morning. She was a thing of beauty. Built in Portugal. Lovely smooth lines, almost like the later clipper ships. They asked permission to come aboard. John Steal welcomed them. He shook hands with both and introduced them to a stunningly beautiful black woman.

"This is Bea Maria," John said. "She sails with me."

The ship was as close to perfect as a sailing ship could be. Every rope, sail, surface sparkling clean. The crew quick and neat. The cousins sailed with John Steal and Bea Maria for eight years.

John Steal and Bia Maria were privateers, pirates, some said.

The cousins learned to sail anywhere in any weather. They learned tides, wind, stars, and they learned to fight. The two of them back to back, never give an inch, never back up made them fierce fighters. Always together.

John Steal would attack any target. He even took a British gun ship twice the size and with twice the canon as the Hasta La Vista. He did it with surprise and speed. "We needed the gunpowder and the new British rifles," he said. John let the British go. With no masts and a hole in the hull.

There were also many slow days when the cousins spent time with Bea Maria. She was a great teacher. The cousins learned to speak Spanish, French, Italian, and Portuguese. They even learned some

English, a language that made little sense to them. She also taught fencing. Yes, fencing with swords. The cousins excelled at this activity.

I guess the time comes for any adventure to end. They spoke to John Steal and Bea Maria about their desire to find wives and have families. John understood and put them ashore at a place in America called Georgia. As they were leaving with their few possessions and weapons Bea Maria stopped them. She handed them a small, heavy wood box. "Your share," she said.

The cousins did not expect this. The box was filled with coins, mostly gold. They'd had eight years of great adventure, good food, and education beyond what any school could offer. They expected nothing more.

"I think we will meet again," John said.

The cousins needed a way to live in a civilized manner, so they hand built a large ship in more or less the Viking tradition. They used mostly white oak and some yellow pine. It had a high pointed bow and a wide, yet graceful stern. The wives they found might be described in much the same way. They named the ship The Hana Maria, after their grandmother.

The cousins did fairly well. Lots of cotton and tobacco going north. Weather along the Atlantic coast was often rough, but they proved to be very reliable. They always delivered.

Around the beginning of their second year, they carried a full load all the way up to the Maine coast. There they spent a few days ashore. They met two big blond twenty year old, old maids.

The cousins were then about twenty-eight years old. The sisters, Enie and Effie were not considered suitable for marriage, because they had opinions and ideas they sometimes expressed.

It was a love at first meeting. Two marriages in a very short time. The cousins built a small, tight cabin aft on the Hana Maria and the two couples sailed happily home to Georgia.

The two couples looked very much alike, you could hardly tell them apart. When weather allowed the couples sailed together using the small cabin at the stern of the Hana Maria.

A time later, less than two years married, an event occurred that changed the couples' lives. A Boston customer - rich and powerful - decided not to pay the cousins for their cargo.

"Big dumb Swedes," he said. "What are they gonna do about it?"

Olaf threw Boston through a door. He did not open the door first. This embarrassed Boston to the point where he challenged Olaf to a duel. Yes, a duel with swords.

"Big dumb Swede. He won't know what poked him," Boston stated.

A clear Saturday morning, a short time later, Olaf and his second, Lars, met Boston and his group of seconds. The duel lasted less than four minutes. Boston on the ground, his clothes in shreds, bleeding badly. His sword was ten feet away from him, Olaf's sword was at his throat.

One of Boston's seconds ran toward Olaf. He fired his pistol at Olaf and missed. Lars shot him between the eyes. Two dead Bostonians. The cousins left Boston quickly. Rumors started about Viking warriors attacking innocent citizens.

The cousins and their lovely wives spent most of the next winter ashore in Georgia, discussing a new plan. Maybe head west - wide open country.

John Steal knocked on their door. "I have work for you and the Hana Maria," he said. "A trip to Ireland, across the ocean. We will sail together. I will escort you and your wives and your cargo. Yes, of course immediately."

Their wives agreed to the adventure. Cargo? Whatever John Steal had in mind. They dumped the Hana Maria's ballast and replaced it with cannon balls. The hold was loaded with rum poured in water tight kegs. On deck they loaded bales of red cloth wrapped in waterproof, oiled canvas.

"What do they do with the red cloth?" they asked John Steal.

"They make coats out of it," John replied.

The trip went fairly well. The Hana Maria loaded heavy, rode low in the water. The Hasta La Vista was always in sight. The Hana Maria unloaded at night in a port with no name. The Hasta La Vista waited off shore.

Both ships sailed south, into beautiful, warm, sunny weather. Captain John Steal declared clothing optional. He thought the Swedish crew would be improved with a bit of suntan. They were. Later, the sisters declared that they never before felt so free.

They arrived on the west coast of Africa. The Hasta La Vista held offshore as usual. She was still a privateer. The Hana Maria sailed into port. A slave market.

"Don't speak English," John Steal ordered. "These people are still fighting the crusades. Tell them you are from Iceland."

For Bea Maria, this was a rescue mission. She wanted to bring some of her people to America where there was plenty of food and plenty of work. Ninety-eight were loaded on the Hana Maria, along with a large supply of food and water. She rode low in the water again. The wind did not favor her on this trip. A very slow passage.

When they left the coast of Africa, they had ninety-eight souls aboard. When they arrived in Georgia, they had one hundred and one. Bea Maria was a great nurse. The sisters, Effie and Enie were experienced midwives. The slaves, Bea Maria called them guests, were all settled in pretty quickly. There was a huge demand for labor in America.

The cousins and their wives decided to head west cross country. They stopped in a place called San Francisco. They built a new ship and did well with cargos of lumber.

Captain John Steal and Bea Maria sailed off into the sunrise.

Oh! You are disappointed. You thought John Steal and Bea Maria met in some romantic cafe or Bistro in maybe Spain or Portugal? Sorry.

A Perfect Moment

By Michael Allen George

It was a long day. I was tired when I parked in my designated spot. In my apartment I opened a beer and lit a cigarette before I remembered I was almost out. I wasn't much in the mood to go out for more, but knew I'd run out long before I went to bed. After I finished the beer, I opened and the cigarette I lit, I went out for more.

I could have bought them at the service station across the street. Traffic was light, so all I needed to do was jaywalk across. Minimal walking. Trouble was, I didn't much like the youngsters who worked that shift, so I walked the couple of blocks to the dairy store.

Cigarettes cost about the same either place, and going to the dairy store meant walking some. But I liked the old guy who owned the place. He was standing behind the counter next to the cash register when I went in. His head was lowered, and he was shaking his head. A severe frown covered his face.

"What's so serious, Bill?" I asked.

"The stupid son of a bitch that runs this country," he sighed heavily. "I just listened to his speech. Part of it, he was talking about the war. Like he served. He made a movie about it, so now he's a damn expert."

A woman, with a loaf of bread in her hand, walked up to the counter. She had a curious look on her face. She was definitely pretty, but I ignored her anyway.

My sigh followed his. "Reagan is expert on only one thing. How to steal from the poor and give to the rich. What he knows about the war wouldn't fill a thimble. It would be good if he did know something. Be good for people to know what it was about. What life was like then."

"You know all about the war, do you?" he asked.

"Not hardly. My old man served. Air corps. Flew waist gunner in a B24. He talked about it some. I think he even liked parts of it. I've studied history too. But no, I don't begin to claim I know all about it. Just bits and pieces."

The lady standing there, waiting patiently for me to shut up so she could pay for her bread and get out of there, spoke up. "I'm curious," she said, "why you want to know about the war? Isn't it best forgotten?"

"A lot of people might think so," Bill told her. "It'd be a wrong thing to do though. We forget what happened then and things like who Hitler was, it could happen again."

"The thing about the war," I said, "about that time, that I think is the most important, is the attitude of the people."

"What's that go to do with anything," she asked.

"Everything," I said. "And I'll tell you if you'll tell me your name. If we're going to have this conversation, it'd be nice to know your name."

She smiled, shaking her head. "You're good," she said, with a smile close to a laugh. "We've seen each other in here before. You've finally figured out a way to ask. It's Lynn. And to tell you the truth, I'm curious too. What's your name?"

I smiled too. "Ray. Nice to finally meet you, Lynn. I assume you already know Bill."

"She does," Bill said. "She even knows me well enough for us to flirt a little."

"Of course we do," Lynn said. "What else would I do with a big, handsome man like you."

It showed in Bill's face that he liked her compliment as she turned to me. "You promised to tell me why someone's attitude was important."

"The depression before the war was ten years long. It was very hard times for most people. Then the war started, and it eased up some. Not because of the war, as most people claim. It was government spending that did it. War was just the catalyst that caused the government spending."

"Reagan says that's near the most evil thing the government can do."

"He's an idiot. Anyway, it was still hard times and we were now in a war. The whole world was in that war. Yet, somehow, most people then were still optimistic. After ten years of depression and now a war, they still believed in a better future."

"They still do, Don't they?"

The answer Lynn got was a double no from Bill and me.

"I don't understand. What's so different?"

"Like I said. Their positive attitude. In 1942 there was a popular song called The White Cliffs Of Dover. We were pretty much losing in 1942. The first line of that song was, "There'll be bluebirds over the white cliffs of dover". It goes on from there, on how everything was going to get better. Now all you hear is a lot of whining about having to work too hard and paying too much taxes. The Liberals are going to cause the end of the world."

"Before we get into this any farther," Lynn informed us, "I have to admit, I don't like Reagan either. I also don't know anything about the war. I still wonder though, if remembering it is important."

"It is," Bill said, "because it's part of us. If we forget all those times in history, like the war, we forget who we are."

A couple of more customers came in, which pretty much ended our conversation. Lynn paid for her bread, I bought a couple packs of cigarettes and we left together.

"I don't suppose you'd let me buy you drink somewhere?" I asked her. I expected a no answer. She was a good five years my junior and very good looking. I was mostly ordinary.

"I think I'd like that," she answered, much to my surprise.

We were both walking, but there was a bar only a couple of blocks away, so it didn't matter. Her apartment was on the way, so she quickly dropped off her bread. Just before we reached the bar, we walked past a delicatessen. I was hungry, and the aroma of many kinds of food reached out and grabbed me. By the time we went into the bar I was near starved.

"It smells good out there," she said. "After we have a couple of drinks, what say we stop at that deli and get some takeout? We can eat at my apartment."

The invitation was a surprise, but one I readily accepted. "That would be really nice," I said. "Especially since I'm already hungry."

She gave me a hard look. "I hope you mean by hungry, you want food. That's as far as my invitation goes."

"I don't expect anything else. I admit, I very much enjoy your company, but that's a lot more than I ever thought I would get from you."

"Get from me? I haven't given you anything."

"But you have. Your company. Your attention. I'm just an ordinary guy who's pushing forty. You're a beautiful young woman who's been giving me her attention. You make me feel good. You are, right now, giving a lot."

She smiled. "I can't tell if that's just a line, or if you mean it. Either way, it's a nice thing to say. And, if I thought you were just an ordinary guy, pushing forty or not, I wouldn't be here."

I just shrugged, not wanting to say something that might make her think I was pushing for something she didn't want.

Our conversation over our couple of drinks was primarily made up of get acquainted small talk, with just enough depth to it to make me comfortable with her. And, of course, like her even more than I already did. Being with her was an altogether pleasant experience.

I don't know how it happened, but I took her hand as we left the bar and walked to the deli. She gave me a sideways glance, but didn't object or pull away.

Inside, still holding her hand, we looked at the menu on the wall above our heads. Suddenly a feeling of total contentment filled me. With her there, standing next to me, I became totally relaxed. I felt as though everything was right between me and the world. Nothing going on out there mattered much. There was no place else I could possibly want to be. It was a perfect moment. I knew in that instant, life couldn't get any better than it was right then, right there. The kind of feeling that only happens once, but that you want for the rest of your life.

"What do you like?" Lynn asked, still looking at the menu.

"You," I said, without thinking about my words. "You, more than you can even imagine."

She looked at me, saw the expression on my face, and jerked her head back. Her eyes went wide.

"How did that happen?" she asked.

I suddenly wanted to kiss her, but said, "You just gave me something I've never had before."

"How could I have?"

"Don't know. You order the food, and I'll buy."

Her face still filled with a curious look, she ordered for us. I fumbled with the money when I paid the bill. I was still alive with the moment when we got to her well-kept apartment. I couldn't take my eyes off her face as we ate. The feeling of that perfect moment lingered through the meal.

"I've never had anyone react to me quite the way you are, Ray," she said. "Are you getting over it yet?"

"No. And I'm not going to. I'll never manage to get over what happened. Or you."

"You have to. You were just supposed to buy me a drink. Now we're eating together, and you're looking at me like I'm your long lost love."

"You are. Don't worry though. I will be good and go home when we finish eating. I don't understand what happened anymore than you do. Whatever it is though, for me it's pretty awesome."

"I didn't do anything to give you any special feelings. Not intentionally anyway."

"I know, and it's okay. I won't ask anything from you. I don't expect anything. I'll just forever be grateful for that beautiful, wondrous moment. And for what I feel now. I think it is going to be part of me forever. It's not something I could forget, even if I tried."

We were strangely quiet until we finished eating. We stayed quiet as we cleaned up the supper mess. She didn't say anything until I was ready to leave.

"Just like that," she said, "with all those feelings, you're going to leave."

"I'm just trying to do the right thing," I answered. "Would I like to stay? Of course I would. But pushing you at all would be wrong."

"Maybe you don't have to push."

I looked at her. She was pretty, smart, and had a friendly, easy going way that I loved. Any other time, and I would have stayed. I didn't want to go, but after what happened to me in the deli, I knew staying would be a mistake. It just wasn't possible that those feelings would ever happen again, no matter how much I looked for them.

If I stayed, somewhere, sometime, I would be disappointed they didn't. It wouldn't be fair to her if I was one day disappointed with our relationship because they didn't. Sooner or later, staying would hurt her, *and me,* then leaving now would. So, I told her I'd be going.

"Are you sure about that?" She moved close. anyway. I kissed her.

I relented, and let her lead me to her bedroom. The night we spent together turned out to be an experience close to that in the deli, when I had the perfect moment. Before it was over, making love took on a whole new meaning. But it was more. I never wanted to let her go. I wanted to keep her in my arms forever. But I was afraid it was a mistake to stay. Somewhere in the early hours I quietly left her bed.

It was a short, perfect moment that I had, followed by a near perfect night. One I was about to walk away from. How could we build a future on something impossible to follow long term?

"Don't leave yet," she said softly then. "No matter what, it is too early to go."

Before I answered, a question ran through my mind. "If stay or go, nothing could be that perfect again, did it make sense to leave her?" After all, this is where the memory of perfection was.

Sam

By Michael Allen George

Dad always said no when I asked if I could have a dog. I persisted. I wore him down, until finally one day he said yes. It happened that a neighbor had a litter of little black mongrels old enough to be given away. The one I picked looked much like a lab, but grew to be less than half the size of one.

Dad, who said he didn't like dogs much, asked me his name when he saw him. I said I hadn't named him.

"Well," Dad said, "he's Sam." And so he was.

It was early summer, and Sam and I spent countless hours roaming a nearby woods. It seemed, for those first few months, whatever we did, we did together.

We only had one problem. He was slow to housebreak. It got to the point that dad laid down the law. Either he was house broke by the end of the month or he was gone. Even more than me, Sam seemed to hear the message. He was trained with more than a week to spare.

Then school started, and I was able to spend less and less time with Sam. At the same time, he and Dad grew closer. Then one day I realized Sam wasn't my dog anymore. He belonged to Dad.

Even so, he and I still did a fair amount together. On the lake, where we spent our annual summer vacation, was the place Sam was the closest to both dad and me. He loved to ride in the boat. Always up front, standing as if he was totally in command of it. His tongue hanging out and his long ears flapping in the wind, he was in his element.

If a fish was caught, he was right there to attack if it got dangerous. Dad and I fished more than anyone else, and no matter what time we started or quit, he was always with us on that boat.

He was a feisty little guy, and considered himself big enough to match any dog, no matter their size. He was, in fact, always ready to take on anyone or anything. Even a gravel truck. The truck won of course, and Sam spent a long time with his rear legs taped together as his broken hip healed.

As time went on, and we all grew older, it seemed as though Sam had always been with us, would always be with us. But like all of us, the years slowly crept up on him and began to show. Still, whenever I saw him, his tail wagged the same as ever.

Then one weekend, mom and dad suddenly had to be gone. There wasn't time to do much else, so they prepared a room for him. It was empty, with the floor covered with newspaper. A lamp lit the room, there was a heavy quilt for him to sleep on, and food and water dishes.

I would have taken him to my house, but Sam didn't care much for my golden retriever, even if she was a female. Instead, I agreed to check on him every day of the four days they were going to be gone.

It all went well until the last day. Up until then, he'd greet me with his tail wagging as always, and anxious for me to pet him, then stay and talk for a while. I didn't make it there on that last day until after dark. He was lying in a corner, and although he tried desperately to wag his tail, he failed.

I knew immediately that something was wrong as I watched him struggle to get up and greet me. He couldn't move.

I sat down next to him and started to pet him. He sighed heavily, then whimpered. His eyes told me he was grateful for my being there. They also told me he knew something bad was wrong, and he didn't want to be alone.

I stayed with him as long as I could, but eventually I had to leave. There was a job to go to in the morning.

Reluctantly, I stood to go. He couldn't do anything but stare at me with those big, oh so sad eyes. There was no doubt he was telling me he wanted me to stay. I wanted to, but felt I had to go home so I could get some sleep. With a heavy heart, I left him.

I didn't sleep well that night. Images of Sam, in that room alone, frequently woke me. When morning arrived and I got up to meet the day, I thought again of Sam, alone all night in that room where I left him. It was hard to imagine the terror he must have felt.

It was then that it occurred to me. If the situation were reversed, and it was me helpless and alone in that room, there is no way he would have left. He couldn't have been pried away. And we humans think we are the special, superior life form on the planet. Just one of the many ways our thinking needs some help.

Taking My Hand

By Michael Allen George

We lived in the country, so the deck was on the front of the house. That's where I was sitting when they drove up. My favorite aunt and uncle. Seeing them was no surprise. For whatever reason, it had been a habit of theirs over the years to unexpectedly drop in. Maybe it was because my wife, Rachel and I, were always glad to see them.

This time the visit was even more special. They brought their daughter, my cousin Lou, with them. I hadn't seen her in way too many years, so it was a pleasant surprise to see her now.

I was always very fond of her, even though she was about seven years younger than me. When we were kids we spent a fair amount of time together. I always owned a car when I was a kid, and I often took her and her older brother along to the beach or horseback riding or whatever activities I happened to be involved in.

I got a lot of static from my so-called friends for doing it, but I frankly didn't give a damn. They were my cousins, and they were going to be part of my life forever. Who knew about other people.

Lou saw me before she even got out of the car, and when she did she rushed up the steps. I barely managed to stand before she reached me. The hug I got was as real and warm as one could get. Then she really surprised me with a big, wet kiss on the lips.

"It's so good to see you, Jerry," she said. "It's been a long time."

"Too long," I agreed. "So what brings you way out here in the country?"

"The folks convinced me to go for a ride with them today. I've been way too housebound since the divorce, and they thought I should get out. They were right."

Rachel, who was busy on the computer doing something for her job, finally joined us. "I'm sorry I didn't come out right away," she said. "I just found out I have to fly to New York tomorrow, to straighten out the mess that's been made of the computer system at our office there."

I was surprised at that. She'd given me no previous indication she was going to do anything like that. But she quickly gave me an explanation.

"I'm sorry, Jerry. I didn't tell you earlier because I didn't know earlier. All this crap just came up."

"When are you going?"

"I'm flying out first thing tomorrow morning."

"Okay. But I think I'll bring the kids along when I take you to the airport. Then I won't have to hurry home."

It was summer vacation, and I didn't want to leave them on their own for too long. And it was just by chance that this was Sunday, and I was looking ahead to a week's vacation.

"Are you not working tomorrow?" Lou asked me.

"No, I'm taking a week's vacation."

"I've got a good idea then. Since you're going to be in town anyway, why don't you come over to my house for breakfast after you drop Rachel at the airport?"

I decided that it might be fun, so I quickly agreed.

We spent the next couple of hours sitting on the deck talking about anything and everything before they went home. We had a simple supper that night, and went to bed early.

Rachel was tense in the morning, and a bit irritable. I asked her why and she only said it was because she didn't like the New York office. It seemed like more than that to me, but I let it ride.

At the airport she asked to be dropped off. She didn't want us to wait with her until she boarded the plane. The kids were making her nervous she said. I kind of wondered what the real reason was, but again, I let it go.

Lou was ready for us, with everything out that we needed to make the breakfast. The two of us went to work on it, and her kids and mine disappeared into the depths of the house.

They quickly returned when the meal was ready, and all showed good appetites. When the meal was eaten and Lou and I finished the cleanup, we decided to take the kids to the beach. It was a warm summer day, and probably the best place to entertain them.

We didn't bring anything along to swim in, but Lou and the kids found enough older things for all of us. I was wearing her ex-husband's swim trunks. For me, the best part of the beach was watching Lou.

There was nothing special about the two piece suit she wore, just a lot special about the way she filled it out. If she hadn't been my cousin, I would have had some evil thoughts. In fact, cousin or not, the suit did raise my thoughts to a few steps above those of a puritan.

Lou was also a bit of a feely touchy kind of person, and tended to sit close whenever we sat on the beach. And that was something we did frequently. Her constant touches, especially the ones that landed on my upper leg, tended to send a special kind of shivers running through my body.

Late in the afternoon we took the kids to a pizza place and let them have at it. They managed the better part of three large pizzas. Lou and I split a medium.

I planned to head for home after eating, but Lou decided we should stay the night. I was hesitant at first, but her smile and the look in her big blue eyes convinced me.

I have no idea what the kids did that evening, but they all seemed content, so I didn't care. Lou and I spent the evening on her back deck, sharing a comfortable love seat.

She sipped a glass of wine and I drank beer. We talked about the past a lot, the future a little, and finally the present. It all went okay until she asked about Rachel.

"Does she travel a lot?" Lou asked.

"Actually, only rarely. This was the first time it was a last minute thing."

"She did seem a bit out of sorts about it, didn't she?"

"Yeah, actually, she did."

"Oh well, it was probably nothing."

There was the problem. It wasn't what Lou said, it was the way she said it. It made me feel something I normally didn't. Suspicious of Rachel and what her trip was about.

Lou seemed to notice that her words had affected me, and changed the subject. We sat out there talking until the kids gave up and went to bed. Then Lou said she thought it was time for us to do the same.

She gave me some of her ex-husband's sweats to wear, then went into the bedroom to change into her own nightwear. To say I was shocked when she rejoined me is a classic understatement. Her nightgown wasn't shear, but it was translucent enough to accent all the parts that mattered.

She laughed when she saw my look as I gaped at her. "That is exactly the reaction I was hoping for, Jerry," she said. "Come now, let's be going to bed."

"I thought I was sleeping on the couch."

"Don't be silly. I have a king size bed. No point in you sleeping on an uncomfortable couch when I have room there for you."

"Aren't you afraid of what might happen with me in your bed?"

"I could stand here and play word games with you, but I don't see any sense to it. Why would I invite you into my bed if I was. Now come."

I did, but lay next to her without making a move. There'd never been another woman since I married Rachel. After a while, I heard Lou sigh.

Taking my hand, she moved closer to me, then moved it over her breast. That was all it took. I kissed her. From there we moved into a wonderland I'd never known before. It lasted a long time, and after it was over it took me a while to realize what I'd done. Filled with guilt, I turned to Lou.

"I'm sorry," I said. "I should never have let that happen."

Lou turned to me. "You don't really," she said, laughing and taking my hand again, "believe that, do you?"

When she moved my hand, I guessed she might be right. She made it difficult for me to believe it shouldn't have happened.

Letters to My Son: A special talent I discovered in high school

By David George

It was the start of my junior year. Up until that point I had been an indifferent student. Yet outside of school I was an avid reader and writer of short stories and poems. The summer before my junior year I decided that I needed to change my ways. I wanted to be the first person in my family to get a college degree.

To embark on this new path, I needed to choose courses that would interest me. Something that involved creative writing seemed like the way to start. I signed up for a journalism course, having no idea what that actually entailed. The first day of class was a huge disappointment. I learned that journalism was weighted down with myriad rules for things like interviewing and gathering information. There were different types (e.g., agricultural and investigative journalism). The subject seemed on the opposite pole from "creative."

I made an appointment with a counselor. I explained my dilemma. He responded, "Well, what do you want to do?"

"I don't know," I said. An idea popped into my head. "How about a shop class?" Though this might have made sense considering my working-class background, in truth I had no interest in shop.

The counselor: "All the shop classes are full."

At this point a thought balloon of unknown origin floated into my head. "How about Spanish?" To this day I have no idea where that came from. I had given exactly zero thought to the issue of foreign languages.

Amend that: I came from a Swedish family and did know a few words in that language. But I had no interest in studying Swedish, even if there were a course in the subject.

The counselor's reaction to my "Spanish" idea: "Are you off your rocker?" He may not have spoken those words exactly, but I'm sure I'm not far off the mark. "Look at your English grades." They were lousy, to be sure. "There's no way I'm going to authorize your signing up for Spanish."

Begging and pleading did not produce the desired effect, so I put my foot down. There was no way I would leave his office until he gave me permission to study Spanish. Now, if this were fiction, I would have to come up with character motivation. Why did the young man want to study Spanish? There was nothing in his background that suggested he would be interested in the subject. But since truth is stranger than fiction, we'll have to forego motivation and stick with the odd circumstance: for some unknown reason that 16-year-old student with a history of lousy grades was determined to sign up for a Spanish class, though he had no idea what the subject entailed nor the cultures it represented. He had never met anyone who spoke Spanish, he had never sampled the food from a Spanish-speaking country, nor did he really know just what countries were "Spanish-speaking."

Suffice to say, the young man wore down the counselor's resistance. He threw up his arms and exclaimed: "Ok, ok. You win. I'll sign the sheet. Go ahead. Take Spanish. But don't come crying back to me when you're flunking out."

So Spanish it would be. Whatever the source of my strange new obsession, the very first day in class I fell in love with the language. After a week, it was a marriage made in heaven. The musical sounds of Spanish were as exciting as rockin' with Chuck Berry (an odd analogy, I know, but I'm trying to think like a 16-year-old in the 1950s). I became fascinated with the grammatical structures. I started conjugating verbs in my head. The first year of Spanish was a breeze. The second year was a hurricane. I became so proficient that the student teacher frequently asked me to stay after school to explain some grammatical concept (e.g., the subjunctive) she would have to present to her students the following day.

To make a long story short, years later I was a college professor… of Spanish. That is, Spanish and Portuguese. The latter language grew out of my love of Spanish. The two tongues are kissing cousins. More romance languages made their appearance. I managed to learn enough French and Italian to get by in France and Italy. To be honest, barely get by.

The moral of this story, if there is one: follow your heart. Trust your instincts. That day in the counselor's office my heart spoke loud and clear and overcame the bureaucrat's authority and preconceived notions. I will not claim that instinct trumps reason. Certainly not. But there are times that instinct, gut feeling, heart shine a light on a path never before explored and reveal special talents previously unknown to those who possess them.

The Kid

By Bud George

Late March - beginning of spring. I had taken a few days off. A few estimates, a few proposals. The kid came down the alley as I was cleaning and reorganizing my truck. A new season. Busy I hoped.

"Mister Anderson," the kid said, "I need a job.

"School?" I asked.

"I left."

I'd seen this kid around town now and then. Big kid, seventeen or eighteen years old. Sloppy dress, too heavy. Glasses with bent frame. Untied shoes. Alone most of the time. I guess he was the lowest kid, the one usually picked on. Public school social order.

"Come and see me Saturday Morning. Nine o'clock," I said.

He did. On time! I told him a little about the work we did. Mostly framing. We were carpentry subcontractors, but sometimes the general contractor. I was the state licensed one. Too cold, we work anyway. Too hot, we still work. Too wet, too muddy, too anything, we work. I laid it on pretty thick.

"Can you live with that?" I asked.

"Yeah," he said.

I hired him.

The first week or so it was a nightmare for him. Couldn't do much right. Cost me time. But it's always that way starting out. My teaching methods were probably a little harsh. Do exactly what I tell you to do. Don't ask, don't question. Later on as you learn you can earn the right to call me an asshole. Many people do.

The kid came back for the next week. Really good. I think we'll stick it out for a while. He picked up skill steadily. Pretty good with basic math and he could read a tape.

Over that season he became a solid carpenter and a damn good worker. He told me about school. Bullied, I think. I talked him into returning anyway.

"Last year," I told him. "You'll need that diploma someday."

"Yeah," he said, "when I run out of ass wipe."

I picked him up one cool morning a while after he returned to school. Dropped him off and leaned against my truck fender to gossip with a neighbor who dropped his daughter off.

A fashionably dressed young man in front of the kid. "Look at them shit-kickin' boots you got there," he said. Then scraped his fashionable sandals over the kids boot toes - leaving wet grass stains.

The kid hesitated a moment, then picked up the fashionably attired young man and set him down on the hood of his BMW. Made a lovely dent.

The gentleman yelled, "My old man's gonna fucking sue you."

"Yeah," the kid said, "your ass print on the hood." He put on hand on the young gentleman's chest to hold him in place. With the other hand removed his fashionable shoes. With which he cleaned his shit-kicking boots.

At that moment a strikingly pretty, small, dark-haired girl slid her arms through the kids. "I need more help with my math," she said.

As they turned to go, the kid said to the young gentleman, "Tell your old man you ran into cry baby Chris today."

The girl laughed. "I don't think I'll call him kid anymore."

They Will Never Make It

A True Story

By Michael Allen George

It was on the way to the farm that Saturday morning I decided we should do it. Dennis was skeptical when I told him what I wanted to do. He didn't think the horses were up to it.

"They don't have shoes," he complained. "If we're ever gonna make them walk that far, they should have shoes."

"It's only fifty miles to the cities," I argued. "They can walk that far."

"What if they can't?"

"They can do it. We've ridden them for nearly a full day before. It didn't bother them any."

"Yeah, maybe, but I've got a lot of chores to do today. It'll be late before we get started. It'll be dark before we get there."

"It won't be that late if I help with the chores. Tell me what to do, and they'll be done early enough."

He did and we whipped into it. The chores took longer than I hoped, but I wanted to go anyway. His folks, uncle Paul and aunt Ruby, didn't think much of my idea when we told them my plan.

"It'll be dark before you get there," Ruby said. "Riding in the dark on the highway will be dangerous. You've got plenty of places around here to ride. You don't need to do anything as foolish as this."

"More than that," Paul said, "those horses won't be able to walk that far. What do you plan to do, when you get stranded somewhere with two lame horses?"

"I don't think they'll go lame," I argued again. "They've never had any problems before, no matter how much we rode them."

"You were riding gravel roads, farm roads, and fields then. This time, most of the ride will be pavement."

"We'll be riding on the shoulder of the road. Most of them aren't paved."

"We don't think you should do this," Ruby said. "But we're not going to stop you. If something goes wrong, you can call us. And if it does, maybe you'll learn something from it."

Back then, in the fifties, the world was safe enough to let two teenage boys attempt to ride a couple of unshod horses from West Union in Carver County to June Avenue in Crystal Minnesota.

So off we went. Dennis and me, riding Lindy and Lancer. Dennis was on Lindy, a mare, and I rode Lancer, a Tennessee Walker. They were both good horses, but when we trotted the horses, I had the advantage. Lancer's special gait was as smooth as was found on any horse. Lindy's was typical, and could be somewhat jarring.

We were also not really prepared for our journey. We left with nothing but us and the two horses. No food and no water. The lack of food was no problem. The horses ate grass and we could go hungry. Water was something else.

None of us got a drink until we got to Chaska, about twelve miles from the farm. There was a small lake there, with a picnic grounds and beach. The horses drank their fill from the lake, and we drank out of a faucet provided for the picnic grounds. Water never tasted better.

We were riding along highway 212 by then, but we were lucky. It was a light day for traffic. The shoulders were just wide enough, so we could ride side by side. It didn't matter that much, because our conversation was close to nonexistent. We were already feeling the sore muscles we were developing from that relatively short time in the saddle.

About the time we got to the Shakopee turnoff, which was Y intersection, Dennis asked, "Do you really think we should keep on going? It's still a shorter ride back home, then it is all the way to your folk's."

"I'd as soon keep going," I told him. "But if you really want to quit, I guess we can."

"I don't know. You think the horses are going to make it?"

"Yes. They still don't seem to be at all tired. I think Lancer would be more than happy to do some running, if I left the reins loose enough."

"Well, that's probably true, but he's nuts for running. I'm surprised he hasn't tried to take off on you yet. Most of the time we ride, he's fighting to run."

"I think he somehow senses that he should save his energy."

"Probably. And we might as well keep on going. If we turn around now, we'll get more 'I told you so's' then I ever want to hear."

We stopped at gas station where they let us water the horses, and I bought us a couple of candy bars. Traffic was heavier now. At the Y intersection we'd just passed, highway 169 joined 212, so that it had nearly doubled. It stayed light enough though, so it didn't spook the horses.

The ride from there to highway 100 was long, but relatively uneventful. We were into the twilight hours by then, and plenty tired. With saddles that had grown considerably harder than what they were when we started out, we were feeling the effects of the ride.

We were okay with the now heavy traffic for maybe a half hour. Then the action started. The first to try and have fun with us was a carload of teenage boys. As the drove by us they filled the air with yells, screams and obscenities. That, however, wasn't enough for them. They came around again and lobbed a few firecrackers at us. Dennis and I responded with our fingers. Lancer did one better and let loose with a large dump in the middle of their noise and stupidities. To the credit of both horses, that was their only response to the mindless wonders.

We didn't get much farther before the adults got in the game. Lots of yells and horn honking. The worst were the truckers, blasting away with their air horns. Again, the horses took it in stride and ignored the almost constant noise.

The only thing that did have a definite effect on them was a freight train. It was a long one, running under a bridge we needed to cross. For that, we dismounted and led them across. Even so, they were plenty shy of it, and it did take a bit of coaxing to get them across.

It was a big relief when we left highway 100. The short ride up 36th Avenue was uneventful, and we were soon riding up to my parents' front yard. We weren't quiet about it, and as we were dismounting, my father looked out the front door.

"Did you," he asked, shaking his head vigorously, "ride those damn horses all the way here?"

I kept my answer simple. "Yes."

"What the hell for?"

"I don't think we know," Dennis answered. "But it was an interesting ride."

"What's the reason, Mike? It could have been dangerous you know. A ride that long, and those horses could have gone lame on you."

"They're fine. They didn't have any problems the whole way."

"Maybe not, but you're going to have to give them a long rest before you ride them back."

"I'm going to need one too," Dennis said, "if I even ride them back."

"Well," Dad said, "I'm sure they're thirsty. Bring them into the back yard, so I can give them a drink."

He found a couple of five gallon pails, filled them, and watched the horses drink their fill.

"So where are you planning on keeping them while they're here in the cities?" he asked as we watched them.

I told him about a friend who had a couple of horses not too far away. The small farm where he lived had a decent size pasture, so I thought he'd let me keep them there.

We rode the horses there in the morning, and he and his parents had no problem with ours staying there for a week.

"I think," Dennis said, once they settled in, "that if you can find someone else fool enough to ride back home with you next Saturday, I'd as soon skip it."

"What if I can't?"

"I'll do it then, but I'd rather skip it. It was a long ride."

I had little hope of anyone being willing to ride with me. At the same time, I decided I wouldn't ask Dennis either way. If nothing else, I'd make the ride alone, leading one of the horses. It would be a miserable ride with one small advantage. Going it alone, I could switch horses a few times, so they wouldn't get as tired.

Determined as I was to make the ride alone, the total lack of a positive response from the people asked about riding with me worried me some. Then I got a pleasant surprise. My brother-in-law, Ron, said he'd love to make the ride with me.

We started out early the next Saturday morning. This time with some water and a few snacks. We took a different route this time, sticking to county roads and avoiding the main highways. It was a longer ride, more than five miles, but the lack of traffic and improved scenery more than made up for the distance.

Ron and I didn't talk much, but he proved to be good company the whole day. Best of all, he didn't complain at all, even though he must have been plenty sore long before the ride was over.

The only mishap we had was when he suddenly realized he'd lost his watch. The band must have somehow broken. We rode back a ways, looking for it, but quickly realized it could have fallen off miles back. It was a big disappointment for him, since the watch was a gift from his father.

But disappointed or not, he continued to be a good riding partner.

Our stop at the lake in Chaska was a big relief. We got a much needed stretch of the legs and the horses were able to drink their fill. We also stayed there long enough to let them chew on some of the green grass the park had to offer.

During the last leg of our journey, from Chaska to the farm, we were both tired. The only thing we looked forward by then was getting there. As we wore down with each mile, the horses seemed to gradually pick up their step. Within a couple of miles of the farm, if someone would have been watching the horses, they would have sworn we were just starting out.

As we rode up the hill, approaching the church, which was less than a half mile from the farm, we found that we had to tighten up on the reins some. For a couple of horses who weren't supposed to be able to walk as far as they did, they had plenty of life in them.

Then, as we turned onto the road that took us to the farm, those two critters exploded. There was no holding them back. Ron and I both knew it was futile to try. We gave the horses their heads and we made that last half mile at a full gallop. All we could do is hang on. The stop at the barn was sudden. It was with a great sense of relief that we both had when we dismounted.

Dennis soon joined us. "After that long a ride, you still made them run at the end."

"Wasn't our idea," Ron told him. "They are the ones who wanted to run. Wasn't much we could do about it either."

"They've been picking up energy for quite a while," I said. "When we got to the church, that was it. They took off. We were both too tired to try to stop them."

"Well, that was the last thing I expected to see," Dennis said. "After tw0 long rides like they just had, I expected them to be half dead when you got here."

"Well," I said, smiling a bit, "I did tell you they could do it before we started the ride."

"Doing it is one thing, finishing the way they did, well, that's something else."

And they were something else. They never showed any kind of problem after being ridden over a hundred miles in one week. I also heard less about all the things they couldn't do.

The truth is though, they surprised me too. They did most of the work on those rides, yet finished a lot stronger than we did. If those rides would have been a contest between us and the horses, I'd have to say, "The horses won."

Not To Be Trusted

By Michael Allen George

Ever since I saw my first cowboy movie, I wanted my own horse. My riding experience was limited to a few times at a riding stable. Places where you mostly played follow the leader, and the guide got upset if you deviated even slightly from their expectations. I loved riding anyway, even if I wasn't much good at it.

I saved money, from the meager pay I got for being a stock boy in a grocery store for two years before I had enough to buy a horse. It was then I realized that I knew nothing about horses, so going alone to buy one was not a wise thing to do. There was only one person in my life who actually knew anything about horses.

When he was younger and still living on the farm, my grandpa trained wild horses for work. It was a task more difficult than training a horse to be ridden. I was told many times growing up, that he was good at it. So I asked him if he would come with me to find a horse to buy.

He agreed, but not with much enthusiasm. Grandma had her own opinion of my going off alone with Grandpa. "You shouldn't be doing this," she complained. "It could lead to serious trouble. Your grandpa is a good man most of the time, but if he makes you stop someplace where he can get a drink, it would not be a good thing. He's not to be trusted when he drinks."

"I think it'll be okay," I argued. "Besides, he's the only one I know who can help me find a good horse. I don't know enough to do it alone."

"Well, I won't tell you that you can't take him with you, but I will tell you, you'd best be careful while you're out there with him. And you most definitely better not let him go into any place he can drink."

"I won't, Grandma," I promised.

My mom told me the same thing about Grandpa when I told her my plans. Like my grandma, she was reluctant to let me go, but wouldn't say no to the idea.

So off we went to find a horse for me. Grandpa and I hadn't ever done much together. The most important activity we'd ever done together before this day was when he taught me how to make his meatballs. Not only were his meatballs different from anybody else's, they were better. I considered them to be treasures, and he knew that. I suspect that was one of the reasons he consented to go with me to find a horse. That, and the fact I appreciated him as a person, and never treated him like an old man.

"I sure do appreciate you coming with me today," I told him when we started out. "I feel real lucky to have a grandpa who's an expert on horses."

"I know some about horses," he said. "But I ain't no expert. The last horse expert I ever knew is dead."

"Really? When did he die?"

"About thirty-five years ago. And that's about how old he was when he died."

"What did he die from when he was so young?"

"Being too damn expert with a wild horse. A man makes too many mistakes when he's too expert. And where that's more than true with horses, it's also true of women. You start thinking you're an expert, you'll get yourself in trouble every time."

I have found that to be good advice all my life. Especially with women.

Him being an expert or not, I was still glad to have him along. From the first horse I got on at the first place we stopped, his advice sounded contrary to what he claimed. It sounded expert to me.

With most of the horses I tried out that day, it only took a few minutes for Grandpa to say no. Even the two that I really liked, that I hoped he'd say yes to, he rejected. I asked him why.

"They were good horses, you were right about that," he said. "They just weren't right for you. Somewhere there's a special horse just for you."

"How will you know when it's the right horse."

"I can't tell you that exactly," he explained. "But I damn well will know."

We were at the last stop for the day, and I was on the third horse. His gait was especially smooth, but at the same time the horse obviously didn't like to be restrained. Everything about him, from the way he held his head, to the way he moved, and his heavy, deep breaths, told me he wanted to run. I loved the horse, but he scared the hell out of me. So, of course, that's the one Grandpa approved of.

"You've got a horse," he said. "That's the best one by far of all we've looked at."

How could I argue. Grandpa did know his horses, and he did like this one. So we asked the price. It was fifty dollars more than I had. Grandpa knew it.

"You're asking too much," he told the man who owned the horse. "He's a sound animal, but you and I both know he isn't but green broke and it's going to take a powerful amount of training to make him worth the price you're asking. The kid'll give you fifty less than you're asking for him."

"How about twenty-five less?"

"That's twenty-five more than he has. From my point of view, our offer is the maximum the horse is worth at this stage of his training. So you can take it or we'll be on our way."

"I suppose you'll want him delivered too?"

"It's a short drive, but a long ride."

"Tomorrow's the best I can do. That be soon enough for you?"

"Tomorrow is just fine. I won't be there, but the kid will."

That settled, we started for home. Because I was curious about why Grandpa picked the half wild horse he did, I asked him.

"It's simple. You've got a lot to learn. The other horses we looked at, and right or wrong, they'd have done pretty much whatever you wanted. The one you bought won't. He'll keep you on your toes and teach you most of what you're going to need to know. By the time you get a decent ride out of him, you'll both be better for it."

I couldn't argue with his logic, and turned my attention back to the road.   We were traveling county roads instead of highways, so we were going to go through some small towns. The first one we went through, he pointed out the local bar.

"Pull in there," he said. "I'm going to have a quick drink."

I thought about all the warnings I'd been given about this very thing as I parked in front of the bar. It was probably a bad idea to stop, but how could I not? Grandpa had just given me a full day of his time. He'd looked at and rejected a lot of horses, and with each rejection, he'd pissed someone off. Given all that, I wasn't about to not stop. Whatever happened, I'd find a way to deal with it.

As I waited for him in the car, I thought about the day we'd had together, and how much help he'd been. He'd also showed me a considerable amount of patience, going from riding stable to sale barn and then to another riding stable most of the day. He was a good man, my grandpa was, and I was grateful to him for what he'd done. And although I didn't know it at the time, the horse he picked out for me, did prove to be just the right one.

So that way, he definitely proved to be one I could trust. Then, to my surprise, less than thirty minutes later, he came out of the bar. He'd only had one drink.

"Okay," he said, "we can go home now."

"I have to thank you again, Grandpa, for going with me today."

"No need for that. It was a good day for me too. Just be sure you take good care of that horse you bought."

"I will," I said. And I did. I wasn't about to betray his trust.

Grab the Other End Abe

By Bud George

No please, no thank you, no, "Can you lift the other end?".
I was new at this - a part-time job. Part-time meant I started work an hour or two after Ken, the boss, and the rest of the crew. Quitting time was when Ken said, "Pick it up." 4:00 PM to 7:00 PM or whatever.

I'd stop at home, eat supper, sleep a couple of hours and go to work at my regular, full-time computer job - midnight to eight AM. Most weeks I worked more part-time hours than full-time hours.

The other end was a flitch beam, about 12 to 14 feet long. Two 2x12 Douglas Fir planks with a solid steel plate bolted between them. I knew from my days of construction work that one 2x12, 12 foot long was about all I could handle. But Ken said grab it so I did. When Ken gave directions, you just did it. No questions, just do it right now.

I got a grip on the end just as he pulled it off the truck bed. I wasn't sure my knees could take the weight. We carried it up the driveway, which was blocked by a pile of sand, used to backfill basements. You did not backfill with bad dirt (clay). I was backfilling with a long-handled shovel and a wheelbarrow (Abe used a long handle - easy on the back). That is how I was elected from the crew to carry the other end. I was closest to the truck.

We got the beam up the drive and slid it onto the deck. The deck is the house floor - (2x10 joists 16" on center) with 5/8 CDX plywood subfloor nailed 8" on center with 8penny sinkers (nails). I learned this stuff much later in that year.

I turned to go back to my backfilling. Ken said, "Up here, we gotta set this header." The flitch beam became a header. A lot of stuff like that happened in construction. Like a piece of two-by-four became studs and trimmers.

Ken set two 8-foot wood step ladders, one at each end of a 12-foot or so opening and said, "Grab the other end, Abe." Abe was my nickname, bestowed on me by Ken my first day in construction. Just about everyone had a nickname, unless you were from some foreign weird place, like maybe St. Paul.

Two good sturdy, wood step ladders -type one- leased for a capacity of two hundred twenty pounds each. At that time, I weighed two hundred ten pounds. Ken was about two hundred thirty. The flitch beam was around three hundred. Interesting math. The third step on Ken's ladder broke on the way up. The two lower ones broke on the way down. As Ken went down, I saw my short life flash before my eyes.

He did not drop the beam. I *barely* held my end. We set the beam on the floor (deck). Ken said said, "You okay?"

I said, "I don't know, Ken." I guess I thought that because I could still talk, everything was okay.

He got another, older, 8 foot ladder in place and we set the beam. Ken had framed an opening just about 1/8 inch loose (large). Each end got two trimmers, supports or posts that were not 1/8 inch short.

I went back to my backfilling. Light work now, and finished out the day. I left the job, and walked to my truck wondering what kind of impossible job Ken would have for me tomorrow.

There was a parking ticket tucked under my windshield wiper.

Letters to My Son: My first big trip From Minnesota to Guadalajara, Mexico, via San Francisco, California

By David George

My first big trip took place the summer after my freshman year in college (1961, age 19). In those days there were no study abroad programs, at least none sponsored by my school, the University of Minnesota. I had studied Spanish for 2 years in high school and fallen in love with the language. I had a friend from Panama and practiced speaking Spanish with him and his family, so I had real-life conversation to supplement the grammar rules I learned in the classroom.

When I started college in the fall of 1960, I was considering a science major. I signed up for a beginning chemistry class that attracted many pre-med students. I also enrolled in an intermediate Spanish class. Though I did well in my first quarter of chem, things went downhill in my second quarter. At the same time, I was thriving in Spanish.

By spring semester, I had decided to spend the summer in Mexico, though I had no idea how to go about it. Why Mexico? I had met several Mexican students in high school and college. I felt a connection to them and their culture. Besides, Mexico was the closest Spanish-speaking country, and my transportation options were limited. I spoke to my Spanish prof, who recommended I travel to the city of Guadalajara. My knowledge of the city amounted to exactly zero. The prof was a close friend of a family in Guadalajara. He suggested I write a letter and propose a 2-month stay with the family. Though I knew absolutely nothing about the family, I took my prof's word that they were *muy simpáticos*, and wrote them a letter with my proposal. Since back then there was only snail mail and the postal service in Mexico was precarious—which I would learn later—it took about a month to get a response. The father of the family —señor Trejo—accepted my offer and stipulated the date on which I should arrive.

How would I get there? My friend Ray was going to drive to California and suggested I join him. Since I was interested in a girl named Sue—no, not "a boy named Sue," Mr. Cash—I decided that San Francisco would be the first leg of my trip. Now, you may be asking yourself, *San Francisco is WAY out of the way on a trip from Minneapolis to Guadalajara. Weren't you concerned about all those extra miles?* (Extra miles: Minneapolis-San Fran 2,000, San Fran-Guadalajara 2,000 = 4,000 // Minneapolis-Guadalajara direct route 2,000 miles. Do the math.) You may ask, *why not fly?* Because air travel was prohibitively expensive. Besides, the thought never crossed my mind that detouring to San Francisco was in any way an inconvenience. I never even checked the mileage. The important thing was the excitement the trip would provide. I came from a working-class family whose members had rarely ventured farther than the neighboring states of Wisconsin, Iowa, and South Dakota. (The exception: my father, stationed on an airbase in England during WWII. In addition, my siblings would later travel farther afield.)

Departure day arrived shortly after the end of spring quarter. When Ray came by to pick me up, I discovered we had a previously unannounced travel companion. Ray's 69-year-old grandpa. He was OLD. Nowadays, many folks that age and older go on long bike trips, jog, work out in the gym, and belong to book and film groups, but Ray's grandpa was feeble and child-like. When we stopped to see the sights, like Mount Rushmore, we practically had to carry grandpa from the car to the observatory (Grand View Terrace). Grandpa also whined constantly.

We were excited to drive through Nevada. We wanted to visit a casino and drop a few coins in the slot machines. The only places where you could gamble legally in those days were located in Nevada. We reached the city of Reno (Las Vegas was too much of a detour). We entered a casino. A chubby security guard approached us, and told us in a friendly manner, also addressing himself respectfully to grandpa, that you had to be 21 to enter a casino and he regretted to inform us that we would have to leave. THE PREVIOUS ACCOUNT IS FAKE NEWS! What the guard actually said was, "How old are you?" Before I could lie—as was my intention—Ray blurted out: "19." The guard: "You gotta be 21 to come in here. Now get the fuck out. Move, before I move you." Ray, a boxer, later told me he had to suppress the urge to punch out the fatso guard. We drove straight out of Reno and headed toward California.

To reach San Francisco we had to cross the Rocky Mountains, a geological wonder I had never laid my eyes on. Snow covered, in Summer yet. When Ray finally dropped me off at Sue's, I was sorry he and I had to part ways, but oh so glad to see the last of grandpa.

Sue and I had almost become an item but ended up as friends. The few days with her were uneventful though San Francisco was a delight.

My trip to Mexico began there. The first bus ride took me to Nogales, Arizona, across the border from its twin city, Nogales, Sonora, Mexico. During the bus trip I imagined a Mexico filled with colored lights and dancing girls. Not that I consciously believed that scenario, but it was an image that took over my fantasy life. When I crossed the border, I saw poverty. Grinding poverty. People living in flimsy shacks. Beggars. I had never seen a beggar in my life (and I came from a low stratum of American society). Street vendors surrounded me, trying to sell me cheap trinkets.

I rushed back to the American side of the border to figure out what to do. I had clearly come to Mexico unprepared, except for my limited proficiency in Spanish. I wandered around the Arizona side, trying to decide how to proceed. I struck up a conversation with another young American. We walked together until we reached his car. He suggested we sit in his car and continue chatting. He was a soldier on leave from a military base. One of his buddies soon showed up, looked at me, sneered, and said: "Who the fuck are you?" Reno redux. I split pronto. I decided to return to the Mexico side.

I waited in the station for my scheduled bus ride to Guadalajara. I noticed a woman acting strangely. She kept standing up and scanning the other passengers in the station; she looked frightened or angry or both. She was dressed all in brown khaki: pants, shirt, jacket, and hat. What was odd about her ensemble was not just the material; everything was completely wrinkled. At one point, the woman jumped up, stared at me, then ran into the bathroom with her suitcase. Some ten or fifteen minutes later she came out, dressed in an identical khaki ensemble, not brown but grey this time. And completely wrinkled. Again, she stared at me.

When it was time to board the bus to Guadalajara, I saw the khaki woman waiting in the same line I was in. I sat in the front row of the bus and was relieved to see that she sat near the back. Our journey began and I soon joined in conversation with a group of Mexican men sitting near me. Suddenly there was screaming in the back of the bus. The khaki woman was berating–in Spanish–a family sitting near her. I understood only snatches of what she was yelling, but my new companions explained that she accused the family members of saying terrible things about her. She heard every word, she claimed. This went on for some time as the family members cringed. My thought was that the woman might not be wrapped too tight... in her khaki... but also that it wasn't very nice to be saying mean things about her, odd though she may be. Time passed as my companions and I chatted, in a mixture of Spanish and English. Suddenly, more shouting from the back of the bus. It was the khaki woman, speaking to us in English: "I hear everything you say about me. You talking about me. You bad people. Don't you talking about me." And so on. But she had never entered our conversation. I hadn't studied psychology yet so I didn't ask my companions, *¿Cómo se dice en español* paranoid schizophrenic? Eventually my companions reached their destination and got off the bus.

As day turned to night, I began to feel lonely, a stranger in a strange land. The bus stopped again and a group of young women boarded.

They soon became my new companions. They didn't speak English so I had to get by as best I could. The important thing to me was that I didn't feel so lonely. Quite to the contrary. I was enjoying the attention from these attractive young ladies. At one point they began serenading me with a lovely song. I didn't understand the words but my spirits soared. I would never forget the melody and their angelic voices. Eventually I heard the song again and discovered the lyrics. The title of the song: *Aquellos ojos verdes*, those green eyes. I, of course, had green—or "hazel"—eyes.

Eventually I arrived in Guadalajara and found the family I would be staying with. My professor had failed to share with me an important piece of information: the father of the family was a Lutheran minister, his church was next to the house, and I was expected to attend services every day. I had been brought up in the Swedish Lutheran Church in Minnesota and now here I was with Mexican Lutherans. Not quite the cultural experience I was looking for. During the church services the parishioners were expected to answer questions posed by the pastor. The first question directed at me was something like, "David, *¿se puede pecar sin hacer nada?*" "Can you sin without doing anything?" My answer, after a very long pause, was: "*El Diablo en la cabeza*"; translation: "The devil in the head." That was the extent of my theological sophistication in Spanish.

There were other Americans who attended the church services. Though they had lived in Guadalajara for years, it became clear to me that their Spanish left something to be desired. One American, a close friend of the family, was a frequent dinner guest. He was a master craftsman of linguistic gems. For example, after dining on pork roast, he declared to the pastor's wife, "*Gracias señora por su puerca comida.*" Literally, "Thank you, *señora*, for your pork dinner." But what it really meant was, "Thank you, *señora*, for your filthy meal."

In spite of my misadventures, I fell in love with Mexico and returned several times in the following years. I travelled to both coasts, visited ancient ruins, and even acquired a rudimentary vocabulary in Nahuatl, the language of the Aztecs.

The Brothers' Ride

By Michael Allen George

We were headed up north for our annual summer vacation. As he was every year, Dad was in a hurry to get to the resort, so we were traveling in the small hours of the morning. Saturday morning.

Mom and dad rode in the front seat, and my brother Sandy and sister Ruth rode with me in the back. They were both asleep, but I wasn't. I was too much like dad, and way too anxious to get there. And again, like dad, I was anxious to get out on the lake with a rod and reel in my hand. Vacation time was fishing time for dad and me.

Then, without warning, the car coughed a couple of times, then died. Dad wisely pulled off the highway and onto the shoulder before the car stopped moving. He slapped the steering wheel and shook his head as if to say, "What the hell do I do now."

I knew we were in deep trouble right away. We were out in the middle of nothing and nowhere. Dad was a lot of things and good at a lot of things, but he was about as far from being a mechanic as a person could be.

That left one solution to the problem. Someone had to go get help. The question was who? Dad was the logical choice, but mom didn't want to be left alone in the car with us kids. That left one choice. Me. The thought of having to go out in the dark alone to find a town or someplace I could get us help scared me. So I talked my brother Sandy into going with me.

He was nervous about it too, but less so than me. At least, when we started out on that lonely walk on that dark highway. We stuck out our thumbs, trying to hitch a ride with the first two cars that drove by us. They didn't even slow down.

A fair amount of time went by before the third car. At the speed it was traveling, I didn't think there'd be any way it'd stop. I was wrong. The driver of the car braked hard enough to lock all four wheels. Even so, he slid on screaming tires quite away past us before he came to a complete stop.

He ground his gears when he put his Buick in reverse. I knew when he got back to us that he was drunk. Drunk enough so he'd have trouble walking if he'd tried.

"Get in," he said when I opened the passenger door. "I don't know what a couple of kids like you two are doing out here this time of night, but you shouldn't be walking along this highway. It ain't safe."

I hesitated a moment and looked at Sandy. He was shaking his head, but got into the back seat when I got into the front. I could tell by the look on his face that, like me, he was scared. Scared or not, both of us wanted to get off that highway bad enough to chance riding with the drunk.

And it was taking a chance. The driver of the car quickly brought the speed up to over one hundred miles an hour. I could see the speedometer from the passenger seat, and as I watched the needle move around, I knew we were in trouble. Especially since he didn't drive in what could be called a straight line. That big old Buick constantly floated from one side of the road to the other. I would have tightened my seatbelt, if the car had seatbelts, but it didn't.

"So what are two kids like you doing out on this highway this time of the night?"

"Our car broke down, and we're going to get help. Dad had to stay with Mom and our sister."

"Help's gonna be hard to find this time of night, but I'll take you where you'll get some."

I just shook my head yes. He didn't see me do it, but he didn't seem to care that I didn't answer him out loud. He was too busy not paying too much attention to where the road was.

I tried closing my eyes, but found I was too scared to not watch where the car was going. I turned to take a quick look at Sandy, and he was quietly sitting there, slowly shaking his head. The look on his face told me he was thinking much the same thing I was. We weren't likely to live much longer. It was only a matter of time before the car hit the ditch and we were dead.

So we were both terrified for the roughly fifteen miles we rode to the next town. Amazingly, the driver dropped us off at the local police station.

"Go in there," the driver said. "They're pretty good guys. They'll help you find the help you need to get your car towed."

Given the fact there didn't seem to be anything open in the entire town, it was a good place for him to drop us off. It seemed strange to me though, that he dared to drop us there given the way he drove. But he was oblivious to it all, and he headed his Buick up to full speed before he was out of town, which is where he was by the time we walked inside the station.

The two cops inside looked surprised when we walked in. The bigger of the two stood as he looked us over, and asked, "Now what can we do for you at this hour of the morning?"

"Our car broke down, and we came here to see if you could help us find someone to go get it."

"Who was driving?"

"My dad. We came instead of him because Mom didn't want to be left alone with us kids out there."

"How far away are they?"

"I don't know for sure. More than ten miles I think. The guy who gave us a ride was drunk, and he was driving so fast I couldn't tell how far we went." Then I told him what highway we were on.

"How fast do you think he was driving?"

"I could see the speedometer. It was over a hundred miles an hour. He kept going from one side of the road to the other."

"Didn't that scare you?

"Yes, a lot."

"You really should have told him to stop and let you out. If he'd crashed, you two would have been seriously hurt, if not killed."

"I know, but it's hard to get a ride right now, and we didn't want them to have to wait in the car too long."

He shook his head, but smiled at my answer. "Okay," he said. "but if something like that ever happens to you again, you tell the driver of the car to stop and let you out."

"Yes, sir," I answered.

"Now, let's see what we can do about getting you some help."

Before he picked up the phone to try and call someone, he asked the other cop who he thought would be the best person to call. They discussed two or three options, then the cop made the call.

He explained the situation to the person who answered. When he finished talking, he turned to me. "Someone will be going out to tow your car in. He owns a garage, so he'll see if he can fix it. We'll meet him out there, then I'll give you all a ride back to town. In the meantime, we'll see if we can get the cafe to make some coffee and put together something for you folks to eat while you wait for the car."

The ride back to the car was a lot more pleasant then the ride away from it was. The cop and I talked about fishing, and even though I was still a kid, just fifteen, he talked to me the same as he would have anyone. Even when he corrected me on some of the ideas I had about it, he never did it like it was a putdown. It was only that there might be another idea on the subject.

When we got to the car, he immediately turned on his flashing lights, made his U-turn and parked behind the car. When mom and dad saw us get out of the cop's car, the look on their faces was perfect. Was this a good thing or a bad one? The cop set them at ease as he told them what was going on.

He finished his explanation with, "Those two boys of yours showed a lot of guts, taking that ride to town. Then they showed a lot of sense when the first place they stopped was at our station. You should be proud of them."

Dad's answer was simple. "You can bet I am."

We waited then, until the garage man arrived with the wrecker. It only took a few minutes for him to hook up the car, make sure it was in neutral, raise it up, and be on his way.

Back in town, we all stopped at the cafe. Mom, dad and I drank coffee. Sandy and Ruth each had a coke. Dad was anxious about the car, so he decided to walk over to the garage to see what was going on before he ate anything.

I was curious too, so I went with him. Inside, the guy who towed it and another guy were leaning under the hood. One of them looked up at dad and said, "we haven't figured it out yet."

So we stood back out of the way and watched them. It wasn't long before the garage owner took off the distributor cap. "Turn it over once," he told the other mechanic. He did. Even I could immediately see the problem. The points were flopping loose. The guy holding the distributor cap just stood back and laughed.

"I don't know," he said, "who worked on your car last. But they surely did screw up. But at least the fix is about as simple as one can get."

And it was. Only a few minutes.

The cop who'd helped us so much already stopped by then. Just to make sure they could fix the car and we'd be able to get on our way. If not, he was prepared to give us a ride to the local motel. Since the car was fixed, he didn't stay long. Dad and I both thanked him again before he left.

When he did, he left Dad and I both with the feeling that sometimes, it's a pretty good world, with even some better people in it. The guys in the garage left us with the same feeling. Their charges for all their help were a simple twenty dollars. The lady at the cafe wouldn't let dad pay for the meal.

Even after all these years, when I think of that night, I always remember the cop, those mechanics, and the lady in the cafe. They all went far beyond their *jobs* to help us out. They always renew my sense of human decency. Something it's so easy to lose in these troubled times.

To Dream

By *Michael Allen George*

I finished the lawn, put the mower away, and went into the screen porch. I was just sitting down in my favorite chair when my wife brought me a beer. She gave me one of her sweet smiles when I took it from her and immediately opened it.

I took a deep drink, smiled back, and said, "I love you."

She nodded her head in response, leaned down to lightly kiss me on the lips, and went back in the house. I watched her go. Even after she had sixty-five years of living, watching her walk away was a gift to my eyes. I was a lucky man to have her, and to have had her in my life as long as I had.

As it often did, that thought led to many others as my mind drifted back in time. One memory popped up, as it usually did when my mind followed this track. The memory of my most awesome dream. A dream that wasn't real.

It had to do with a young lady I was sure I was in love with. A love she knew nothing about. She couldn't, because she didn't even know me. I was just a customer in the small grocery store where she worked, primarily as a cashier. My fixation with her started the first time I ever saw her. I stopped into the store to buy cigarettes. They weren't such a forbidden item as they are today, although it's been a long time since I've used them.

She barely noticed me, and completed our transaction quickly and efficiently. Much quicker than I wanted her to. It wasn't just that she was extremely pretty, it was more than that. To me, there was some kind of glow around her and about her. She was special, I knew, from the first time I saw her. I instantly became fixated on her, and all day, every day, she filled my thoughts and dreams.

She worked days, so every day, on my way to work in the morning, I stopped in that small store for my cigarettes. I never bought any extra packs, because I couldn't face the day without seeing her. We sort of were becoming acquainted, but not well enough for me to dare to ask her out or anything. But at least she was kind of friendly toward me, and almost always had a smile for me.

Then one morning she was waiting on an older lady when I went in. So I went down one of the aisles so she'd be alone when I bought my cigarettes. A young man came in while she was waiting on the lady. As soon as she finished up with her, she got a serious frown on her face, one like I'd never seen before. And by then, I'd been buying my cigarettes from her for nearly six months.

For a reason I didn't understand, her frown really bothered me, so I watched the young man closely. She shook her head no to him and that's when it started for me. He lifted his arm and I saw the gun in his hand. It was one of those automatic types with lots of bullets. I knew I had to do something. There was no way I was going to let him hurt her.

I'd played some baseball in high school. I was a pitcher. I had a decent arm, not great, but decent, so I grabbed a can off the self I was next to. For some odd reason I remember that it was a can of Campbells Cream Of Mushroom soup.

The kid heard me, and turned toward me. It was what I wanted him to do, so the gun wasn't pointing at her. Then, at the same time I let fly with the can of soup, he fired. His aim was way off, and the bullet barely scratched my left arm. The good thing was, the can that flew out of my right hand wasn't off. It hit him in the face, right at the bridge of his nose. It knocked him senseless and he dropped his gun.

I was on him before he fell. I slammed him back against the counter and held him up while I hit him. I continued to do so until his face looked quite pulpy. When I let him drop, she pulled some paper towels loose from a roll under the counter and handed then to me. I used them to wipe the blood off my hands. Mister pulp-face was lying quite still on the floor.

Then she noticed the blood seeping from my arm. "Oh my god," she said, "you got shot." She turned a bit pale.

"I don't think it's serious," I said. "I doesn't really hurt. It only stings a little."

"But you got shot. I was watching you when he was asking me for the money. You made noise on purpose, to make him look at you. Why did you do that? He could have killed you."

"He was pointing his gun at you."

She just stood there, staring at me with her mouth open, as she pulled some more towels loose for the blood on my arm. By then, the store manager had come out of the back room and joined us.

"What the hell is going on?" He asked, glaring at me.

She nodded toward me, "He just kept us from getting robbed, and me from probably from getting shot. Go call the police."

He left for the back room where the phone was. She motioned for me to roll up my sleeve, then helped me do it when I had trouble with it. "I don't know your name," she said as she used the towels to wipe the blood away. "I think, since you probably saved my life, I'd like to know it now."

That's when I noticed the look in her eyes, but I managed to answer her anyway. "Greg," I said, "Greg James, Lynn." I knew her name because she always wore it on a tag just above her left breast.

She was firm, yet still gentle as she wiped the blood away. As I suspected, the wound was little more than a scratch. But the way she was looking at me, it seemed normal that she was treating it more like it was a mortal wound.

Great as it was to have her seeing me that way, I felt like I didn't deserve it. I was sure when I grabbed the can of soup that the odds of my getting seriously hurt were slim. She thought otherwise.

"I think I owe you a lot, Greg," she told me. "More than I can repay. I'd like to try though. I think you like me, don't you?"

"I sure do, but you still don't owe me anything. And I sure don't want to ever take advantage of you because you think you owe me something."

"I guess it'd surprise me if you did. I've noticed the way you look at me when you come in here to buy your cigarettes. *Every day.* No one stops for cigarettes that often. But when this is all done, and the day is over, why don't you come by here and pick me up. We can go out and have a hamburger and a beer or something."

"Okay. I think I'd really like that."

I decided then that I was in no mood for work that day, so I called my boss, told him what happened and that I got shot. He didn't argue when I told I wasn't coming in. Probably not for a couple of days.

That's when the police arrived. They treated us decent enough, even though they wondered about the would-be robber's face. They questioned Lynn and me about it, making us repeat our story several times. Even so, they called an ambulance for me when they called one for mush face, insisting that my arm be properly treated. So after they were finished with the interrogations, I was taken to the hospital.

When they finished with me, I took a cab back to the store to get my car. I stopped to confirm my date with Lynn while I was there. She'd decided to finish her workday, and suggested I pick her up at the store that night.

That was some careful thinking on her part, I thought. She didn't really know me, and this way I wouldn't know where she lived. I couldn't really blame her. Most men would happily take advantage of the situation. I didn't have any plans beyond spending a pleasant evening with her. I didn't even so much as consider anything beyond that. From my point of view, she was way out of my class. With her looks, she could have about any guy she wanted. I figured I was just too ordinary for her.

She suggested a nice little bar that served great burgers. Then she surprised the hell out of me when she slid over to the middle of seat when she got into my car. I thoroughly enjoyed the feel of her body next to me on the way there, but still didn't think we'd ever go beyond this simple date.

We weren't very far into our meal when she said, "If you don't mind, I think we should call it a night after we eat. After all that's happened today, I don't feel up to doing much else tonight."

I was disappointed, but I said, "Whatever you want. I'm grateful for the time with you, however short it is."

"Don't be silly," she said. "I'm enjoying my time with you too. I've wished for a while now that you would ask me out."

"Really? That surprises me. I never would have thought you'd even be slightly interested in me."

"Why do you say that? I think you're more than just interesting. You seem to be a genuinely nice guy. You're always so polite and soft spoken when you come in the store. And even though you look at me the way you do, you've never made me feel uncomfortable."

"I'm glad of that. That's the last thing I'd want to do to you."

"What you made me feel mostly, Greg, was flattered. I'm pretty sure I'm the main reason you stopped for cigarettes every day. Yet, you were always a gentleman."

"I tried to be. With you, I never expected to get beyond the dream stage."

"What do you mean? The dream stage?"

"I didn't think anything with you would get any farther than my dreaming about it. Be it day or night dreams."

"Were they nasty?"

"No, nothing like that. They were more like what we're doing now. The closest to nasty they got was you holding my hand."

"How long have you been having them?"

"Since the first time I saw you."

She shook her head, smiled, and took a big bite of her hamburger.

I tried to make the meal last, but she'd have none of it, and a short time later we were leaving the bar.

"You don't mind taking me home, do you? I normally ride the bus to work."

"Of course not. I'd be glad to take you anywhere."

"Even heaven?" she asked, then laughed.

When we got to her apartment building, I walked her to the door, then opened it and said, "I really did enjoy tonight. Thank you."

"You sound like you're leaving," she said. "Don't you want to come in for a while?"

I think my mouth must have dropped open, because she chuckled before I could answer her. "I'd love to," I told her when I did answer, "If you want me to."

"I wouldn't have asked if I didn't."

So I went in, still with no expectations. She gave me a beer and opened one for herself, then sat close to me on the couch. Because she did, I felt confident enough to put my arm around her. When I did, she lifted her face toward me. I kissed her. Her response was strong enough to surprise me. So I kissed her again. She totally surprised me when we broke it.

"I'll get towels ready for you. You get the first shower. It's too early in our relationship to take them together.'

The rest of the night was one spectacular time. I was in bed when she finished her shower. She was only wrapped in a towel, which she dropped before climbing in next to me.

We were slow to start, and built a large fire before I finally moved over her. She was more than ready and a soft, satisfied growl escaped her. I only lasted a little over a minute, but stayed where I was. She smiled when, a short time later, I moved again.

It proved to be the most incredible time I could have had, and after I slept sound through the night. So sound, I woke up wondering how I could have such an incredible dream.

I was alone in the bed, and found myself wishing passionately that the dream had been real. I turned over and stared at the ceiling. Something was wrong. It wasn't my ceiling. Then I smelled bacon frying and coffee percolating.

"What the hell?" I thought. "What's happening?"

Then she came into the bedroom, with a hot cup of coffee for me. "I took you for one who drinks it black," she said. "But I'll bring you some cream and sugar if you like."

I reached for the cup of coffee. "Black is fine," I said. The joy and thrill of seeing her standing there overwhelming my senses.

She could see the effect she was having on me and a broad smile filled her face.

"I woke up thinking it was a dream," I told her. "You are infinitely better than any dream could ever be."

"I'm glad," she said. "I wanted to be, because so are you."

And that was my dream that wasn't real. It was life that was real. But even so long ago, it's still like yesterday. It's a for sure thing that dreams are often good.

The memory stirred something in me, and I left my favorite chair and joined my wife in the kitchen. I walked up behind her and wrapped my arms around her. She turned her head to face me, a look of anticipation in her eyes.

"Remember," I asked, "when you told me to take the first shower? We couldn't take them together you said, because it was too early in our relationship. It was the dream again. It's not too early today, is it?"

"For you, Greg, it's not too early. And it'll never be too late to dream."

A Warm Summer Day

By Bud George

The job was a two story atrium, timber framed, mostly glass (3 sides), shed roof with four roof windows. The type that operate and had inner screens.

It was a four men crew. Me, the boss, Ken, Bill (at one time known as wild Bill), and Dick, who had the ability to move around partly framed buildings like a squirrel.

The new addition, placed on the south side of the existing house required us to remove a large section of the existing roof. Normally we most likely would install a heavy ridge beam, which in this case would have been about twenty-eight feet long. But there wasn't enough room for a machine to maneuver or handle a beam that long, two and a half stories up.

The solution was to site build a girder truss the full width of the building using twelve inch LVLs. Double LVL at the ridge (about six feet above floor) truss webs single twelve inch LVL.

The temperature that day was ninety plus and very humid.

We removed both gable windows and set up scaffolding to move materials into the attic. Most of the cutting to size and shape was done on the ground. The temperature inside that attic that day was very near one hundred twenty degrees. We took turns, rotating through about ever twenty to thirty minutes.

We got the thing (as our crew named it) built, nailed, bolted, and finished. We then proceeded with the timber framing. Another hot, very still, summer day. Dark, tornado weather.

Ken was on the ground, the saw/man. Bill and I were decking the roof. Dick was moving materials. Bill and I spotted a huge, black weather front moving toward us, coming out of the southwest. We yelled out to Ken. He looked up and said "Nah! We got a little time yet." He was not correct.

The storm began with rain. Ken came up the ladder with a big tarp. Dick was on the roof by then. Then the storm hit. Wind gusts. We are trying to hold the tarp down. It lifted Bill off the roof deck, and started sliding him off the edge. He drove his twenty ounce farming hammer through the plywood and held on with both hands. Dick wrapped his arms around the brick chimney. The chinaman's hat blew off the chimney and cut his forehead, luckily pretty minor. The wind lifted the tarp up with Ken and me on it. I started sliding off - one leg and one arm hanging off the side. Ken grabbed me by the nail belt and pulled me back.

We heard the ladder go with a loud crash. A short time I'm sure, but it seemed like an hour, the wind eased off. The rain let up and Dick found a way off the roof. He did a temporary fix on the badly bent ladder and we climbed down.

We were completely soaked. About as ugly as a bunch of wet cats. Ken said, "Help me set a layer of felt and some battens on that roof and we'll call it a day. This never happened. Leave early - *never!* Ken's moto, start early, work late.

Anyway, we did get the roof secured and we did leave early. I was kind of thankful for the rain. I did not have to explain how I got my pants so wet.

The Expert

By Michael Allen George

"He's an expert," Derrick said, when they asked me to help with a day of cutting firewood. "He's an engineer. He rebuilt his chainsaw. He really knows what he's doing."

"You don't even need to bring your chainsaw," Gene, Derick's construction company partner said. "He'll do all the cutting. All we need you to do is help load the truck."

"So," I answered, "he's cut a lot of wood?"

"I don't know about that," Derrick said. "I just know how smart he is. He's the kind of guy who can probably teach you a thing or two. You're going to be surprised how good he is with a chainsaw."

"Whatever you say," I told him. "I'm sure he'll show me how."

I let it go at that. There was no use in arguing about it. If they wanted to believe that rebuilding a chainsaw would teach someone all they needed to know about cutting firewood, there was damn little I could do to convince them otherwise.

So off we went to cut firewood in their fifty acres of oak woods. It wasn't something I was looking forward to, and would have turned them down if they hadn't already let me cut a few cords of wood there.

The expert got to the woods about thirty minutes after us. The first thing he did was set his fairly old chainsaw on the ground, start it, and then try to tighten the chain. It wasn't working too well so he grabbed the saw's handle and tipped the back up to get a better angle. The problem with that was the fact that nothing will dull a chain quicker than running it in rocky ground. He finally got the chain a little tighter and shut the machine off.

When he made no effort to sharpen it, I said, "Aren't you going to sharpen it? It's too dull to cut anything now."

"No, it isn't. I sharpened it before I left home."

"While you were trying to tighten the chain you ran it into the ground. So it's dull now."

"You know," he told me in no uncertain terms, "I don't need any advice from you. I'm an engineer, and I think I know better what I'm doing than you could ever possibly know."

I didn't bother to answer him. He was the expert, after all. Instead, I took my chainsaw out of my truck. I already had no doubt about who was going to do the cutting. And there was little chance it would be the expert.

As I knew he would, he proceeded to show me what cutting wood was about. He picked out a good size oak and tried to cut the notch. He didn't get much more than an inch into the tree before the chain was smoking heavily. I just watched him, shaking my head.

"Well damnit," he complained. "This makes no sense at all. I just sharpened the chain."

"Like I said, it's dull. It'd be a good idea to sharpen it now."

"I can't. I left my sharpening tools at home."

"You mean you thought you could cut wood all day without sharpening your chain. You'd be damn lucky to go a couple of hours without the chain needing sharpening."

"That's not true."

"You're sure about that, huh? So, are you going home to get your sharpening tools, or are you going to run into town and buy some new ones?"

"Home is too far away, and I hate to waste the money on new tools. Don't you have some I can borrow?"

"No, I surely don't. But I will sharpen your chain for you."

"I can't let you do that." He gave me his best serious look. "I rebuilt that saw myself, and I don't like anyone else messing with it. You'll have to lend me the tools.

"Not hardly," I said, no longer trying to keep my opinion of him out of my voice. "You're the kind of a guy who could screw up a wet dream, so there's no way you're going to touch any of my tools."

His face started with red, and as it moved to purple, I half expected him to take a swing at me. That's when Derrick stepped in. "Let him use your tools," he told me, his voice filled with the authority he thought he had over me.

"Not going to happen," I answered. "I'll sharpen his chain, but he'll not be getting near my tools."

"He's not going to hurt them any. He's an engineer. He knows all about tools."

"I'll sharpen his chain. Anymore bullshit and I'm out of here."

Derrick knew I wasn't kidding, so he told the engineer to let me do the sharpening. After having done that job a few hundred times in the past, it didn't take me long.

The engineer went back to the tree he originally started on. With a sharp chain, he managed to cut a notch. He had two problems though. The notch was in the wrong place and it was too small. If he tried to take the tree down, it would not fall where he wanted it to, no matter what he did. He cut the notch on the south side of the tree. The tree was leaning heavily east. If he tried to make the second cut, I knew the tree would twist as it fell, and hang up on standing trees long before it hit the ground.

Not only would that make it tough to take down the rest of the way, it would be dangerous. So I told the expert about the problem, and how to get around it.

"Ain't no way," he snarled back, "I'm gonna cut another notch. The trees gonna fall where I want. That's what the notches are for."

"Okay," I said. "But when the tree starts to go down, get yourself and your saw the hell out of the way. It could get dangerous."

"You are so full of shit," he complained. "You're just trying to make me look bad, telling me how to do things. Now get out of my way. I've got some real man's work to do."

I turned my back on him and started to walk away. That's when I saw Derrick checking out my chainsaws. "Mind if I use the small one to trim some brush," he asked.

"No, but be careful. I know the saw seems small, but it could take a hand or foot or even a leg off just as quick as the big saws. So keep two hands on it."

"No problem," he said, "I can handle it."

The tone of his voice gave me a sinking feeling. It sounded like I had a second expert on my hands. If there was anything I didn't need, it was another expert.

The sound a tree makes before it falls is distinct when it's taken down properly. The sound it makes when the whole process has been screwed up is something else.

I turned in time to see the tree being cut down, twist around, snap loose, and drop off the stump. The expert was sitting on his backside about two feet from the new stump. His chainsaw lay on the ground, under the cut end of the not quite fallen tree. The chainsaw's bar was bent nearly in half. So much for the expert showing me how to cut wood.

My small chainsaw was running now, so I looked over to see how Derrick was doing. As I suspected, he was cutting brush with one hand. Even worse, he was cutting over his head. Trouble waiting to happen.

I knew it was an exercise in futility, but I walked over and told him, "I now you think you can handle the saw really well. Trouble is, what you're doing is extremely dangerous. Lots of people have been hurt and even killed pulling the batshit nonsense you're doing now. Keep it up, and it's a near guaranty you're going to get hurt."

"Not going to happen. I know what I'm doing."

"Don't ever say I didn't warn you."

I stopped talking. I didn't even tell the idiot expert what I thought of engineers. I just went to work on the large oak tree hung up tightly in some other large oak trees. I ignored everything else around me until I finished bringing it down, one chunk at a time.

With that done, I looked around for Derrick. I asked where he was. "Oh," someone told me, "Gene took him to the hospital, to the emergency room. He cut himself with the chain saw."

"Was he hurt bad?" I asked.

"All I know is, he was bleeding pretty good."

"Great," I thought. "That's all I need."

I had someone point out where Derrick was when he got hurt. I found my small chainsaw there. The chain and bar were indeed bloody. All I wanted to do at that point was get the hell out of there. Instead, I decided to help out and cut down a few more trees. I trimmed the trees as best I could, then cut them in pieces small enough to handle.

The expert didn't say a word to me the whole time. I figured he was probably putting together an expert opinion for Derrick on how I did everything wrong.

I waited for nearly another hour before Derrick finally returned, his left hand heavily bandaged. "Don't even say a word," he said as he got out of Gene's car.

So I didn't. I gave him a big smile instead. He frowned back.

"I just cut some more trees down," I explained, "trimmed them as best I could, and cut them into loading size pieces. I also left a hatchet to trim any other branches I might have missed. You want a better method, go buy yourself a chainsaw. Take the expert along so you get just the right one."

"I'd like to have you stick around, to help finish up," Derrick said. "I bet you would, but I think I've done enough for one day. You've got enough help to load. And I've learned enough wood cutting expertise to last me awhile."

Derrick could tell from the sarcasm in my voice that there'd be no use in arguing with me. So I loaded up my tools made one hell of an expert type exit.

Rae's Smiles

By Michael Allen George

She was coming up the hill. I was walking down. My sister was with her. She introduced us when we came abreast of each other.

"This is your new cousin, Rae," she said. "Rae, this is my little brother, Al."

"Hi," I said, looking into her beautiful blue eyes. She had freckles, and from that moment I loved freckles.

"I think I'll like having so many new cousins," she said. "So I guess it might be okay my mom got married."

She was referring to the fact her widowed mother had recently married my uncle.

"I think it's okay, too," I said, already knowing she would be the new cousin I'd care the most about. And I always did, even if I was only seven then, and she was six.

"Well," my sister said, interrupting my rapt fascination with Rae. "we better get going."

"It was nice to meet you, Rae," I said.

"I liked meeting you, too," she said, then smiled. A smile that pushed a glow through me.

I watched them for quite a while as they walked away, up the hill.

❧

It was right after the war, and for a lot of families, still a hangover from the depression. Not much money. The first time we visited them, they were living in a small, rented house, which had begun its life as a chicken coop. We started playing outside, but when it got dark, we moved inside. We played in the tiny bedroom where Rae and her brother Benny slept. My younger brother and sister were there with us.

There wasn't much we could do in that small room, so we decided to play moms and dads, which consisted of nothing more than lying down next to each other in the single size bunk beds. My sister and Benny lay down on the lower bunk. Rae and I were on the upper bed.

We just lay there quietly for a while, until Rae said, "I think it will be nice to grow up. Then we can be real moms and dads. Would you like to be a real dad with me?"

The fact that I had no idea what that involved made no difference to my answer. If it meant doing something with Rae, it was something I wanted to do.

"Yes," I told her, "I would like being a dad with you."

"Good," she said, turning on her side, facing me. She smiled and rested a hand on my arm.

Then mom opened the bedroom door and told us it was time to go home. Everyone else in the family was ready to go. I felt as if I could stay there forever.

The family farm where we lived for a while during the war, after dad enlisted, had been rented out for a few years. My uncle and his new family moved there when the most recent tenants left.

We made our first visit a few months later. As young as I was when we lived there, I still fell in love with the farm, and was anxious to see it again. I was, however, even more anxious to see Rae. It had been almost two years since we'd seen each other, so I wondered what it was going to be like to see her again.

We were only there for the afternoon, so I tried to get her away from everyone for a while. I didn't manage it. She was nice enough, but not much interested in doing anything with me.

I soon gave up, and spent the rest of the day walking around, alone, getting reacquainted with the farm. I was glad to be there again, but disappointed with the day. I didn't spend any time with Rae.

◦◦∞◦◦

It was summer and I wanted to go out to the farm. Not just for an afternoon. I wanted to go for at least a week, if they would let me. Maybe even longer if it was possible.

After a couple of weeks, dad decided he had enough time on Saturday to take me out there. My uncle didn't mind my being there. The first crop of hay was ready to bale, and since his new children weren't all that anxious to help, he hoped I'd be willing.

I was. Anything that would allow me to stay on the farm. I had a lot of friends at home, but there was no place like the farm. Along with being in the country and having fields and woods to roam in, it had something even more special. It had Rae.

Even though she was rather cool toward me, I still wanted to be where she was. It didn't matter that she didn't seem to care about me one way or the other. The sight of her still filled my heart with feelings that otherwise didn't exist.

I tried to help in any way I could when I first got there. But I didn't really do much until the hay was baled. My uncle hired another farmer to do the baling. He did it on shares, taking a percentage of the hay as pay for the job.

As the hay was baled, it was dropped to the ground. We drove around the field and picked up the bales. Rae drove the tractor, my uncle threw the bales on the hay wagon, and I piled them. I was a long way from full grown, so every bale was a struggle. Yet I somehow managed them. My biggest problem was Rae. She left a lot to be desired as a tractor driver.

My uncle had moved most of the bales together in piles scattered around the field. Rae drove up to each pile and stopped. I piled the bales as they were thrown onto the wagon. The problem arose when my uncle finished throwing the bales on the wagon ahead of me getting them piled. Then Rae's lack of ability with the clutch appeared. She tended to snap it, which often knocked me on my back.

It knocked the wind out of me. I also tended to let out a howl on my way down. She usually turned around when it happened. At first. she looked worried. When I didn't get mad, her look turned into a sheepish grin.

Luckily, she didn't knock me down every time, but it was a long day.   When we finished and were walking to the house, she said, "I'm sorry I made it so hard for you. I'm just not a very good tractor driver yet. And thanks for not getting mad at me."

She smiled, so it was all worth it.

I hadn't been to the farm for a while. It wasn't that I didn't want to go so much as it seemed impossible to get anyone to take me. It wasn't until my aunt was in town for a visit that I got the chance to go.

The problem was, she wasn't going all the way home. From her visit, she was going to work. Her job as a cook in a small diner was in a town a good twelve miles from the farm.

My bicycle provided the solution. It fit in the trunk of her car, so I rode with her, then got on my bike and rode it the rest of the way to the farm. It was a long ride and I was tired when I got there. All the same, I was excited. No one knew I was coming, so I was especially anxious to see how Rae would react when she saw me.

I didn't see anyone around and my uncle's truck was gone. I found out later that he and Benny had gone to the feed store.

I went in the house and could hear the piano playing. I walked into the living room. Rae was making the music. She didn't hear me come in, so I clapped my hands a couple of times to tell her I was there.

She turned around, looked at me with a frown, and said, "On, it's just you."

My heart dropped heart into my stomach as I watched her turn back to the piano. It didn't prove to be my best visit to the farm.

For the next couple of years, Rae was never unfriendly. It was more like I didn't exist in her part of the world, wherever that was. For me, the feeling was a simple sense of loss. And by the time this day arrived, I'd long given up on us even being friends.

My whole family and visited the farm on a beautiful Sunday afternoon in July. We got there just after a typical Minnesota thunderstorm. The rain came down hard, so we knew the creek would be running full. Benny and Rae suggested that since the creek would be running full from the storm, we should go swimming. We were all for it. But we knew our parents wouldn't be.

Without telling any of the adults what we planned, claiming we were just going for a walk in the woods, we went to the creek and went swimming. Due to the lack a swimming suits, we went in with our clothes on. I've often wondered over the years if Rae knew ahead of time what the result would be.

We had the usual fun time playing and splashing in the fast running creek, but the most fun for me was when we got out of the water. I don't know why, but it seemed as though no one else noticed Rae. I did, and it was beautiful. The memory of what I saw is still beautiful.

Her wet blouse was now totally translucent when it touched her skin. She wasn't wearing a bra. So she had to continually pull it away from her body so her perfect, just the right size, breasts didn't show.

As we walked back to the farm, I was in front of the group. Rae was directly behind me. I couldn't help it and constantly turned to look at her, trying to catch the times when her blouse settled against her chest. Each time I caught a glimpse of her breasts. I marveled at the sight of them. And each time I stared longer.

The last time I looked, just minutes before we got back to the farm, she caught my eye when I turned around. Her blouse was tight against her skin. She knew what I was looking at. I think she knew all along what I'd been looking at. She cocked her head to one side, waited a moment, then leisurely peeled the blouse away. The view disappeared. But before it did, she looked me in the eye, then gave me a wide smile.

This time my heart didn't drop. This time, it nearly leaped out of my chest. The look in her eyes took my breath away.

Then she said, "Swimming was fun today, wasn't it, Al?"

"Yes," was the best answer I could come up with.

The blouse dried a short time later, and it was as if it never happened. We never got the chance to talk to each other that day, so I didn't know how she really felt about what happened, except that after I started to exist for her again. Nearly exist.

School was out for the summer and the only thing I wanted to do was go out to the farm. I was working part time for my dad in the grocery store he managed, so I had to be home on Fridays and Saturdays. But the farm is where I wanted to be. I didn't care what I did when I got there, it was still the only place I wanted to be.

I didn't expect any kind of special greeting when I got there. Benny, now Ben, seemed glad to see me. If nothing else, he knew my being there would relieve him from helping my uncle in the fields. I was always my uncle's first choice for a helper.

I didn't see Rae right away, but when I did, I got the impression that she was almost glad to see me.

I didn't do anything particularly exciting the first week that summer. Most days were spent cultivating corn. We used an old horse drawn cultivator, modified to use with the tractor. I drove the tractor and my uncle rode the cultivator.

In the evenings we watched television. The last night I was there Rae sat next to me on the couch. Shortly before bedtime I felt her hand touch mine. I wrapped mine around hers. Just before we left the couch, she gave my hand a squeeze.

It filled me with a sudden sensation I'd never felt before. I couldn't believe it. Rae liked me.

When they took me home, Rae asked to ride along. Something she never did. Life got even better. We held hands all the way, occasionally giving each other a squeeze.

"When are you coming back?" she asked when we got close to home.
"I'm going to take a Greyhound right after work on Saturday night."
"That's good."

I was in love. Totally in love. Especially when she smiled her goodbye that night.

I counted the minutes, each of which felt like an hour, until I could return to the farm. As I told Rae, I was so anxious this time that I didn't wait until I could get a ride. Saturday night, after work, I took a Greyhound bus to the closest town. I thought my mom told them I was coming, so I expected someone to pick me up when I got there. No one came, so I started walking. All the time I was hoping they'd come and pick me up on the road. But they didn't. I walked the entire five miles.

Rae wasn't home when I got to the farm. She was babysitting. The people lived two miles away. My uncle wasn't too keen on my going there, so he declined to give me a ride. I walked.

She was surprised when I got there, but glad to see me. "You walked all the way here just to see me?"

"I did. I walked all the way from town too. No one picked me up when I got off the bus."

"Does that mean you like me?"

"A lot. I like you a lot, Rae."

"Good, I'm glad." She smiled. It was a full smile.

We sat on the couch, holding hands while we watched television. I was in my own little heaven. I had everything in the world I wanted, and only one thing I wanted to do. It took until shortly before the people she was babysitting for came home that I worked up the courage.

I put my arm around her, nudged her chin toward me, and kissed her. There was no resistance. Only an enthusiastic response. I kissed her again, then left so she wouldn't get in trouble for having company.

I kissed her a few more times before we went to bed that night. When I did, sleep came slow. The world was now too full of wonder to sleep.

We had a fabulous summer. With my aunt working the afternoon shift as a cook in a diner, and an uncle who always went to bed early, we had little in the way of adult supervision.

We never did anything beyond a hell of a lot of necking. With the exception of the one special night when Rae let me open her blouse and fondle her breast. She wasn't wearing a bra. It wasn't something we never talked about, but I don't think she cared for bras because she rarely wore them. Which was fine with me. Especially that one night I was allowed to touch.

"I don't think I'm supposed to let you do that," she said after a while. "So you should stop now."

I did.

We spent every minute together we could, and soon were helping each other with our assigned chores. Rae did the milking, so I learned how. There were ten cows to hand milk, morning and night. So I got up an hour early to help her in the morning. When I got in early enough from helping uncle in the fields, I also helped with the evening milking. I was never good at it, so the most I ever milked was two. She milked eight, and often finished up my second cow. And my two were the easiest to milk.

I took her to the county fair. We went with the rest of the family, but were allowed to wander off by ourselves. I'd managed to save a little money from the meager pay I received from my part-time job, but managed to spend most of it on her that day.

The summer went by fast, as summers always do. Too soon it was time to go back to the much, on my part, dreaded school. Weekends for me were made up of a single day because of my job. Once it started, we didn't see each other again until our fall break for teachers' convention. Dad let me take the weekend off from work, so I spent the four days on the farm. My aunt was now working days, so Rae and I had little time alone.

The one saving grace was the fact it was corn picking time. In those days, the two outside rows of corn needed to be picked by hand, so it wasn't lost when the picker ran over them.

The picking was easy. Just snap off the ear, then throw it ahead in the middle of the two rows. When you reached the pile, you started to throw the ears ahead again. The piles were picked up later.

The corn was high enough, so the pickers couldn't be seen from outside the field. Rae and I volunteered to do the picking. We both knew how to work, and could move down the rows fairly rapidly. We were slow anyway. As we reached a pile, we often stopped.

The first time I stopped, Rae asked, "What's wrong?"

I shrugged, then took her in my arms and kissed her. She didn't argue or ask again. Not even when we got near the end of the row.

"Let's rest," I said.

She smiled, and said, "Okay."

We lay down together, and managed to do a lot of kissing while we rested. When I got carried away at the end of the second set of rows, and put my hand on her breast, she gently removed it.

"Someday that'll be okay," she said, "but not today."

My uncle gave me a ride home. Rae had to stay home to help her mom with something. I didn't even get the chance to kiss her goodbye.

It was a long winter. I only got to see Rae once. When spring finally came, my dad decided to buy a better car. The trade-in value of the old one wasn't much, so I convinced him to sell it to me. I'd already passed my driver's test, so I had a license.

As soon as the car was mine, I drove out to the farm the next Sunday. To my great disappointment, Rae had gotten a part-time job at the diner where her mother worked. I had to go back home before I got a chance to see her.

When school was finally out and I got out to the farm, I knew right away that things had changed. Rae was friendly, but it definitely wasn't the same kind of friendly as before. I finally talked her into going for a ride and took her to a place I could park out of sight of the road.

"What's wrong?" I asked her.

"Nothing's wrong exactly. We just can't do what we did before."

"Why? What did I do wrong?"

"You didn't do anything wrong. I've been going out with someone else. So I can't do with you what we used to do."

I didn't know what to say or do. At that moment I don't think there's anything anyone could have said that would be more devastating. She knew by the look on my face the effect of what she to me.

She tried to smile. It didn't work.

❧

I continued to go to the farm. I still loved the place, even if I felt a little lost every time. The rare occasions I saw Rae she was nice enough, but there was an obvious wall between us.

I figured there was no hope of ever resuming any kind of real relationship between us, so I didn't attempt to start one.

Then one evening when I was at the farm, she called from some kind of school affair saying she needed a ride home. I volunteered to pick her up. Ben rode along.

When we picked her up, she moved to get in the back seat.

"Don't be stuck up," Ben told her. "Ride in front."

She got in between us. Having her so close was disconcerting to say the least. I held tight to the steering wheel to keep my hands from shaking, but couldn't do anything to calm the flip flops going on in my stomach.

"So how have you been, Al?" she asked. "It's been a while since I've seen you."

"I've been just fine," I answered, my words sharper than I wanted them.

"Are you mad at me?"

"Why do you ask me that?"

"Your tone of voice. You sound a little bit angry."

"I'm not. I'm fine."

"Okay, if you say so."

We were quiet until we got to the farm. Ben got out of the car, and without a word went into the house. I was planning on heading for home right away, so I stayed in the car. To my surprise, so did Rae.

"I'm sorry, you know," she said, "that things didn't work out for us."

"Not as sorry as I am."

"Do you think, maybe, that we can be just friends?"

"I don't know, Rae. It's hard for me to think about us at all. So mostly I don't."

"I often think about you. Don't you want to remember the good times, the fun we had?"

"I'll never forget a minute of it. Not anymore than I'll ever be anything but sad that it's over."

"Isn't there anything I can say to make you feel better about it?"

"Not one damn thing."

"I'm sorry you're so upset about it. What can I do to make you feel better?"

"That's not something you really want to know."

"Yes it is, Al. I do want to know how to make you feel better."

"You sure about that?"

"Yes."

I put my arm around her and kissed her. To my surprise, she didn't pull away. She responded. I followed the kiss with another, which led to more. Soon, it was the same as it was that one special summer.

"I would like it if you would be my girlfriend," I told her. "And go steady with me. You're the only girl I care about."

"I don't know," she answered. "Maybe." She smiled. It was the kind of smile I remembered. "Can I tell you next time I see you?"

"Sure. I'll wait. You're too important to me not to."

"Okay, Al. But I have to go in now. Mom's already going to be full of questions about what I was doing out here so long."

She kissed me one last time and smiled as she left the car.

I drove home confident that it was good between Rae and I.

For too many unimportant reasons, I didn't see Rae for another two weeks. When I did, it was to live through the results of her mother's advice. I wasn't good enough. Rae just looked at me with sad eyes. I left her standing alone in that farmhouse kitchen and went home. To say I felt terrible, that I was lost and empty, is only part of it. This time, I knew, it would never be. In only two weeks, I'd gone from having everything to having nothing.

It took a long time, but we became friends again. Although it often seemed to be a guarded friendship. All grown up, with families and all the standard things one does, didn't matter. Not even when we got together for various family get-togethers. There was always something going on between us.

One year we even went on vacation together. To Yellowstone Park. Her husband fixed up a van to be a camper of sorts. It worked good for them to sleep in, but while we were driving it wasn't the greatest. Because of the design, only two rode in normal car seats up front. Everyone else rode way in the back. Because the van tended to sway some, the discomfort was doubled.

I wouldn't have minded it if we'd ever had a seating arrangement with Rae's husband and my wife up front, leaving us alone in the back with the kids. But her husband made sure we never were allowed in the back alone. Not even with the kids there. And it didn't matter that he could watch us every minute. He didn't like the idea of us sitting close together.

We all seemed to enjoy the trip anyway. Once we got to Yellowstone, we moved from campground to campground. Most days, her husband wanted to go fishing. Of course, he wanted me to go with him. I wasn't all that anxious to do much of anything. I'd just finished a few months of long hours and hard work on the job and wanted only to rest. So most days, after following him up some small river or another, we'd split up. The idea was to find different fishing spots. Instead, I'd crawl under one of the huge pine trees and go to sleep.

The one day I did fish, I only caught two small trout. Then, shortly before it was time to quit for the day, I felt a creepy feeling on the back of my neck. I was standing at a spot in the river where the banks on both sides were fairly high. I was down low, next to the river.

I couldn't shake the feeling, so I turned around. Standing there, up high on the riverbank, watching me intently, was a huge brown bear. There was no doubt as to who was in charge of the situation. It certainly wasn't me.

"Well," I said to him, "I guess you can take whatever you want. We both know there ain't no damn thing I could do about it. So if you'll just tell me what you want, I won't argue."

He looked at me, shook his head as if to say, you're boring. Then he turned around and walked slowly away. I thought about telling everyone about my little adventure, but decided the hell with it by the time I got back to camp. I knew it was one of those little things that would never have any meaning for anyone but me.

One of the campgrounds where we stayed was close to a trail up the mountainside. I begged off from fishing one day, and with only a quart jar of water, hiked up the trail. No one else was on it, so it was a good hike. The problem I quickly had was water. It was soon gone, and I was angry with myself for being so unprepared. Hiking with only a quart of water along was stupid.

I continued up trail after the water was gone until I reached a plateau. I rested on a downed fir tree to decide if I should go any further. Part of me wanted to keep hiking, and never go back down to the real world.

The other part, the one that was so damn thirsty, said I should go back down. I argued with that part of me until I remembered Rae was at the bottom of the hill. The way I thought of her at that moment was something pulled out of the past. It was enough, though, to start me walking back down.

Rae was the first to see me when I walked into camp. "Al," she said, her voice bright, her eyes shining, "we were beginning to think you got lost up there." She followed with a wide smile and looked into my eyes for only brief moment.

Overall, it was a good vacation. We got to see a lot of new country, and I did get a decent amount of real rest. But by the time we got home Rae's husband was tired, crabby, and impatient with everything and everybody. So the only thing I missed when we parted company was Rae.

∞

The years flew by. The children grew up and marriages failed. We both remarried. Me to a woman I was far more compatible with than the first wife. Rae, to a part-time evangelical preacher. I got along with him okay, but here was very little in the world that I agreed with him on.

Almost all of what he believed and thought he knew was stupid. The worst thing of all was what he did to Rae. She developed a lump in her breast. He told her that it was nothing to worry about. The cure was simple. Wear a crystal around her neck and pray harder to God. A year later she finally went to see a doctor. She ended up with a full mastectomy.

She fought the cancer every way a person could. She went into remission for a while, then the cancer came back. This happened a number of times. He never seemed very concerned about it, confident as he was that the Lord was going to cure it.

Then, mercifully, he had a heart attack and died in the hospital. We went to his funeral, but I didn't see Rae for a long time after he died. I thought of her often though, and finally gave her a call.

"I've often wondered about you, Al. It's been a long time since we've seen each other."

"I know. I'd sure like to get together sometime soon."

So we made plans to have dinner together. We both assumed my wife would come along.

When I brought it up to her, she said she thought it would be better if it was only Rae and I. She knew that Rae held a special place in my heart, and thought that at this stage in our lives we deserved this one night out alone.

Rae was surprised when I met her alone. When I explained why my wife wasn't there, she just shrugged it off. All through the meal our talk was mostly of family and the usual day to day things one does. It wasn't until the third glass of wine that I steered the conversation to our past.

At first, Rae tried to avoid talking about our summer, but I finally got her into it by talking about the time we picked corn together. That got her laughing. We kept the conversation light, but we talked about the past for a while longer.

"I remember when I met you," I finally said. "You were only six and I was seven. I fell in love with you the instant I saw you."

"You couldn't have. We were too young for that."

"Maybe you were, but I wasn't. And not only that, I'm still in love with you. I have been since that moment. I always will be."

She didn't answer. The look she gave me wasn't surprise as I expected it would be. It was more curious. As if she were trying to figure my motive for saying I was in love with her.

So I told her. "I'm not trying to make a pass at you, Rae. It's only that I've always wanted to tell you how I feel. I'm not looking for anything."

We were quiet. She stared at the table to avoid looking into my eyes. It was only after several minutes passed that she finally looked up.

The look on her face was almost that of a person who'd just learned that something valuable they lost, shouldn't have been.

"I guess, Al," she said, "it just wasn't meant to be."

She smiled, but tears were welling in her eyes.

We saw each other a few times and talked on the phone often. Everything seemed good. Then I didn't hear from her for a couple of weeks. The phone call came midmorning that day. It was her brother Ben.

"I think you'd best come to the hospital," he said. "It's Rae. She's had a relapse. The doctors don't give her much time. A couple of days at the most."

He told me the hospital and the room number. I told my wife what was going on and left for the hospital. Several people were in her room when I got there.

"Al," she said in a strained voice when I walked in. "I'm so glad you came." She looked around the room. "Please, everyone, give Al and me just a few minutes to talk. Then you can all come back in the room."

Everyone one there looked surprised at her words. Several shook their heads. But they all left.

I moved next the bed. She took my hand. "You said once that you always wanted to tell me something. Now, I *have* to tell you something."

I leaned closer to her. It was difficult to hear her as her voice grew weaker. She gave my hand a slight squeeze.

"I love you, Al. I always have. I always will. Maybe it wasn't meant to be, but it should have been."

She squeezed my hand again. That was all the time they gave us. They poured back into the room.

I released her hand. They crowded around her.

She watched me as I backed away.

A lone tear rolled down her cheek. I held mine back.

Her smiles were gone.

Along with all the years we didn't have.

By Michael Allen George

The Longest Days

Remember the longest days
When creeks were rivers
And farms seemed like home
Summers were younger then
Tobacco tasted new.
Cracking nuts in attics
And drinking sour root beer.
Each day started new
Unlike today when the only
Sparkling is a glass of wine
On a misty night and
Mornings begin with heads
Filled with work to be done,
Old thoughts and
Other things forgotten

Morning

Light breezes drifting
Through the window
Flowing past curtains dancing on
Scents of wild apple blossoms.
Roosters crowing in alarm
At a rising sun casting
Its first rays on the giant elm
With a tire swing in hand.
Muffled bangs from frying pans
Set on the stove follow,
While the sudden aroma of coffee
From porcelain percolators
Makes one hunger for the bacon
And eggs now frying,
Burying the thoughts of all else

Save the soft scent of the hay
To be baled today.

Corn Picking

She laughed as they lay
On those crispy-crackling
Corn leaves covering
The black clay ground.
Their intentions were honest
When they went to the field
On that warm October day
And they did pick some corn
But what they remember
Are the laughter and the leaves.

Fence Walking

Late night and past time
For a small boys bed.
He follows the man into
The star filled night,
Downhill passed the old red barn
To lowland with misty ground fog.
Along farm roads leading to
The meadow where the creek
Runs low in summer.
Stopping at a corner post to rest
While listening to the night sounds.
Saying nothing before moving
On the dew wet grass
Slapping the boys' thighs.
He stops for a moment
Before hurrying along,
Trying to match the stride
Of a man who again
Has room enough to walk.

Walk The Beam

By Bud George

"Abe, you and Abe decide who is going to walk that beam." You see - Ken gave everyone a nickname. Since my given first name and Abes first name were the same, to avoid confusion we got the same new name!

About the beam - that front beam. It was at the moment 8 feet above the second deck of a two story house we were building. We, when possible, framed exterior walls in a horizontal (laying down) position. We included sheathing, headers, window and door openings, and exterior soffits and facia.

We raised the walls with wall jacks (a come along which mounted on a steel pipe four inches in diameter with a steel cable). This wall had a ten foot soffit. An eight foot wall with a ten foot soffit - ten foot high. The beam was to rest on four 6x6 solid redwood columns about twenty-two foot long (beam dug into four concrete pier footings with 1/2 inch bolts.

We did not have the full-length redwood columns. We built temporary columns using multi layers of spliced shorter lengths of 2x6. These we set on short lengths of 2x10 and 2x12, because we had to leave the concrete footings for the redwood that we did not have that morning.

Abe and I set the wall jacks (the bottom of the jacks had a foot-hinged that we nailed to the floor, and a hook at the top to catch (stop) the top of the wall in its vertical position.

Ken checked the temporary columns for plumb and added a few more braces. Ken and Abe each operated a wall jack. I held onto a fourteen foot 2x4 that was nailed to the top plate of the wall. My two hundred and ten pounds was to act as a counter weight for the ten foot soffit and that beam. It did not.

The temporary columns bowed when the weight of the soffit and beam dropped on them. The nails holding the wall jacks into the floor pulled. But the columns held. We quickly braced and adjusted the wall and spent the rest of the day framing and setting walls and doubling top plates.

The next day Abe and I moved and set joists as Ken cut, moved rafter material for Ken to layout and cut. We moved 4x8 sheets of plywood to the second floor deck. This was 1/2 cdx for the roof deck. It was all lift and carry by hand.

There was no forklift, no boom truck, no compressor, no nail guns. Just Abe, Abe, and Ken. It was late November. Cold, but no snow yet. We needed two more days.

About that damn beam twenty feet from the ground - I lost. I got the beam about twenty feet from the ground. Abe won. He got the rear of the building. The house was a walkout. About thirty feet to the ground. Maybe I won.

To set (install) the rafters I set a 2x10 between the front wall plates and the beam and crawled out to the beam. Then walked on the beam to set the rafters. Abe did the same on the back wall. Ken handled the center ridge. I told Ken that I thought I might apply for a high wire circus job that I was pretty sure I qualified for now.

Next day colder. Ken set to cut plywood as necessary. Abe at the rear and me in front again. Snap a chalk line for the top of the first course of cdx. Nail it off completely. Toe hooked over the top to keep from sliding off. Snap a second line three feet on top of the plywood. Install first course of roofing underlay. Nail 2x4 toe hold on top of that.

We did okay that day. Watertight roof. It snowed eight inches that night. We still had windows, doors, siding, and exterior trim to do. But I did not have to walk that damn beam again.

Letters to My Son: My Closest Friend Throughout the Years

By David George

I have been blessed with close friendships throughout the years. Friends from Brazil, Mexico, Spain, Israel, and other places. I'm going to talk just one, an American.

My oldest and closest American friend, dear son, is your honorary Uncle John Berninghausen.

John and I met as undergraduates at the University of Minnesota. Our first contact was a Spanish play we acted in. We didn't take to each other at first. I thought he was arrogant and, well, I'm not sure what he thought. Perhaps the fact that we were from different social strata was an initial impediment to friendship. He was from an academic family and I from the working class. Somehow, we became close friends. We had many interests in common, such as foreign languages, politics, and the arts. We were also political liberals, at a time when universities were not necessarily so.

One thing I remember fondly is that John introduced me to Bossa Nova, which fed my growing interest in Portuguese and in Brazil. I don't have to tell you how important that was.

Over the years John and I met in various and sundry locations. When it came time for graduate school John enrolled at Stanford. I visited him many times in Palo Alto. When I moved to San Francisco in 1970, we met there frequently and usually headed to China Town. Since John had been in China and was now working on a Ph.D. in

Chinese, he knew the cuisine well and could order our food in Chinese (Mandarin).

Later on John got a teaching gig at Middlebury College. And wouldn't ya know, I was hired there in 1978 to teach Spanish and Portuguese. You can be sure that John had a hand in my hiring. Now living and teaching in the same place, we saw each other on a nearly daily basis. I got to know his lovely wife Alice and his great kids Gayle and Eric. I became Gayle and Eric's honorary uncle, just as John is yours. And I can't fail to remind you that you had your brief moment in Middlebury when we went on a canoe camping trip (I won't mention Lyme's Disease).

In 1985 I was hired by Lake Forest College. Bia and I moved to a campus apartment in Lake Forest (we moved to Evanston in 1989, a year before your birth). John and I saw each other occasionally when he would attend conferences in Chicago. We spoke frequently on the phone and when the age of the internet began, we were able to exchange emails.

John and I have met up many times in recent years (pre-pandemic). We've met in Minneapolis and Evanston. We continue to talk on the phone and exchange messages and emails.

We will be friends to the end.

Only An Allegory

By Michael Allen George

Chris sat in his makeshift office in the basement of his three bedroom Rambler, wondering what he was going to do next. Nearly twenty years teaching science at the same high school, and suddenly he was unemployed. Fired for answering a student's question honestly. Sometimes the truth hurts he knew, and this time it had hurt him bad.

It wasn't because he wouldn't find another job. It was more because he loved teaching, despite its meager salary and long hours. There was a special joy in seeing a child's eyes light up when they discovered something new. Nothing could fill a teacher's heart more than awakening the urge to learn.

That was what was so frustrating about this. He'd seen that light in the eyes of several children when he'd taken the time to answer the question. The question asked by the son of the school's principal. The question about Noah's Ark and the flood. The single question which turned into many.

It was a class discussion about the environment, and how conservation of all resources was becoming critical, with fresh water near the top of the list.

That's when the student said, "But God won't let us run out of water." Then he asked, "Don't you read the bible? It's the absolute true word of God. He can make water anytime he wants. Didn't you ever read about Noah and the flood?"

"Yes, I have. It's an interesting story, but just a story. It's what is called an allegory."

"What's an allegory?"

"In this case, it's a story that tries to tell us that we should behave or we will be punished."

"How can you say it's just a story? It's true. It happened."

"Throughout history, there have been a lot of flood stories, because there have been a lot of floods. That said, however, a flood large enough to cover the whole earth is highly unlikely. To start, where did the water come from to make the flood, and where did it go after the flood?"

"God took care of all that. Whatever he wants to happen, happens."

"Okay then, who built the ark? Was it Noah or was it God?"

"The bible says that Noah did."

"How did he manage to build it, and how long did it take him. It would have taken an immense amount of wood to build it. And the time for him to do it alone would have been considerable. He didn't have any modern tools to work with. Any kind of saws or chisels would have needed constant sharpening. The support beams he'd have needed would have been incredibly large and difficult to handle, even if you didn't consider how heavy they'd be."

"So, I guess God must of helped."

"But it doesn't say that in the bible, does it?"

"Maybe not," the kid said, his frustration with the teacher starting to show. "But it doesn't have to. If that's the way it was, that's just the way it was."

"Okay, I'll give you that. The thing is, the size of the ark doesn't compute. It wasn't anywhere near big enough. The space for the animals inside for each one was about the same as a dishpan that would fit in your kitchen sink. Not quite enough for an elephant. Given that problem, where was the food and water stored with no space left? Forty days and forty nights meant that a lot was needed."

"God took care of that. He took care of everything."

"What about all the lifeforms that live in water. What happened to them."

"Nothing. the world was covered with water. They did what they always do. They swam around in the water."

"There's a big problem with that though. If the salt in the water where saltwater critters live is diluted too much, they can't survive. If fresh water where freshwater critters live becomes too salty, they can't survive. With all that rain, all the water was mixed. So for some the water wasn't salty enough, for others it was too salty. Did God want all of them dead, too?"

"It didn't happen that way. The water stayed the same."

"You're sure about that?"

"Yes. I go to church, so I know the truth."

"I go to church, too. Every Sunday."

"That doesn't matter," the kid said, his confidence coming back. "You go to a Lutheran church, so you're not a true believer. Only Evangelicals are."

"That must mean you believe God knows everything that has ever happened. God knows everything that is happening. And God knows everything that is going to happen."

"Of course I know that. I thought even you Lutherans knew that."

"Some Lutherans do. Some don't. What was God's reason for creating the flood, or didn't he have one?"

"He did it because people were so sinful that God wanted to start over with people who weren't sinners. That's why he picked Noah and his family to start over."

"But since God knows everything that is going to happen, he knew it wasn't going to work. It surely didn't. So why did he do it anyway?"

"Because it was his will."

"It was his will to put not only the human race but trillions upon trillions of other lifeforms through the terror, pain, and agony of an extremely cruel death, only because he felt like it? You have a pretty poor opinion of God, young man."

"The truth is what the truth is."

"Yes it is. That's why I believe God, the creator of it all, exists on way too high a level to have ever done any of it. The story is just an allegory, plain and simple."

That was the end of the discussion, and before the end of the day, the end of Chris's job. The end of his teaching career. And as he sat there in his basement office, mulling over what happened, he knew he should have kept his theological views to himself.

To start with, being a teacher, he should have known better than to try to explain anything to the kid. Trying to explain an idea, or to teach someone too stupid to learn, was difficult at best. Because this subject involved religion, it was simply impossible.

The only saving grace was the fact that his time teaching was already limited. Science was a subject on its way out in the public school system run by conservative evangelicals.

That's when the phone rang. An old friend was on the other end when Chris answered it. She was the head of an environmental group that was growing fast.

"What can I do for you?" Chris asked.

"It's more what you can do for us. We've been selectively recruiting people for our organization. We were at the school today to do just that. We learned what happened to you. Now that you're unemployed, how'd you like to come to work for us?"

"I don't know. What would I be doing?"

"Working with a group we've recently started. Its purpose is finding new and better ways to deal with the worsening water crises. We really need people like you who already know the problem and can both speak about it and teach it."

"What does it pay?"

"A fair amount more that you make now."

"Well, my wife will like that."

"Does that mean you'll take the job? But before you answer, I have to tell you the name of the organization. I think you'll appreciate it. Maybe even like it."

"Really? So what is it?'

"We call it Riding The Ark."

Sunday Nights

By Michael Allen George

It was times like this that my father said, "Sunday nights are always lonely." And for him, they often were. I think part of that came from the war. There, men like him were often alone, especially on nights like Sundays, even when they were stuck in a crowded barracks.

When he came home, he always relished having family around. Especially Sundays. Early on it was parents and siblings, and on rare occasions, friends. As time went on, it was more and more his own family, and as we grew up, married, had kids, he lived for those Sundays when we had impromptu gatherings. In those days it could be just one of us with our families, some of us, or on the best days, all of us.

The strange thing for me though, was when one of those days ended. The happier the day, the more of us who were there, the sadder he became when it was over.

He would sit down in the only easy chair he ever sat in, sometimes sip a cup of coffee, and pet his dog. There was always a dog there, totally loyal to him, and offering his head for dad to pet.

Mary often commented on it. She loved dad, but she had a hard time excepting the way he seemed to sink down those Sunday evenings. When we visited her folks and it was time to go, I think they celebrated our leaving. And there never was a dog around for anyone to pet. They even found it somewhat disgusting that we always had a dog. Animals of any kind should live outside. Never in anyone's home, or even anyone's heart.

But over the years, Mary found their attitude toward dogs disgusting. Before we got married, the only pet she'd ever had was a tank of guppies.

When I told her I wanted to get a dog, she was totally undecided, so it took me a while to convince her we should get one.

It all changed within hours of bringing home the first puppy. She quickly fell in love, and of course, the pup adored her. I was pals with the long succession of dogs that passed through our lives, but Mary was always first, always the one they most looked out for, and most of all, the one whose attention they most wanted and needed.

Our latest dog, Fred, who we rescued just days before his execution date, was especially bonded with Mary. Even as we aged and our bodies began to show the ravages of a long life, his bond with her grew ever stronger. He and I were buddies too, and I was at the age where I very much appreciated his company, especially on our morning walks. But after those walks, it was always Mary he looked for.

When she got sick and was bed ridden, other than our walks and his time to eat or go outside to relieve himself, his time was spent with Mary. Sometimes on the floor next to the bed, other times on the bed.

She slept a lot of the time, but when she was awake and lucid, I would often hear her talking to him. When I'd look in on them, he'd be staring at her with rapt attention, the look in his eyes carrying the impression he understood every word.

He even stayed with her at the end. And when the day came that the ambulance took her away, some of the life seemed to leave him as they moved her from the bad to the stretcher. Everything about him, from the way he moved to the look in his eyes, said that he knew she was never coming home again.

She lived a few more days in the hospital. I wanted to take him to see her, as much for him as for her, but they wouldn't allow it. Every night I came home after she was gone, he was at the door to greet me. He asked for nothing, other than to be close. He knew I needed the comfort he gave me as badly he needed to know I would come home after I left every day.

The day of the memorial service was the toughest. For both of us. And hardest of all, was the impression I got when I left for the service, he was afraid I wasn't coming back. The look in his eyes when I did return said it all. From then on, he hated to leave my side, even for a moment.

In the end, though, he gave me more comfort than I gave him. So it was hard when he began showing his age. It started after Mary had been gone for nearly four years, and now five have gone by.

Last night, somewhere around 3:00 AM he woke me up, needing to be taken out to relieve himself. Lately, he'd been sleeping all night on the floor, but when I brought him back in he wanted to get up on the bed. He couldn't manage it alone, so I helped him up. When I got in the bed, he curled up with his back as tight against me as he could get it.

It was a bit uncomfortable but having him close was worth any amount of discomfort. I fell asleep again, and it was near 7:00 AM when I woke up. Fred was in the same position he was in when I fell asleep. He was gone.

It was like him, I thought. The last two things he did in life was ask to be taken out so he didn't leave behind a mess, and ask to get up on the bed to be close at the end time.

The first thing I did was let the tears flow. Then I wrapped him in plastic, and took him out on the back forty, near a stand of pines we'd walked by in the morning so many times.

There were several markers there, where so many old friends like him rested. I still remembered all of them. They were all special in their own way, but this time was the hardest. Not only was he a great companion, he was the one who seemed to help keep the memories of Mary so fresh in my mind. The only thing that eased some of the hurt was the knowledge that he and Mary would be close there. That's where I spread her ashes, just as she asked me to do. "So my memories," she said, "and the memory of me, will be close when you need them. And so my spirit will be with them, those friends who filled our lives with so much love."

Even so, life felt like nothing but empty. I simply couldn't decide what to do next. In the past when I lost a dog, I got another one. This time, though, I wasn't sure I should. At my age, the dog would likely outlive me. Would it be fair to put a dog through that, sensitive as they often are.

On the other hand, however long I lived and the dog spent with me, it would probably be a lot more time than if I didn't rescue it. So whether or not I got another pup was going to be a tough decision, which I'd have to put off until tomorrow. It isn't something I can rationally do now. I was filled with the understanding of how my father felt when he said, "Sunday nights are always lonely." Because too much was gone, and it was Sunday night and I was lonely.

Best Reason

By Michael Allen George

Friday night and I was tired. It was a long day and an even longer week. All I wanted was a couple of beers, then home, a long hot shower, something simple to eat, and a little television before bed. It was a good way to spend a Friday night. Something I'd been doing for about seven years now. Ever since, with my blessing, she walked out the door.

The only trouble was, even after that long, I thought of her every Friday night I stopped for a beer, knowing I could without having to listen to her bitch after I got home, about my stopping. She never thought it was okay for me to do much of anything without her. The truth was, I liked taking her with me. It was only on Friday nights that I wanted the simple freedom of a couple of beers alone.

The trouble this night, I was later than normal. My partner insisted we set the last beam before we quit for the day. When I saw how crowded the bar was, I almost left. All the tables, booths, and bar stools were occupied, and I was in no mood to stand while I drank my beer.

While taking one last look around, I noticed a small table with a lone woman sitting there. Hoping she'd understand my desire to sit while drinking a beer, I walked over to ask her if I could share her table for a short time. I leaned down closer to her but didn't see her face until she turned to answer my question. To say it was a shock when is about the best I can do.

She gave me a half smile, shook her head no, but said yes. I fumbled with the chair as I sat down, staring at her the whole time. She looked every bit as good as she did the last time I saw her, nearly seven years ago. She was the first to speak.

"So, how are you, Dale?" she asked. "It's been a long time."

"I'm fine, Rebecca," I answered. "This is a totally unexpected surprise."

"Not a good one, I imagine."

"I don't know if it's good or bad. Not yet anyway. I was just thinking about you. That makes seeing you all of a sudden an even bigger surprise."

"So I managed to ruin your night even before you saw me?"

I sighed as I decided to leave. Fighting with my ex-wife, who I hadn't had any contact with for so many years, wasn't my idea of a way to spend a quiet Friday evening. I stood to go.

"I'm sorry I bothered you, Rebecca," I told her. "I won't bug you anymore." I turned to leave.

Unexpectedly, a look of disappointment swept across her face. "I'm the one who should be sorry," she said. "Please, sit down. I didn't mean to offend you. I just figured that was the way you felt about me, so I stupidly said so. I'd like it if you stayed."

Not sure it was a good idea, I sat down again. Staying there wasn't a hard thing to do. No matter what had happened between us, the years hadn't changed the fact that she was a treat for the eyes. Looking at her reminded me of how long it had been since I'd been out with any woman, good looking or not.

The waitress made a quick stop at our table. I ordered a light beer and she ordered another glass of white wine. "It's only my second," she said. "I usually have two when I stop."

"I remember. You didn't like it when I ordered a third beer."

"I didn't, did I," she agreed, then said something I never would have expected. "Tonight, though, since I'm drinking with you maybe I'll have a third glass. It isn't up to me how many beers you drink."

Why she would drink a third glass because she was with me made no sense. I was sure she had no love, or even a remote fondness for me, so why was she trying to be nice?

"I can remember when it mattered a lot if I stopped for even one beer."

"I was younger then. It wouldn't matter now."

"What? You mean if we were still together?"

"Yes, I mean if we were together now, it wouldn't matter. Now I understand how much a little wind-down time can mean at the end of the day. Especially Fridays. Now it would probably be you getting upset at me for stopping on my way home for a couple of glasses of wine."

"No, I think it'd be more like we both stop and are more relaxed when we get home. Or better yet, we meet someplace and eat together. Even back then, I would have liked that."

"Really. I always thought the main reason you stopped was to avoid coming home."

"It wasn't. It was like you said, to unwind a bit. I know that being a carpenter isn't the same kind of stressful as what you do, but it can have its own moments."

"I understand all that now. I just wish I would have while we were still married."

"You almost sound as if you wish we still were?"

"There are days, Dale, I wonder about it. Sometimes I think we are like the people in Anne Murray's song, Somebody's Always Saying Goodbye. You know the line, "We could have had it all, if we'd only tried.""

"When we split, we both figured we didn't have much of anything. A couple of cars too old and worn out to talk about, and a house with an underwater mortgage."

"I know, but it's the sentiment. Whatever did you do with that house anyway? Just walk away?"

"I kept it. I finally got a new mortgage, so the payments are easier. And I've been doing a little remodeling as time and money allows."

"I'd have thought you'd get rid of it."

"I thought about it," I said, this time surprising her, "but I always liked the house and the neighborhood. And it was filled with too many good memories."

"Really? You have good memories of living in that house. I didn't think the memory of anything connected with me was good."

"There are a lot of them," I said, then downed my beer. Her last comment came across a little too sarcastic for me, so I got up to leave. "Most of my memories of you are good, and I think I'll keep it that way."

"Please, Dale, sit down. I wasn't trying to be offensive. It's just that we were both pretty bitter when we split, and life being what it is, I didn't believe you could possibly have any good memories of me."

Against what at the time seemed to be my better judgement, I yielded to the look in her eyes. There was something there that said she seriously wanted me to stick around. She managed a smile when I sat down.

"Thank you," she said, "for understanding. Now, how about I buy us supper? You still like a good hamburger, don't you?"

"I do. A bacon cheeseburger with greasy fries is about as good as it gets."

"It's a good thing to see, when some things don't change."

She bought us a meal. She ate the same thing as I did, with one small difference. My burger was a double meat. Hers wasn't.

As busy as it was in the bar, it took quite a while for the food to come and when it did, we ate slow. The conversation between us got even friendlier, and before either of us realized it, the evening was used up and the nighttime crowd was in the bar. Then the band started. They weren't that great, but the third song they played was a slow one.

She didn't ask. She stood and took my hand. "Let's," she said.

"I don't know," I argued. "It's been a hot day and I was sweating a lot. I probably don't smell too good."

"Doesn't matter." She pulled me to my feet.

I didn't try to hold her close. After a long day pounding nails, I really was afraid of offending her. She made it clear when she moved in close that she really didn't care about that.

Quickly, much faster than I thought possible, holding her was a familiar thing. A very pleasant, familiar thing. The feel of her breasts against my chest might have been enough, but so much of her was so close, the inevitable happened. It embarrassed me some, but when she felt it she momentarily tilted her head back. She had a smirk on her face when our eyes met.

It was an odd thing for a band like that to do, but they played three slow songs in a row. By the third, we were pretty comfortable dancing together. Her head rested on my shoulder, and shortly into that third song, I felt the moisture. She was crying. Silently, but crying. It felt like she was holding on as if her life depended on it. For me, it felt like something lost was returning. But I forced myself to take it all as some kind of illusion.

When the song ended, she lifted her head and we kissed. Where the passion came from, I wasn't sure at that moment. It was simply there, in full force. It took a minute or two after we broke it, before we walked back to the table.

We stared into each other's eyes for a while before talking. I spoke first. "I know there's no good reason for it, but you could stop by the house."

"Are you leaving now."

"I thought it might be a good idea."

"Because of what happened out there?" She nodded at the dance floor.

"That's part of it."

"What else is there?"

"The way I feel right now. I don't see how the future could hold anymore for us than what we've just shared. So before we get serious with something we probably can't share, going home might be the best."

"I guess you're right."

"You could stop by the house though. See what I've done to it."

"I could, and I would if I could see any reason to. But I can't. There is no reason to. It's funny. If this was the first time I'd ever met you, I might decide there was a reason to go look at your house. Given our history, it probably isn't."

"You're right. There's really no reason, good or otherwise, for you to stop."

"No, none at all I guess."

"Well," I said, "thanks for a great night. I've enjoyed your company." I stood and turned away.

"Wait," she said, "I'll walk out with you."

She held my hand on the way to her car. When we got there, she turned to me. "You can kiss me goodnight now."

I did. That led to a second and a third, the passion building with each one. But she stopped it there and pushed me away. Her eyes were filled with tears. "I wish I could find a good reason, Dale. If I could…" She quickly got in her car, started it, and left.

I tried to figure out my own feelings as I watched her go. They were mixed. I really would have liked it if she'd agreed to stop at the house. But part of me wondered if we actually could do it better if we tried again. Along with that was the realization that I missed her for the entire seven years she was gone. A lot more than I cared to admit. Even to myself.

It was with a bit of loneliness that I drove home. I was feeling sad when I got there, so I knew my heart would feel as empty as the house, even before I went in.

Then, to my surprise, I didn't find out if it did or not. A speeding car turned into my driveway. Rebecca got out and I heard her door locks click when she closed hers. Her keys were in her purse by the time she reached me.

There were no preliminaries. She literally threw her arms around me and kissed me. Then she laughed.

"Sometimes," she said, "the best reason is no damn reason." She took my arm. "Now show me *our* house."

Of course, I did.

To Gain Control

By Michael Allen George

To control her while they rolled her into the institution for dying, otherwise called a nursing home, she was tied tightly to the wheelchair. They were certain it was a legitimate tactic to use on an elderly woman who refused to cooperate. They were wrong, but didn't really care. They had her where they wanted her now, and that was all that mattered to them. What didn't matter a damn to them, was the fact she was their mother.

For her, this was the final indignity. It was even worse than the time in the courtroom with the macho judge and their team of lawyers. She was ruled to be too incompetent to call her own lawyers, so she faced the legal inquisition without legal representation. And because it was all about money and control, they won handily.

Now here she was in a nursing home, where she was soon to be locked into her future cell. They were sure they had her so beaten now that she wouldn't even try to open the case again. She'd simply give up and let them take total control over the company she and her husband spent a lifetime building. It was now a corporation worth over a billion dollars.

What they, her children, didn't know, was that she suspected for a long time they were planning something. They were sure, now that she was confined to a wheelchair, she was defenseless. They somehow confused a physical ailment with her mental capacity. Never mind that she was running a billion-dollar corporation and doing a superb job of it. They also never suspected that she would have them watched.

She, being a few steps ahead of them their whole adult lives, did have them watched, and watched closely. All three of them. Both sons and the daughter in the middle. So she knew all along about their basic plans for her. Plans, had they had their mother's intelligence, they would have known they never needed. Before they decided they couldn't wait until it was the right time to take over, taking over was exactly what their mother had planned for them.

They didn't have it, however, and therefore made the biggest mistake possible. They only managed to do one thing right. They made their move quicker than their mother expected, and now had her locked up for good. Or so they thought.

For her it was only a temporary setback. As soon as one of her lawyers failed to contact her, her own plans would be set in motion. She knew, without any doubt, she would be out of her personal hell hole in a day or two. In the meantime, she would find some small personal delight in what her children would find when they began their planned takeover of her company.

What they had in front of them was nothing. In a short time she had liquidated all of what they once would have inherited, including the company. Most of the cash she generated while she liquidated, she donated to various environmental groups and the ACLU. None of her children cared about, or even thought about, the environment. They'd consistently complained to their mother that she'd always given too much to those groups.

So now she felt it was the best way to dispose of their inheritance. And being essentially conservative, they all hated the ACLU. Not only did they lose nearly everything with their premature move to gain control, it all went to places they hated.

So it was with a great deal of delight she faced the children as her lawyers and new bodyguard escorted her from her short-term prison.

"How could you do this to us, Mother?" her older son asked as she walked past them on her way out.

"With superior intelligence," she said, "and because of the lack of any kind of human decency on your part."

"But it was our heritage. It never would have happened if you'd have been willing to give up control of the company when you were no longer capable of running it."

"But, as you can now see, I was capable. So now, because of your greed and rush to gain control, you'll never get it. There is no way you can recover what's gone."

"You're so unfair, Mother."

"You bet, and tying an old woman to a wheelchair is fair. Fair will be when your children do that to you. All three of you. I've set up a large endowment for each of them, which they can only collect after all three of you are permanently placed in nursing homes."

Letters to My Son: How Has the Country Changed During Your Lifetime?

By David George

The answer to this question could fill several libraries. So I'll limit my response to a few anecdotes about technological change.

A) Television

The first significant change I was aware of concerned television. Though TV broadcasts date back to the 1930s, I first saw a TV program probably in the late 1940s. A family in our neighborhood got the first set. It consisted of a large box-like piece of furniture with a tiny screen embedded in the front, probably the size of an I-phone screen. One night the kids on our street crowded outside in front of the living room where the TV was showing a program of cartoons. How we were able to view the miniscule screen from outside is a mystery to me. But I do remember being transfixed. Cartoons, which I had only seen in a movie theater, were flashing across a screen in someone's living room! Unforgettable.

It would be a few years before my family got a TV. I'm sure the sets were quite expensive, and my family was close to the poverty line. But get one we did, eventually. I'm not sure of this, but there were only three channels to choose from: ABC, CBS, and NBC. Sound familiar? So fights over what to watch were minimal, perhaps even non-existent. My favorite program was Howdy Doody, a puppet that sat on the knees of a man named Buffalo Bob. They both dressed in western style. There was a live audience called the peanut gallery and a theme song that began, "It's Howdy Doody time." Classic.

TVs were black and white. But when my father found an ad for turning our black and white into a color TV, oh the excitement. Father signed up for the …whatever… and we waited with bated breath. A package arrived. Inside was a sheet of plastic with three colored strips on it. My father placed it over the screen and voilà! A color TV. Three static strips of color overlaying the screen. Scams and the suckers who fall for them are nothing new.

B) Computers

Even more significant was the age of computers. My first contact with computers was in an office at the University of Minnesota where I worked as an undergraduate. Data was collected via computers and stored on punch cards. I'm not sure how all that worked because I was never allowed on the computer team. That was reserved for well-behaved student workers.

I first interfaced with computers in 1970 when I worked in the free clinic at San Francisco Hospital as a bilingual—actually trilingual—clerk-typist and medical interpreter (the latter position wasn't official – a long story). Information on patients was stored on a mainframe (I think). To register patients information had to be retrieved from the computer. Only employees above clerk-typists in the hierarchy were allowed to get the info. That always caused a delay in registering patients, some of whom arrived a very poor shape. But since it was the "free clinic" most of the employees cared little about the patients. I decided to take matters into my own hands and learn how to get patient information from the computer. A woman in the insurance division was one of the few with empathy vis-à-vis the patients and she agreed to help me with the registration delay. We sat down in front of a screen and keyboard, and she explained codes and sequences. I took voluminous notes and after a few days I could operate the system. It speeded things up significantly and patients on repeat visits always looked for me to register them. It didn't take long before the bosses found out what I was doing. I was told in no uncertain terms to keep my hands off the computer keyboard. I didn't obey and continued to retrieve information surreptitiously.

A decade would pass before I next interfaced with computers. I was now teaching at Middlebury College. Faculty were granted access to the college's mainframe to enter their research material and store it on the computer. Only a few of us availed ourselves of this privilege. I took the first baby steps in learning how to use a program that would change my life: a word processor. It was cumbersome but clearly a huge leap ahead from typewriters. Though you had to type in commands for everything on the keyboard (!@#$%& etc), there was a life-changing function called cut-and-paste. You could change anything in your text without having to white out or worse, start over!

It wouldn't be long before personal computers would hit the market. In the early 1980s there were zillions of brands. To name a few: Commodore, Osborne, Tandy, Texas Instruments, Timex, not to mention IBM and Apple Macintosh. My brother Mike gave me my first tutorials on personal computers. I don't recall the brand but he got me started. When I was hired by Lake Forest College in 1985, part of the deal was that the college would pay for my own home computer. I had to choose from all the brands. A Middlebury colleague who knew a lot more about computers than I almost talked me into buying an Osborne. In the end—lucky me—I chose an IBM. It wouldn't be long before the only remaining brands on the market would be IBM (or PC as it's now called) and Apple.

From 1985 on I did everything on the computer: class preparation and grading (spread sheets soon hit the market), scholarship (essays, followed by books). Soon would come the internet and email and all the other stuff you, dear son, have been familiar with all your life.

I could go on and on: tablets, cell phones, Alexa etc. The list is dizzying. But let me end with another anecdote. In the 1980s Brazil passed a computer law called *Lei da Informática*. It meant that Brazil would develop its own hardware and software. Nothing would be imported. But there was a problem: only a few companies that had an "in" with the government were awarded concessions to produce computers and software. No free market for computers. No competition. The upshot: the only thing available on the market were extremely expensive and crappy computers that you had to program yourself. And since the gringo, meaning me, was the only one in the Zonis family with any experience, I spent significant time during my visits to Brazil programming computers. Yes, me, I was a computer programmer. People soon concluded that the computers and software produced under the *Lei da Informática* were a waste of time, and they began purchasing MACs and IBMs smuggled into the country. The *Lei da Informática* was soon put out of its misery.

There's so much more to tell, not only about computers but about other changes I've witnessed in my lifetime: changes in society, personal identity (from homophobic slurs to LGTBQ), feminism, politics, war (WWII, Korean War, Vietnam, Middle East etc), health care, art. I've lived through nearly 80 years of change, almost a century! For some things I could say, *Plus ça change plus c'est la meme chose* (racist, venal politicians is a good example). But let's end on an upbeat note: living through all these changes has been challenging and exciting. I can't imagine you answering this question when you're my age! *Boa sorte, filho querido*

Peanuts

By Bud George

A few days ago I came home to find a cute little chipmunk sitting on the arm of my favorite outdoor chair.

"Hey, Chippie," I said by way of greeting.

He looked at me and said, "My name is Ralph."

Needless to say, I was shocked, taken aback. I have not had a conversation with a chipmunk since we smoked a lot of those mushrooms. So I answered,

"How they hanging, Ralph?"

Ralph rolled his eyes and informed me, "Nothing hanging, nothing banging."

"Gotta be able to move quick, think quick. Where's that girl with the peanuts?" he asked.

"Well," I said, "that would be Liz. She's in California."

"What did you do?" he asked. "Ask her some stupid anatomical question?"

"No no," I answered, "She lives in California."

"Well," he said, "say hello for me - tell her to stop by anytime and bring peanuts."

Letters to My Son:
What famous people or important people have you encountered in real life?

By David George

This question is easy to answer: oodles of famous people, mostly in Brazil but also in Argentina, Chile, Mexico, and France. And a few in good old USA. Through my work as a scholar specializing in Latin American culture I met–and in many cases became friends with—writers, actors (film, TV, and stage), directors (ditto), and critics. Not to blow my own trumpet, but in my prime years as a scholar and translator, I achieved a measure of distinction myself. Ahem. But I'll focus on one such person whom you, dear son, came to know in childhood: Edla van Steen.

I met Edla 50+ years ago in São Paulo where I was spending a year on a Fulbright Fellowship. Edla had recently given up a promising acting career—a real beauty, she had even been a "cover girl"—and was transitioning to writing. I had frequent encounters with Edla and her then husband Ennes at parties hosted by the American Consulate, which administered the Fulbright program. Eventually Edla and Ennes began inviting me to parties at their beautiful home in the chic Morumbi neighborhood. It was a gorgeous house with an infinity pool in the hills overlooking São Paulo. Ennes, an architect, had designed the house (you yourself spent time in the house and the pool in childhood).

I was still a pup, age-wise, and often found myself speechless when was introduced to some famous actor or actress from a movie I had seen recently. There were always writers present at the parties, which is what I was mostly interested in.

In time I became an "honorary" family member, not just with Edla and Ennes but also with their three children: Ricardo, Anna, and Lea. Invitations to parties were extended to Saturday family luncheons, which I was fortunate to be a part of for the rest of Edla's life (she "shuffled off this mortal coil" in 2018). Back to the Fulbright years: Edla's writing career was just beginning to take off and I was privileged to read her early stories and her first novel.

After a year in Brazil, I returned home, spent a year playing hippie in San Francisco, and eventually started a theater career in Minneapolis. I made my living (barely scraped by would be more accurate) translating newspaper articles and other documents for government agencies and individuals (e.g., a Ph.D. thesis on cryopreservation, from Portuguese to English). Somehow Edla and I lost track of each other. Somehow (part 2) a letter from Edla reached me years later after I had returned to the University of Minnesota for doctoral studies.

After I passed my doctoral exams (oral and written), I received another grant for thesis research in Brazil. Back in São Paulo again, "out where a friend is a friend…" I quickly reprised my role as honorary family member. Meanwhile, Edla had achieved renown in her writing career, and we began talking about my translating her work. Here's an irony: though I had made my living as a technical translator for several years, I had no experience as a literary translator. Though Edla's stories had by this time been translated into several languages, she wanted to give me a shot at it. Maybe because I was a "family member," or maybe because she trusted my judgement (sure fooled her). The first story I translated was published and we were off! Over the years I translated (and published) two of Edla's novels, three books of short stories, and individual stories in edited collections. I also wrote about Edla's fiction and drama (yes, she was also a playwright) in essay collections, journals, and newspapers. I also wrote (in Portuguese) a preface to one of her books.

Edla and Ennes eventually divorced. Though it was a sad occurrence, she later remarried. Her new husband: Sábato Magaldi, Brazil's most renowned theater critic. Sábato and I became friends and he helped me with my research on Brazilian theater, research which produced five books and numerous articles and essays. To return the favors, I published an article on Sábato's career and lavished praise (well deserved) on him in my books.

As an honorary member, I have been involved in other family projects (e.g., translating and/or critiquing Ricardo's film scripts).

All goods things come to an end, and Sábato left us five years ago and Edla three years.

I will always treasure our time together.

Now that I've finished this tale about "famous people," I realize that the only thing that matters is friendship. The "famous" part is irrelevant.

P.S. Here's something from an email I sent to a mutual friend on the day of Edla's passing: "Losing a dear friend and mentor of 50 years standing is hard. My only consolation is that I was here when Edla departed and was able to share tears and fond memories with family and innumerable friends. Ella was much beloved, lived a memorable life, helped so many people—as did Sábato—and the fantasy of the two of them reuniting today is a comfort."

Rhubarb And Lilacs

By Bud George

Drove to Minneapolis this morning - had coffee with breakfast and another cup driving. When I got to Lake Street I really had to pee, but nothing was open. All burned out or boarded up. What could I do? Well, I stopped near an alley - might have been Bryant Avenue.

Went up the alley and found a Lilac bush behind a garage, unzipped, and aimed at a little patch of Dandelions. Then I noticed a black guy on the other side of my lilac bush. He was pissing on a Rhubarb plant.

"Hey," I said. "How's it going?"

He looked up from the Rhubarb and said, "Man, I tell you I'm ready to crash. Really beat. Been up all night for a week."

"Doing what?" I asked.

"Well," he said, "you know, driving back and forth and picking up stuff here and there.?

So then I asked him, "Hey, you guys got another riot planned soon?"

"Oh hell no," he said. "Gotta wait until the liquor stores and drug stores open again."

"So - what else you got planned?" I asked.

"Well," he said, "we are gonna demand all cops the city hire from now on are female, and they gotta train them way different."

"Whadda you mean?" I asked.

He explained. "Like right now, a party gets a little loud the cops come and break it up. Not good - a real waste."

"What are you gonna train them to do instead?" I inquired.

"Simple," he answered, "the cops would join the party for a while. Kick back. Have a nice glass of Dago Red or Mad Dog. Maybe dance a little. Be way better community relations. I don't understand why you folks are in such a hurry to get to work in the morning anyway."

"So, what else you gonna ask for?" I asked.

He said, "We gonna improve cop cars for new black cops. Better stereos, I'm thinking. Probably Esculates with wire wheels - sharp - Style - look good - feel good."

"Well," I said, "sounds like you gonna be plenty busy."

"Yeah," he said, "home to bed now. Have a good day."

"Thanks. Good talking to you," I said as I zipped up.

He walked in the opposite direction, to an Impala - low to the ground in back. No license plate. I headed the other way.

"Shit!" I thought. "I hope my truck still has tires on it."

A Rainy Day Chipmunk

By Bud George

"Go outside. Don't go far. We are leaving soon." The three of them went outside.

Jenny said, "The canoe is way out at the very end of the dock."

Luke said, "We better move it onto shore."

Josh was running out on the dock to move the canoe. The sky was dark and looked like rain, maybe? As they climbed into the canoe the rain began. The sky got darker and the wind blew. They untied the canoe from the dock. The wind blew a great gust and pushed them away from the dock, out into the lake.

"Paddle for shore," Jenny yelled.

"Paddle for shore," Luke yelled.

"Paddle for shore," Josh yelled.

It didn't work. The wind blew. They could not see the dock because of the hard rain. They could not see the cabin.

"Paddle for shore," they all yelled. It didn't help.

They heard a very loud clunk and felt the canoe go sideways. It had hit a big floating branch, the canoe slid sideways onto shore. They were safe, sort of, and very wet.

"Tip the canoe on it's side," Jenny said. "It will shelter us."

The canoe was a pretty good shelter from the rain.

"I'm hungry," Luke said.

"I have an orange," Jenny said.

They ate the orange.

"I'm still hungry," Luke said.

"I have four crackers," Josh said.

They each ate a cracker.

Josh gave the last one to a chipmunk who had taken shelter with them under the canoe.

Luke said, "I have some peanuts. We can have them for a snack later."

After a while the rain stopped and the sky cleared up a bit.

Jenny said, "We better peddle back to the cabin."

Just as the kids were getting into their canoe, the adults came rowing up in the big, flat bottom, fishing boat.

"Oh! We were so worried about you kids," they said.

The adults were soaking wet. The kids were pretty dry.

"We had food," Josh said.

"We had shelter under the canoe," Jenny said.

"That chipmunk took our peanuts," Luke said.

Tractor Ride

By Michael Allen George

It was a typical July, midweek afternoon in my part of Minnesota. My daughter and granddaughter were over to work in the garden. They always said I was too bossy to work with, so I was watching their efforts from the glider on my front porch.

My house was even older than me, so it was a real porch. The kind you see damn little of nowadays. No glass, no screens, no extra doors. Just a low railing and a place to sit. And on days like this one, an especially good place to sit, watching someone doing the work that was getting increasingly difficult as I aged.

Suddenly I heard a scream, then my daughter yell, "No, no, don't drink that! *It could kill you*!

My granddaughter was about to drink out of the hose. I couldn't help it. I laughed. Loud. My daughter heard me and turned to give me one of her I'm going to kill you looks.

"Water from a hose won't hurt you unless it's been sitting in the hose for a very long time," I told her. "Even then, it's not likely to do much harm."

"That's your opinion," she answered. "I know for a fact, it's dangerous."

"I must be dead then," I joked, pinching myself, pretending to check and see if I was still alive.

All I got was another dirty look and they went back to work. The exchange between us got me thinking back. There were so many things we did on a regular basis when I was young, that are pretty much forbidden now, that it sometimes seems a miracle that I've not only lived this long, but even survived into adulthood.

For me, it went beyond hose drinking, riding in the back of a truck, smoking, and so many other standard no nos. I spent as much of my time as I was allowed on my Uncle's farm when I was a kid. There, half the things I did would be considered a hazard now.

For one, he used to send me to the store, located about a half mile from the farm, to buy his cigarettes. Thing was, he let me drive his two-ton cattle truck. That wouldn't sound like anything, except I was only around thirteen when I started doing it. I was still a bit of a runt then, so the foot pedals were a reach. That might have been the serious part, if it wasn't for the fact the truck's brakes didn't work.

I also wasn't much good driving in reverse, so I always drove around the block, a distance of four miles. The good thing was, I never had any kind of incident or accident when I went to the store. I never had an accident during all the hours I spent driving a tractor either.

There was, however, one time that could have been a disaster while driving the tractor. My uncle's farm was relatively small, and he only owned one small tractor. A wide front, three-point hitch, Ferguson. It was always kept parked on the top of a hill so we could give it a rolling start, since the starter didn't work. I remember getting up to a pretty good speed sometimes, before it started.

Then came the day it wouldn't start. He had just completed a tune up, new points and plugs, and had evidently done something wrong. No matter what he attempted, he couldn't get it running again. So, he decided to tow it to the local mechanic.

Since all he had to tow it with was an ancient pickup and a ten-foot length of chain, I was elected to ride the tractor and steer it. It went okay until we reached a long, steep hill down into a creek valley. We stopped at the top of it, and I was lectured about the use of the tractor's brakes to control the downhill speed.

It was a bit of a tedious run down that hill, because I found if difficult to maintain a steady speed. We made it down with a few close calls, but nothing serious happening.

At the mechanic's, Uncle told him about the problem. The mechanic nodded, then lifted the distributor cap off the tractor. That's when I noticed the missing finger on his right hand, and the two from his left. All missing after different accidents that happened while he was repairing something for someone.

He loosened the points, used a bent in half paper match to get the proper gap, tightened them down, and replaced the cap.

"Should be good to go now," he said.

"How much?" Uncle asked.

"Two-bits ought to do it."

Uncle paid him, then pulled me a few feet. I let out the clutch on the tractor, and it popped right off. Uncle unhooked the chain and said, "Now you be really careful on the hill. You have to keep the speed down."

I told him I would, and he took off. I put the tractor in fourth gear, its highest gear, and took off. I drove flat out, which on that tractor wasn't all that fast. Being a typical young (13 years old) male, I quickly got impatient. I liked driving the tractor, but the six-mile drive seemed awful slow.

Then I reached the hill. I stopped at the top, and thought, "What the hell, why not," and started down. I pushed in the clutch and let it roll free. Before I had the chance to react, I was moving a lot faster than the tractor was designed to move. I didn't dare let the clutch out, for fear of what the sudden change in speed would do to the motor, so I eased into the brake. I knew braking hard could start me sliding, and that could easily lead to disaster in the deep ditches on both sides of the road.

By this point, the front wheels of the tractor were literally beginning to dance. I knew I had to do something, so I eased out the clutch and put more pressure on the brakes. It didn't come close to stopping the tractor, but it did slow it enough to give me some control the rest of the way to the bottom of the hill.

I didn't stop the tractor until I was completely out of that creek valley. When I did, I took several deep breaths and waited for the shaking to stop. The rest of the way back to the farm I was satisfied with the tractor's slow speed.

When Uncle asked how the trip home went, I told him just fine. I also always paid better attention to what he said after that, when he gave me any kind of instructions. He was, I believe, a wiser man than I'll ever be.

Why then, one might wonder, did he sometimes give me such heavy responsibilities? Mostly, I think, because he trusted me. Maybe more than he should have that one time, but none of us is perfect.

Overall, I believe the trust was well founded, and made life better for the both of us. It's something that's seems to be getting lost now. Enough so, I knew it wouldn't do any good to point out to my daughter how much water she drank out of a hose when she was helping out in the garden when she was a kid.

So I got up and left the porch. In the garden I picked up the hose, turned on the water, let it run a while, the took a nice big drink. My granddaughter laughed like hell.

Time

By Michael Allen George

Seeing them together, it was obvious they were sisters. Sylvia, the oldest by a year, was beautiful, and carried an air about her that made men want her. And want her now. There wasn't many she couldn't have, if she wanted them. Which she didn't. She was satisfied with her very rich husband who gave her all the things she wanted. At least, that's what I believed.

The younger sister, Susan, my wife, was very pretty. She was attractive to men, but the kind of woman you can be satisfied with if all you get in bed is a snuggle. There's something cozy and warm about her. She's fun to simply snuggle with. That said, the other things about sharing a bed were more than just fine between us. Better in fact, then they ever were with Sylvia, who I dated before Susan, and I got together.

Not to say Susan broke us up. That was Sylvia's husband, the very rich Herbert J. Johnson. He was born into a moderately wealthy family, and at age eighteen was given a gift of one hundred thousand dollars from his parents to start his adult life with.

He went to college, but also invested most of his money. He didn't do well in college, but he did great with his investments. So good that he was rich by the age of twenty-one, about a year after he gave up on college. By age twenty-two he met Sylvia and easily convinced her that he was a far better prospect than I was. Especially since I only earned a middle-class income working as a computer programmer.

I was naturally upset when she broke it off with me, but it didn't last long. Susan changed it. I think she initially called me more to spite her sister than to get together with me. As fate would have it, we hit it off extremely well and nine months later were married. A year, almost to the day, before Sylvia and Herbert married.

They came to our wedding and we went to theirs, but in both cases it was performing a sense of duty on each sister's part more than wanting to share something. And sharing something wasn't anything I expected when we agreed to visit them in San Diego.

They'd moved there five years previous because Herbert somehow was sure the climate there was perfect. This would be our first visit to what turned out to be their mansion stationed in a bay off the Pacific Ocean. This time we could drive, rather than fly. I hate airports, so for me the five hundred or so mile drive from Tucson beat the hassle of going through any airport. Even if the Tucson airport was super simple to navigate.

We'd been invited to come visit by Sylvia in the past, but I'd always come up with an excuse for turning her down. I never had any interest in visiting them, and Susan didn't much care either way, so we didn't. But now we were close enough to drive, since I'd been transferred to Tucson from our main office in Minneapolis.

By driving, we could leave at anytime during the visit, if we found our time around Herbert got too disgusting. He simply put on too many airs, and was an altogether an uncomfortable person to be around.

That proved to not be a problem. When we arrived at their impossibly huge house, we only saw Herbert for about fifteen minutes. He was busy, he claimed, and had to get back to work. Since he was retired already, I asked Sylvia what kind of work he was doing.

"He's managing his stocks and his money. It's what he does. He often doesn't eat and he never sleeps more than five or six hours a night. He worries that he could lose it all if he doesn't stay in control."

"You mean," I said, "he spends most of his time managing his money?"

"Just about all his time, actually."

"You're kidding, right?"

"No, I'm not. That's part of the reason I wanted you to come. Our family is still in Minnesota. I rarely see any of them. Only two of my old friends have visited. I get lonely sometimes, living in this big house with no company."

"Does Herbert know that. If you lived with me, I can guaranty you wouldn't get lonely."

Sylvia could see that I meant it. It brought on something weird. For her anyway. She blushed. That was enough for Susan. She needed to put her hand over her mouth to keep from laughing. I quickly made another comment to keep Sylvia from noticing.

"For me, it would be a waste of time to do what he does. There's a hell of a lot more to life than constantly worrying about money."

"Yes, but if he didn't do what he does, we wouldn't have this house. We have so many things now that we wouldn't have if he didn't make the money he makes."

"I guess. The thing is, though, what do you do with all those things you have? You don't seem to be enjoying them much."

"I enjoy them as much as anyone."

"Do you? How? Do you really enjoy this monster house you live in?"

"Well, yeah. Maybe not as much as when we first moved here. But I still do. I admit, we've been talking about downsizing. Herbert says the overhead costs are too much. He doesn't like spending his money on things like that."

"What does he like spending his money on?"

She blushed again, embarrassed this time over the answer I was about to get. "Not much. It seems that the more he makes, the less he spends. The one thing he hates most is paying taxes. He firmly believes the government is stealing his money. That's the main reason we haven't sold this house. We'll have to pay capital gains taxes if we downsize, because now the house is worth a couple million more than we paid for it. He's not ready to do that. The taxes will be a lot more than the overhead cost on the house, so he isn't ready yet to do it."

"That makes no sense to me at all. If you don't live at least more or less the way you want to, if you don't spend as much time as possible doing things you enjoy doing, it's all pointless."

"That's partly true. But in our case, we wouldn't have all that much if he didn't work so hard."

"The problem as I see it, Sylvia, is simple. You have a lot of stuff. What you don't have is much joy in your life. Susan and I don't have near the stuff you have, but we do have a fair amount of joy in our life."

Susan finally joined our conversation. "That's right, Sylvia, we do. And if we don't find some around here pretty damn quick, we're going to be on our way back to Tucson."

"Yes, you're right. What is it you'd like to do?"

"How about a ride in that big boat you've got parked out there?"

"I guess we could do that. I have to go tell Herbert though. He normally doesn't want me to take it out alone."

"Go tell him then," Susan directed. "If you must."

It was an obvious struggle, but Sylvia did her best to ignore Susan's last comment, and went to get permission to use the boat.

"It's fine," she said when she came back. "I'd rather not stay out too long though. Herbert's not feeling too good right now."

"If that's the case," Susan said, "we can skip the boat ride."

"No, no, we'll go."

So we did. Sylvia drove the boat initially. When she'd maneuvered it out into the main channel, she offered to let Susan run it. Susan was all smiles over that idea, and readily accepted Sylvia's driving instructions. As soon as Susan was in control, Sylvia took my hand.

"Let me show you around the cabin," she said. "We won't miss anything as long as we're still in the bay."

I followed her down into the cabin. She didn't show me anything there. She took me directly into the sleeping quarters, turned to face me, then wrapped her hand around the back of my neck. I let her pull me down to her and kiss me. Without thinking, I responded to it. To several of them actually.

"If we're quick," she said, "we can make good use of the bed." While she was talking, she moved my hand to her breast.

"That would be an easy thing for me to do, Sylvia," I told her. "I haven't forgotten how good that was between us way back then. But I won't. I love Susan, and I can't do that to her."

"I was afraid of that. I had to try though. It's been a long time."

"You mean Herbert doesn't get away from his money tending long enough for even that?"

"Sorry to say, no, he doesn't."

"I have to wonder, is the man insane, an idiot, or simply stupid? There's no way I'll ever be able to understand his approach to life. What the hell good is all that money, if you throw away the one thing you actually have in life?"

"Are you saying that sex is the only thing we actually have."

"No, not at all. Sex is great, one of best things there is. But the only thing we actually have in life is time. A very short time at that. So, what really matters is how we spend that time."

"What are you now? Some kind of damn philosopher?"

I had to laugh at that. A computer programmer a philosopher? Couldn't happen. "No," I said. "I'm just a person who realizes what matters. There's more to life than things. And it actually does boil down to one thing. You have only a very limited time in life, and you really ought to make the most of it. Spending all of it counting your money just doesn't cut it."

"I guess I know that. I just don't know how to deal with the situation I'm in right now."

"If it was me, I'd get a divorce. Because the truth is, there's no way you'll ever be happy in the situation you're in now."

"I can't do that. I still care about him."

"I'm sure you do, but that's enough of that. Let's go back up and enjoy the boat ride."

The rest of the ride went by without much happening. Not even much conversation. When we returned to the house, Sylvia immediately reported into Herbert. When she returned, she was a bit pale and seemed to be a somewhat shaken. I asked her if something was wrong.

"It's Herbert," she said, a slight tumble in her voice. "I think something serious is wrong, but he won't stop working with his computer. He says what he's doing right now is too important."

"Well, if that's the case, whatever is wrong with him can't be too serious. I can't see even him risking his life for a few dollars."

"I can," Susan said. "But I'll tell you what. I'll go see if I can motivate him enough to get away from his computer for a while."

She had a mischievous grin in her face when she went to see Herbert. Her grin was gone, and she was shaking her head when she returned a short time later.

"What a simple-minded grump," she said. "I tried everything I could think of to get his attention. He wasn't interested. I finally told him that we were planning a threesome, but that we'd like to have him join in. He said no, he couldn't get away right now. But that we should all enjoy."

Even Sylvia was surprised. "He said that? We should enjoy a threesome?"

"He did, but I don't think what I said registered. He was concentrating so hard on playing with his money."

That's when Herbert joined us, looking not much better than death warmed over. He also had an extremely annoyed look on his face. "What the hell are you three planning?" he growled. "It better not be what I think it is." Apparently, Susan's teasing finally registered with him.

"What the hell do you think it is?" Sylvia growled back.

"Susan said you were going to have a threesome."

"So, what if we do?"

"You can't do that. Susan is your sister."

"That the only reason?"

"No, you just shouldn't even think about such a thing."

"Why not? You're too busy to do anything, and I'm getting tired of it. You don't need to spend the rest of your life playing with your money. There are too many other things to do."

"You're just being silly." He looked at me. "Tell her how important what I'm doing is. You're a responsible man, so you should know."

"Actually, I think she's right. You're wasting your life and the little time you have to live it. The real truth is, all your money doesn't mean shit."

"That's nuts. I've got plenty of time to live my life. I just have to take care of what I need to take care of right now." He turned to Sylvia. "Where's the Tylenol? I've got a terrible headache."

"I'll get some for you. How many?"

"Three. This one is really killing me." Herbert was right. That was the most accurate statement he'd ever made. He suddenly grabbed his head, gave out a small groan, and fell. He was dead by the time he landed on the floor. He'd just stroked out. Everything has its price. The price he paid for living for nothing, but his money was a heavy one. The time he might have had was now gone.

It was total chaos for the next few days. We stayed with Sylvia as long as it seemed she needed us. The last day it became obvious she didn't need us anymore. She spent it working on Herbert's computer. She only left it long enough to tell us goodbye.

"Are you going to be okay now?" Susan asked her just before we went out the door. "We can come back anytime you need us."

"I'll be fine," she answered. "As soon as I get control over all the things Herbert was always working on." With that, she turned and hurried off to Herbert's office. She had money on her mind, so now time was no longer a concern.

"What a waste," I thought as I watched her fine young body walk away, happy that the sister who looked so much like her lived in a very different world. Susan held my hand as we walked to our car.

Three Days

By Michael Allen George

We were close from the time we met. We were six years old. Ann and her family were near the last to move into the brand-new neighborhood. All the houses were either story and a half or three-bedroom ramblers. Not at all fancy, but given where most families living there came from, rather luxurious for them and us.

We were the same age, our birthdays being only a month apart. Mine was May, hers in June. We played all the usual kid games then, but often as not we'd leave the rest of the kids and find a place to be alone. We had a park close by, with a few wild spots, so that was easy.

The rest of the kids weren't interested in coming with us. Finding a pond where you could watch the frogs and turtles, or simply a quiet place to talk an enjoy each other, wasn't at all what grabbed their attention.

As time passed, we graduated to movies, drive-ins with good hamburgers and fries, and our favorite, the library. We both loved to read, and history and the natural science topics that captured both our imaginations. For fiction, she preferred romances. I loved my westerns.

We were sixteen before we shared our first kiss, and I didn't make love to her until the night before we both left for college. Colleges on either side of the country.

Summers and holidays, when we came home, we spent every possible moment together. Strangely though, we never made love that whole time. Something in her was changing, and it wasn't until we both graduated that she told me. Our relationship would never be what we'd both expected all the years we were friends and almost lovers. She'd found another way to live.

So this day, with a lifetime used up, was the saddest time I'd ever experienced. When I entered the church, her best friend Betty greeted me with a warm hug and a kiss on the cheek. It helped, but I was still close to breaking down when I walked up front.

People often talk about how alive the dead look lying in their coffin. As I stood there, starting down at her, I heard that comment a couple of times. Sadly, she only looked dead to me. Dead and out of my life forever.

Our friendship was sometimes difficult over the years, and there was never enough time together to suit me, but it was always there. Looking at her now, I once again wished it could have been different. That we could have had a life together. A home, kids, all of it.

Given the lack of all that, she gave me one thing that was and still is by far my fondest memory. It was less than a week before she was going to, in her own way, leave us. We were having lunch in the neighborhood bar. Bacon cheeseburgers and greasy fries.

Tired of my somber mood and extremely sad eyes, she smiled and said, "Okay, Al, I'll give you three days. After we finish eating we'll go home, pack, then head north. We will spend the next four nights and three days together. Just the two of us. I know it's not enough, but it'll have to do for both of us. All I ask is that we do our best to grab the moment, and try not to think about the rest until the days are gone.

So off we went, up north. In Minnesota, the term 'up north' refers to any number of places. For us this time, our up north consisted of a small lake cabin with a sitting area, a kitchenette, and a bedroom with one double bed. She sat down on it as soon as she saw it. She looked up at me and smiled.

"It's not as big as what we'd find most places," she said. "But I think it will suit us just fine for our three days together."

Her comment surprised me, but what followed surprised me even more. I'd expected a totally platonic relationship when she suggested the three days together.

"We don't have much time," she said, leaving the bed, "so let's waste none of it." She unbuttoned her blouse as she moved close. "You too." She finished her last button.

I took her advice, and quickly we were joined together on the bed. We'd only made love once, years before, and as good as it was, it was a bit clumsy. This time was different. It had the strong feelings of the first time, yet flowed as if we'd been together for years. Perfect is the only way to describe it. It stayed perfect for all the time we were there.

Later, we dressed and went for a ride in the small boat provided with the cabin. It was midweek and early evening, so there were fewer boats on the water than there might have. That gave us a chance to see more critters than we might have seen on a weekend. Something we'd enjoyed together since we were kids. The highlight was the eagle who plunked a fair size fish out of the water no more than a hundred feet from us.

After we left the lake, we went in search of a place to eat. We found a roadside steak house. It was once common in rural Minnesota, but like all good things, was a lot less common now.

Because this meal was special, as was everything we did during this very short time together, we ignored the prices on the menu and both ordered fillets. They couldn't have been better.

It was a quiet meal. Frequently our eyes met, and that seemed to be all the conversation we needed. We didn't talk much when we got back to the cabin either. Instead, we simply lay together in that double bed, holding each other when we weren't making love.

We spent the rest of our time together in much the same way, never straying too far from the cabin. Instead, we took a lot of walks. On one of those walks, we passed a couple as we crossed a bridge over the river channel that ran to another lake downstream. I had my camera along, so I asked them to take a picture of us. The first was the usual, with us together, arms around each other.

"One more," I told them.

I kissed Ann with all the passion in me. That was the one she wanted when I developed them later. The lady taking the picture had a broad smile on her face when she handed me back the camera. So did her husband.

As always with the best things in life, the time quickly ran out. Three days had come and gone. When we climbed into bed together that last night, I was so filled with the terror of losing her that I literally trembled.

We made love with a kind of slow anticipation. It lasted a long time. I held her after as she lay with her back to me. I could feel her trembling this time, and when I touched her cheek, it was wet with tears. I didn't say anything to her, but mine flowed along with hers.

For the last time ever, we made love just before leaving in the morning. She ignored seat belts and rode tight next to me on the very quiet ride home. I kissed her goodbye when I dropped her off at home. She cried again. I held my tears back until after she disappeared into the house.

Three days. Not much to last a lifetime. But it was what we had, and I never forgot a moment of it. I was wondering if she remembered it the way I did. I somewhat doubted it, given the busy life she'd led. She taught full time and was also always busy with church activities. The busyness was over now though. Now there was just the service to be performed.

And that was something that only the memories could get me through. After it was over and I was ready to leave her friend Betty searched me out again.

"I'm so glad I found you," she said. "I almost forgot to give it to you. It was hers, and she wanted so much for you to have it." She handed a gold locket to me. "I never saw Ann without this on. From the time she entered the convent, until she gave to me to give to you, just before she died, she had it on."

It was a fairly large, plain gold locket, with only what seemed to be some small scratches on the back. It was difficult to open, but I managed it. Inside was the kissing picture we had taken on the bridge. I took a deep breath, trying to control my emotions. I looked closer at the back. The scratches turned out to be a simple engraving. It said, *Three Days!*

All that time. All those years. She remembered it, probably much the same way I did. Why was it that we never had what we should have had? I looked at the picture again, then the engraving. Three Days. Just three days. It was too much to accept. The tears started flow at the same time a total emptiness overcame me.

Letters to My Son: How did you get your first job?

By David George

The response to this question will be oblique, meaning there's no direct answer. What I can tell you, dear son, is the story of my early work experiences.

My first "job" was unpaid peon labor on my uncle Paul's farm. From the time I was—guesstimate here—8 years old I spent a good part of the summer on the farm, picking berries and apples, milking cows, helping my Aunt Ruby decapitate chickens, and joining a bucket brigade to empty the septic tank (disgusting!).

My first paid gig came about at around age ten. What I recall is that my brothers and I went to a kind of staging area where farmers picked up day laborers. When we were selected, we were driven to the farm to hand pick vegetables like potatoes and carrots. What I remember about the work was spending the day on my knees digging in the dirt with my bare hands. We were paid in cash at the end of the day. You may ask, weren't there child labor laws back then? I don't know, but if there were nobody enforced them.

When I got a little older, say, age 14, I began working in Stillman's supermarket in Minneapolis as a carryout boy. An aside here: Stillman's was Jewish owned and almost all the customers were Jewish, some of them survivors of the Nazi concentration camps. Working at that job I learned about Jewish culture, food, language (swear words in Yiddish were fun!), and the Holocaust.

In my adolescence I was also an occasional carpenter's helper, house painter, and farm laborer. I hired out to do the really heavy work like lifting hay bales from the field to the hay wagon. The latter job in particular gave me physical strength that lasted well into middle age.

I don't look back at my childhood and adolescent labor in a negative way. Quite the opposite: those experiences instilled in me a solid work ethic that allowed me to go to college, which I paid for with the proceeds of my various and sundry jobs. And you know the rest: graduate school, Ph.D., college professor.

Two Times To Tucson

By Michael Allen George

We got a late start. The lady who bought our house was supposed to come by with the down payment. She was late. We were into the afternoon by the time the guy who brokered the deal came by to tell us she wouldn't be there until tomorrow. We told him to mail us the check. Thankfully, he did.

I knew we wouldn't get far, but we started out anyway. No matter what, we'd be sleeping in a motel. I decided staying in Minnesota made no sense. We'd be better off with a couple hundred miles of the trip completed when we did.

So we left our home, and started out for our new home. Way down in Tucson, Arizona. Eighteen hundred miles in a Uhaul truck pulling a Uhaul trailer. The trailer had a forty-five mile an hour speed limit written on the fenders. A limit I ignored the whole trip. I could only ignore it just so much though. Anything over sixty-five miles an hour, and the entire front end of the truck started shaking. Not just the front wheels. It was the entire front end that shook. Hard enough to throw the truck into the lane to our left. Never the right, always the left.

We made it as far as Des Moines our first day. Dark was pushing in, and I was already exhausted. Too little sleep the night before, finishing the loading in the morning, and the two-hundred-mile drive.

Ruth wanted to keep on going. "They won't rent us a room anyway," she claimed.

She was sure no motel would rent us a room because we had a dog, and we were turned down once because of it. I stopped anyway.

"I can't drive that far straight through," I told her. "As tired as I am, I really shouldn't drive any further now."

"Well, go ahead and try to get a room. But they're not going to rent you one."

"Maybe not, but we're going to try. Grab Atlas," Atlas was the dog, "and come in with me."

Inside the motel office the young lady spent a couple of minutes oohing and awing the dog, then happily rented us a room. Also happily charging us an extra ten dollars for him.

After settling in, I went out and got us some takeout. We were in bed early and up the next morning just as early. I filled the truck at the first truck stop, and we got coffee and some breakfast sausage there.

Traffic was heavy and the closer we got to Kansas City the heavier it got. We were still in rush hour traffic when we got really close, so we stopped in a rest area. I wanted to wait another hour before I braved the traffic around the city. It was always a horrible drive, and at rush hour it went beyond that.

I napped through the hour and felt a hell of a lot better when I woke up. Traffic was still heavy as we circled the city but seemed somehow subdued.

Not having any idea why, I was beginning to feel as though something weird was happening. The only thing I could figure was my driving a strange truck with a dancing frontend, pulling an overloaded trailer with a forty-five mile an hour speed limit on it. That, and maybe the fact we were leaving a place we'd lived our entire lives and going somewhere we actually knew little about. Only that Ruth's mother lived there and that our house would be close to hers so we could help her. She was suffering from dementia.

Things got even stranger at the next stop for gas. As I filled the truck, I overheard bits and pieces of the conversation a couple of guys in the next bay were having. Something about a probable war somewhere. I shook it off as a likely Middle East conflict. But it got stranger.

"Where you headed?" I was asked when I paid the fee as we left the Kansas Turnpike.

"Tucson," I told her.

"I wish you luck," the lady said, shaking her head.

"That was weird," I thought as I pulled away from the toll booth.

I didn't need gas at the next small town I drove through, but I noticed that every station, large or small, had a lineup of cars and trucks waiting to buy gas. That told me there was for sure something really wrong somewhere.

I hadn't had the radio on, because I like to be able to hear the road noise and the sounds of the vehicle I'm driving when I'm on the highway. I turned it on now.

The voice talking said, "The first tower hit has collapsed, and according to reports from the scene, there's a danger the second tower is going down soon."

I was getting out onto the Kansas prairie by then and the radio signal was failing fast. I heard something about New York and the twin towers before it failed completely. I searched for another station.

We were in Kansas, so there wasn't much for a real station. All I could find was a religious station. The lady talking claimed to be Reverend someone or the other. She was quick to tell us the entire problem.

"New York City," she claimed, "is now facing God's unforgiving wrath for their sinful ways. For too long now, they have allowed homosexuals and too many other deviants to exist in their city of sin. What happened today to those towers is a direct result of their wicked ways."

It was the only station I could get so as much as I wanted to turn it off, I left it on. Her being an evangelical, I knew that most of what I'd get would be nonsense, but I hoped she would mix in a little news with her crap.

I drove through a couple more towns, with every gas station packed with vehicles lined up for blocks to buy gas. Finally, by the next town I had no choice. I had to stop, and there was only one station. It was located on the other side of the road. I did the only thing I could do and turned in. I figured it could be hours before anyone let me in the long line.

Then, what I considered a near miracle happened. A car was just leaving the gas pumps. The guy in the car who was behind it, got out and waved me in. It was with a huge relief that I pulled in. I looked at the guy as I removed the hose from the pump, and mouthed a good dozen thank yous. He returned them with a smile. I've met a lot of nice people from Kansas, but he's at the top of the list.

The strangest part of all that, was the fact that no one yelled or honked their horn. I guess they all felt for anyone unlucky enough to be traveling on that day.

There was one negative about it though. The price of the gas was two dollars a gallon higher than what it was the last time I bought it. After that, once we got out of Kansas, although every gas station or truck stop, we went to was busy, the waits were never very long. And the gas prices hadn't gone up.

I also got real stations on the radio with real people talking. Thankfully, no more evangelicals. As I listened to the news come in, it was hard to believe how much devastation had happened. At that point, I only had one goal. Get to our new home. What ever happened after that, would happen. I just wanted to see that home first.

Ruth didn't have near the feeling of urgency to see it. She'd flown to Tucson alone just two weeks before. There, she found and purchased our new home. So she sat calmly, frequently napping, with Atlas on her lap doing the same thing.

We made it into New Mexico that day. The first motel we found with a vacancy was difficult to drive into, with turning around even more difficult. It was super cheap, and they didn't charge extra for the dog. The guy running the place and I talked about the events of the day before I left the office. We couldn't help but wonder what was going to happen next.

The room was typical motel. Small, but surprisingly clean and comfortable. I got us some takeout from a restaurant across the road and after a much-needed shower, was in bed a short time later.

I slept straight through but woke up about four-thirty. I was anxious to get on the road, so I woke up Ruth and we were soon on our way. It was a quiet but hurried ride through New Mexico. We stopped for gas just outside Deming, and I felt a little more relaxed then. We had enough to take us all the way to our new home.

But relaxed or not, I was anxious to get there. I pushed it hard. Hard enough to wonder if the wheels were going to fall off the trailer we were pulling. I even passed a few semis. Something I rarely did, especially driving a strange vehicle.

We made one more stop. The rest stop in Texas Canyon, about sixty-five miles from Tucson. It's full of beautiful rock formations, and always worth the little time it takes to look.

After I used the restroom, I walked by a young couple trying to sell a camera. They were apparently broke and couldn't drive any farther without gas money.

I didn't have any use for the camera, but looking at the desperation on their faces, I remembered the guy in Kansas who let us in to buy gas when we were desperate. So even though we didn't have much extra cash, I decided it was payback time. It wasn't much, but I gave them ten dollars. The look on their faces was worth a lot more.

Even though we didn't have that many more miles to go, I continued to push it hard. When we finally reached the outskirts of Tucson, the drive on Interstate 10 to the west side seemed endless. When we finally made our turnoff, and got close to home, I stopped at a convenience store and picked up a case of cold beer.

"I'm not going to tour our new house without a beer in my hand," I told Ruth.

"That's good," she agreed. "I want one too."

Atlas didn't say anything, but I'm sure he approved of the idea.

I opened the beer and one for Ruth as soon as we stopped in front of the house. I took the first sip as I walked in the front door. No beer has ever tasted better. A feeling that despite all that was going on in our country and the rest of the world, it was all going to be okay for us.

We were home again. A strange one yes. But still, it was home. Whatever happened next didn't seem as important as the fact that whatever it happened to be, we were at home to face it.

We got the call about eight that morning. Dad died. Ruth got me on the next flight to Minnesota. But with all the airport stuff and renting a car when I got there, along with the heavy northbound summer traffic, it was eight in the evening when I got to my folk's.

Mom had a houseful. A bushel of questions was immediately thrown at me. Everything from 'How was the flight?" to 'You must be hungry?' to 'It's getting late, is it okay with you if we head on home?'.

It was okay, so most everyone left. My younger brother hung around, and we had a few drinks and talked about Dad for a while. Mom was still up when he left. It took some coaxing to get her to lie down on the couch and get some sleep. The shock of his dying was still controlling her, and she wasn't quite sure what she should be doing.

It took a week to get through all that needed doing and have the funeral. I had already decided to take her home with me, so it was just a matter of convincing everyone else that it was a good idea to take her all the way to Tucson. Some totally agreed it was a good idea, and the rest reluctantly agreed, as long as it was temporary.

My sister and I went through all her stuff, packed up what we thought was necessary, and loaded the rental car. Extremely overloaded is a better way to describe it. We also had Mom's cat along. A fourteen-pound black cat who hated the carrier he had to ride in, and the car even more.

Mom and I left for Tucson at two-thirty AM two days after the funeral. She managed to sleep for the first couple of hours. As soon as she woke up, she said, "You must be tired. We should stop for the day."

I'd planned to take three or four days to make the drive, not ten or twelve, so there was no way I was about to stop that early. She was tired, but still out of it as a result of Dad's death, so she wasn't completely aware of what was going on. So I was able to somewhat satisfy her with my promises to stop soon.

The toughest thing to handle were the bathroom breaks. Mom was using a walker, and not handling it well at all. For the past two years she'd slept sitting up, just in case dad needed something. So her feet and legs up to her knees were badly swollen and had literally turned purple.

Every time she had to go into a ladies room, be it a truck stop or a rest stop, it was a sweat it out worry for me. A few times, one kind lady or another saw her problem and helped her with the in and out.

The cat was another problem. He refused to eat, drink, or eliminate. He didn't even want to leave his carrier when I opened it up on a grassy spot at a rest stop.

So it was a long haul until we finally reached the Kansas turnpike. The ride through it went smoothly enough, until I missed my exit, and had to back track several miles.

By then, I was willing to stop for mom, so I looked for motel for the night. I found the perfect one. It had a service station on one side of it and a McDonald's on the other. So I was able to fill up the car, check us into the motel, then walk to McDonald's for our supper after mom was settled in. It was the kind of place I always look for when I'm traveling.

Once again, mom wanted to sleep sitting up in a chair, but I convinced her to get in bed. There were two queen size, so sleeping in a chair was rather nuts. When she did get in bed, it was only minutes before she was asleep.

We had a cat box, and food and water dishes with us, so I set then up in a corner. I put the cat and its open carrier close by and hoped for the best.

I woke up early again. I'd actually slept for nearly five hours, but it was still only three AM. I sat on the edge of the bed, watching mom in her bed, with a sleeping cat next to her, for about ten minutes. I wanted to get back on the road, but I also didn't want to drive too tired.

My urge to get going won the argument. I gently woke mom and told her that if she didn't mind, I'd like to get an early start. She didn't mind at all. Even the cat didn't complain, and was no problem to put back in the carrier. He drank most of the water I'd left in his dish, ate some of his food, and made good use of his cat box.

Mom also made good use of the bathroom while she had the chance. She was a bit slow dressing, but we were on the road again in decent time. We started with over a thousand miles left to drive, so I had no expectations of making it home that day. My goal was Las Cruces, New

Mexico. That would leave somewhat more than three hundred miles for the third day.

I figured that making that drive in three days, with a cranky cat and an old woman in as bad a shape as mom was, was doing pretty damn good.

The day quickly began to fill with shaky stops to use toilets, requests to stop for the day, and a cat who wouldn't do anything but occasionally complain.

This leg of the trip was state highways, so there were no rest stops. Most of the service stations left something to be desired, so it seemed as though the struggles with mom doubled.

Add to those struggles, I, for whatever reason, started to get sleepy. So I had to make periodic stops to get out and walk around some, just to wake up.

By the time we reached Las Cruces, I knew I couldn't go any further. Then, driving through the city, we hit a construction zone. The direction signs were terrible, and soon I was lost. I was traveling west, so I stayed on westbound streets. After what seemed like forever, and some bad language my part, we finally reached interstate 10.

Once I was on it, I decided to go a little further before stopping for the night. I drove until I needed gas again. This time, Mom refused to use the toilet. I decided it was okay. It wasn't going to be long before we found a motel.

I drove past a few, and decided I didn't want to stop in any of them. Then we reached the Arizona border. There was a rest stop coming up, so I asked mom if she wanted to stop. I told her it might be a while before we reached another place to go. She said she'd wait.

That was fine by me. I'd made another decision. No motel. We were going home. I also decided I was going to get us there and soon as I could. My foot got really heavy on the accelerator. The rest of the way, I consistently did what I normally rarely did. I passed a lot of semis. I was moving a consistent eighty MPH, except when I was driving faster.

We didn't stop at Texas Canyon. After that, it was under an hour to home. Pulling into our driveway was a huge relief. I'm not sure where Ruth was when we went in, so I called out, "Is anybody home."

Ruth came running into the room. "I thought you were in Las Cruces," she said.

"No," I told her, "we're home."

Home! What a wondrous place to be. After that ride, nothing could ever feel better that being home.

It must have felt good to mom too. She slept for fourteen hours her first night there. Then called it her home for the next nine years.

Mama Don't Let Your Babies
Grow Up To Be Builders
By
Bud George

Two new houses in an upscale western suburb. Both split entries. Fairly simple houses, but another crew had started them. Lots of mistakes and barely out of the ground. Deal was, we'd build them on shares. Our crew, me, Ken, and Bill. Big crew of three.

Dick and Ken had met with the local inspector, who was very happy to see these houses finished. He'd had many complaints over the summer. The lots, the yards looked like hell. Lumber piled here and there. Lots of tall weeds. Lots of mud.

And so it began. Thirty days, but no one warned us about that suburbs noise ordinances. We start on Friday and by Sunday morning a cop was waiting for us as the sun came up. No noise Saturday or Sunday morning before 11AM.

The two crews learned very quickly how to work in teams. Alone, or a couple of times, all six of us. Dick's house had the deck on it when we started, but front knee wall was in the wrong place. There was no room for a brick ledge (brick front). We helped him move it back four-and one-half inches. It took a couple of hours.

We started way behind. No deck, no joists, and we had to build the center bearing wall and set a steel beam to carry the joists and cantilevered exterior deck. We got it decked, exterior walls, sheeting, interior walls balancing crew size from house to house as needed.

I was helping Dick's two carpenters install the roof deck while Dick was next door on our until showing Ken a different way to set trusses. I thought we were pretty good at it, but instead I was nailing plywood.

I didn't mind installing roof decking and the three of us were making real good time. And at the same time trying to convince Chris (who drove a Dodge) that Jim (who drove a Chevy) and I (who drove aa old F150 Ford) we were correct on insisting the spelling for the Dodge was really only three letters.

Every once in a while, I glanced over at the house next door. Looked to like Dick was picking our up our truss setting system. We pushed hard, all of us. Short breaks and sometimes no breaks. We got both houses completely done in twenty-eight days.

Time for a payday. The bank stopped the financing. They would not loan on houses on piling as these were. We were all by now pretty broke, pretty pissed off, and pretty frustrated. But what could we do? Nothing very quickly. The legal system, it seemed, worked on years, not days or months.

I walked to my old, paid for F150 and unscrewed the dome light cover. I had disconnected it several years ago. I had a tightly rolled one hundred dollar bill tucked into the bulb socket. I was low on gas.

Pushing It

By Michael Allen George

It was just past 1:00 AM when I kissed Susie goodnight and headed for home. Staying any later would have been pushing it. My luck has never been good enough to stay past closing time. I went directly to bed when I got home. My shower could wait until morning.

The house we were building was less than a mile away, so I could sleep until seven and still get to work on time. This morning, it didn't matter. My boss, Jake, was fifteen minutes late. Caused by a hangover, I was sure.

He was crabby and in a hurry, the same as most mornings. Whatever it took, we were going to get the roof deck on and nailed down tight. No matter that it was already pushing ninety-five degrees with one hundred percent humidity.

He was better up high than I was, so he worked up top and I stayed on the ground to do the cutting and feed the material up to him. We moved along okay for about an hour. I was sweating profusely and already feeling very dry, so I told him, "I'm going to stop a minute for a drink. Be a good idea if you did too."

"I already drank some water. Get your drink and let's get moving. We have to get this roof decking on today."

I knew it was hopeless to argue with him, so I let it slide. When Jake was in a hurry, the whole world was supposed to be in a hurry.

In less than an hour, I needed another drink. When I stopped for one I was told to hurry it up, and no, he wasn't thirsty. This time, his lack of drinking anything concerned me. Working the way we were, what he was doing was extremely dangerous. Dehydration is nothing to play with. And working up high where he was, made it doubly dangerous.

On my third stop for a drink, he finally came down off the roof. He didn't look good at all. His skin was dry now, bright red, but kind of pasty looking. His eyes looked sunken and he seemed a bit short of breath.

He drank some. Not enough, but it beat what he had been drinking. Back on the roof, he continued pushing it. I was getting close to calling it a day. He couldn't keep up the pace he was setting without me, and I figured it would make more sense to let him get pissed at me, or even fire me, then it would keep going the way we were.

I knew I'd be okay. I was drinking enough, and my end of the job wasn't as hard as his. For him though, it was getting downright dangerous. It was a lot hotter up on that roof, and he hadn't drunk near enough water.

My next drink break, I took extra time, even though he bitched the whole time. I ignored him. He didn't know it, but his body needed a little extra time to catch up with itself.

What he got wasn't enough though. The numbers he gave me for the next cut I had to make were way off. When the plywood I cut for him didn't fit, he got pissed and threw it to the ground.

"Try to cut it right," he yelled.

"When you give me the right numbers," I answered, "I'll do just that very thing."

"Well, damnit…" he started to say, then grabbed both sides of his head with his hands. "My head…"

He was way up high by this time. The last thing he wanted to do was fall. So whatever his problem was, he should have sat down. He didn't. He tried to walk the roof instead. It was just steep enough and slippery enough to cause him to slip. Right off the edge of the roof. He landed on his back and was busted up pretty good, but he survived.

I did the only thing I could do at that point. I called 911. Quicker than what I'd have thought possible, the ambulance and two cop cars were there.

One of the cops talking to me was a little bit pushy. "So, you say he just slipped and fell?"

"Yes, but before he did, he grabbed his head like it hurt really bad. He did it sudden like, after he got pissed because the last piece of plywood I cut didn't fit."

"So you got into a fight?"

"No, I was on the ground." I went on to tell the cop about Jake pushing too hard and not drinking enough water.

When I finished talking, one of the ambulance guys who was close enough to hear what I said, told the cop, "The guy on the roof probably was suffering from heat stroke or heat exhaustion. A bad headache and/or disorientation are common symptoms. So it's likely that he did simply fall off the roof."

"Okay," the cop said, "that makes sense." He looked at me. "You're off the hook. Now I'm on it. I have to notify the next of kin about his accident."

"There's only his wife," I said. "They didn't have kids. If it'll help any, I can go and tell his wife. She'll need a ride to the hospital anyway."

"I would appreciate it," the cop agreed.

I waited until they told me which hospital he was going to and hauled Jake away. Then I left to tell his wife. I couldn't help but wonder then, what Susie would say when she answered my knock on her door at this time of day. She was used to seeing me only occasionally at night.

Letters to My Son: Did you consider any other careers?

By David George

This is an easy one, dear son. I did indeed consider another career: theater director (actor, designer).

It all began during my undergraduate years (my freshman year, to be specific). A Spanish professor planned on staging a Spanish play and spread the word among the students that he was looking for actors. Well, not real actors, just students who knew enough Spanish to deliver lines in a believable way (sort of believable). I was one of the chosen. I had a small part. I even remember my line (maybe I had more than one – not sure): "Señor Jordán, ¡hay que pactar!" In spite of my small role, I loved the process of putting a play together, from the first cast reading of the script to opening night butterflies.

In each subsequent undergraduate year I played a role in a Spanish play. I got better and had a larger role each time.

There were no more plays in graduate school, but when I first went to Brazil as a Fulbright scholar I fell in love with Brazilian theater. I began fantasizing about working in theater. So when I returned from my first year in Brazil, that's exactly what I did (well, not exaaaactly – upon my return I ended up playing hippie in San Francisco). It was upon my return to Minneapolis that I stumbled into my theater career.

I ran into an old friend who was doing a Spanish play and asked me to be in it. Though the play itself was no masterpiece (that is, the play, by Federico García Lorca, was a masterpiece, but the production was a flop; the director, unfortunately, had serious problems that created a mess). But there's a happy ending: a REAL actor, Mim Solberg, a friend of the messed-up director, was the lead in the play. She invited me to a REAL theater she worked with to participate in a workshop.

I showed up for the "workshop," which turned out to be a tryout for a new play. Though I was no great shakes as an actor, I was a good reader. So I got a part. And thus began my theater career.

The play was titled "Nicotine Phallus." It was as bad as it sounds. I include a slightly fictionalized version of the play in my novel: here's an abbreviated version:

The group began reading "Nicotine Phallus." It didn't make a whole lot of sense. There was no discernable plot. Just characters with allegorical names like Establishment, Government, Church, Truth, Lie, Innocence, Pig. Each character had a rambling, garbled speech.

Pig started out with, "I am Pig. I am law. Law is flaw. Streams of ratshit horseshit pigshit. I will smash you kill you lock you up. Throw up. Gag. Vomit running through the streets."

And on it went, each character making less and less sense. Then, on the very last page of the script, according to the stage directions a green Martian—that was me—climbed down a rope from the ceiling to the stage, and spoke:

"Corrupt humanity, I have come from the red planet, traveled through the asteroid belt, sliced through outer space, and descended in a ball of fire through your Earth's atmosphere. I have come, oh deceitful Earthlings, to save your blighted souls."

Then all the characters were to fall to their knees weeping, lights out, the end. The director made me read the lines over and over, each time with a different instruction:

"Read it like a professor… like a doctor… like a priest… pretend you're me.. get your ass in gear… you want I'll kick your ass." (The director pretended to be a badass, but he was in fact afraid of me – he knew if push came to shove, I could easily kick his ass.)

No matter how I read the passage, it sounded false, amateurish. If there was any so-called truth in those lines, I couldn't find it. I did get chuckles and giggles from the other actors. Finally, the director put an end to my humiliation.

"Ok, folks, listen up. Those are your roles you just read. Feel free to change the lines if you want. Jock (that's what the director actually called me), you're gonna be the Spaceman. But you don't get to change any lines. Your lines are perfect. The best ones in the whole play. Harold Pinter couldn't improve them. You dig?"

As time went by I became a member of the theater and got to play roles in Shakespeare (Macbeth) and Checkov (The Seagull). I also played roles in plays written by members of the theater. My best role was a crazy Spanish waiter. I had a talent for comic roles; for serious "dramatic" roles, not so much.

As I slowly came to understand that my acting skills were limited, I tried my hand at directing. I was happy to discover that I was good at it. (I later discovered that I was also a good light and set designer – but that's a story for another time).

Years passed and I began thinking about graduate school, about unfinished business; to wit, completing my Ph.D. work.

I had started a Spanish language theater (El Teatro Nuevo) that presented plays in high schools and colleges. After a presentation at the University of Minnesota, the chair of the Spanish Department invited me out for lunch. When he discovered that I had done a few years of graduate school and had been a Fulbright Scholar, he asked me if I wouldn't like to join his department as a Ph.D. candidate and he offered me a T.A. position. I accepted.

For the first year or so I did both Ph.D. studies and theater. I even directed a very successful play in the Spanish Department. But realizing I couldn't keep wearing two hats, I decided to focus exclusively on my Ph.D. studies. In a few years I was Dr. David George.

I began my teaching career and Middlebury College and ended it at Lake Forest College. In both schools I occasionally directed Spanish plays (and even one French play).

My most significant theater experience took place in Brazil, in 1984. I was in São Paulo with a grant, researching Brazilian theater (I had started writing about the subject). I was invited by the Escola de Comunicações e Artes (Universidade de São Paulo), to teach an acting course. I decided that the best way to teach acting would be to stage a play. There was a great deal of skepticism: "How do you, a foreigner, think you're going to produce a play in 3 months?"

Well, I did it. The actors were at first unhappy with my methodology: a lot of hard work, meaning actually rehearsing the play. They wanted to talk—and talk and talk and talk—before we even began the rehearsal process. It's not that I didn't want to talk, but we only had 3 months—I only had 3 months—to stage the play. I was called a "cultural imperialist," my methodology "nazista." But in short order the actors came around. We were actually getting shit done. We might even produce a full-length play.

At the end of the 3-month period we opened the play to acclaim. The São Paulo Ministry of Culture offered to subsidize a tour of the play to theater festivals in the city of São Paulo and beyond.

It was during this 3-month period that I met someone you might know: a lovely lady named Bia. And here, with this happy ending, we bring down the curtain.

The Ivory Machete

By David George

Marfil Márquez arrived an hour early for his shift at Land of Lincoln College. He parked his vintage VW Rabbit behind Facilities Management, which he was fond of calling Facilities *Mis*management. That's where the bosses sat on their thrones, so he never uttered his *injuria* in their presence. There was a time it was called Buildings and Grounds. Back then, Marfil and his fellow employees had benefits like health insurance. Now they were contract workers.

Marfil took in the smells of autumn, the musk of decaying vegetation and the sweet acrid scent of burning leaves. He walked around to the trunk and pulled out the bag containing his work tools.

Handyman skills were a source of pride for Marfil. He could fix any machine on campus and take on the most complicated tasks without complaint. He gladly worked the early morning shift the other contract workers dreaded. But Marfil believed orders should make sense. If there was a quicker and more efficient way to complete a task, then official procedures be damned, and the bosses, too… He regretted allowing the word "damned" to enter his thoughts and he whispered a silent prayer of contrition.

Despite his skills and work ethic, the bosses were not fond of Marfil. The fact that he tried to enlist the maintenance staff into a work-stoppage to demand the return of benefits was *el colmo*, the last straw. How had Marfil kept his job until now? Most likely because he was on friendly terms with a professor in the Language and Linguistics Department. The administration, not so much. In fact, Dean Gaborski's secretary had sent Marfil an email last Friday—today was Monday—commanding him to appear in the dean's office at the end of his shift. Marfil had committed it to memory:

To: Marfil Márquez, Facilities Management Custodial Division

From: Susan Campbell, Office of College Dean Gaborski

Your impertinent behavior has come to Dean Gaborski's attention. More important, the dean has been informed that in your application for the position at Facilities Management, you were not truthful about your activities prior to your employment at the college. Therefore, the dean has instructed you to attend a meeting in his office, immediately after your morning shift next Monday. Failure to heed Dean Gaborski's instruction will have serious consequences.

Had someone he confided in about his sinful past betrayed him? If this was his last day on the job, so be it. He whispered the well-worn prayer: "God grant me the serenity to accept the things I cannot change, the courage to change the things I can, and the wisdom to know the difference."

Marfil headed to the chapel for his morning worship. The chapel was not part of his custodial territory and therefore out of bounds. Over the years, however, he had surreptitiously accumulated keys to every lock on campus. He inserted the antique key—its head in the shape of a cross—into the brass lock and inched open the massive wooden door. Using his iPhone flashlight, he found his way to the organ bench. Not that he intended to play the organ. Marfil's fingers performed a short air dance above the organ keys. The prayer began with the one phrase he knew in Latin, a remnant of his childhood in the traditional Catholic Church of the Dominican Republic. *Patri fili spiritus sancti.* Marfil continued in English. He wasn't sure if the Lord had language preferences but decided that Spanish would not be appropriate in a house of English-language worship. *Forgive me, Lord, for my misdeeds and bless and protect those I harmed in the Evil Time…*

After exiting the chapel Marfil headed to the administration building. He would take the extra time afforded by his early arrival on campus to give the dean's office special treatment. Not that it would make any difference, but perhaps the dean, seeing his office sparkling clean, would dismiss Marfil with *un poquito de respeto*. He held on to this thought even though Dean Gaborski had a reputation for disrespecting everyone, even the faculty. Marfil unlocked the front door of the administration building and trudged up the three flights of stairs to the dean's office.

Marfil never took the elevator. Taking the stairs was for him an act of penance. For how many years had he performed such acts? Atonement for a dreadful secret past, a gang member in the Dominican Republic in his teenage years, followed by his move to Chicago at age 18 when he joined the Latin Kings. His Evil Time lasted until he took a bullet during a shootout. Convalescing in the hospital, he began reading the bible. That put him on a path that led him away from the gang life and turned him into *un siervo del Señor*, a servant of the Lord.

Marfil put those thoughts aside when he reached the third floor. He looked toward the end of hallway where the dean's office was located. *Curioso….* Light filtered under the office door and spilled into the hallway. Why would the dean be in his office this early? He had a reputation for arriving late, especially when the president was away on a fund-raising tour. Marfil walked softly down the hallway. Despite his 6-foot 250-pound frame, he was light on his feet. A gift he attributed to a childhood spent on a soccer field and dancing at celebrations in a Santo Domingo shantytown.

He approached the door and listened. Not a sound. Knocked softly. No answer. Turned the doorknob. Unlocked. Pushed the door open partway and looked inside.

The Public Safety office, once known as Campus Police, shone like a lighthouse on the edge of campus at that early hour. No one in living memory could recall the "lighthouse" rescuing anyone from danger on that bucolic campus surrounded by wheat fields in western Illinois. The only sounds in the office were intermittent radio calls—"All clear at the Student Union"—and the clatter of fingers tapping on a computer keyboard. Assistant Safety Officer Chris Baldoc occupied the desk with the computer, in reaching distance to the communications equipment. The inner sanctum was the realm of Chief Alice Conklin, normally occupied at this early hour by Sub-Chief Roger Griswold. Baldoc was bigger than life, both physically and vocally, while Griswold was scrawny and sarcastic.

Griswold entered the office looking sweaty and rumpled, said "Sorry I'm late," and entered Chief Conklin's office.

The phone rang and Baldoc picked it up. "What? Say again." His grating voice penetrated the walls of the public safety office and raked across the soccer field to the cluster of dormitories on middle campus, but since the students were on break no one heard him. "I can't understand you,' Baldoc continued yawping. "What? Say again. I can't understand you. What?" Words bubbled out of the speaker, incomprehensible to Assistant Baldoc. Except for *"Dios." Why does the person keep saying "goodbye"?* the assistant asked himself. There was a moment of silence. "They hung up on me."

Roger Griswold thrust out his bald head. It balanced precariously over his scrawny neck, which always gave the impression that his thin frame would topple over. "What was that all about, Chris?"

"Sounded like a crazy person, Rog. Had an accent. I think talking, like, half in Spanish. Anyway, the caller ID said it was from Dean Gaborski's office."

"You mind running over there and checking it out? You can take a golf cart if running is too much for you." Griswold asked.

Baldoc said, "No problemo. Be good to stretch my legs. Been sitting in this chair so long my ass fell asleep."

The chair squeaked as Baldoc lifted his ample frame and stretched his limbs. He headed across campus and entered the administration building. He contemplated the flight of stairs that reached the third floor, padded his belly, then called the elevator. As he walked down the long hallway toward the dean's office his lumbering footsteps echoed in the hallway. When he reached the office, the door was ajar. He scrunched his face, reached for the door handle, then withdrew it. He backed away as if to return to the elevator, reconsidered, the pushed open the door.

Dean Gaborski was tied to a chair, surrounded by a pool of blood. Next to him a large knife seemed to coil like a rattle snake. Baldoc took in the scene in silence. He retreated to the hallway, stationed himself outside the elevator, lifted a generous portion of his belly, reached under, ripped the walkie talkie from his belt, and made a distress call.

"Listen up, everybody." He seemed to realize there was no emotion in his voice. He turned the intercom off then on again. He filled his voice with a tone of panic. "Emergency, emergency. Get your asses over to the administration building. Third floor. Dean Gaborski's office. It's horrible. Looks like a murder. Call Chief Conklin at home. And call county Sheriff Olsen." There were squawks in response but nothing comprehensible. Baldoc kept an eye on the stairway and the elevator and listened for approaching footsteps.

Baldoc heard the sound of someone running up the stairs. Roger Griswold crashed through the stairway door and shouted in his partner's face.

"What's going on, Chris? Did I hear you say 'murder' on the walkie-talkie?" In spite of the shouting, anyone listening would have thought the questions sounded rehearsed.

"It's Dean Gaborski. You shoulda seen the humongous knife, the blood…"

"What in the bejeezus we waiting for? Let's get our butts down to Gaborski's office," Griswold commanded. He moved quickly, his hands sliding along the wall as if gravity were now horizontal. His thin frame sounded like sandpaper scraping against the brick wall.

Baldoc seemed unable to move, stuck in a quicksand of indecision.

"Get moving, you mutt," Griswold growled.

The two men crept down the hallway and halted before the dean's office door. Griswold's hand fluttered to the doorknob and twisted it clockwise. He opened the door an inch at a time and maneuvered his bald dome into the office. His head drooped sideways nearly to the floor, as if he were about to throw a gutter ball. His eyes gripped the scene, the body deflated, the blood, the knife glistening with streaks of red, the atmosphere infused by the stench of feces.

Griswold closed the door. Turning to Baldoc, he spit out his words.

"How many times I told the administration we should be allowed to carry sidearms? There's a goddamn machete. Who on campus has one of those? That, you know, that... Anyways, we better wait til Alice Conklin and Sheriff Olsen show up. Let's move back to the other end of the hall. Just in case the perp is still around. Let the sheriff deal with it. Goddamn I wish I had a gun. Got one at home. Like to shoot the fucker right through his black heart." Griswold felt something stirring in his stomach as he spoke.

The howl of a siren erupted in the distance. The elevator door opened and out stepped Alice Conklin, so quickly she nearly knocked her two colleagues over.

"What's going on, Griswold?" she asked.

"It's Dean Gaborski. His throat's been cut. Oh my...." Griswold's thin body folded like a wet matchstick, the round dome of his head rolled down, and he vomited on Conklin's cowboy boots.

"You idiot. Get a hold of yourself. Baldoc, fill me in. And if you throw up on me like Griswold did, I'll shove my boot down your throat."

"Well, see, chief. I got this call, like, on our office line, you know, the equipment is kinda outdated, don't you know. And well..."

"Just get to the point."

"Sorry, chief. Well, I get a distress call from Dean Gaborski's office. I run over here, take the stairs three at a time..."

"Fat chance," Conklin scoffed.

"So I open the office door and there's the dean tied to a chair. There's blood everywhere. And there's this huge knife. So I come back to the hallway and call it in. Griswold shows up and he seen it too."

"I don't understand. Who made the call?"

"Who called? I was kind of excited and... well ... I guess it was..."

His answer was cut short by the approaching siren. A vehicle came to an abrupt stop outside, followed by the sound of feet running up the stairs. Sheriff Rich Olsen burst into the hallway. Conklin relayed the situation to him. The sheriff hurried down the hallway and into the dean's office. He quickly approached the body to check for vital signs, taking care to avoid touching the machete lying next to the chair. The sheriff spoke up. "No pulse. The victim has bled out. I'm going to have to tell the M.E. we have a murder victim for her."

Linguistics professor Joseph Archer, dressed in a frayed bathrobe, was drinking his first early morning cup of coffee. His cottage, situated on a bluff overlooking the Mississippi, afforded a striking view of the autumn foliage, the red and orange maple trees a gouache of flowers streaming down the riverbank.

The view failed to move Joseph Archer this morning. His usual sleep remedies had failed him. The dean's voicemail churned in his brain.

"Professor, this is Dean Gaborski. Let's cut to the chase. It's time you stop making excuses for the janitor Marquez. This is what comes of not doing thorough background checks. Turns out, he is not only insubordinate, but dangerous as well. I just learned about his record, which I'm sure you knew all about and for some perverse reason chose to keep to yourself. The fact that you're the senior member and chairman of the Language Department doesn't give you the right to shirk your responsibilities. You professors, my god. Is it true what they say? Overeducated, overpaid, and underworked. Be forewarned: I am now in charge of this case and I intend to set things right. Do not, I repeat, do not interfere."

The professor heard a tap on the door, an odd occurrence at any hour in his solitary life. He opened the door and a figure from Hieronymus Bosch stood before him. It was a large-framed man dressed in mud-covered overalls and a torn shirt streaked with dark red stains, his face knotted in a grimace. Professor Archer scrutinized the face and reached a tentative conclusion.

"¿Marfil? ¿Eres tú?"

The man dropped his head and tears moistened a small section of the porch he stood on.

"Marfil? Is it you? Talk to me. What's the matter?"

The man looked at Joseph, his lips trembled, then the words tumbled out. "*Es terrible, profesor.* I didn't murder the dean. I just found him there, dead. *El machete*...I...I..."

Professor Archer dropped his coffee cup which shattered on the floor. He took a step back.

"The dean? Murdered? Are you sure?"

"It wasn't me. *Soy inocente.*"

Professor Archer searched Marfil's face, took a deep breath, regained his composure, took his friend by the arm, and gently pulled him inside the cottage and into the kitchen. "*¿Café?* Or would you like something stronger? *Algo más fuerte.* To take the edge off." Marfil looked at him, his face gradually relaxing. "That's right, Marfil. You don't drink alcohol. How about a cup of tea? I'll heat the water."

Professor Archer busied himself preparing the tea and encouraging Marfil to recount his disturbing tale. He poured the tea into a white and blue flower-patterned cup, which he nudged into his visitor's hands. "Drink the tea. *Toma el té.*" Marfil sipped the tea. It seemed to calm him.

"Professor..."

"Marfil, you know you don't have to call me 'professor'. Just call me Joseph. Or Joe. Now tell me what happened."

"I went to the dean's office extra early..."

"Why extra early?" Archer asked.

"I wanted to clean it until it sparkled. I was supposed to meet with him today. I wished to make a good impression. Halfway through straightening up I took a break and left my tools and machete in the office. I went over to the Student Union to get a snack out of machine. I was gone about a half hour. I returned and...*¡Dios mío! ¡Dios mío!*"

"Calm down, Marfil. Take your time. Was there anyone else around?"

"I cannot say. Nobody will believe me. When I returned to the office the dean was tied to a chair. All bloody. My machete was right next to him. I had the idea I could drive him to the hospital. Then I thought, I should not move an injured person."

"Injured? So he wasn't dead?"

"I do not know. I guess he was probably dead. So I put him down and called Public Safety. I am not sure I made any sense. I waited for them to arrive. I finally heard someone coming up the elevator and walking down the hall. I panicked."

"Why did you do that?"

"I do not want to get shot."

"But, Marfil, campus safety officers don't carry guns."

"That is what most people think. It is like when I was in the gang. I told you about that. You are one of few people who know about my younger days in Santo Domingo and Chicago. So I could hear the person running and puffing in the hallway and the elevator made that dinging sound. Then some more people arrived and opened the door."

"Did you show yourself at that point?"

"No. I climbed out the window and down the fire escape. I ran quickly. I tripped and fell into a ditch, picked myself up and..."

"Why didn't you stay and tell them what you've explained to me?"

"Everything from my past came back. It is like I am still a violent gang member, and the police cannot wait to get their hands on me. Like I am not *un siervo del Señor*. Like He cannot hear me anymore."

Marfil paused, took a sip of tea, and put his hand on the professor's arm.

"Do you believe me, professor?"

"I believe you, Marfil. I know you're a good man."

"You have always been *muy simpático*, professor...Joseph. That is why I came to you. I trust you."

As Marfil drank his herbal tea, Archer noticed red stains on the cup.

"You believe me, professor, but the Public Safety men and the sheriff will not. I left my tools in the dean's office. Including my machete, *mi marca registrada*."

"Your trademark. I know. The students think it's cool all the things you can do with the machete."

The machete was central to Marfil's pride. It served to clear brush, cut wood, chop compost for the Environmental Studies garden, remove invasive plants, even to prepare meats and vegetables for student barbecues. He didn't like to think about how he had used the machete in what he thought of as his Evil Time.

"Marfil, why don't you take a shower and change clothes? I'll put out a clean shirt and pants for you. They'll be a little tight, but I think you can squeeze into them."

"I do not want to be a bother, professor… Joseph."

"It's not a bother. You'll feel better after a nice bath. Let me get you a towel and some clean clothes."

Archer asked Marfil to leave his muddy clothes outside the bathroom door. He had an ulterior motive for his request. To place Marfil's clothes in a plastic bag to protect evidence… just in case. *Am I betraying his trust?* He hoped not. While Marfil showered, Professor Archer called his lawyer, Russell Hamilton, and explained the situation. Hamilton assured Joseph that he was doing the right thing. He recommended they call County Sheriff Olsen. If Marfil was a suspect or person of interest, Hamilton would represent him. Turning himself in with a lawyer present would make a good impression and at least delay incarceration. They would discuss the legal complications at a later time.

"Just one thing, Joe."

"Yes?"

"Don't be offended but… did you have anything to do with the dean's…"

"What kind of a question is that, Russ?"

"It's just I know you hated the guy. Look, if there's any question about this you know I've got your back."

"I appreciate that. But it's Marfil who needs your help."

When Marfil returned, showered and dressed in a clean but tightly fitting pair of khakis and a dress shirt, Joseph asked him to sit with him again.

"I have something to tell you. I just talked to a friend of mine. His name is Russ. He's an attorney. He's going to talk to the sheriff about the situation. If the authorities are looking for you, the best thing is to turn yourself in. Russ is highly respected in the community and with him representing you, well, it'll help a lot."

"Go to jail? *Dios mío*, I cannot go to jail. They will kill me in there."

"Marfil, I promise you they won't. Russ will make sure they won't lay a hand on you. You have my word. *Palabra de honor.*"

"I thought you were my friend, professor. Do you have any idea how cops treat Black men and Latinos? And I am both. I am Dominican but as far as they are concerned, I am just another Mexican… how do you say it… illegal alien. I am an American citizen, but the police around here could care less. *Que Dios me libre y me guarde.*"

"Sheriff Olsen is not that kind of cop. He's a fair-minded man. We can work with him."

There was a knock on the door. Archer stood up. "That must be Russ. Just hang on a minute. He'll explain everything. Be right back." Archer left the living room and went to the front door. He let the lawyer in. When they entered the living room, Marfil was nowhere in sight.

"Marfil," Joseph called out as he searched through the house. "Marfil. My friend Russell is here. He's going to help you."

"I believe your friend has flown the coop, Joe." The professor and the attorney heard a sound behind them.

Marfil walked out of the kitchen holding a butcher knife.

Sheriff Olsen, Campus Chief Alice Conklin, and Roger Griswold stood outside the dean's office as the M.E. examined the crime scene. Chief Conklin had sent Chris Baldoc off on a search of the campus.

"Ms. Conklin, why do you keep that Baldoc character on your crew?" Sheriff Olsen asked.

"He's all I can afford. Minimum wage. And Griswold here keeps an eye on him. He's harmless."

"To get back to the matter at hand, you're saying the machete belongs to one of your custodians?"

"That's right, sheriff. That bag of tools is his, too."

The sheriff shifted his weight from one foot to the other, which set off a jangle of metal against metal: handgun, handcuffs, flashlight, truncheon. Griswold rubbed his round dome as he looked enviously at the equipment denied to him as a minor leaguer in the cop business.

"So, Ms. Conklin. Tell me more about this custodian. We need to get a bulletin out on him asap."

Griswold answered for her. "He's a Mex. A Black Mex. Not too many of those around."

"He's African American and Mexican? Never heard of that before. What's his name?"

"Something like Merfel."

"Stop interrupting me, Griswold. It's Spanish, sheriff. Marfil. Means Ivory. I have no idea where he got a name like that. We're waiting on Facilities Management to send over his file."

"What's the holdup?" the sheriff asked.

"They can't find his file. Go figure." Chief Conklin said.

"Give me a description, then. I'll call it in."

"As I said, sheriff, he's Black. Salt and pepper hair cut short. Around six foot. Heavy set. Assuming he's wearing his regular outfit, it's grey coveralls. The college's logo is on the back. Shouldn't be that hard to identify him. I mean, how many people of color we got in our county? Especially one's got a Spanish accent."

The sheriff said, "One more thing. What kind of car is he driving?"

Alice Conklin scratched her chin. "That's the thing. His car is still parked behind Facilities Management. He might've taken a bicycle. There's a broken chain by one of the bike racks."

"Any chance he's still on campus?" the sheriff asked.

"Damn. Never thought of that."

"Ok, so here's what we're going to do, chief. Your team searches the campus and mine will check out other leads. And get that file to me, for Christ's sake."

Alice Conklin walked toward the elevator. A voice floated out of the dean's office.

"Sheriff, we've found something you need to see."

Marfil walked out of the kitchen brandishing a butcher knife. Joseph Archer moved protectively in front of Russell Hamilton.

"Marfil. What are you doing? *Larga ese cuchillo.*"

"I am sorry, professor. I cannot put the knife down. I need it for protection." He made a wide berth around Russell and Joseph, moving in the direction of the front door.

"Where are you going, *compadre?*"

Marfil stopped in front of a Frida Kahlo print. "I have to get away, professor. I will go back to Chicago, back to my old neighborhood in Humboldt Park."

"But Marfil, you left that behind years ago. You're a new man, a good man. You have to stay and face this. Russell and I can help you. We'll call the pastor at your church. He'll vouch for you."

Marfil lowered the knife. Tears glistened in his eyes. Joseph moved closer to him. Marfil jerked the knife back up and pointed it at the professor, halting his forward movement. "I am sorry. I am going now. *Que Dios me perdone. Adiós.*" He rushed to the front door and exited the cottage. Archer scurried after him and tripped over a bicycle lying by the porch. From his prone position he watched Marfil jump into Archer's vintage 1960s VW van, a relic from his long-ago hippie period. Before he could reach him, Marfil put his hands under the dashboard, started the vehicle, and drove off. Archer ran back inside.

"He just took off on your old beater, Joe. How'd he get the keys?"

"It's an old trick. He must have used aluminum foil to hot-wire the V.W. Let's follow him in your car to see where he's going."

"Aluminum foil?"

"I'll explain later. Let's get going before we lose him."

"Slow down. We're not cops. We have to report this."

"Just give me your keys. Make yourself at home."

"The hell with it. I'm going with you."

Archer and his attorney hurried out to a yellow electric Smart car parked in the driveway and headed off... in search of someone they hoped was not a murderer.

Marfil drove through the bitter light of early morning as the sun peeked its bloodshot eye over the horizon. He headed in the direction of campus. Because the students were away on fall break, a dormitory seemed like a good hiding place. Marfil regretted threatening the professor and his friend and lying about going back to Chicago. But he needed a diversion, time to figure out what to do. A possible safe refuge presented itself on the outskirts of the campus, Frank Lloyd Wright Hall.

Marfil parked the VW behind a hedgerow out of sight of any campus buildings. He entered the dormitory by using the knife he took from Professor Archer's kitchen to jimmy the lock, a skill he learned in his past life. He walked softly down a hallway, hoping none of the students had stayed behind during the fall break. There was no way to know, since his custodial territory did not include student residences. One by one he checked the rooms. All empty. The basement would be the best place to hide. That would be his home until he could come up with a plan. Some of the students kept small refrigerators in their rooms, which hopefully would provide a source of food.

Sheriff Olsen entered the dean's office, summoned by the M.E.'s voice. Marge Benson was in her mid-thirties, her hair covered by netting, wearing a polo shirt with "Forensics" embroidered on the lapel.

"What's up, Marge?" the sheriff asked.

"The lab has found two sets of fingerprints on the machete handle."

The sheriff paused. "Which means… we now have two suspects? But wait… Is it possible one of these campus minor leaguers picked it up?"

"I assume their prints are in the system so it would have to be someone else," the investigator responded. "The fingerprints in the system ID your custodian, Mr. Márquez. He's got a rap sheet, stuff that happened a long time ago. Seems he was an enforcer for a Chicago gang called the Latin Kings. His weapon of choice was, get this, a machete. The other prints aren't in the system."

"Thanks, Marge. Keep me posted. I have to go back to my office to coordinate the search for our person of interest."

Archer and his attorney were unable to pick up Marfil's trail. On a hunch they drove to the train station. If Marfil's plan was to return to Chicago, the logical step would be to catch the early train. Archer and his companion entered the station and looked around the waiting room. There was no sign of Marfil. They approached the ticket booth.

Archer addressed the person in the ticket booth.

"Can I help you?"

"I'm looking for a passenger taking the train to Chicago. He's a large man, African American. He's wearing khaki pants and a blue dress shirt."

"Sorry. Haven't seen anyone like that."

The two companions left the station and drove back toward Archer's home. *Had Marfil returned to the cottage? With the butcher knife?* Archer asked himself.

Sheriff Olsen sat in his office with his western boots up on an oak roll-top desk, which barely afforded room for his computer. He wore a cowboy hat with a gold star and braid. The sheriff pondered the morning's events. The case seemed open and shut. Though he was almost certain the perp was the African American custodian, the fact that there were two sets of fingerprints troubled him. A search of Márquez's apartment had come up empty. The phone on the sheriff's desk rang and he picked it up.

"Sheriff," his assistant said, "it's Marge on line two."

The sheriff switched to line two. "Hi Marge. Anything new to report?"

"We searched the dean's computer. Turns out it wasn't password protected. We found a note in Word written this morning."

"What does it say?"

"That's the thing. We can't read it. It's in Spanish."

"Sounds like it's our perp. Talk to Public Safety. See if there's someone who can translate it for us."

Joseph Archer sat with his attorney in the living room.

"If he's not taking the train to Chicago, I doubt my old VW would make it that far. I mainly drive it between home and campus. So I'm guessing he's parked my van on campus."

"Where else could he be going, Joe?"

"Although it seems unlikely, maybe he went back to his apartment."

"Where's that?"

"It's in town. An efficiency right by the library. He's a volunteer. Drives the bookmobile."

At that moment Archer's cell phone vibrated. He answered the call.

"Yes?"

"Professor Archer?"

"Speaking."

"This is sheriff Olsen calling."

"Hold on a minute."

Archer muted his iPhone and turned to his attorney. "It's the sheriff. Should I talk to him?"

"No reason not to, Joe. See what he wants."

"Sheriff? What can I do for you?"

"It's a long story, professor. Don't know if you've heard. There's been a murder on campus. Our investigators found a note that might be a clue. Problem is it's in Spanish. Would you translate it for us?"

"A murder? Who?" He tried to sound alarmed but feared the sheriff would call his bluff.

"First, just read the note." Archer detected impatience in Olsen's voice.

"But sheriff, who was murdered? Can't you at least tell me that?"

"We're waiting to notify the next of kin before we release the victim's name. Sorry. Can we send it to you, professor? What's your email address?"

"Of course, sheriff. Glad to be of help. It's *Archer@LandofLincoln. edu*. A murder? On our campus? That's awful." The look on his attorney's face suggested his feigned surprise was not very convincing. Archer shrugged his shoulders and told the sheriff he would report back asap. He assumed Marfil had not been apprehended. Archer explained to Hamilton what the sheriff had told him as he set up his computer which sat on a small table in his home office. He logged on to his email account and opened the sheriff's message:

> *"Professor Archer. Thanks for agreeing to help us. Here's an attachment with the message in Spanish. Call me as soon as you have it translated."*

Archer clicked on the attachment and downloaded the document. It was a confession. From Marfil. The gist was that he was sorry for killing the dean. He didn't mean to do it.

Archer turned to his attorney. "Look at this, Russ."

"What, Joe?"

"Sheriff Olsen's email."

"What does it say?"

"It's an attachment in Spanish. Marfil supposedly confessing to the dean's murder."

"Why 'supposedly'?"

"There's no way Marfil wrote this."

"How could you know that, Joe? It's in Spanish, right? How many people around the college know Spanish besides you?"

"Some of my students. But they're off on fall break. Oh, and of course there's Alice Conklin. She studied Spanish with me years ago. Here's the thing: the language is very formal. No, that's not it. More like stilted. Marfil speaks Spanish fluently, but it's very colloquial. A lot of it is what we call Spanglish."

Russell sat down next to Joseph and looked at the computer screen. "So what's your point, Joe?"

"Looks to me like it's a machine translation. Probably Google Translator."

"How could you tell?"

Joseph stood up and began pacing. "I'm a linguist. Trained to decipher modes of discourse."

"Modes of discourse? Talk English."

"Let's say, different styles. Speaker's educational level. Profession. Country of origin. Machine translations stand out like a sore thumb."

"If you're right, this sheds a whole new light on the murder. It's too bad you didn't find this out before Marfil ran off. At least you can share your analysis of the note with the sheriff's office. Explain why you don't think Marfil wrote the note."

Roger Griswold followed the order to search the campus for the custodian. He had first driven to his house to arm himself. His gun was an old-style Colt revolver inherited from his father. A quick check of the pistol revealed no sign of rust. What about the ammunition? Did it have an expiration date? The best thing would be to check out the gun. Since his house stood alone in the neighborhood, a test should go undetected.

Griswold loaded the pistol and, in his backyard, fired a shot into the air. The pistol didn't jam, or worse explode. So far so good. Next, a target, a bottle on a fence post. It took four shots to hit and shatter the bottle. "Just let that Mex bring a knife to a gunfight," Griswold said to himself. Campus cops were not supposed to carry firearms. But if anything happened, like the perp putting up resistance, he was ready and willing to do what had to be done.

Griswold drove back to campus, now armed with a pistol, and began his search. His hunch told him that if the perp was hiding on campus he'd choose a dormitory, since the students were away on fall break. Griswold first checked the residences closest to middle campus and found nothing suspicious. He worked his way to the perimeter, to the farthest dormitory out, Frank Lloyd Wright Hall. Clutching his pistol, Griswold unlocked the main door and entered.

Marfil rested on a mattress in the basement storeroom. Time creeped slowly along. His thoughts turned to life back in Chicago. A vision assaulted his memory and tightened his throat. A bloody hand was splayed on the table. Marfil held a machete that swung slowly back and forth above the hand of the man who, he was told, had information about a Judas cooperating with the police. The Latin Kings wanted the informant's name, whatever it took. Marfil was the man for the job... He cut the scene short. He wept as he prayed, begging the Lord for forgiveness, wishing he could tell the man at the table how sorry he was. A flood of images from the dean's office seeped into his prayer.

Griswold looked down the first floor hall and listened carefully. Nothing seemed amiss. A door that didn't match the entrances to the student rooms opened on a stairway that led to a basement. Griswold began climbing down as quietly as he could, stopping every few steps and inclining his rounded dome to listen. The basement included a large open space and a single doorway. A faint rustling sound slid from under the door.

A noise from outside invaded the storeroom space. Marfil approached the door, which crashed open. A man rushed in. Marfil reached for his knife. A blow to the chest knocked him backwards, down on the mattress. One by one his thoughts and memories faded, like fireflies blinking out across a darkening field.

The meeting in Campus Chief Alice Conklin's office included Sheriff Olsen and College President John Hunisak, who had just returned from his fund-raising tour when news of the murder reached him. The president spoke first.

"Alice, since you're the one with most complete picture, what're your thoughts about this mess?"

The president self-consciously averted his gaze from her tight jeans. "Well, Mr. President, I wouldn't call it a mess, more like a debacle. First, you've got the dean, his throat cut in his own office. Then you've got the suspect Marfil who managed to escape on a bicycle, for god's sake. And then there's Joe Archer. There's a lot that ties him to this… mess."

"Joe? I could come up with a long list, but mild-mannered Joe Archer?"

Alice crossed her arms and thought a moment. "He's probably Marfil's best friend on campus, besides the students who love his barbecues. They're both Spanish speakers and Joe is interested in Marfil's Dominican culture."

The sheriff gave her a look of surprise. "Dominican? I thought he was a Mexican Negro."

"That's what a lot of people think. I don't mean to lecture you, but a lot of Hispanics have African heritage, especially if they're from places with a history of slave culture, like Cuba and the Dominican Republic."

"How do you know all this stuff?"

"Years ago, I was a Latin American Studies major here. Getting back to Joe, he hated the dean."

"Folks, there's something I better share with you," President Hunisak said. "Everybody hated Gaborski. Don't let this out of the room, but I was looking for an excuse to fire him."

"Here's another thing that stays in this room," Alice added. "The dean was working on a way to fire Joe Archer."

"Where did you hear that?" The president asked.

"His secretary and I share secrets. She told me."

"But Archer's going to retire in a year. Two at most. What would be the point? Not to mention it would be my decision, not Dean Gaborski's."

The sheriff entered the fray. "Your college is starting to sound like a looney bin. Hope you got a good supply of straitjackets in storage… Sorry, bad joke… What about that note on the dean's computer?"

Alice said, "That's a tricky one. I mean obviously if the murderer leaves a confession on the computer in Spanish, that brings Joe into the picture. But what if it's a ruse, a way to deflect suspicion? I mean, who would purposely leave evidence at the scene of the murder they committed?"

"What about one of your crew, Alice?" the president asked.

"I know most everyone on campus. None of them liked the dean. But I can't see any of them had a reason to kill him. Although I have to say Griswold was always complaining about campus cops not allowed to bear arms. Nor did he appreciate the dean making jokes about his bald head. And Baldoc resented the dean always mocking his potbelly"

"What's any of that got to do with cutting someone's throat?" the president asked

"By the way, where is Griswold? And Baldoc? They should be participating in this meeting," the sheriff asked.

At that moment the door to the sheriff Olsen's office slammed open and Griswold stumbled in, his bald head covered with blood.

Conklin, Olsen, and Hunisak rushed to aid Griswold. They placed him on the floor and the sheriff called 911. Alice held her face close to his and asked, "Can you talk, Roger? What happened?"

"That Mexican janitor attacked me with a knife. So I shot him."

"Where is he?" the sheriff asked. "Is he on campus? You said you shot him. Is he alive?"

"Last I saw him he was lying on the basement floor in Wright Hall." Griswold pulled himself up and sat in a chair.

"What are you doing? Lie back down," Olsen insisted.

"I'm ok. Just a scratch on my scalp. The blood splashed from where I shot Marcus, or whatever his name is."

The sheriff picked up the phone. "Marge, call emergency and tell them there's a gunshot victim in Frank Lloyd Wright Hall. In the basement. And tell my deputy Alex to meet me at the entrance… yes… on campus. Tell him to wait outside… No, he's not to enter until I get there." He turned to the others. "Sorry, folks. I gotta get things under control. Let's meet again in my office, say, in an hour."

"Speaking of office, I've got to get over to mine. I haven't been there yet." The president exited.

After the sheriff and the president had left, Alice asked her underling, "What the hell were you doing with a gun? You know the rules."

"Damn good thing I had one. You'd be picking me up in pieces instead of bitching at me. Not to mention who knows how many other people I saved by putting a stop to his killing spree."

Alice handed him a box of Kleenex. "Clean yourself up, Griswold. So, how do you know he's killed anyone?"

He wiped off his face, made a bloody ball, and threw it toward the wastebasket next to the sheriff's desk. The ball sailed in a high curve over the desk, bounced across the stacks of white paper, and left a trail of red drops

"Nice shot there, Lebron."

"Don't give me a hard time. I been through enough for today."

"Fine. Get your ass to the health center. You need to be checked out. I'm heading over to Wright Hall."

Sheriff Olsen arrived at Wright Hall and found his deputy, Alex Sanders, standing over Marfil Márquez, who sat on the front steps. A large patch of blood had soaked into his shirt front. Olsen and his deputy approached him slowly. His head hung down and he gave no indication he noticed them. They stopped a few feet away and noticed a pistol and a knife lying at Marfil's feet.

"Marfil," the sheriff spoke, "get down on your knees then lie flat. Put your hands behind your head."

"Take a close look, sheriff. The knife is broken in half and the pistol is in pieces. Griswold tried to shoot me with his old grandfather gun and it exploded. A big piece hit my chest. I tried to defend myself with the knife, but it broke in half."

"Doesn't matter. Down on your knees."

Marfil stood up. "Do what you must. I am going to the chapel and pray. You want me out of there it will have to be in a *cajón*. A coffin."

Marfil stood up. The only sound was his feet brushing lightly on the sidewalk. A gunshot cracked open the silent afternoon. Marfil dropped like a rag doll.

The sheriff and his deputy looked at each other in consternation.

"Got the Black bastard. He ain't getting away this time." Baldoc stood proudly holding a Glock 22, a string of smoke curling out of its barrel.

"Put down that gun. What the fuck you think you're doing?"

"I'm doing what nobody else had the balls to do, sheriff. I just solved a big problem." His attempt to thrust his chest forward succeeded in calling attention to his bulging midriff.

"Drop that gun and get the fuck down on your knees. Now!"

At that moment Alice Conklin arrived on the scene.

"Come on, sheriff," Baldoc attempted to put an arm over the sheriff's shoulder." I'll share the credit with you. We'll both be heroes." Olsen pushed him away.

Alice entered the conversation. "Get down on your knees, Baldoc, or I'll put you there myself."

"You're gonna put me down? A middle-aged broad who couldn't give up her coed life."

Alice walked directly toward Baldoc. His facial muscles stiffened. He raised his Glock. She kicked him squarely in the crotch. His gun pointed up, went off, and dropped to the ground next to its owner. The bullet pierced a second-floor window in Wright Hall.

"You mind handcuffing him?" the Sherriff said.

An ambulance pulled up at the entrance to Wright Hall.

Sheriff Olsen's office was becoming increasingly crowded. The sheriff presided, his boots on his desk. His secretary sat next to a large window, the afternoon light dimming imperceptibly. She took notes of the meeting and as a backup had her iPad recorder activated. The sheriff's deputy stood at attention by his side, his hand loosely covering his pistol grip. President Hunisak sat in a straight-backed chair, his expression stern. Archer and his attorney sat next to the president, one on each side. Alice Conklin stood by the office door, swaying slowly from one foot to the other. Griswold and Baldoc sat forcibly next to the old-fashioned radiator, secured by handcuffs.

"First item," the sheriff began, "is that Márquez is in the hospital, and it looks like he's going to pull through. Though he's not ready to talk yet. We can thank Baldoc for being a lousy shot with that Glock he carried ILLEGALLY, otherwise Márquez wouldn't have a word to say. We're all here to see if we can get to the bottom of this mess. It's either us or the state police take over the investigation. That would lead to my resignation. You may not give a damn but it's my career. So no b.s. I catch anybody in a lie and I'll take out another pair of handcuffs. I've got a drawer full. And I'll lock you up with today's heroes, Baldoc and Griswold."

"Sheriff, I object to this…"

"Speak when you're spoken to. That means the two of you. Got it?"

"Yessir," Baldoc and Griswold responded in unison.

"Good. Now that we've got that settled, everybody raise your hand if you didn't kill the dean."

Everyone but Olsen's secretary raised their hand.

"Marge, did you kill Dean Gaborski?"

"Sheriff?"

"You didn't raise your hand."

"Oh, sorry, I was busy taking notes and making sure this iPad is recording properly."

"That's fine, but just to make everything clear… did you?"

"Did I… Oh, no, of course I didn't."

"Next order of business is Márquez. Hamilton and Archer are here to speak on his behalf. Who wants to start?"

Hamilton stood up holding a yellow legal pad, faced the group, cleared his throat, and began. "Ladies and gentlemen. We are faced with a great injustice. The onerous duty has fallen to me…"

The sheriff cut him off. "Knock of the courtroom theatrics, Mr. attorney. This is between us. It's not official. So just say what you have to say. And put away that legal pad. Just looking at it gives me heartburn."

"Alright, sheriff. In the first place, Marfil is a man of peace. And deeply religious."

"My old man was a preacher and he used to kick the shit out of me," Baldoc whispered to Griswold. The sheriff looked around to see who had spoken out of turn but said nothing.

Hamilton went on. "Marfil's past misdeeds and his subsequent thirty years of saintly behavior are a testament to his character. Even the biblical prophets had skeletons in their closets."

"We're not here for bible study, counselor."

"Let me give it a try," Archer said. "I know Marfil better than anyone on this campus. We've been friends for nearly three decades. I can assure you he is a man of goodness and empathy. He would never hurt someone purposefully. If somehow, some way, he had anything to do with what happened to the dean, it would have to be an accident. And I say 'if' because I don't believe he had anything to do with it."

The meeting was interrupted when Marge's iPhone vibrated. She looked at the screen. "My apologies but this is a call from the crime lab." She listened for a few minutes. "Thanks for bringing me up to speed. The sheriff needs to hear this."

Sheriff Olsen placed his boots on the floor and turned to his assistant. "Ok, Marge, now what?"

"Well, sheriff, apparently there has been a mistake. A big mistake. There aren't two sets of fingerprints on the machete. There are several."

The sheriff breathed deeply, clenched and unclenched his fists, looked at kaleidoscopic light streaming through the late afternoon window, and spoke slowly in a deep cavernous voice. "So. How. In. The. Fuck. Did. That. Happen?"

"Seems they hired a new trainee to give the medical examiner some backup. They put the trainee on the case to give him some true crime experience…"

The sheriff slammed his fist on his desk. "Is this a murder investigation or a goddamn Halloween party? Sorry, Marge. Didn't mean to startle you. Did they say anything about DNA?"

"They're working on that. Kinda looks like there's several people's DNA on the knife as well."

"So that makes everybody in this room suspects. And who knows who else. This meeting is over. Looks like I'm going to be spending some time with the M.E. My deputy will be in charge of the office here. Chief Conklin, I'm deputizing you. Do you mind partnering up with me? Everybody else, I'll be in touch."

The group filed out of the office toward their various destinations. The sheriff failed to notice Griswold whispering: "Let's get our asses over to the hospital and finish off that murdering Mex." Unbeknownst to the sheriff, Griswold had used a pick he always carried in his pocket to unlock the handcuffs. A loud clanking filled the room, the two campus safety officers jumped to their feet, and ran out of the room.

Marfil lay on his hospital bed, his head encased in a large bandage, his right arm handcuffed to the bed frame. A doctor sat next to his bed and spoke to him. "Well, Mr. Márquez, you're a lucky man. The bullet grazed your head but did no serious damage. I'd say you could probably go home in a few days, but that's up to the sheriff. How's the pain? Need anything?"

"Thank you, doctor, but I don't take drugs."

"I'm talking about pain relief, not intoxication. But it's your call. Just press that button to your right to summon the nurse if you need anything."

"I appreciate it, doctor. But my right arm is chained up and the button is on left. I can't reach it."

The doctor thought for a moment. "I see what you're saying. Somebody goofed. Let me see if I can find someone who can change your position. Be right back."

A hospital maintenance worker solved Marfil's problem by attaching the handcuff to a chain with a lock to allow more freedom of movement.

Marfil heard the elevator doors on his floor open and close when two men barged into his room and shut the door. It was Baldoc and Griswold.

They approached Marfil's bed. "Ain't this convenient," Baldoc said. "He's already locked down."

"What do you want? You both already shot me. Going to shoot me again?"

Griswold laughed. "No need for that. One of them nice fat pillows will do the trick. We smother you and they think you died of natural… whatever. But first we need to know what you seen the morning Dracula bit Gaborski's neck."

"I vant to drink your rich red blood." Baldoc laughed at his own joke.

"Shut the fuck up, you idiot. So, amigo, spill the beans."

"That's right. You're a beaner so spill 'em."

Griswold slapped him across the face. "I told you to shut up, Baldoc. So zip it. I'll do the talking. Now, señor Marcheese, answer my question. Pour fayvor."

"You think I'm afraid of you two? I used to eat punks like you for lunch."

Baldoc moved his face close enough so that Marfil could smell his fetid breath. "The beaner's a vampire and a cannibal. How 'bout that?"

Marfil moved his left arm under the blanket and considered throttling his tormentor. "After, I went to get a snack I looked up and saw from the ground people moving in dean's office. I climbed up to the balcony and saw through the window you two with the dean tied to a chair. I heard you talking. Like, 'who ratted us out?' I listened more and got the idea that the three of you were drug pushers fighting over a drug deal gone bad. I saw too much of that during my evil time, my gang years. It always ends bad. I was trying to figure out how to get my tools and machete out of there when fat man here grabbed my machete and started swinging it around and it slipped out of his hands and sliced the dean's neck. I always keep my machete sharp like a razor. But not to kill someone like you two evil ones. You should get down on your knees and pray. Ask God for forgiveness."

"So that's your story? Bullshit." Baldoc closed his right hand over Marfil's throat and began squeezing. "You're the one better start praying, tortilla lips." With his left hand Baldoc pulled the pillow from under Marfil's head and placed it over his face. The two campus cops heard deep-throated laughter from beneath the pillow.

An arm snaked out from beneath the blanket and a hand gripped Baldoc's throat. Griswold laughed when he heard choking sounds but soon realized Baldoc was emitting them. He pulled off the blanket and saw Baldoc's neck in Marfil's grasp. It reminded him of a python choking an alligator. He seized the arm throttling his accomplice and soon found himself in the grasp of Marfil's other arm, the recently installed chain encircling his neck. The hunters, now become desperate prey, were unable to extricate themselves. Marfil's grasp on their throats made it impossible for anyone outside the room to hear their panicked gasps. Their constricted throats and thrashing, the shock of turning so quickly from inquisitors to martyrs, began to deflate their resistance and their bodies settled slowly into the bed, like a child's toy sinking into the asphalt on a scorching summer day.

A knock on the door froze the execution on the bed. Alice Conklin and Rich Olsen took a step inside the room and stopped cold. Alice and the sheriff experienced the same first impression: a bizarre orgy.

"What is god's name is going on here?" Hearing Alice's voice Marfil released his tormentors and they both rolled off the bed.

"This murderer was trying to kill us," Baldoc cried in a barely audible voice. "You got here just in time. I thought we was done for." Griswold's voice sounded like a dog chewing a lacerated tennis ball.

"I can't understand you. Can you explain what this is all about, Marfil?"

Marfil repeated his story of Dean Gaborski's murder and explained the struggle in the hospital room.

"I had been hearing rumors about methamphetamine on campus," Alice said.

Baldoc cried, as he slowly regained control of his voice. "It was all the dean's doing. He roped us into it. We were trying to talk him into letting us out of the whole deal. But we didn't kill him. We're innocent."

"Yeah, we're victims," Griswold embellished. "We deserve a medal for stopping a dangerous drug gang. And this bean… I mean… this character here was the gang leader."

Alice looked at Marfil and he gave her a smile that made her think, *beatific*, though she wasn't entirely sure of the connotation that word suggested.

"First things first," Sheriff Olsen said in an authoritative voice. "Let's get these two ne'er-do-wells cuffed again."

"But what about the Mex?" Baldoc whimpered. His partner added in the same wounded child tone: "He's the drug king and he tried to murder us."

"Alice," the sheriff said, "would you like to do the honors?"

"My pleasure, Rich." They had never addressed each other with their first names. Alice felt her face burn. Was she blushing?

"You two, bellies on the floor, hands behind your back. You know the drill."

"You know, Ms.… Alice, anybody watching you from the outside would take you for a bona fide police officer. There's a new position opening up in the sheriff's department. If you're interested, I'll put in a good word for you."

"I am interested. Let's talk about it once we get this mess here straightened out."

Alice Conklin and Sheriff Olsen interrogated the three perps—though they were increasingly convinced Marfil was not a "perp"—and the medical examiner's office called in more test results. The crowded fingerprints on the machete were easily explained by the fact that during a barbecue the week before spring break Marfil had allowed several students to take turns cutting the meats and vegetables. Marfil explained that he only rarely wiped the machete clean. The flavor from one barbecue to another builds up, he said.

The others involved in the case made their appearances and congratulated the sheriff and the campus chief for their good work. Deputy Alex Sanders announced that he had been offered a job in a larger precinct and had decided to accept. He thanked the sheriff for "all you've done, all you've taught me." Alice suspected that the sheriff had already been informed of Deputy Sanders' departure and that he and Olsen had put on a performance for her benefit. Joe Archer and Russell Hamilton were especially interested and spent an hour listening and asking questions. Joe and Marfil exchanged a *fuerte abrazo* and discussed Marfil's future plans, which in spite of his innocence did not include Land of Lincoln College. President Hunisak made a perfunctory appearance and stayed long enough to make sure he would suffer no political consequences.

When everyone had left and the prisoners taken away, Alice and Rich found themselves alone in the hospital room. They made a pretense of looking for more evidence but in fact were looking for an opportune moment. That moment came when back-to-back they lightly bumped into each other, turned about, encircled their arms around each other, and shared a long-deferred kiss.

Before leaving campus for the last time, Marfil made an early morning visit to the chapel. He sat before the organ and began to pray:

Patri fili spiritus sancti. Lord, forgive my mortal sin. I promise it will be my last. I will spend every hour of every day thou grantest me to do Thy work. Because Thou seest all Thou knowest I killed the dean with my machete after his fellow drug dealers left him tied to the chair. Drug dealers. A filthy gang. As if this was not a clean God-fearing campus but a den of iniquity like what I left behind in Chicago all those years ago. Forgive me, Lord. Perdóname, Señor, perdóname.

Problems With Pestergas

By Michael Allen George

Chapter 1

Alex Askew wanted a paper route, but they were hard to come by in 1950. Every kid who was over twelve wanted one and he had just turned twelve in April. So he spent a lot of time looking for other ways to make some money.

If he wasn't mowing someone's lawn, he was searching for returnable pop bottles that were thrown away. Ditches along the highway and neighbor's garbage cans yielded some. The local dump though, was his best source. The problem with that was the dump man. He didn't allow kids in the dump, so Alex had to be careful not to get caught while he was there. Even so, he found enough to make it worthwhile.

On those rare occasions when he had enough money to go to the store to buy a Popsicle, he'd take his sister, Caroline, who was nine, with him and buy her one too. It never occurred to him that taking the short trip to the store could get him in trouble. Even more than getting caught in the dump would. The trouble started on a morning bicycle ride home from the store.

Alex got on the bicycle first, then took the Popsicles from Caroline. He held up the bicycle with his free hand and legs as she got on. As soon as she was settled on the bars in front of him, he handed the Popsicles back to her.

"Don't drop them, Caroline," he warned, "'cause Lester will get mad if you do." Lester was their older brother.

"Lester's always getting mad."

"I know, Caroline, but he did help me find the pop bottles at the dump. If he wouldn't of gone with me, I probably wouldn't of found enough bottles to buy you a Popsicle too. He found four and I found four."

"Okay, Alex, I won't drop them. What're you gonna do with the penny you got left? Give it to Lester?"

"No, Lester got to keep the extra penny last time we had one. I get to keep it this time. Then all I need to do is find two more pop bottles and I'll have a nickel. I can buy a candy bar or some popcorn or another Popsicle with a nickel. Now keep your feet out of the spokes."

"I know that. You always tell me that. Every time you give me a buck on a bike you tell me to keep my feet out of the spokes. Why do you always tell me that?"

"So you don't put your feet in the spokes."

"Well okay, I won't! Don't ride too fast."

"I never ride fast on Lester's bike."

"That's 'cause he yells so loud."

"No it isn't. It's mostly because Lester's dumb bike is so slow."

"I bet that's not why. I bet it's 'cause he yells."

"Shut up, Caroline."

"Okay."

"And don't drop the Popsicles."

"You better hurry, Alex. I don't want them to melt either."

"I already told you, I don't ride fast on Lester's bike."

"I know. He yells too much."

"Oh, shut up, Caroline."

"Okay. You know, I'm sure glad they finally got banana Popsicles at Bagette's store. I like banana Popsicles."

"Rootbeer's better."

"I don't like rootbeer so good. Rootbeer Popsicles taste mostly like pop. Banana's best."

"They are not. So shut up, Caroline."

"Okay. Why did Lester want orange? They always got orange Popsicles at Bagette's store."

"Lester likes orange."

"Oh."

Because Alex was so busy talking to his sister, he didn't notice the police car creep up behind him as he rode down the middle of the street. The cop was only a few feet behind the bicycle when he turned on his siren. Its sudden wail startled Alex. He swerved to the side of the street and hit the curb. They toppled over.

"Did you get hurt, Caroline?" Alex asked.

"Just my leg got broke…and part of my arm."

"Good," he said, knowing if she said she broke something, she was okay. "Pick up the Popsicles then. Boy, I hope Lester's bike didn't get scratched too much. He'll really yell if it did."

"What do you think you were doing, Young Man?" the cop asked, after pulling his short, bulky body out of his car and hiking up his pants by the waist band with his rather spindly arms.

Alex continued examining the bicycle without answering. He was far more afraid of his brother, Lester, than he was of any policeman. After all, his father told him many times that policemen were nice people, who were only there to help. His father hadn't yet met Pestergas Hunter, Robinsdale's new Juvenile Officer.

"Young Man," he said, his voice and a pulsing vein in his bulbous nose showing his irritation with Alex, "I asked you what you thought you were doing."

"I wasn't doing anything," Alex answered, still more concerned about Lester's bicycle than the cop. "Boy, I sure hope Lester doesn't find too many scratches."

"You'd better show me more respect," Pestergas whined, wrapping his plump hands around Alex's arms and picking him up, making the bicycle fall again.

"I bet you made it get scratched good that time," Alex complained. "Lester's really gonna yell now."

"You have far more serious things to worry about," Pestergas warned, struggling to keep the natural squeak out of his voice, "than your bicycle. Now, I want you to tell me exactly what it was you thought you were doing!"

"I didn't think I was doing anything wrong," Alex answered. "I was just riding my brother's bike."

"I don't think he was doing anything wrong either, Mister Fat Policeman," Caroline said. She tended to be more honest than tactful. "Why do you think Alex was doing something bad?"

"You two delinquents," Pestergas sputtered, the lumps on his big nose turning red, "sure do have sassy mouths. I've got half a mind to take you in. I can't understand how parents can let their children run wild and break the law. They always turn into juvenile delinquents like the both of you. Now you tell me this instant," he shook Alex, "why you broke the law?!" He shook him again. "Why did you?"

"I didn't know I was going fast," Alex said, looking for an answer. "I thought I had to be going a lot faster to be speeding."

"Speeding? Speeding!"

"Alex wasn't speeding," Caroline explained. "Lester yells at him too much if he goes fast on his bike. Sometimes, when Alex's bike isn't broke like it is now, he might even race Lester. Then they both go fast. Alex doesn't ever do that on Lester's bike, 'cause Lester yells. Lester always wins when Alex races him too."

"Now see here, Young...."

"I think Lester's probably smarter too," Caroline continued, ignoring Pestergas's interruption, "I don't always say so, 'cause then Alex yells. So you see, Alex wouldn't never speed on Lester's bike. Can we go now? The Popsicles are getting melted."

"So, Young Lady," Pestergas growled, his voice a poor imitation of an angry poodle, "you want to go because your Popsicles are melting. I'll show you what to do about your melting Popsicles." He grabbed them out of her hand and threw them into the street.

"You're a mean man!" Caroline yelled.

"Why'd you do that?" Alex asked. "She didn't do anything to you! Even if we were speeding, she wasn't riding the bike. You don't need to be mean to her."

"You'd better watch your mouth," Pestergas warned, shaking a finger under Alex's nose, "and change your attitude. Now get in the car. You too, Young Lady. I'm going to show you two what we do with lawbreakers in Robbinsdale, Minnesota. After all, these are modern times, and if you delinquents can only learn the hard way, then that's the way we'll teach you."

"I didn't do anything," Alex said. "I wasn't speeding, and I didn't break any other laws either."

"You know very well that you did break the law, and it wasn't speeding. The law you broke was far more serious than speeding."

"I don't know what law you're talking about."

"Are you going to have the gall to stand there and try to tell me that you don't know it's against the law to ride double on a bicycle?"

"I wasn't riding double. I was only riding one bike."

"You were riding that little brat."

"I was not riding her. I was riding the bike. She was just on it with me. Besides, she isn't a little brat. She's my sister."

"I don't care what or who she is! Get in the car!"

"I can't get in a car with a man," Caroline told him. "My mom told me not to ever do that. She said men do nasty things in cars."

"I'm not a *man*!" Pestergas sputtered. "I am a police officer. And now *both* of you are under arrest."

"Are we going to jail?" Caroline asked, her tears increasing. "I don't want to go to jail."

"It definitely means exactly that," Pestergas smiled, "you are going to jail. If your parents don't want to teach you not to break the law and sass police officers, then I certainly will."

"You mean you're really going to take us to jail," Alex asked, "because I gave my sister a buck on my brothers bike? That's kind of dumb, isn't it?"

"Don't you ever call me dumb!" Pestergas screeched, raising his hand as if to hit Alex. It shook as he tried to control it. "Now get in my car. I've had enough of this. What you did *is* against the law."

He put Alex in the back seat and Caroline in front. She huddled as close to the door as she could. Pestergas dumped the bicycle into the trunk of the car, then slammed the lid down hard. Alex shuddered, thinking about all the additional scratches on the bicycle, sure that if he ever got out of jail, Lester was going to kill him.

But Alex was wrong, because when he was free again, Lester surprised him by being mad at Pestergas Hunter.

"Boy," Lester said while examining his bicycle, "I'm going to get that guy. "There's scratches all over the place. Dad should have killed that guy, instead of only yelling at him."

"He told Hunter to leave us alone."

"Didn't Dad call him any names?

"Dad was yelling so loud I couldn't hardly tell what he was saying, but Dad said something funny to Hunter."

"What was it?"

"I can't remember exactly what Dad said. It was about cutting something of Hunter's off, then stuffing it down his throat."

"What was so funny about that?"

"'Cause when Dad said it, Hunter jerked away from Dad, and he wouldn't stand by Dad again. I don't think Hunter will be mean to us now. He seemed scared of Dad."

"I don't care if he isn't mean to us, Alex. I'm going to get him anyway. Dad didn't do enough to him. He scratched my bike. He should have to buy me a new one."

"We could scratch his police car."

"We should do a lot more than that to him. He made Caroline cry too."

"We make Caroline cry sometimes."

"Alex, sometimes you're so stupid I can't stand it. It's different when we make our sister cry. We're her brothers. He's a cop and cops ain't supposed to do things like that. So no matter what, I'm gonna get that Hunter."

Chapter 2

Alex's best friend, Quick Chase, came over a short time after Alex was released from jail.

He was wearing a sweatshirt, dyed a splotchy orange, jeans bleached almost white, with orange lightning bolts sewn to the sides of the legs, and a blue beach towel, tied around his neck and hanging down his back.

It wasn't unusual for him to be wearing something weird. He loved to dress in costumes and his mother was an excellent seamstress, so he frequently did. They seemed to go along with his name, which he explained to Alex when they first met.

"My name is Quick Chase," he told Alex.

"How'd you ever get a name like Quick-Chase?"

"I have a special name. It is a very good name given to me by my mother."

"Why is it special?"

"Because I was named after the special way I was born."

"What way was that, Quick-Chase? My mom told me that there's only one way to be born. She said it hurts too."

"I am not so sure she is right. My mother has told me the story many times. I was born because one time when I was not born yet, my father gave my mother a quick chase around the house. He caught her, and it was very much the wrong time. So then, I got to be born."

"That doesn't make any sense, Quick-Chase."

"What does, when you live with grown-ups?"

"Why does your dad chasing your mom have anything to do with being born?"

"My mother said it is because we are Catholic."

"I don't get it. Catholic is just a church."

"I do not know why it is Catholic either. She did name me Quick Chase though, and it is a good and special name."

"What's your last name, Quick-Chase?"

"Quick is my first name and the name my mother gave me. We already had the name Chase."

"Did you ever ask your mother what the story she tells you about your name really means?"

"I have asked her many times. She only laughs, then tells me I am too young to understand. She always tells me I will know what it means when I grow up. I believe her and so can you."

Alex still wasn't sure the story was true, only that it sounded like a story Quick Chase would tell.

"I am an atomic war hero today," said Quick Chase, who was called Quicker by all of his friends, about his current costume.

"What are you, Quicker?" Alex asked, wondering what he'd thought up this time.

"I am an Atomic man. I am a war hero. I was blown up by an atomic bomb. It made me a war hero and a crime fighter. I am stronger than superman."

"Where did you get this idea, Quicker? I've never heard of an Atomic Man."

"Alex, do you never read comic books?"

"Only when I've got enough money to buy them. In the summer, I spend most of my money on ice cream and Popsicles. That's what Caroline and I were doing when that cop arrested us."

"What cop?"

"The new juvenile officer. He arrests kids who give someone a buck on their bike."

"He sounds stupid. I should zap him with my atomic sword."

"What's an atomic sword, Quicker?" Alex asked, even though he knew the answer was going to be a made-up story. When Quicker explained things, it usually was one of his stories.

"They work like bombs do nowadays. Atomic bombs are what we used to win the war with."

"I thought we won the war by fighting with Germans and Japanese."

"We did fight with those Germans. That is for sure true. But we beat the Japanese with atomic bombs. Fighting them helped, then we really got them with the atomic bomb. Atomic bombs are very, very powerful bombs."

"I know that, but we dropped a lot of bombs during the war. My dad was one of the guys who dropped them, remember?"

"Your father probably doesn't know much about the atomic bombs though."

"He does too. He learned about them in the army."

"When I go in the army, I am probably going to be an atomic soldier."

"How do you get to be one of them?"

"You go where they blew up an atomic bomb. All the radiation it makes falls on you, and that makes you super strong."

"I thought it killed you."

"Not always. Sometimes it changes your muscles in a way that makes them get really strong."

"That doesn't make any sense, Quicker."

"Yes it does, you see, because it seems as though radiation can change your muscles with special rays. They are called gamey and batty rays."

"Quicker, I know for sure now, that you're just making up some new words."

"No, Alex, I am not. My father said that someday all the electricity and stuff like that, in the whole world, will be made out of atomic stuff. He says that atomics are good, not bad the way some dummies say. He knows all about everything, because he sells insurance."

"I bet if they do that," Alex said, wondering how anyone could think up such nonsense, "we'll get blown up when we turn on the lights."

"No, Alex, I do not think that will happen."

"Why not? If the atomic bomb blew up enough in Japan to win the war, why won't they blow us up? I bet what happened to Japan was, some guy went and turned on the lights."

"No, that is not what happened. We blew up Japan by dropping atomic bombs on them. They use a different kind of atomics to make electricity."

"Maybe they might, Quicker, but I'm not going to be the first one to turn on the lights when they use atomic stuff to make electricity."

"My dad said that pretty soon we will have atomic refrigerators big enough to keep a whole house cool all summer. That's how good atomics will work."

"I don't believe you. Even if there is, it won't do us any good." Alex frowned. "We don't even have a regular refrigerator yet. All we have is an icebox. I bet we aren't ever gonna be rich enough to get a refrigerator. So we aren't ever gonna have a refrigerator for our whole house."

Just then, the boys heard a familiar sound. The iceman was driving past.

"Come on, Quicker," Alex said, "let's get some ice when he stops."

"Okay!"

As soon as the iceman took a block of ice out of the truck and carried it into Alex's house, they climbed into the back of it. As always, there were a lot of small pieces of ice scattered on the floor. They grabbed several of them and scurried out. The iceman yelled at them and they ran down the street. Quick Chase was sure he looked great with his towel-cape streaming out behind him.

They didn't run far. They knew the iceman wouldn't chase them, even though they never saw the grin he always had when he yelled. They didn't know that he considered it to be a normal part of life for kids to take the wasted pieces of ice in the truck. He'd done it himself as a child. He only yelled because it made getting the ice an adventure for them.

"This sure is good ice," Quick Chase said.

"It is," Alex agreed. "Sometimes I think it's almost as good as a Popsicle."

"One thing I know for sure. It is a lot better than the ice we get out of our refrigerator."

"Yeah, well at least you can get ice any time you want some. I wish we had a real refrigerator so I could do that."

"You have ice in your icebox, Alex. Ice which is the same as this good ice. Are you not allowed to have some of that good ice when you want it?"

"No, not in the summer, and that's the only time I want it. My mom says that if we eat the ice, there won't be enough to keep the icebox cold until the iceman comes again. So she doesn't ever let us have any."

"Do not worry, Alex. I am sure the day will come when you have a refrigerator. I do not think it will be too long before everyone in the neighborhood has one."

"Golly, I really hope so."

Chapter 3

When Alex stopped in the house to get his baseball glove, his mom was on the phone. She looked upset, almost like she might cry.

"Who was that?" he asked when she hung up. He always worried when she got that look on her face.

"Your dad."

"Did he yell at you or something? You don't look too good."

"No, he didn't yell."

"What's wrong then?"

"He just heard from the National Guard. He's being called back into the service. He's going to be sent to Korea."

"Why does Dad have to be in this war too?" he asked.

"I don't know," Mom answered, her voice tired.

"Why are they making him go?"

"Because he's in the National Guard, and his unit's been called up. When they call up a guard unit, they usually take everyone who's in it."

"Why? It ain't fair. He helped beat the Germans, so that ought to be enough. He shouldn't have to fight any more wars."

"You're right. He shouldn't have to. He might anyway. They'll take anyone who's trained. Fair has nothing to do with it."

"Why are those guys making us fight another stupid war?"

"I don't know what this war is about, and I seriously doubt anyone else does either. It seems to me that wars get fought mostly because men like to fight them."

"Geez, I sure don't see why we're in a war again. It doesn't make any sense to me at all."

"It shouldn't, Alex, because war never makes any sense."

"Why does everyone keep on having them then?"

"Alex, I just don't know the answer to that. I don't know the answers to any of your questions. So please don't ask me another one. I've got enough to worry about right now, without trying to answer them."

"But, Mom......"

"Please, Alex, stop now. I'm too tired, too worried, and way too scared for any more of this. Go outside or something."

"Ah, you aren't scared, Mom. Grown-ups don't ever get scared."

"Where did you ever get that idea, Alex?" She shook her head and stared at the ceiling for a moment. "Grown-ups get scared all the time, just like kids do. Growing up doesn't stop all your fears."

"Why are you scared, Mom?"

"Right now, if your dad does go, how am I going to take care of you kids? How am I going to pay the bills? We probably won't be able to keep this house. Where are we going to live if we can't keep it?"

"We can move to the farm with Grandma and Grandpa."

"That's out of the question. They're too old to be able to cope with all of us. I'm not about to live in the country. I grew up there. That's enough."

"Gee, Mom, why......"

"No more of that, Alex. Just tell me, if you can, what we will do if your dad goes to this war and gets wounded, or even killed. That's what scares me the most."

"I suppose we won't ever be getting a refrigerator now." Alex didn't like to see things change, but a refrigerator was one thing he really wanted.

"What?"

"Does Dad having to go to the war mean we won't be getting a refrigerator?"

"Is that all you're worried about, Alex?"

"I'm not worried about it. I was just wondering."

"Alex, I told you we might lose this house. How would I know about a refrigerator? All I know now is that your dad might have to go to Korea."

"Where is Korea?"

"It's next to China, and not far from Japan."

"Does it mean we're fighting with them Japs again?"

"No, we're fighting North Korea. And don't call them Japs. They're Japanese."

"They used to be Japs."

"Only when they were at war with us. The war with them is over, and they're our friends now."

"That's stupid. First they bomb us, then they get to be our friends. Who are those North Koreans?"

"They're the Koreans who live in the northern half of Korea. They attacked South Korea, so we're helping the people of South Korea."

"Why'd the north guys do that? They're the same kind of people, aren't they?"

"In our Civil War, Alex, we were all Americans, and it didn't do a thing to stop the killing."

"We were trying to free the slaves. So why are we fighting there? Do the Korea guys have slaves?"

"No, the North Koreans are Communists, and they want all of Korea to be Communist."

"Those damn Communists are always causing trouble, aren't they?"

"Watch your mouth, Alex, unless you want it washed out with soap. One more word like that is all it's going to take."

"I'm sorry, Mom, I didn't mean to say it. Only those guys make me so darn mad. They're always causing trouble, and now we're not getting a refrigerator, just 'cause they started a war. I hate them da......darn Communists."

"Careful, Alex."

"Ah, heck. Okay, Mom. I sure hope Dad doesn't have to be in this war."

"So do I, Alex. Why don't you go out and play now?"

"It isn't gonna be any fun playing, when I know we aren't gonna get a refrigerator."

"Your play, Alex, will be the same, whether or not we get one. You should be careful too, about what you wish for. Sometimes when you get what you want, it turns out to be something different than what you thought you wanted."

Alex wondered as he walked to the park, how something he wished for could turn out to be something he didn't want.

He found the neighborhood kids at the only baseball field in the park. They were arguing with some older kids from the next block over about who was going to use the field. Ralph Bradley, the oldest and biggest kid there, was the leader of the other group.

"Ain't no way," he said, "I'm gonna let you brats play here today. We're gonna use the field."

"But we were here first," Lester argued.

"Tough!"

"I have an idea," Quicker suggested. He was wearing the baseball uniform his mother made for him.

"What's that, stupid?" Ralph asked.

"Well, simply this. We do not have enough kids for two teams and neither do you. We should choose up sides, then we can all play and have a real game."

"We could do that," Ralph said, a smirk on his face, "but we ain't gonna. The only way I'll let you guys play, is us against you."

"That will not be a fair game. All of you are older and bigger than us."

"Maybe," Ralph smirked. He liked to beat smaller kids. "But it's the only way you're gonna play any ball today."

"Let's go home," Lester said. "We'll play tomorrow."

"Not if we want to, Stupid," Ralph said.

"I think we should play them," Quicker said. "So what if we lose."

"I suppose we might as well," Lester agreed.

Ralph took his team aside to tell everyone where they were going to play. Lester did the same with his team. After he picked the first eight positions, he had three kids left. Caroline, one of her friends, and Alex. Lester hesitated a moment before settling on Alex.

"I guess you are going to play right field, Alex," he said.

"I don't want to play at all," Alex argued. "Besides, right field is too far to throw the ball, and I can't catch fly balls. Let Caroline play. She's better than me anyway."

"I keep telling you, Alex," Lester said, "you got to play all the time, and learn how to keep your eye on the ball. Then you'll be able to catch them. So play. Ralph plays too rough for little girls."

"That is right, Alex," Quicker added.

"Sally and Marsha are playing."

"That is different. They're as old as us."

"I'm not good enough to play against those guys."

"You should practice and play more, then you would be. It does not matter. We are going to lose anyway."

"I don't want to practice and I don't want to play. I'm going home."

"Ah, dog-gone it, Alex," Lester argued, "I want you to play."

Alex hesitated a moment before answering. "Well," he finally agreed, "okay, I guess I'll play." He did it, only to please his brother.

Two innings were played before Alex got a chance to do anything. His first play was a low fly ball, which he missed. When he picked it up, he threw toward second base, where the base runner was headed. The throw was way off and flew by the second baseman. The pitcher picked it up in the infield. He threw the runner out when he tried to turn his sure double into a triple. Ralph Bradley cursed the runner when he left the field.

"That was one real smart play, Alex," Quicker told him on their way in, when the inning was over. "It was real good thinking, throwing the ball to the pitcher instead of second base. It was a good throw too. The runner would have stopped at second and had a double, if you would not have fooled him."

"Oh yeah," Alex answered, not bothering to tell him that his clever play was only a bad throw.

"Does your dad have to go and fight in the war in Korea?" Alex asked Quicker, while they waited to bat.

"No, of course not. He is way too valuable to be sent to war. He sells insurance."

"I sure wish my dad was doing something special, 'cause he has to go. If he does, we ain't ever gonna get a new refrigerator."

"Oh, that is too bad, Alex."

The players in the outfield always relaxed when Alex went up to bat. They knew there was little chance of him hitting the ball out of the infield. It was the bottom of the seventh inning when they paid for it.

The first two pitches to him were slow, high, and outside. He swung at both of them and missed. He hesitated on the third pitch, then swung the bat late, hitting the ball hard. The line drive stayed on the right field line, barely over the first baseman's glove. It landed fair and rolled deep into right field. The right fielder didn't expect Alex to hit anything, much less to right field, so he was way out of position.

Alex ran all the way to second base before looking for the ball. The right fielder was picking it up, so he ran for third base and Quicker him waved home.

"Slide, slide, slide!" Lester yelled as Alex raced for home.

Alex didn't want to slide. Sliding hurt. But the infield was rough and he tripped in a rut as he neared the plate. The fall sent him into a headfirst dive, and he came in under the catcher's tag.

"Great hit, Alex!" Lester yelled. "Great slide too! You sure are playing good baseball today."

Alex didn't argue as his team pounded him on the back. He was more concerned about his skinned-up hands and how much they hurt.

At the top of the eighth inning, Ralph Bradley's team was ahead by three runs. The first batter hit a fly ball to left field and was out. Ralph followed and singled to center. The next batter was the left-handed hitter Alex feared. He moved around in right field until his team quit yelling at him to move to a better position. The center and left fielders moved as far toward right field as they dared.

The first pitch was a ball. The second was hit, a high fly to right field. Alex constantly shifted his position, trying to keep his eyes on the ball while he tried to figure out where it was going. He was sure he would miss it, and get hit on the head the way he usually did. He hated fly balls. They always hurt when they hit him on the head.

When he finally decided where the ball was going, he knew it would land behind him. He turned so his back was to the ball, and with his gloved hand outstretched, he dove toward the spot the ball was headed for. It landed in his glove. The sensation of having it land there and not on his head was shocking, but he got up quickly. An equally shocked Ralph was almost to third base, so Alex's throw to first got there way ahead of Ralph, even if it did bounce a couple of times before it was caught. Alex had a double play and the side was out.

"That was a real heads-up play, Alex," Quicker told him. "It was great ball playing."

"I'm just trying, Quicker, and being lucky too," Alex answered, glad he'd accidentally caught the ball. "I sure wish my dad didn't have to go in the war. I bet we'll never get a refrigerator now."

"Why on earth, Alex, are you worrying about a refrigerator when you are playing terrific baseball?"

"Because I want us to get a refrigerator."

"I would much rather play good ball, than have a refrigerator. Baseball is far more important than any refrigerator could possibly be."

Lester joined them and slapped Alex on the back. "Great play," he said. "From now on, you're always gonna be on my team."

Alex smiled, knowing he'd gotten a real compliment if Lester gave it.

Quicker's team scored two runs in the bottom of the eighth inning, so they were within one run of a tie. They managed, barely, to keep Ralph's team from scoring in the top of the ninth. Alex was up first in the bottom of the ninth. He hit a bloop single over the second baseman.

The next batter hit a long, high fly ball to left, where Ralph played. Everyone on Alex's team was yelling at him to run, thinking the ball wouldn't be caught. Alex wasn't so sure, and didn't want to make an out like he usually did, so fear held him on first base. Even the batter who hit the ball was screaming at him to run. Alex still refused. Ralph made a running dive at the ball and caught it in the webbing of his glove. Alex tagged first and ran to second. Ralph was back on his feet and pulling the ball from his glove. Alex knew he had a chance to make it to third, but decided to stay where he was. Ralph's throw to third base was a perfect strike, and would have easily gotten Alex out had he run.

The next batter struck out, and Alex tried to remember what he should do with two out. Not sure, he decided to run if the next batter took a swing at the ball. It seemed like the logical thing to do. He took a big lead on the first pitch. The catcher noticed, and knew he'd throw Alex out if he tried to steal third base.

The batter swung on the next pitch and missed. Alex made a tentative move toward third, and the catcher rifled the ball down there. Alex dived back to second. He got up and took an even bigger lead. The catcher grinned, knowing Alex was going to be an easy out. He was too slow to make it to third. The batter swung and missed and Alex started toward third, then changed his mind. He tripped as he tried to change directions. His fall caught the catcher's eye as he threw to third, and the ball flew off to the right of the third baseman. Alex was up and on third base before they could make a play on him.

The catcher turned his back on the pitcher, kicking the ground, disgusted with himself. Alex took a big lead off third, and the pitcher threw the pitch high and wide. The catcher rifled the ball to third, forcing Alex into a headlong dive to make it back.

His hands were really hurting now, so he took a shorter lead. He didn't want to do any more dives. All he wanted was to have the batter get a solid hit, so he didn't have to make any decisions about what to do. All he would have to do then is run for home.

The next pitch crossed the middle of the plate, and the batter swung and missed. The catcher, who was keeping one eye on Alex, missed the ball. It rolled toward the backstop. Not knowing what else to do, Alex ran for home. He reached home plate behind the pitcher, who was as confused as Alex, and forgot to tag him when he caught the ball from the catcher. Alex slid home safe. The pitcher's throw to first was late, because in his confusion, he forgot the batter could run on the third strike if the catcher misses or drops the ball. The runner was safe, and the score was tied.

Alex was suddenly a big hero who didn't care. His last slide was feet first, and now there was some skin missing on his thigh. He ignored the adulation, shaking his hands as he limped in circles, trying to ease the pain.

He didn't want to be a hero. It hurt too much. All he wanted was a refrigerator.

While his team cheered, Ralph's team yelled at each other, with Ralph yelling the loudest. They were upset and shaken from the turn of events. A definitely inferior team, with the worst right fielder in the neighborhood, had tied the game. And the right fielder was responsible. Even so, they were still sure they'd win.

The next batter was going to be almost as easy an out as Alex was supposed to be. The only reason Marsha batted second in the lineup, was because she owned the catcher's equipment. The first two pitches were low and inside. She swung at both and missed. The rest of her team, except Alex, who wanted very badly for the game to be over, picked up their gloves, ready to go out in the field. They were sure the game was about to go into extra innings.

The pitcher was every bit as sure as they were, and didn't put anything on his last pitch. The batter put everything she had into her swing, and from the sound of the bat when it made contact with the ball, they knew there was no point in chasing it. The batter did that when she finished rounding the bases.

Alex was delighted to have the game over. He didn't want to get hurt again, and he knew he'd somehow screw up if it continued.

Ralph Bradley shook a finger at him and said, "I'm going to get you for this. You better watch out."

Alex knew he'd have to avoid Ralph for a while.

"Boy, Alex," Lester said on their way home, "you sure played good ball today. You played better'n most of the guys who play all the time, and I sure ain't never seen you do that before."

"No I didn't, Lester. I was just lucky."

"You were a lot more than lucky. You did some real smart base running. Pretending to fall down was the best one. That really messed up their catcher. Catching that fly ball was great. The way you threw Ralph out was even better. I ain't ever seen anybody play a fly ball better'n that."

"I didn't do anything special. I don't think I'd of got Ralph out, if he wouldn't of thought I couldn't catch the ball."

"It doesn't matter. You still played it perfect. I bet the kids won't pick you last, the next time we play."

"I hope they do. They don't yell so much when you do something wrong, if you're picked last. I don't really care about it right now though. I just wish we'd get a refrigerator."

"Ah, I don't think Dad's going to really go to the war this time. He doesn't want to go. In the last war, he wanted to."

"I bet he does want to go. Then he can be a hero."

"No, I don't think so. Being a hero in a war ain't so much fun as it is in baseball."

"It ain't much fun being a hero in baseball either."

"It is too. I'd sure like to play as good every time, as you did today."

"You go ahead and play like that all the time. You can be the hero. I don't want to. My hands hurt too much."

When they went inside the house, they were warned not to ask any questions if they wanted to stay there. Lester went back outside and Alex went upstairs to his room. He spent the rest of the afternoon reading comic books. He didn't want to take a chance on going outside again. Some fool might organize another game. Like, God forbid, football maybe.

He didn't go downstairs until he was called for supper.

Chapter 4

Alex and Lester went out after supper, and stayed out late to complete a particularly hard game of pump-pump-pull-away. They were on the way home and arguing loudly about who the biggest loser was when the nine o'clock curfew siren rang.

They didn't hear Pestergas Hunter's car creep up behind them and stop, with its headlights already turned off. He got out and closed the door quietly. He would have caught them if he hadn't wanted to scare them by yelling, "Stop You! Stop in the name of the law!"

The boys ran the instant they heard his voice, each in his own direction. Alex heard Pestergas's steps close behind him as he cut through a neighbor's yard. It was too dark to see much, but Alex was sure he would be caught with him so close. Then Pestergas stumbled and fell over a back yard picket fence. It gave way under his heavy weight, and Alex scrambled over it. As he ran, he heard Pestergas curse as he struggled to free himself from the fence.

Alex ran to the end of the alley, cut through another yard, then out into the street again. Lester crawled out from under a hedge to greet him. "Where's Hunter?" he asked.

"He's stuck on Bissel's fence. He fell on it and broke it. I hope Mister Bissel gets him for doing it."

"He won't. Grown-ups never get cops."

"I sure wish we could get Hunter right now."

"His car's still here, Alex. Let's let the air out of his tires."

"Yeah, that's a better idea. Then he'll have to call a tow truck."

"Come on, we better hurry up."

Pestergas Hunter never guessed they would go back to his car, so he gave them a lot of time while he searched for them at the far end of the block.

While Alex let the air out of the tires, Lester checked the front door of the car. In his haste to arrest them, Pestergas had left it unlocked and the keys in the ignition.

"Hey, Alex," Lester whispered, "that nitwit left his keys in here."

"We probably better not steal it, Lester. Dad will get mad at us for that. Besides, the front tires are flat now."

"I don't want to steal it. We can take the keys though. It'll really fix him, 'cause then he'll for sure have to walk somewhere."

"If we take the keys, we should lock all the doors too."

"That's a good idea, Alex. Let's turn on the headlights too. Dad told me that leaving the lights on can run down the battery. And look at all those switches. Quick, lock all the other doors, then we'll turn on all the switches before we lock this door."

They were nearly home before they heard Pestergas scream, then swear, over the wail of the car's siren. They turned to watch him standing in the flashing red lights, trying to open the car doors. They cut through another yard, went down their alley, and into their house via the back door.

Their parents were outside in the front yard, as were most of the parents on the block, watching Hunter smash a car window to get inside it to turn off the lights and siren. Alex and Lester went outside through the front door.

"I think you boys better go to bed now," Dad said quietly. "It's getting late."

"Okay, Dad," they agreed, knowing it would be best not to argue.

They got ready for bed quickly, turned out the light, and looked out on the street from their open, upstairs bedroom window. Their parents were laughing, so they leaned close to the window, holding their breath as they strained to hear what was being said.

"Do you really think," Mom asked, "that it was our boys who did it to him?"

"One can only hope, Honey," Dad answered, laughing harder than ever. "One can only hope."

Chapter 5

After the incident with his car, Pestergas hunter became a regular visitor to the neighborhood. To escape his constant harassment, all the kids started riding their bicycles, so they had a decent chance of escaping him. Alex tried to fix his, but couldn't manage it on his own. He finally asked Lester, who was making one of his constant adjustments to his own bike, to help.

"Okay, but you got to bring it here. I'll help you when I'm done with mine."

Alex went out to the garage, got his bike, and wheeled it over to Lester.

"Alex," Lester said as he finished with his bike, "sometimes you gonna have to learn how to fix your own bicycle."

"I'm getting better at it. I just can't do it alone."

"I don't think you're getting any better at all. But all right, what's wrong with your bike? Mine's almost fixed."

"The chain won't stay on. I can't get it tight enough."

Caroline limped into the back yard before Lester could answer, dragging one leg behind her. She was wearing her roller skates, and one of them was popped loose from the toe of her shoe.

"Will one of you guys please tighten my skate for me?" she asked. "I can't never seem to get it tight enough."

"I'll do it," Alex said.

"Think you can?" Lester asked. "You can't do anything else right."

"Oh, Lester," Caroline giggled as Alex tightened her skate. "You talk so silly sometimes."

"Go roller skate, Caroline," Lester told her. He turned to Alex. "Now what's wrong with your bike?"

"I can't get the chain tight enough to stay on."

"I don't understand," Caroline said, "why you boys are always fixing those bikes. You should get roller skates. Then you could play, instead of always having to fix things. Roller skates are much better than bikes."

"Roller skates ain't no good for nothing," Lester growled. "They don't go fast enough to get away from Hunter. Sometimes bikes do."

"They're good, Lester. Roller skates are big bunches better than bikes. Bikes always break."

"Ah, Caroline," Alex said, "you only say that because you don't know how to fix your bike."

"I would never say they were better because I don't know how to fix my bike." She gave Alex her best smile. "Will you fix my bike for me?"

"What's wrong with it?"

"It's got a flat tire."

"Okay, go get it."

"Will you please get it for me. I can't push it so good with my roller skates on."

"Oh, all right, Caroline. As soon as I get my bike fixed."

"Go get her bike, Alex," Lester told him. "I'll see what's wrong with yours. Caroline, you go back out on the sidewalk and skate. It's hard enough for me to fix all these bikes, without having you hang around in the way."

"Okay, Lester."

"Yeah, Caroline, you'd better go skate. Lester's getting crabby."

"You'd be crabby too, Alex, if you had to fix three bikes every time. I sure wish I had an older brother to fix my bike."

"Gee," Caroline said, "he is crabby. I think I better go skate."

"Dad-rat it, Alex, get over here. I need help to get this damn chain tightened."

"What do you want me to do, Lester?" Alex asked.

"Pull on the back wheel."

"Which way?"

"Dad-crap it! Don't be so damn dumb! You pull it backwards. You ought to know that by now."

"I forgot, Lester," Alex said, pulling back on the wheel. "I thought you could adjust it."

"The adjustments don't work right. And dad-gum it, Alex, you got to pull a lot harder than that."

"I'm pulling as hard as I can."

"It sure as heck ain't hard enough. You got to pull the wheel far enough back to make the chain tight."

"I can't pull any harder."

"You got to."

"You pull it then, Lester. I can't pull any harder."

"Come here then, Alex. I'll pull on the back wheel. When the chain gets tight, you tighten the nuts. Let's get this bike of yours fixed, so I can go riding."

"I want to go too. As soon as I fix the tire on Caroline's bike."

"It ain't my fault you told her you would."

"Yeah, I know, but girls can't do anything without us boys helping them."

"Girls can do lots of things," Lester said, grinning. "They just can't fix anything."

"Mom does though."

"That's different."

"I guess so. I wonder why she knows how."

"She's a grown-up, Alex. It's hard to know why grown-ups do what they do."

"Yeah, I think you might be right there."

"I'm going riding," Lester said as soon as Alex had the nuts on his bicycle tight.

"Will you help me fix the tire on Caroline's bike?"

"Fix it yourself. I'm real sick of fixing bikes. I'm going riding." Lester left.

Alex took Caroline's bike apart, repaired the tube, then went inside the house for something to eat.

Alex was on his way out of the house as Lester returned from his ride, got off his bike, and let it fall. He pushed Alex out of his way as he went inside. He was obviously upset about something, so Alex followed him in.

"What's wrong, Lester?" Alex asked.

"Ralph Bradley."

"What did he do?"

"He and one of his friends knocked me off my bike and beat me up."

"Why'd they do that?"

"Because we won the baseball game. He said he's gonna beat you up too. He's really mad that we won."

"That don't make no sense. It was just a baseball game. Why does he want to beat up on us?"

"I don't know. I guess he likes beating up kids smaller than he is. I ain't the only kid he ever beat up. You're gonna be lucky he if all he does is beat you up. He really hates you, because you played so good."

"I'll try to stay away from him. I sure wish I was bigger, 'cause I'd like to beat the heck out of him."

"You better not ever try, Alex. He's much bigger than you, and he'd really mangle you."

"Maybe me and you should catch him and beat him up together. He sure isn't bigger than both of us."

"Naw, I don't think so. He'll get more of his friends and then they'll all beat on us. All of them are older and bigger than we are."

"Then what are we gonna do, Lester?"

"There's nothing we can do. We just got to not let him catch us."

"How're we gonna that, Lester? He can run faster than us, ride his bike faster, and do just about everything else faster. I think the only way we can keep away from him is to stay in the house all the time. Even if we do, he'll get us at school."

"I ain't gonna stay in the house. I'm gonna try to think of something to make him stop."

"Well, you better hurry up, Lester, or else we're gonna get clobbered one of these days."

"Maybe, but I want you to get out of here and leave me alone. I'm trying to think of what to do."

Alex left Lester, rode his bicycle over to Quicker's house, and from there the two of them went riding. A few blocks from home they passed Ralph Bradley riding his bike the other way. Ralph turned around and caught up with them.

"Hi there, Chicken's little brother," he said to Alex. "What do you think you're doing?"

"I'm riding my bike," Alex answered, trying not to look at him. "What does it look like I'm doing?"

"It looks like you're gonna wet your pants, you're so scared." Ralph laughed at his own joke. "It's like this, you chicken kid, I don't want you riding no bike around here. This here is my street. You better go home and stay in your yard with your chicken brother. I don't like you guys."

"You don't own this street, Fatso," Alex answered, feeling almost as much anger as fear. "I'm riding my bike anywhere I want to."

"If you don't do what I tell you to do, I'm gonna beat the hell out of you, just like I did to your chicken brother."

"I don't like you either, so go jump in the lake."

Ralph suddenly reached out and pushed Alex over. He got up, more angry now, then afraid.

"You ugly fatso pig!" Alex screamed as Quicker raced away.

Ralph jumped off his bike, then slammed his foot through the spokes of the front wheel on Alex's bike. "That's what I do to baby chickens," he said, a big smile on his face.

"You damn rat," Alex threatened, "we're gonna get you."

"You ain't gonna get nobody. I'm gonna pound your face into mush for saying that."

Alex backed away.

"Stand still," Ralph laughed. "You can't get away."

Alex stopped, terrified now of what was going to happen. Ralph moved in fast, his fists flying in all directions. One of them managed to find Alex's face and he went down. Ralph danced and jumped like a boxer, letting Alex lay there. He rolled away, wiping a hand across his face as he got up. He looked at the blood on his hand and it made him furious. He charged blindly with both hands swinging wildly. Ralph was so surprised by the move that he hesitated. Alex caught him on his chin with a lucky, although solid, right hand, staggering the bigger kid.

Alex moved in again and they stood toe to toe, trading punches. Ralph's fists landed more often than Alex's, but he didn't know what to do with him. He'd terrorized smaller kids for a long time, and this was the first time one ever fought back, and seemingly without fear. Ralph slowly began backing away as Alex continued to press him. The blows Ralph's weakening arms landed had no effect on Alex, other than make him angrier and more determined. Finally, Ralph tried to wrestle Alex to the ground, but before he could manage it, Quicker returned with Lester. Ralph turned tail and rode off at top speed.

"Where are you going, you damn chicken?!" Alex screamed at him.

Lester studied Alex, somewhat awe-struck. "Were you really fighting him, Alex?" he asked.

"You bet, and next time, I'm going to get him. I'm going to beat him good."

"We'll get him, Alex," Lester promised. "We'll for sure get him. He can't be beating my brother up."

"Gee whiz, you guys," Quicker said. "I do not think you should try to get him. I think you should stay away from him. I think all of us should stay away from him. He is very much too tough for us."

"You stay away from him, Quicker," Alex said quietly, "if you want to. Me and Lester are going to get that guy. He ain't really so tough as you think he is. He's beating us up just because we won the baseball game, and because we're smaller than he is. Me and Lester together are tougher than him, and we're gonna get him."

"That's right," Lester agreed. We're for sure gonna get that guy."

They spent the rest of the day trying to decide what would be the best way to get Ralph, but hadn't made any definite plans when they went to bed that night.

Chapter 6

Life changed for Alex after the incident with Ralph Bradley. Quicker was sent out of state to visit some relatives while his parents went on vacation. Pestergas Hunter continued his regular patrols through the neighborhood, arresting kids for the slightest provocation, and Ralph tried to catch and beat up anyone who played against him in the baseball game.

Alex felt dejected and alone, and even the new family moving in across the street didn't give him much hope that he'd have anything new to do.

He watched them from the curb on his side of the street, hoping they'd have a boy close enough to his age to give him someone to play with. He was sure a girl, if they had one, wouldn't want to do anything with him. Girls always liked Lester and the other older boys better than they liked him. Besides, girls giggled too much. Almost all the time it seemed.

As he thought about all the fun things he'd do if they did have a boy, the family arrived in a new Buick convertible. The only child with them was a girl. She was close to his age, but she was still a girl. He was disappointed, though not surprised. Very little, he was sure, would ever turn out the way he wanted it to.

He hated the new people for having a girl rather than a boy, and he sat glaring at their house for quite a while. When he was ready to leave and go inside his own house the girl came outside. She crossed the street, stopping in front of him.

Alex looked up at her, immediately noticing how her small nose wrinkled at the top of her smile, how shiny her red hair was, and how it seemed to sway gently when she moved her head. Most of all, he noticed her penetrating green eyes, staring directly into his. Boys did that sometimes. Girls never did.

"Hi," she said, keeping her smile, "I'm Darlene."

"Hi. I'm Alex," he answered, "and I live here." He pointed to his house, small in comparison to the one she moved into.

"Your cute, Alex, and I like cute boys. Are you busy doing anything?"

"No."

"Good. Do you want to go over to that house they're building at the end of the block? I'll bet the carpenters are going home soon. It's fun to climb around inside them."

"Sure." What else could he say to a girl who called him cute? No other girls called him cute. Besides, she wanted to climb around in the new houses. Girls didn't do that. Not the girls, anyway, as pretty as Darlene.

As they started down the block, Lester came out and joined them. "Where are you going, Alex?" he asked.

"Over to the new house." Alex didn't want Lester around. Not until he and Darlene were friends first.

"Who are you?" Darlene asked Lester. Alex was sure she was interested in him now.

"I'm his older brother, Lester."

"Hi, Lester. I'm Darlene. I just moved in."

"Oh, nice to meet you, Darlene. What're you guys gonna do at the new house?"

"Climb around after the carpenters go home," Darlene told him. "Want to come along?"

"Naw, I never do that stuff anymore."

"Okay, Lester," she said, taking Alex's hand. "We'll be seeing you."

"Why are you going over there with him?" Lester asked, trying to give her what he considered his most charming smile, "Playing around in new houses is kid stuff. There are a lot of things you could do with me that are more fun, Darlene."

"We know it's kid stuff to play in those houses," Darlene said. "But Alex and I are kids. So goodbye, Lester." She led Alex away.

Alex couldn't believe what happened. Girls didn't choose him over Lester. Most girls wouldn't even talk to him after they met Lester. Having her hold his hand was nice too.

As soon as the carpenters picked up their tools and left, they went inside the house. The carpenters had completed the roof framing, but hadn't nailed the roof sheeting on yet.

"Let's climb up there," she said, pointing at the rafters, "and swing on those suckers."

Alex loved climbing around new houses, and swinging from floor and ceiling joists, but not rafters. Rafters were too high.

"I don't want to go all the way up there," he said.

"How come?"

"They're way too high. I'm not so good at climbing. I always feel like I'm going to fall when I get up there."

"Come on, Alex, we won't fall."

"But..."

She left him standing in the middle of the floor, and started working her way up the angled bracing on the back wall. From there she pulled herself onto the ceiling joists, and then half walked, half crawled up the rafters to the peak of the roof.

"See, Alex," she said, "it isn't hard."

He was scared all the way up, but even more afraid of not going up. She might not like him if he didn't.

"See," she said when he got to the top, "I said it wasn't hard."

"Right."

"It's nice up here. Sit down and relax."

Carefully, he sat down facing her, his legs straddling the roof ridge, the way hers did. He was grateful he didn't have to continue standing.

"You're brave, Alex," she said, smiling.

He felt his chest swell. "So are you."

"No I'm not. I'd never do anything that scares me. Not the way you just did."

"I'm not real scared."

"It's okay. I don't care if you're scared. You're even cuter when you are."

Alex smiled, then slipped a leg over the ridge board, and holding one of the rafters with both hands, slid free of the ridge. He moved hand over hand down the rafters until his feet reached the ceiling joists. He waited until Darlene came down, then climbed back up to the ridge and down again.

They continued climbing around inside the house until it was time to go home for supper.

"Can you go out after supper?" she asked when they got home.

"Sure."

"Come over and get me then. We'll play some more."

"Okay!"

Alex ate as fast as he could, then went back outside. Lester went out with him.

"Where are you going, Alex?" Lester asked.

"Over to Darlene's."

"Mind if I go with you?"

"No," Alex answered, surprised Lester bothered to ask. He usually didn't ask Alex anything like that.

Darlene was sitting on her front steps, waiting for Alex. "Let's steal some apples," she said. "I haven't done it for a long time. I bet you know where to steal some, don't you, Alex?"

"Sure, I know a lot of places," he said, pleased she asked him and not Lester.

As they walked, Lester tried to take Darlene's hand. She pulled away and moved closer to Alex. He glowed.

As they passed a small, white house on Alex's side of the block, Darlene stopped them. "They've got apple trees there, in the back yard," she said. "Why don't we go get some of them?"

"We can't steal apples there," Lester explained. "Old man Foster will call the cops if you mess around in his yard. Then we'll have Hunter around again, trying to arrest us."

"Who's Hunter?"

Alex told her about Pestergas.

"If we're careful, he probably won't catch us," Darlene said.

"I ain't going in his yard," Lester complained. "I'm not in the mood to go to jail tonight."

"That's okay, Lester, you go home. Alex will go with me. He's brave."

"You ain't going in his yard, are you, Alex? Dad'll get mad if you get arrested."

"Well," Alex said, deciding he'd rather get arrested than disappoint Darlene, "if Darlene is going to steal those apples, so am I."

"You're nuts, Alex."

"You're always saying that, Lester, when you aren't saying I'm dumb or chicken."

"Well you are, most of the time."

"Don't pay any attention to him, Alex," Darlene said. "We'll show him how brave you are."

Darlene led the way through a neighbor's yard, to the alley behind the house. They were careful to stay in the bushes as they crept up to the back fence. She climbed it first, with Alex right behind her. He went up the tree first. They filled their pockets, and were down and out of there quickly, without incident.

Alex took her to a secret place in the lilac bushes to eat the apples. They each ate a couple, then stashed the rest for the next day.

"I think you and I will be good friends, Alex," she said. "You're not like other boys, always grabbing at me."

"Why would I grab at you?"

"You know, to touch me where you're not supposed to."

Alex shook his head in disgust. "Course I won't. Where ain't I supposed to?"

"You know, here and here."

"I only did that when I was little. When we used to play doctor."

Darlene laughed. "I think that was different, Alex. Little girls are different."

"I know. They don't have any chest."

"They're called breasts, Alex. Unless you're crude. Crude people call them boobs."

"I heard my dad call them that once. Mom got mad at him for using bad words in front of us kids."

"Well, it's not really a bad word, it's just crude."

"Either way, bad word or crude word, I won't grab them."

"Good. Not unless I decide I want you to, anyway. I think I better go home now. Mom likes to have me come in before dark. Will you walk with me?"

"Sure."

She took his hand again, on the walk to her house. Somehow it felt different this time. It gave him a slight twinge in his stomach, a chill up his back, and made him glow all over.

After she went in, he walked across the street to his house and sat on the front steps, watching the stars slowly appear in the night sky. They filled him with a sense of wonder, almost as much as holding Darlene's hand did.

Chapter 7

Alex was ready to go outside, anxious to go over to Darlene's, when the telephone rang. Mom was busy in the kitchen, so he answered it.

"Alex," Dad told him, "you're coming down here to get something for you kids."

"Can't Lester go?"

"No, you're the one I'm talking to, so you're coming. Don't argue, and let me talk to your mother now."

Alex called his mother to the phone and she talked to Dad for a few minutes. When she hung up, she gave Alex bus fare and told him to go to the corner to wait for it.

"How come Dad's got something for us?" Alex asked. "Is he going to Korea now?"

"No, that hasn't been decided yet. Now go, or you'll miss the bus."

The small grocery store Dad managed was in Minneapolis, on lower Broadway, near Washington Avenue. When he got there one of the cashiers, who was bagging potatoes, wiped off her hands and gave him a couple of ginger snaps from one of the bulk cookie jars.

"What am I supposed to get, Mrs. Rosengren?" he asked her.

"You have to go back and see your dad," she answered, grinning.

The article he was to pick up was sleeping in a cardboard box. She was a plump, yellow kitten with light brown stripes, who quickly taught Alex that it was futile to try to keep her head in the box. He rode on the bus, holding the cardboard box on his lap, with the kitten's head poking through the middle of the closed flaps. He didn't care about her head, only that everyone on the bus laughed when they saw her. He was embarrassed because he wasn't sure whether it was her or him, they laughed at. It was a great relief to get off the bus.

"Now that you have the kitten home," Mom said, "I think it would be a good idea for you to go outside and find your brother and sister. I'm sure they'd like to come home and see their new kitten."

"I guess they would, Mom."

"Okay."

As soon as Caroline saw the kitten, she scooped it up and hugged it tightly to her chest. She held on even tighter when it squirmed to get away. "I'm naming you Sunshine," she told the kitten.

"No you ain't," Lester argued. "That's a stupid name for a cat."

Caroline squeezed so hard the kitten could barely breath. When it couldn't get away any other way, it raked its claws across her hand. "Mean cat!" Caroline yelled, letting it jump free. "I ain't naming you nothing."

"She isn't mean, Caroline," Alex said. "You were hurting her."

"I don't care. I'm not going to name her. She can just be a dumb old no-name cat now."

"She's not going to be no no-name cat," Lester said. "I think she's tough, and she's gonna grow up to be tough and mean. Them are the kind of cats I like. So I'm naming her Tiger. She's even got stripes like a tiger."

"I don't want her to be named Tiger," Alex complained. "I went and got her so I get to name her. Her name's Misty."

"Alex," Lester said, "if you like that name, you're stupid. My cat's name is Tiger."

"It's my cat too," Caroline said. "So I'm gonna to name my cat No-Name. That's the best name for cats who scratch."

"Tiger is its name," Lester threatened. "If you guys don't like it, I'm gonna beat you up."

"If you beat me up, Lester," Caroline said, "I'll tell Mom on you. My cat's name is No-Name, because I want to name it that."

"I wish I didn't have nothing but brothers. Brothers are much more fun than sisters. You can beat up on brothers once in a while."

"If you beat me up, Lester, because I don't like your dumb cat name, I'm gonna tell Mom on you too."

"Boy, Alex, you're sure getting to be like no brother at all. I can't hardly ever beat up on you without you telling Mom on me."

"I'm still naming my cat......" And the debate over the kitten's name continued the rest of the day. When their father came home from work it still had three names and was a thoroughly confused kitten.

Each of the kids wanted to be the first to suggest their name for the kitten to their father, hoping he'd think it was the best. But none of them dared to say anything to him before supper.

As he always did, he sat down on his chair to read the paper while he waited for supper to be put on the table. This time the kitten climbed onto the chair, curled up on the newspaper in his lap, and started purring.

"Well," he said, "you really think you're some kind of duchess, don't you." He gently lifted the kitten from his lap and set her on the floor. "Now stay there, Duchess, until I finish reading the paper."

The kitten looked up as if it liked the name he called it, then curled up near his feet and purred itself to sleep. The kids heard an audible sigh from Mom. The kitten finally had a name, and it hadn't come from any of them.

Chapter 8

Lester had great hopes for Alex's ball playing following his big game, so he kept after him to practice and play more. He and Alex were out in the front yard, playing three corner catch with Darlene. Lester was trying to teach Alex how to keep his eye on the ball when it was thrown to him, when Caroline came out to watch.

She had her new camera along, but stuck her hand in her jacket pocket to touch her two extra rolls of film before she decided to take any pictures.

"Alex," she directed, "will you please try harder to catch the ball next time? I want to take a picture of you catching it with my new camera."

"I'm trying to catch the darn thing, Caroline," Alex answered, wishing everyone would quit worrying about the way he played baseball. "You know I'm not very good at catching. Take Lester's picture. He's the one who's good at catching."

"I already did," she explained. "I took Darlene's too. Taking their pictures was easy. Now I want to take yours. So stop making it so hard, and please catch the ball."

"What do you think I'm trying to do?"

Alex dropped the next three balls.

"Alex, pul-leeze stop it!" Caroline yelled. "How do you ever expect me to take your picture, when you keep on dropping the ball?"

"Ah, it's your fault. I keep forgetting to watch the ball when you point your camera at me. Take Lester's picture again. He likes to look at pictures of himself."

"I don't either, Alex," Lester argued, "so don't say I do."

"Sure you do, Lester."

"Alex, if you don't shut up about it, I'm going to pound you to a pulp."

"I want you guys to stop fighting right now!" Caroline instructed. "I'm trying to take pictures. Alex, you have to throw the ball real high to Lester, so I can take a picture of you throwing it. I'm going to take a different picture of Lester catching it. You must throw the ball high enough, so I can rewind my camera before the ball gets to Lester."

"Caroline, you know I can't throw the ball that high."

"Will you at least try, Alex? Please! For me? I am your sister, you know."

"Okay, I'll try."

Alex threw the ball as high as he could, and Caroline took a picture of him throwing. She didn't rewind the camera fast enough to take Lester's picture when he caught the ball.

"Well, Alex," she said, "you need to throw the ball again. You didn't throw that one very high. I still need to take a picture of Lester catching a ball you throw."

"You already got one of me throwing the ball, so let Darlene throw the one Lester catches. She throws much better than me."

"I know she does, Alex, but the picture must have Lester catching a ball you throw. The pictures will not be right, if Lester catches a ball Darlene throws."

"Why not? Lester will still be catching it."

"Will you please listen to me one time! The pictures simply will not be right that way, unless you are the person who threw the ball. So throw the dumb ball!"

"Okay, I'll throw the ball again. I'm not very good at it though."

"Everybody knows that, Alex, so you don't have to keep telling us. Please now, throw the darn ball."

Alex put everything he had into the next throw. The ball went up very high, in the general direction of Lester, then flew past him and into the street. It landed in the middle of the windshield of Pestergas Hunter's police car. The glass cracked and Pestergas stopped. He was angry when he got out of his car.

"Somebody's in real trouble now," he said, sticking out his chest, grabbing his pants, and hiking them up over his hips. "Yes sir-ree, this time there's real trouble. I've got evidence too," he pointed at his windshield, "right here on my car."

He grunted as he stooped down to pick up the ball. He flipped it in the air a couple of times, catching it with one hand, then grinned.

"And here's the rest of my evidence. All you kids with baseball gloves, come over here to my car. You're all under arrest for the destruction of police property."

"Mister fat policeman," Caroline said, "they didn't mean to break your window. Alex just doesn't throw so good."

"Young Lady," Pestergas growled, "you can't call me fat. I'm an officer of the law, so now you are under arrest too."

"No, I certainly am not!"

"What? What did you say? You can't say that! I arrested you. When I arrest you, you can only say what I tell you to say. I represent the law."

Caroline stuck out her tongue at him. "Run, Lester! Run, Alex! Run Darlene! I'm going to run too. My dad said we should never let you arrest us again. So there!" She stuck out her tongue one more time, then ran.

It took Pestergas a moment to decide Caroline would be the best kid to chase. She was the slowest, and the least dangerous. He caught her in the alley behind her house.

Alex was waiting near his police car when Pestergas returned, carrying a screaming and kicking Caroline on his shoulder.

"So, you returned to the scene of the crime, huh, Boy," Pestergas grunted, breathing heavily. "It's a good thing for you that you did. Now, I won't charge you with fleeing the scene of a crime, the way I will with those other two."

"You ain't charging me with a darn thing, you fat-faced dumbo," Alex told him. "All you're gonna do is let my sister go, and give her her camera back."

"Don't talk to me that way, Boy. I get angry when brats talk to me that way. You won't like me when I'm angry."

"Just put my sister down."

"You can't talk to me that way, with that tone of voice. I'm part of the law and I will not stand for it. You must get in the car now, because you're under arrest. We're taking a ride downtown to the station."

"I ain't under anything, Stupid. You left your keys in the car again. So you better put my sister down now, or I won't give them back to you."

"Oh no. Oh damn, I did forget them. What'd you mean, again? Oh my, I know who you are now. You're one of the brats who wrecked my car a while back. You are now in a lot of serious trouble." He dropped Caroline and reached for Alex. Caroline grabbed her camera and ran. Alex backed away.

"I've finally got you," Pestergas bragged. "You're in real serious trouble this time."

"You ain't got me and you ain't gonna get me either."

"Oh yes I have. I've got you good and you can't get away this time."

Alex kept one eye on Pestergas, and one eye on Caroline, as he backed away. When she was well down the street, and cutting through someone's yard, he ran.

It was close, with Pestergas right on his heels. When Alex could hear his heavy breathing, he ended the chase by throwing the cop's car keys into a neighbor's hedge.

Pestergas's mouth dropped open, then hung there as he stood gasping for air, wondering how a mere boy would dare to throw away police property. Was it any wonder the world was so rapidly going to hell?

The mere boy, who was more intelligent than Pestergas, continued running at top speed. Pestergas discontinued his pursuit. He was too winded to run any farther. Then he made another mistake, by resting before he looked for his car keys.

Darlene was hiding in the hedge and picked them up. Pestergas was so surprised to see Darlene get up and run that he didn't bother to chase her.

The kids met in their hideout in the Lilac bushes that ran between the alley and the highway. An old manhole there, with a loose cover, served as a perfect spot to hide the car keys.

When they told their parents about the happenings of the day, Lester, Alex, and Caroline were told to try stay away from Pestergas Hunter in the future. After, that is, they were assured the cop would never be allowed in the house to arrest them.

Darlene was confined to her house and yard for a week.

Pestergas Hunter was reprimanded by the police chief for damaging police property, and the cost of the windshield and new car keys were deducted from his pay. The judge Pestergas saw, to get an arrest warrant against the kids, refused to give him one. A few weeks before, Pestergas had arrested the judge's three-year old granddaughter for riding double on a tricycle with a four-year old.

Chapter 9

Quick Chase got a new puppy when he came home. Alex wanted one too, but his dad said no. Not right now. Not even after he promised to share it with Lester and Caroline.

"There's too much to worry about right now," Dad told him. "We still don't know whether or not I'm going to Korea, and your mother and I are worried about polio. We've got enough to do without having a puppy underfoot."

Alex tried not to worry about all that. He just hoped they wouldn't take his dad away, and he was sure polio was something other kids got. So far, none of the kids on his block had gotten it.

Instead, he was determined to have fun playing with Quicker's new puppy, Duke, even if he couldn't have one. He and Quicker and Darlene were going to take Duke out in the woods and play around the old apartment house ruins.

The ruins were never an apartment house. They were only the remains of a dream. A ten acre site where someone went broke trying to build apartment buildings. All that was left was a big hole in the ground, concrete footings, and part of a cement wall, much of which was knocked down over the years by the kids who played there.

To most adults, it looked like a worthless piece of wasteland, covered by sumac, spindly maple saplings, thorn bushes, and weeds.

To the kids who lived near it, it was a place of mystique and joy. If they tired of playing in the old apartment hole, there was a pond, commonly known as the swamp, deep enough to fish in. It was full of bullheads mostly, but fish none the less. It was even rumored over the years that, occasionally, some of the braver boys actually went swimming in it.

Alex left the house that morning wearing his favorite jeans, with holes in the knees, and a well worn shirt. He stopped in the kitchen on his way out of the house to grab a couple of apples and a piece of cheese out of the ice box.

"Alex," Mom asked, as he raced out the back door, "where are you going?"

"Me and Quicker and Darlene are taking Duke over to the ruins."

"Be home before supper."

"Okay, sure, I will, Mom. Bye."

Quicker was waiting for them when Alex and Darlene got to his house. He was wearing an old, wide brimmed hat, with an ostrich plume stuck in the hat band, a white shirt, and pants two sizes too big for him, which were dyed pink. A wooden sword was stuck in his belt.

"Why are you dressed like that, Quicker?" Darlene asked, giggling. She hadn't known Quicker long enough to be aware of his love of costumes.

"I am a Cavalier today, Darlene," he said. "I work for the King. I find bandits and cut their guts out with my sword. This is Duke, my trusty sidekick. He eats their guts."

"Why are you wearing that stuff, Quicker?" Alex asked. "I thought we were going over to the ruins with Duke."

"Alex, my friend, we are. That does not mean I must dress in rags as you two are. As a Cavalier I will have more fun. I shall run up and down the hills, through the woods, and around the swamp. I will be slicing up those bandits the whole time. Duke shall follow me to protect my back, and to eat the dead bandits."

Darlene giggled again.

"Sometimes I wonder about you, Quicker. Where'd you get them pants?"

"My kind mother made them for me. They are beautiful, are they not?"

"Sure they are, Quicker," Darlene told him, struggling not to laugh.

"Well....yeah, sure, they're great," Alex said, "but let's go."

"Yes, let us do that. Come, Duke, trusted sidekick."

Duke didn't care much about being a sidekick, trusted or not, but in his excitement to go somewhere, he tended to kick his heels high in the air as he ran down the street ahead of the boys.

"Duke sure is excited about going," Alex said.

"I am sure he is, Alex, his being a dog and all. It is one more reason why dogs are much better than cats. They go places with us. Cats do not do anything they do not want to do. So most of the time you cannot take them with you."

"I don't care," Darlene argued. "Cats are a lot more cuddly than dogs."

"You used to like cats, Quicker," Alex said.

"I was young then."

"You're still young, Quicker. It wasn't that long ago that you were trying to kill buses, because one of them killed your cat. You should have seen him, Darlene. He used to chase them and try to kill them with a stick."

Darlene giggled again, never doubting that Quicker would do that.

"That is true," Quicker said. "I still consider it at times."

"You wouldn't really?" Darlene asked.

"Possibly not."

"Probably is more like it," Alex said.

Duke stayed ahead of the boys all the way to the ruins. When they got there, he was chasing something around the bottom of the hole. The kids slipped and slid as they scurried down the steep banks. The animal Duke was chasing was gone when they reached the bottom.

"I wonder what he was after," Alex said.

"I do not know. I want to find it, so I can kill it with my sword."

"What do you want to kill it for?" Darlene asked, taking Quicker literally. "It's probably a squirrel or something. Whatever it was, it hasn't done anything to you."

"That might be true, but killing it will give me practice. I need practice with my sword to better defend us, and to do a more better job of killing all the bandits I chance to meet."

"All you need practice with, Quicker," Alex said, "is using your brain. I don't want to see you killing any animals either."

"I don't ever want to hear about you killing any animals," Darlene said. "Killing animals for no reason is mean thing to do."

"Oh, sometimes you guys get so serious. Of course, I will not go around killing any animals."

"That's good," Darlene said, "because in the woods, all animals are supposed to be here. We're not even supposed to hurt them, so you sure shouldn't be killing them."

"Let's go see what Duke's doing," Alex said.

They looked around for Duke. He was stalking something behind the crumbling, cement block wall. Suddenly, the something jumped out and dashed across the hole to the other side.

It was Alex's cat, Duchess. The boys went after her and caught her halfway up the bank, with Duke right behind them. Alex picked her up just before Duke got his mouth around her.

"No, Duke," Alex yelled, trying to hold onto his terrified cat, who was trying equally as hard to claw her way free. "Hang on to him, Quicker!"

Quicker grabbed one of Duke's long, drooping ears, using it as leverage to hold him off the cat.

"I got him now," Quicker said.

"What am I gonna do with Duchess?"

"Whatever it is you do, you better hurry up and do it. Or else Duke is going to get loose and eat her."

"I guess I'll have to let her go."

Alex dropped Duchess and she ran off into the brush. Later, she showed up again as a yellow blur streaking by them. Duke immediately took up the chase, barking constantly as he and the cat tore up and down the banks, through the rubble, and around the ruins.

"I sure hope he does not catch her," Quicker said. "He will hurt her for sure if he does."

"I don't think he can catch her," Alex answered. "It looks like she's faster than he is."

"She is faster," Darlene said. "Smarter too. Cats usually are."

"Oh no, she could not be," Quicker argued. "She is only a cat. A very lucky cat."

"I don't think she's lucky, I think she's faster."

"And smarter!"

"That could not be. Dogs are better and faster than cats."

"Not always," Alex said.

"Oh, yes, always," Quicker proclaimed.

"Quicker, you're always saying always. Look at the way Duchess is fooling Duke. He isn't smart enough to catch her."

"Look at that. Duke is catching up to Duchess."

Duke got within a foot of Duchess's tail. She made a hard right turn. He tried to stay with her, then stumbled and nearly fell. He returned to Quicker's side, panting heavily and hanging his head. Duchess followed him back to the kids and rubbed against Darlene's legs, purring and smiling.

The rest of the day Duke and Duchess ignored each other as they played among the ruins until close to suppertime.

They were halfway home when Pestergas Hunter showed up. He stopped his squad car in front of them, blocking the service road they were on. The kids tried to ignore him by walking around him and into the park. Alex knew that if they could get to the lilac bushes, they could lose him with no problem.

Pestergas wasn't going to be outdone this time. He got back into his car. He chased them with it through the park. The kids gave him a good run for it by dodging around trees and bushes. They didn't give up until they were too tired to run any farther.

"Now I have you little heathens," Pestergas roared, "for fleeing the scene of a crime, as well as the crime itself. You are all under arrest."

"What crime did we commit this time?" Alex asked, so angry about being caught he really didn't care.

"You use the wrong tone of voice, Boy," Pestergas snarled. "I don't like you."

"I don't like you either," Alex answered.

"You just committed another offense, in addition to walking your animals without a leash and fleeing the scene of a crime. Insulting a police officer is against the law."

"Is there anything that isn't?"

"That is all I'm going to take from you," Pestergas yelled, reaching for Alex. "Now get in the car."

Alex was holding Duchess, and as Pestergas's hand touched his arm, she pushed the claws of both front paws deep into the cop's hand, then bit the end of his thumb to the bone. He screamed, Quicker, Darlene and Duke took off, and Alex and Duchess ran in the other direction.

Pestergas continued to scream for a while, then got into his car and drove away. He headed for the local hospital, sure he was about to die of rabies or something equally deadly.

Chapter 10

In the constantly hot summer, the threat of polio continued and grew ever more prevalent. More and more it confined kids to their own neighborhoods. In Alex's house there was even more worry as the time for Dad to leave for Korea grew closer. Then they got a short break in the weather.

A thunderstorm woke Alex. The sun was up, but it was dark as night, except when lightening flashed across the sky. A harsh wind slammed huge drops of rain against the house, and a welcome chill filled it. He curled up under the covers, wishing he could stay there all day.

Although the storm abated early in the morning, the rain continued, and was still falling when Alex got up.

Caroline was outside, building dams along the curb in front of the house with one of her many friends, using sand, dead worms, and other debris.

They'd completed several of them, with a small lake behind each one, when Ralph Bradley rode by on his bike. It was the first time he was seen since the incident with Alex. He knew Caroline, and when he saw what she was doing, he turned around and rode his bike over her dams, smashing them. Caroline screamed as he rode through.

Alex and Lester heard her and ran outside. Ralph turned around to finish destroying Caroline's creations. Caroline grabbed a stick, washed down the street by the rain, and poked it into the front spokes of his bike as he went by her. The bicycle stopped instantly, but Ralph kept on going. He flew over the handlebars and landed face down in the muddy water along the curb.

Alex and Lester jumped him as he started to get up. Lester hit him in the face and Alex worked on his stomach. As soon as it was obvious that Lester could handle him, Alex got up and walked over to Ralph's bike. He kicked the spokes out, doing the same thing Ralph did to his bike. The only difference was, Alex destroyed both wheels on Ralph's bike.

"Don't you dare ever touch one of us again," Lester warned as he let the bully up. "If you try, we'll beat you up worse than this time. If you ever hurt my sister again, I'm gonna beat you up so bad you'll be really lucky if you don't die."

A badly shaken Ralph, with tears in his eyes, limped away without a word, half carrying and half dragging his mangled bicycle.

"We got him," Alex said, "just like I said we could."

"I bet he comes back though," Lester worried. "He'll be bringing a bunch of his mean friends with him if he does, and they'll probably beat the hell out of us. That don't matter none though, 'cause I'm glad we got him."

"Maybe he'll come back, and maybe they'll beat us up. If they do, we'll get him again, and really hurt him next time. We can't quit now. We aren't gonna quit! Not until he gets tired of us hurting him, and he quits this crap."

"I wonder, Alex, if he's ever gonna quit."

"Oh, he'll quit. We might have to break both his arms and his legs and maybe his neck, but he'll quit sometime. He has to, if he doesn't want to get hurt really bad."

"I don't really want to hurt him bad, Alex. I just want him to stop fighting and being mean."

"I know. Getting hurt is no fun."

"Yeah, no matter what kind of hurt it is."

Chapter 11

Alex found his mother in the kitchen crying. "What's wrong, Mom?!" he asked. "Is Dad going to Korea now?"

"No, and it's nothing for you to worry about right now," she answered, "so go outside and enjoy yourself while you can."

"Mom, I know something is wrong. You don't ever cry when there isn't. Why won't you tell me?"

"Please, Alex," Mom said again, her tears now making small rivers on her cheeks, "go outside."

"But, Mom...."

"Alex, please go out now. We'll talk about it later."

He knew from the tone of her voice that she wasn't going to tell him anything, so he went outside and looked for Lester. He found him sitting in their hideout in the Lilac bushes, across the alley behind their house.

"Mom's crying, Lester," Alex told him, "and she won't tell me why. Do you know why?"

"Caroline's sick."

"Mom doesn't cry just because we get sick."

"I heard Mom on the phone. She told Grandma that Caroline's got Polio. A lot of kids have been getting it, you know."

"Do you think Caroline is going to die, like some of the kids already did? Is that why Mom's crying?"

"She's crying 'cause Polio is a real bad disease. Even if it doesn't kill you, it can cripple you so you can't walk. Sometimes it cripples you so bad you can't even breath without a machine to help you do it."

"That means Caroline could die, doesn't it? You know, I like having a brother much better than having a sister, but I sure don't want Caroline to die."

"She ain't for sure gonna die, Alex. Mom told Grandma it might be a light case, whatever that means."

"If her Polio is like everything else around here, I bet she's going to die."

"No! I don't think she's gonna, Alex!"

"Why not? Didn't it kill some of the other kids around here that got it?"

"Sure it did, but not all of them, and none of them other kids were Caroline. You ought to know that Mom won't let Polio kill Caroline."

"Maybe she won't die then. Mom's kind of tough."

"You doggone right she is, Alex."

Alex continued to worry anyway. His concern grew when his mother was still crying after the doctor came and went, but it wasn't until the ambulance came that he got really scared. It took Mom and Caroline away and that meant Caroline was for sure very sick.

His grandma come over to help right after Mom left. Even outside, sitting on top of the shack he and Lester built with Dad's help, years before, he could smell the pies and biscuits she was baking. But he was afraid now that Mom might not come back either. What would they do if she got Polio. Without her, life would be impossible. How would he and Lester manage if Mom and Caroline died, and Dad went to Korea? The thought was terrifying.

He didn't think he'd mind so much getting sick. Even if it was Polio. At least when he was sick no one yelled at him. No matter what he did. He just didn't want to die. Being crippled would be even worse, he was sure. How could he ride his bike or climb trees if his legs didn't work? That wouldn't be any fun at all. If he got Polio without Mom there, he was sure everything bad that could happen to him, would happen.

So it was a huge relief when Mom came home, late the same day. She was still upset, and only told him that he and Lester had to stay in their yard until Caroline came home from the hospital.

"How come, Mom?" Alex asked.

"Because we're quarantined."

"What's that?"

"It means you've got to stay in the yard. Caroline's very sick, so no one wants you to play with any of the kids around here. They're scared you might make them sick too. People are afraid of families with Polio."

"I don't feel sick, Mom."

"I know, Alex. You need to stay in the yard anyway."

"Who said I do?"

"The doctors and the police."

"I hate those doctors. And why would the police say such a dumb thing? I thought the police were supposed to be nice. Except Hunter!"

"They are nice, most of them anyway. You still have to stay in the yard. Mr. Hunter will be the policeman who'll be watching you, to make sure you do. They've put him in charge of enforcing the quarantines. Now go outside and find Lester and tell him to come home."

"Okay, I'll find him, but I hate this, and I hate the police. Especially Hunter. They're really mean, making him the one that's going to watch us."

"They're not just mean, putting him in charge. They're insane. But after all, this is Robbinsdale. Now go outside and find Lester."

Alex left the house to find Lester, who was in the Lilac bushes again, eating apples.

"Where'd you get the apples, Lester?" Alex asked when he found him.

"I swiped them."

"Can I have one?"

"Yeah, only one though. I've only got about ten left."

"Thanks. Mom says you got to come home now. We've got to stay in the yard until Caroline comes home from the hospital. Or else Hunter is going to arrest us."

"I bet we don't really need to. I bet you're telling me a lie 'cause I got more apples than you."

"No, I'm not telling you a lie. If we don't go home now, someone's gonna call the police so Hunter can take us to jail, so I'm gonna go home."

Lester reluctantly left his apples and followed Alex home. He didn't really believe he'd have to stay in the yard, so he went inside the house to check Alex's story with Mom. He kicked the back porch when he came back out, then picked up a rock and threw it at the garage.

"Those stupid police," he complained, "ain't nothing but a bunch of idiots."

"Mom told you, didn't she, that we've got to stay in the yard."

"Yes, she told me, and it isn't fair either. The police are mean, and Hunter is the worst."

"You're right, Lester. He's the worst. What should we do now?"

"There's nothing to do in the yard."

"We could play in the shack. We've had lots of fun in there sometimes."

"Yeah," Lester said, smiling. "Like that time, we were in there with Stacey Larson."

"Don't you remember, Lester. You wouldn't let me come in there that time."

"Oh, yeah, that's right. I wish she wouldn't moved away."

"Okay, but you've got to tell me why it was so much fun in there with Stacy Larson."

"I ain't never gonna tell you that, Alex. You might tell Mom."

"Oh, heck. I sure wish I'd get to do secret stuff like you always do."

"You will, Alex. Maybe we can get Darlene to come over and go in the shack with us? She just lives across the street. I bet she could sneak over here."

"Oh, no, we won't do that. Darlene's my friend, and you better be nice to her, and never do any secret crap with her either."

"Okay, Alex, I won't. But it sure was fun with Stacey Larson."

"I don't care. We're never doing anything like that with Darlene."

They walked around to the front of the house and sat on the front steps. Pestergas Hunter drove by and parked across the street, watching them.

He didn't get out of the car, and with nothing else to do, the boys took the time to make faces and some really good gestures at him. His face turned bright red, and they could see that he was talking to himself, but he stayed where he was. It was good to know the man was a coward.

Chapter 12

Pestergas Hunter's police car slid to a stop at the side of the road, with its front bumper hung on the curb. He got out, slamming the car door to illustrate his power, and walked over to Quick Chase.

"Now!" Pestergas said, waving his stubby little finger close to Quicker's nose, "I want you to tell me, Young Man," he tried to sound tough, but his voice tended to squeak, "what it is that you think you're doing with that dog and cat?"

"If I may be so bold as to ask, Sir," Quicker said, struggling to keep a serious expression on his face, "will you kindly point out to me which dog and which cat it is that you are referring to?"

"That dog and that cat," Pestergas sputtered, jabbing his finger in the general direction of Duke and Duchess, who were barely past the puppy and kitten stage.

"Oh....that puppy and that kitten. And here I thought you were referring to my dog and my cat."

"You're going to have to tell me, Mister, how I could be referring to any other dog or cat. There are no other dogs or cats anywhere around here."

"Please excuse me, Sir, for saying this, for I beg to differ with you. My dog and my cat are right here, behind me." Quicker turned and pointed, allowing himself a quick smile while he had his back to Pestergas.

"Listen here, you can bring yourself a lot of trouble by smart-mouthing me."

"I fail to understand what you are saying, Sir."

"Listen you brat, I've had about all I'm going to take from you. I ought to rap you upside the head."

"Excuse me, Sir. It is wrong to call a man of honor a brat. It is even more wrong to threaten to hit him upside the head. When you do so, you put flannel shirts on everything I am fighting for in this war."

"War?! What war? Are you kids having gang fights? I don't allow gang fights in my town."

"Gang fights? You dishonor me. And worse than that, you dishonor Washington's army. Here we are, fighting a very tragic, though required, revolution, and you insult us. In the future do not insult me, General Washington's brave and most trusted aid, with such talk. Not when we have so very recently got the British on the run."

"What're you saying? Is that the name of the gang? The British? Where'd they get a name like that?"

"Gang? Who is speaking of gangs. Where did you get that uniform? Perhaps it should be red. Perhaps you are one of the many dirty, traitorous and treacherous, redcoat spies."

"So, the kids in the other gang wear red jackets, huh? I sure am glad you decided to cooperate with me. Now I can arrest every kid in town who's wearing a red jacket. I can see, from this new information, that I'm going to be very busy for a while. Do all the kids in your gang wear the same outfit you've got on?"

"Sir, the men of the revolutionary army supply all of their own uniforms. While they are all similar, each one is unique."

"It won't be hard to find them anyway. I'll just arrest every kid in town with a hat like yours. They'll be easy to spot, with those big feathers on them."

"Very few in Washington's army are given the honor of wearing a hat such as mine. Only those few of us who are leading this revolution are given the privilege of wearing one."

"Revolution huh? It sounds real commie to me. So does all your talk about redcoats. What are you revolting against? The school, I'd guess. So what're your plans with it? You gonna burn it down or what? I'll be warning the school officials about your plans as soon as I finish arresting you, and have you safely locked up."

"I do not understand, Sir. Do you actually intend to arrest me?"

"I most certainly do."

"For what crime, may I ask?"

"To start with, it was because you were out here with your dog and cat, and because neither of them are on a leash. Also, I don't see a license on either one of them. Now I can surely see that you're guilty of far more serious crimes. Being involved in the Communist conspiracy is the single worst crime anyone in America can commit nowadays. You're obviously a part of it. Hurry up and get in the car. I've got a lot of people to warn about this. It's got to be stopped before it gets too far out of hand. Freedom is going to be preserved if I have to put every damn kid in this town in jail."

"I do not believe, Sir," Quicker said, frowning at Pestergas as he realized the joke had gone too far, "that I am going to allow you to arrest me. I have not done one thing wrong. I am a good soldier."

"That's it, Kiddo. Now I've got you for resisting arrest. I've taken all I'm going to take from you, and when I get done with you, you're going to be an old man before they let you out of prison. Get a hold of your dog and cat. Then get yourself and them into my car. And hurry it up! You don't want to make me angry. You won't like me when I get angry."

"No, I will not do what you ask."

"Don't be giving me any of that, you commie brat. Get over here!"

Quicker backed away from Pestergas, drawing his wooden sword as he did. Pestergas reached for his gun, certain he needed to protect himself. Quicker moved in on him, exactly as he'd imagined himself doing to evil men for years. With one lightening stroke, he whacked the gun with his sword, sending it flying into a distant weed patch.

Pestergas stood there, dumbfounded, unable to decide whether he should go after Quicker or his gun. He made his decision when Quicker raised his wooden sword and snarled at him. He dove into the weed patch after his gun, knowing it was the safest move to make when he was up against a dangerous weapon.

Before Pestergas could come up with his gun, Quicker scooped up Duchess with one hand, called Duke, and left him trying to get his gun out of the weeds.

Quicker had played enough games, stole enough apples, and rang enough doorbells, to be an expert at using alleys, back yards, and bushes for escape. By the time Pestergas removed enough weeds from his face to see, Quicker was nowhere to be found.

Stealthily, Quicker made his way through the neighborhood, working his way toward Alex's house. He met Darlene in the alley, coming out of the kids secret place in the lilac bushes.

"Hi, Quicker," she said, then noticed the look on his face. "What's wrong? You look scared."

"Oh," he said slowly, clearly, and carefully, "it is nothing serious really. Someone tried to kidnap me."

"What?!"

"Yes, it did happen. The man said he was a Communist. He wanted me to take him to the school, so he could blow it up. I hit him with my sword and knocked the gun out of his hand, then ran for my life. I lost him in the alley. I am sure he is still looking for me."

"Oh my God!" she said, "we better do something about it. They're always talking on television about the dangers of communism. I guess they know what they're talking about."

"No, I don't think we should. I think I'll go home."

"At least tell your mom what happened."

"She's not home, I'm afraid."

"You can't go home alone, Quicker. He might go after you. My mom isn't home either, so let's go over to Alex's. His mom will know what to do. She's smart."

"We might get Polio there."

"Don't be silly. If we're gonna get it, we'll get it anyway."

"Well, okay."

Darlene carefully led the way to Alex's house. She knocked hard on the back door until Alex's mom answered it.

"I brought Duchess home," Quicker said, handing the cat to her.

"Well, thank you, Quicker," she said, "but you kids shouldn't come over here when we're quarantined." Then noticed the look on his face. "What's wrong? You look scared."

"It's horrible," Darlene answered breathlessly, "Someone tried to kidnap Quicker."

"What?!"

"They really did. The man said he was a Communist. He wanted Quicker to take him to the school, so he could blow it up. Quicker only got away by hitting him with his sword to knock the gun out of his hand, then ran for his life. The communist is probably still looking for him. No one's home at our houses, so we came here."

"Oh my God! I'm calling the police."

"That is okay, you definitely do not need to do that," Quicker said. "Can we just stay here for a while?"

"Yes, I think you'd better come in. You kids are lucky I'm not at the hospital today. If Alex's father hadn't taken the day off to go see Caroline, I'd have been there. God knows what would have happened then."

Quicker and Darlene went in, and while Alex's mom called the police, Darlene told Alex about the near kidnapping. Mom was white and shaking when she hung up the phone.

"Quicker," she said, "you're definitely staying here, inside the house, until your mother gets home. Darlene, your mother just drove in the driveway at your house, so you run home now. I'll watch to be sure you get there safely. Alex, you don't go outside again until this is all over. The police have already gotten reports of a Communist gang roaming around, and planning to attack the school. They're afraid it won't stop with that. They said a police officer has already been attacked."

"Does this stuff you're talking about mean the communists are attacking us?"

"No, I don't think so."

"I bet they are, Mom. Pretty soon bombs are gonna be dropping all over the place. Quicker, do you think the commies are gonna be dropping atomic bombs on us?"

"I do not think so. If they do, we will drop atomic bombs on them. Our atomic bombs are bigger than theirs, and they will really get wrecked. I do not think they want to get wrecked."

"I bet they don't care about getting bombed. They're just like those Japan and German guys. They like to drop bombs on us. I bet Dad's gonna for sure be in a war again."

"Now, Alex," Mom said, "there's not going to be another war."

"That's what everyone said after the last one, but there's one in Korea right now. And you just said, Mom, that the dirty Communist rats are gonna attack the school. If the communists blow up the school, then we gotta have a war with them. We can't go around letting them blow up everything without having a war. Everyone will think we're chicken if we do. If they think we're chicken, they'll be blowing up all our stuff."

"No one is going to think we're chicken, Alex. I'm sure the police will catch the gang, whoever they are, before they do any serious damage."

"I sure hope the police do catch them, Mom. But maybe," he smiled, "they won't catch them until after the school gets blown up."

"That's terrible, Alex, to want the school blown up."

"I guess so. I sure wouldn't want anybody to get blown up, but I wouldn't care if the school did."

"You'll still have to go to school, Alex. You'll just be going somewhere else."

"Maybe the Communists will blow up all the schools. There won't be any place for me to go then."

"I don't think that will happen, so quit your dreaming."

"Ah, heck. It doesn't seem like anything good ever happens. I bet those dumb Communists can't do anything right. Can me and Quicker go outside?"

"No! Of course not. Not after what just happened."

"The Communists aren't gonna hurt us."

"No, Alex. No one is going outside until all of this is settled. So don't ask me again, unless you want to spend the rest of the day in your room."

"But you should let me go outside and try to get some of those communists."

"You're not going to go outside because I don't want you to get hurt. Now take Quicker up in your room and play checkers or something."

"Ah, heck. I don't ever get to do anything fun. I always have to go in my dumb room."

"Alex!"

"Yeah, Mom, I'm going. Come on, Quicker, let's go play checkers."

"I like checkers," Quicker said on the way to Alex's room. "My father taught me how to play. He was the Grand National Champion checker player of Rattlesnake County, Texas, when he lived there."

"I didn't know your dad ever lived in Texas, Quicker."

"He did not live there for very long."

"Did he sell insurance when he lived there?"

"Oh no. He hunted Mexican bandits for the bounty on them. He was very good at catching them too. That is part of why we are rich now."

"I didn't know you were rich. You don't look rich, and your house isn't that much bigger than ours."

"We do not tell everyone we are rich. My father wants it to be a secret."

"Why does he want it to be secret?"

"So no one can steal his money. It is why we own only one car. If we owned two cars, then everyone would know how rich we are."

"Well, I heard my mom and dad talking once, about buying another car. Mom said she'd rather spend the money on something else, even if we did have enough money for two cars."

"Well, your mother does not really need a car all the time. My mother would like to have another car, because she really needs one."

"What for, Quicker?"

"She is very busy. She needs to go to her bridge club twice every week, she goes to the beauty shop a lot, and she must go shopping almost every day."

"My mom doesn't go to any beauty shop. Why does your mom go all the time?"

"So she can be beautiful."

"Gee, Quicker, don't you think that maybe she ought to go to a different one. I don't think the one she goes to is helping her much."

"That is exactly what my father sometimes says. Shall we play checkers now? I feel like beating you."

"You ain't gonna beat me, Quicker."

"I certainly am."

"Nope, not today. Not at checkers. Lester taught me how to play, and he's really good. He even beat my dad a couple of times."

"Maybe, but today I will prove to you that I am better."

Alex beat Quicker five games in a row.

"I told you," Alex said, setting up the board again, "Lester is good."

"It is true, Alex. You are a very good checker player. I think it was probably your father who taught you how. Not Lester."

"Now you listen here, Quicker, Lest...." Alex's argument was suddenly interrupted.

The police came.

Mom let the young cop in. He had a boyish face, freckles, and a shock of blond hair hanging in his eyes. She sat him down at the kitchen table and gave him a cup of coffee. Then she brought Quicker in to talk to him.

"Was the commie kidnapper," the cop asked a somewhat nervous Quicker, "wearing a red jacket when he jumped you?"

"Yes, Sir!" Quicker answered. "He sure was. It was a very bright red one."

"And he was packing a gun?"

"He certainly was. It was a very large gun."

"Did he have a knife too?"

"Ah, ah yes, come to think of it, he certainly did."

"Was the knife he carried long, almost like a sword?"

"Ah, yes, I do believe it was. Yes, it was long, very much like a sword."

"Do you remember what the man looked like?"

"Oh sure, I remember him well. He was a real big man who looked mean. He had a long scar on his face." Quicker ran his finger down the right side of his face. "It was very much the type of scar a pirate or a burglar might have."

"What else can you remember about him?"

"Nothing that I can think of right now. I am sorry. I guess I was too scared to notice much, when he tried to take me away with his gang."

"What gang is this? This is the first time I've heard about anyone seeing his gang."

"It was the gang he had with him in his car. His car was red, and filled with mean looking guys. A lot of them had scars too. They were all wearing red jackets."

"All of them were wearing red jackets?"

"Yes, Sir, they sure were."

"That's strange. They'd have to know how easy they'd be to spot, dressed that way."

"My father told me that all of those communists are called Reds. It is because they like red, and wear it all the time. Red is the color they use for almost everything."

"Excuse me," Mom said, "for interrupting." She looked at the cop. "Can you tell me who the officer was, who was hurt earlier today?"

"Sure, it was Pestergas Hunter, Ma'am," the cop answered. "He said almost the same thing about a gang of communists as the kid here just told me."

"He said a gang of Communists, riding around in a red car and wearing red jackets, attacked him?"

"He mentioned the jackets, but he didn't say anything about the car. He was kind of confused after he escaped and came back to the station."

"How was he hurt? Was it a serious injury?"

"No, it wasn't anything serious. He had a bad bruise on his hand."

"Can you tell me exactly how it happened?"

"Well, Ma'am, I can only tell you what he told us. He said he went for his gun after he was attacked, but they got the best of him. They knocked him down and stomped on his hand. Why all the questions?"

"Oh, I have reasons. Personal reasons."

"How personal?" The cop smiled.

"I know what you're inferring," Mom said, leaving the table, "with your question and your insipid grin. If I were you, however, I'd get my small mind back on track, and be a lot more careful with my insinuations. I think you'd better consider the source of all this information you're getting about communists. There are people in your police department, you know, who are little more than idiots."

"Now, Ma'am, I don't see what you're getting so excited about. I wasn't inferring or insinuating a thing."

"Then wipe that dirty smirk off your face."

"Now, Ma'am, let's not be this way."

"Right now, Officer," Mom told him, raising her voice. "I mean right now! You're making a huge mistake, trying to make an association between me and that pig, Pestergas Hunter. I've heard of his reputation, and I'll never understand how someone as stupid and ugly as he is could acquire it. Our family was forced to deal with him, and the only thing he'll ever get from me is contempt, and regrets that we ever met him. Now get the hell out of my house!"

"Now, Ma'am, don't be acting this way. I have a lot more questions for the boy here."

"That, you idiot, is too damn bad!" Mom was yelling now. "How can you people be so stupid? Is it a requirement that you be a moron to work on the police force in Robbinsdale? My God, we're in the 1950's. You'd think that in these modern times, people would have reached some sort of maturity." She pulled him off his chair, then pushed him toward the door. "Now get out of my house, before I throw you out." She shook her head, a pained look on her face. "Communist conspiracy to blow up the school? Now I've heard just about everything."

The cop looked at her, his face full of confusion and disbelief. "I hate to have to tell you this, Ma'am, but it certainly looks like there is. This is a very dangerous time for us. Hell, for the world."

"Save your hogwash. Peddle your nonsense somewhere else. And tell that simpering fool, Pestergas Hunter, to stay out of our neighborhood and completely away from my children. We have enough real problems without putting up with his nonsense."

"Okay, Ma'am, I'll go now, but you're making a real big mistake here. The FBI knows how to deal with you commies."

"You are a total fool," Mom said, assisting the cop out the door. "Just a total damn fool."

With the young cop safely out of the house, she turned her attention to Quick Chase. "Okay, Quicker," she said in a no-nonsense way that only a mother can do, "you've got to tell me what really happened to you today."

"I already said what happened."

"No, Quicker, you did not. You told some pretty good stories, but you haven't told me what really happened."

"I did tell you."

"Come now, Quicker, let's get to the truth. Did that stupid cop try to arrest you for something?"

"No. I have never before seen the policeman who was here."

"I didn't mean the cop who was here. I mean Pestergas Hunter. He's short, chubby, and kind of ugly. Did he try to arrest you for something?"

"How did you know it was him?"

"We've dealt with him before. Haven't we, Alex?"

"Yeah," Alex said. "I don't like him at all. He's a mean, rotten rat."

"So, Quicker, please tell me exactly what happened."

Quicker told her the truth this time.

"All right, Quicker," Mom told him, "it's time for you to go home. Straight home, and take off your costume as soon as you get there. Stay in the house with the doors locked, and don't let anyone in until your mother gets home. It would probably be a good idea to stay inside for the rest of the day. From now on, stay away from Pestergas Hunter. He will do nothing except cause you trouble. That's all he ever does."

"Are you going to tell my father about this?" Quicker asked, his voice filled with fear.

"I will talk to your parents. When I explain to them what really happened, and who and what that idiot Hunter is, I'm sure they'll understand. Now leave by the back door and stay in the alley. Try not to let the police see you."

"Okay, I will do everything you told me to do. I sure wish you would not tell my father about it."

"It'll be okay, Quicker. I'll do all I can to make your parents understand."

He nodded and quickly left.

The rest of the afternoon was quiet. That evening, shortly after Alex's dad came home, a man from the FBI arrived. Dad wasn't home long enough to know what happened earlier. Alex answered the door.

"FBI," the man said, holding up his badge. "Are your parents home?"

"Oh, yeah," Alex said, suddenly afraid they'd all be put in jail because the young cop called them commies, "just a second. Hey, Mom," he yelled, "the FBI is here."

"What?" Dad asked. "Who the hell is here?"

"It's only the FBI," Mom said, her smile telling him to relax. "I've been expecting them."

"Well, damnit," Dad said, "what's going on now?"

"It's nothing serious, Dear." She smiled at him again. She invited the man from the FBI inside.

"Can I get you a cup of coffee or something?"

"No, I don't think so," the FBI man said. "I'm here on a very serious matter. I'd guess you know what it's about. People in this country who are accused of being Communist are almost always sent to jail. Thank God."

"Don't be ridiculous," Mom told him, shaking her head at his folly. "We're not Communists. My husband is a veteran of World War Two, will probably be going to Korea with his National Guard unit soon. We're very loyal Americans. This whole thing is so silly I'm having a hard time believing it."

"There is nothing ridiculous or silly about a Communist conspiracy to blow up the schools."

"That's the point," Mom laughed. "There are no communists here to blow up the schools. There is no plot. This whole thing has come out of a simpleminded cop, and the very vivid imagination of a child."

"What are you talking about? What do you mean? The report I have says this is a very serious and dangerous situation."

"I'm aware of that. Now let me tell you what really happened today, and what is really going on in our fair city of Robbinsdale."

Mom told them about the day. They listened intently at first, but in a short time she was constantly being interrupted by their laughter.

"So all this happened," the FBI man said, wiping the tears of laughter from his eyes when Mom finished the story, "because that damn fool cop wanted to arrest a dog and a cat?"

"It did."

"I guess I'll have to do something about the idiot."

"I sure wish you would," Dad said, "because if you don't, I'll have to."

"I want to get that mean skunk, Hunter, too," Alex said.

"There'll be none of that, Alex," Dad said. "You got him once, and that was enough."

"What did the kid do to him?"

"I think it would be best," Dad said, "to leave it at that."

"Sure, I understand. I guess all I need now is the name of the boy who was involved in all this today."

"I'd rather not give it to you," Mom said.

"I can surely understand why, but it'll be nearly impossible to prove what happened without his side of the story."

"Could you please try?" Mom asked. "Or at least give me the chance to talk to the boy's parents first."

"Okay, I'll wait until you talk to them, but I'll need to know who he is before this is settled."

"I guess that's fair. It's likely the boys parents will be calling you, regardless."

"That'd be the best. Good night now."

"Good night."

The next day, Quick Chase and his parents talked to the FBI and everything was straightened out. Pestergas Hunter wasn't suspended, only because it was felt he was needed for the Polio crisis.

Alex and Quicker talked about what happened the next day.

"I know one thing for sure," Quicker said during their discussions. "I am never going to be in the Revolutionary War again. I believe the next time I fight in a war, it will be in The War Between the States. Then my enemies will wear blue, instead of Red."

"I think you mean the Civil War," Alex corrected. "Your enemies in that war will be wearing gray. That was what the southerners wore."

"Oh no, Alex. I will wear gray. I will fight for the south. The true and proper name of the war is, The War Between The States. My father has often explained it to me. He has told me, correctly too, that the north was a bunch of communists, trying to take freedom away from the states."

"Quicker, it was the north who won the war."

"That is it, you see. We still have not beaten those communists."

Chapter 13

Darlene slipped around the block and met Alex in the back yard. They talked about Quicker's adventure, then Alex broke the rules by going down the alley to their secret spot with her.

"At least," she said, "Hunter won't find us here."

"He better not, or else I'm gonna get into a lot of trouble."

"He won't, and even if he does, I bet you can outrun him, Alex. He's fat and ugly and slow. He isn't cute and fast like you."

Alex blushed. "Do you really think I'm cute?" he asked. "No girl has ever told me before that I was."

"I think you're real cute. I want you to be my boyfriend. Do you want to be?"

"Sure!" Alex said, grinning widely. "I really like you."

"Good, I really like you too, and now you're my boyfriend. But you know what, Alex, I think I better go home for a while. I don't feel really good."

"Are you getting sick?"

"Naw, I'm just kind of tired. After I take a nap, I'll come back and get you."

"Okay."

She held his hand on their slow walk home.

Darlene's mother took her into the doctor shortly after she got home. She was diagnosed with Polio and went directly into the hospital from there. Three days later she was dead.

For two days after he was told Alex didn't leave his bed for anything, other than to use the bathroom. He couldn't eat anything, even though he wanted to, because everything he put in his mouth gagged him. All he could manage was to force down a little water. It was two more days before he left the house for anything except Darlene's funeral. By then he didn't care what Pestergas Hunter did to him. It was hard for him to care about anything, with the big empty hole left inside of him from the death of his beautiful friend, Darlene.

So when he went out the first time, and no one was around, he walked down the alley. He found Lester and Quicker in the secret place in the lilac bushes, eating apples.

"Alex," Lester said, glad to see his brother outside again, "do you want an apple?"

"Sure. Where'd you steal 'em?"

"Over in the next block."

"Ain't you worried about Hunter coming around? If he catches you stealing apples, you know he'll take you to jail. That guy doesn't like us much."

"He is no longer so much of a worry, Alex," Quicker explained.

"Why not? Isn't he a cop any longer? I know he shouldn't be after what he did."

"He's still a cop, but we have him figured out. He still comes down the block all the time, only he always comes at the same time. There is never more than a few minutes difference in the time he comes. So it is not difficult to avoid him. We simply steal the apples when he is not here."

That afternoon though, Quicker got careless. Pestergas caught him crossing the street. The cop arrested him for jaywalking.

Quicker was grounded for a week. Not for what he did, but because he let Pestergas catch him.

The next day their mother came outside to tell them, "Your sister is coming home today. I'm going to the hospital to get her now."

"How come she's coming home already?" Lester asked. "I thought she was going to be in the hospital for a long time?"

"Your sister is a very lucky little girl. Everything is okay. She's well now." She left to pick up Caroline at the hospital.

That afternoon most of the kids from the neighborhood came over to see if Caroline had anything wrong from having Polio. Although it was disappointing to some that she didn't, they had fun making a grand parade around the block. Caroline led it, with Lester and Quicker, who was granted a temporary reprieve from his grounding for Caroline's homecoming, close behind her. Alex stayed at the very end. He couldn't quite manage to have any fun, and soon got tired of the struggle and went home.

"What's the matter, Alex?" Mom asked when she saw his sad face.

"Nothing!" he answered.

"Are you sure?"

"Well, maybe. I wish Darlene was still in the hospital, and not dead."

Mom turned her back to cry.

Chapter 14

Quicker spent his week at home trying to figure out a way to get even with Pestergas Hunter.

"We must find a way to get Hunter," Quicker said the first time he saw Alex, Caroline, and Lester after regaining his freedom. "I was doing nothing wrong when he arrested me. I was simply crossing the street. There were no cars driving on the street. There was nothing on the street other than me. Even Hunter was not on the street when I crossed. He was waiting for me on the other side. So, you see, we must get the rat!"

"I sure am getting tired of having him chasing me," Lester complained. "Quicker's right. We gotta do something about him."

"I agree," Alex said, letting all the anger he felt toward the world show. "I hate that miserable cop being around. We can't do anything anymore. He even chases us when we play baseball."

"I don't like fatso either," Caroline said.

"Caroline," Lester told her, "you better get out of here. This ain't none of your business."

"It certainly is too. I hate that guy too. I want to help you get him. He tried to take my camera away from me."

"If you promise not to tell Mom anything, Caroline," Lester said, "then you can stay."

"I promise."

"What can we do to get him?" Quicker asked. "I tried to think of something all week. I did not get any good ideas."

"We could wreck his car again," Alex suggested.

"Naw," Lester argued, "we better not. Dad told us not to. Besides, I think we should do something worse."

"We should find his house," Caroline said, "and put a dead skunk in it."

"He stinks so bad," Alex said, "I bet he probably wouldn't even smell it."

"No matter what," Quicker complained, "we simply must do something. I am very tired of staying home all the time."

"I got an idea," Alex said.

"What is it?" Lester asked.

"It probably isn't such a good idea, Lester."

"Then why'd you say you had an idea, if it probably ain't a very good one?!"

"Please, Lester," Quicker requested, "do not yell at him. We need to get some ideas, even one as silly as the ideas Alex usually has."

"Don't you go calling me silly, Quicker. I'm not in the mood for that crap right now."

"You boys should stop fighting," Caroline told them. "How are we going to figure this out, if you continue to fight all the time? Alex can't tell us his idea when you yell at him so much. I think Alex has good ideas sometimes. Sometimes, he even has the best ideas. He was, after all, the one who thought of taking fatso cop's keys when he captured me. If Alex hadn't of done that, I bet I'd still be in jail....maybe. So I think you should listen to him and his ideas that are good, sometimes. How do you ever expect him to tell them to you if you don't ever shut up? I just don't see why you all talk so much. Why can't you ever listen...."

"Shut up, Caroline," Lester said. "We are trying to listen to Alex. It's kind of hard when you're talking all the time."

"Well, Lester, I was only trying to tell you...."

"Shut up, Caroline," Alex said.

"Oh, okay, Alex, if you want me to, I will. Don't you think that you should tell us your idea?"

"If I can still remember it."

"Oh good," Caroline said. "I really want to hear your idea. I think you get good ideas, sometimes. Are you going to tell us your idea now? I sure hope...."

"Shut up, Caroline."

"Okay, Alex."

"Tell us your idea, Alex," Lester said. "Before she opens her mouth again."

"Yes," Quicker agreed, "please do."

"Okay, here it is. I was thinking that what we can do to him, is do what he's doing to us."

"How can we do that?" Lester asked. "We can't arrest him. We can't chase him. We ain't cops, he is. So how can we do to him, what he's doing to us?"

"I don't mean all that. I mean we should watch him all the time, like he watches us."

"What'll that do?"

"I don't know for sure, except he's so dumb he might do something he isn't supposed to. If we watch him, we might catch him, and then maybe we can get him into trouble."

"You were right," Lester said. "It's not a very good idea. It's a really dumb idea."

"Alex," Caroline said, "you have good ideas sometimes. That was a real dumb idea this time."

"Can I say something?" Quicker asked.

"Sure," Lester said, "if what you got to say ain't as dumb as Alex's idea was."

"Well, Lester, I do not think Alex has a dumb idea. I believe it is a very good idea. It is a good idea because Hunter is so stupid. You do agree with that, right?"

"Yes."

"For sure."

"You bet."

"Okay, we all agree he is stupid. If he is as stupid as we are sure he is, then he will for sure do something wrong, sometime."

"Yeah, maybe," Lester argued, "but even if we catch him doing something wrong, what can we do about it? We're just kids, and nobody will believe us."

"Caroline has a camera. If we can take his picture doing something wrong, they will have to believe us."

"I get to take the picture though," Caroline said, "I don't want you guys wrecking my camera."

"We ain't gonna wreck your camera," Lester told her.

"You might, so if I don't get to take the picture, then you can't use my camera."

"You take the picture then," Lester said. "First, we gotta have one to take, and I don't see how we'll get the chance. We ain't gonna be able to watch him that much, without him catching us watching."

"I've already watched him some," Alex explained. "I followed him on my bike, one time after he came around here looking for us."

"What does he do?" Lester asked.

"Mostly, he drives to Bagette's store and buys stuff."

"What kind of stuff?"

"Pop and potato chips, candy bars, peanuts, cupcakes, and things like that."

"Is that all you ever saw him do?"

"No. Once he went over to the motel next to the highway, down past Bagette's."

"When did he go there?"

"Last Wednesday or Thursday, I think."

"What'd he do there?"

"It does not matter," Quicker said, interrupting the brothers. "Motels are not much of anything, other than a whole bunch of bedrooms. What could he possibly do wrong there?"

"I'm not sure, Quicker. What did he do in there, Alex?"

"I don't know. I waited a long time for him to come out. He never did."

"That's all you ever saw him do, Alex?"

"Yeah, that's about all. Maybe he went to the motel to eat. He bought a whole lot of stuff at Bagette's that day."

"Was it different than the junk he usually buys at Bagette's?"

"It was about the same things he always buys, he just bought a whole lot more of it. I bet he got four bags of potato chips. They were big bags too. Boy, he sure is lucky, getting to eat all that stuff."

"Maybe," Quicker suggested, "he goes to the motel to visit someone who lives there, and they help him eat all his good things."

"People don't live in motels, Dopey. They mostly go there to sleep."

"They could live there if they wanted to, Lester."

"I don't think they could, Quicker. Those rooms are too small to do much except sleep. What else could anyone do in a real small room filled up with a bed?"

"I think," Caroline said, "there is some kind of bad thing you can do there. I heard Mom and Dad talking one time, about bad people who go to those places. I remember, 'cause Mom got kind of mad when Dad laughed about it."

"What kind of bad things do people do there, Caroline?" Alex asked.

"I don't know. They was talking words they don't never say when they know we're around."

"I think Caroline's right," Lester said. "I'm pretty sure now, I know what he does there. We'll have to watch him until we know."

"I do not think he does anything bad there," Quicker said. "but maybe he steals things at Bagette's store sometimes, then goes to the motel to hide what he steals."

"Yeah, you bet, Quicker," Lester said, "maybe that's why he goes there."

"Lester," Caroline said, "sometimes you don't get very good ideas like Alex does. Alex told us a good idea. We should spy on dumb Hunter. We can follow him to the motel place and peek in the window and take his picture."

"Caroline," Lester said, "for a girl, you got a good idea."

"It's a better idea than what you've gotten," Caroline argued, "even if I am a girl."

"I think we're gonna for sure get Hunter this time," Alex said.

"I think so too," Lester agreed.

"I most certainly hope we do," Quicker said.

"Yeah, but I think we better plan how to follow him."

When they had their plans laid out, the kids went home, agreeing to meet again in the morning.

Chapter 15

Alex joined the other kids at their hideout in the lilac bushes, as they'd planned. Since they already knew the times Pestergas Hunter patrolled they set up a relay system, using their bicycles, to watch him.

Quicker followed him first, to the end of the block. Lester picked him up there, and stayed with him to Bagette's Store. Alex and Caroline followed him from there, as far as they could.

It was on the third day of spying that they followed him to the motel.

Pestergas parked in the back and went inside the motel from there. The kids tried to look in the back window, near the door he went in, but the blinds were drawn tight. The window was open though, and Alex put his ear close to the screen to listen. He heard a woman's voice.

"If you aren't the dearest little man," she said, "I don't know who is. I do so love the treats you bring me, Pestergas. They are such a delightful energy pickup after. One would think my husband would understand that. However, the idiot doesn't."

Pestergas laughed. "It's well known your husband isn't the brightest cop around, police chief or not. I, on the other hand, do appreciate the stimulus of good food, and," he laughed again, "the delights of a full figured woman."

"Oh, Pestergas..."

"Enough talk now, Woman. You alone have picked up my energy. So come here, I've got plenty to spare."

"My now, are you in a hurry today, Pestergas?"

"Can't you see that?"

She giggled.

Nothing they said made a bit of sense to Alex, so he took Caroline around to the other side of the motel, where it faced the highway. The blinds on that window were closed, only not quite as tight. He strained to see in the dark room. When his eyes adjusted to the poor light, he could make out the forms of two people on the bed.

Alex was excited until he told Caroline about it.

"Alex," she said, "you know we still can't do nothing to him. It's too dark to take pictures of them."

"Yeah, you're probably right, Caroline. I sure was hoping we were gonna get him this time. I guess we better go see what Lester wants to do."

"Okay, Alex, but don't be so sad. Lester might know what to do.... maybe."

"I sure hope he does."

Lester wasn't happy when Alex told him what they'd learned. "Dad-crap it," he complained, "I don't see why stupid Hunter couldn't of been doing something really bad in the motel. How are we gonna get him in trouble for wrestling with the police chief's wife? I wish you could've seen inside the windows better, Alex, so you guys could've taken some pictures."

"What're we gonna do, Lester?" Alex asked.

"We ain't gonna do nothing. We can't."

"I think we should keep watching him," Quicker said. "We know when he goes to the motel now, so next week we can be ready for him."

"How can we be more ready than we were today? If it's too dark in the room, we still can't take pictures of him."

"I know that very well, Lester. However, it is my opinion that we should keep watching him. We will continue to try to think up a way to get him, and maybe one of us will think of another way."

"I....maybe, might be thinking of a way," Caroline said.

"Now, Caroline," Lester told her, "we can't be wasting our time with no silly, little girl junk right now."

"Lester," Alex argued, "we haven't got any good ideas, so maybe we should see if Caroline's got one."

"Yes, I will agree to that," Quicker said.

"Okay," Lester agreed grudgingly, "Only if you don't talk too much, Caroline. It hurts my head when you talk as long as you do sometimes."

"Okay, Lester, I'll try not to. Do you guys remember when I told you about Mom and Dad, and they were talking about people doing bad stuff when they go to them motel places?"

She waited a moment, until each of them gave her an affirmative nod.

"Good. I'm not sure what the bad stuff they do is, but I remember Dad saying something about not having clothes on. You guys know our moms and dads don't let us go outside, or be in front of each other naked. Not brothers and sisters anyway."

"So what, Caroline? How can we get Hunter in trouble for that?"

"Well, I think it's okay if you get naked with the person you're a mom or dad with, but I don't think you're supposed to do it with someone who's a mom or dad with someone else."

"I know," Caroline said, talking fast so Lester wouldn't interrupt her. "Let's put a dead skunk in their room. When it stinks them out, then I can take their picture. Even if we don't get him really good that way, we can get him some."

"You know, Caroline," Lester said, "that's kind of girl silly, but not real girl silly, so it might work. To get him some, anyway."

"We gotta find a dead skunk though," Alex said.

"Maybe we should find two dead skunks," Caroline said, "so we can put one in his car too."

"How are we gonna do that?" Lester asked. "I bet he locks his car doors."

"We have a simple solution to that," Quicker said. "We still have his car keys."

"That's right," Lester agreed. "You know, maybe we can get him yet. What we gotta do now is find the dead skunks."

"That isn't gonna be hard. There's lots of them on the highway by the dump. It seems like the dump is full of skunks in the summer."

"Alex," Quicker said, "that is because the skunks go there to eat rats, and the dump is full of rats. My father told me that."

"Ah," Alex said, "your dad is always telling you silly crap."

"That's for sure," Lester agreed. "Skunks can't catch rats. They stink so much the rats can smell the skunks, before the skunks could ever get close enough to catch them."

"You guys are wrong. Everything my father says is true."

"Oh no it's not, Quicker," Caroline argued. "Not everything. I remember when you said your dad told you that you were born with your diaper on. Everybody knows babies are born naked."

"On no, they most certainly are not. My father told me, when the stork brought me, I was fully dressed. He sells insurance, is a Republican and a good Catholic, so he is always right."

"I don't care what he is," Alex said, "you didn't come from any stork, Quicker. You came from the inside of your mom's stomach. Didn't he, Lester?"

"Not Quicker," Lester said. "I think the stork, or something, probably did bring him."

"Nobody comes from the stork."

"You think about it, Alex. Quicker could have."

"See, Alex, I told you so."

"I guess you're right, Lester. Some kind of thing probably did bring him."

"You guys are being silly again," Caroline said, "so stop it. We've got to plan really good, about getting the dirty man, Hunter."

Chapter 16

The kids got bad news that night. When Dad came home from work, he told them that it had been decided. His National Guard Unit would be leaving for Korea in a little over a week. After supper, they went outside to talk about that and Pestergas Hunter.

"I guess we better not do anything now," Lester said. "Not until after Dad leaves anyway."

"Yeah," Caroline agreed, "we better not. We don't want to get into any trouble now. I think Mom's really worried already."

"She'll worry more after Dad's gone," Alex argued. "And if we get in trouble then, Dad won't be here to help us. I think we better try to get Hunter now, before Dad goes. Otherwise, we might not ever get him. When he knows Dad's gone, he'll really get mean."

"I never thought of that," Lester said. "I guess we better get him while we can."

"Yes," Caroline agreed, "we better."

They made the best plans they could, and for the next week, while they weren't watching Pestergas, they searched the highway for dead skunks. Before the week was over, they had four of them buried in paper bags in a shallow grave in a small patch of woods near the motel.

Rather than follow Pestergas the day they expected him to go to the motel, they waited in hiding for him to arrive. When he was safely inside, they went to the back window to listen. The woman was already there. Quicker put two of the skunks in the back seat of Pestergas's car. Alex and Lester took the largest skunk to the window in front. They left the fourth one in its grave, in case they needed it.

When they removed the screen and looked in, Pestergas and the woman were already undressed.

"Man oh man," Alex said as they stepped back from the window, "I've never seen a naked lady before."

"Me either. I thought they were supposed to look better'n that."

"Yeah, she is kind of bouncy, isn't she?"

"I guess we can throw the skunk in now."

"I got a better idea, Lester. Do you still have some rope in the bag on your bike?"

"Yeah, I use it when I pull the wagon to the store."

"Go get it, would you?"

"Don't you think we should hurry up and throw the skunk. They might smell it if we don't."

"Go get the rope first. It doesn't stink so bad as long as we keep it in the paper bag."

Lester went for the rope. Alex looked in the window again while he was gone.

"Boy," Alex said when Lester got back, "those two sure are doing some weird stuff. I've never seen anybody do anything like that before."

Lester looked in the window while Alex tied the rope around the skunk.

"I think, Alex," Lester said, "that you're right. They're doing some real weird stuff. Why've you got the skunk tied to the rope?"

"Now, when we throw it, we'll throw it on the bed with them. If we pull the rope slow, they'll think it's alive. It ought to scare them, and I really want to scare Hunter."

"Good idea, Alex. Do you want me to throw the skunk? I throw better'n you do."

"Sure, so long as you get it on the bed. When you pull it back, go slow. We want to scare them really good."

Lester's aim was perfect, and the dead skunk landed on Pestergas's back. He felt it land, and when it started to move, the woman saw it. They both screamed,

As the skunk moved across his back, the woman pushed Pestergas away, then ran for the motel room door, holding her nose. He was right behind her. They forgot their clothes.

Without thinking about the risk he was taking, Alex climbed through the window, closed and locked the motel room door, and went through Pestergas's pants for his car keys. He left the motel room as fast as he went in, then followed Lester to the hidden bicycles.

Pestergas and the woman quickly realized they were standing outside, stark naked. Finding the door locked, they ran for his car. Quicker had left the doors unlocked when he put the skunks inside it, so they got in without the keys.

"Oh my god," the woman screamed, "do something. I can't stand the smell in here. I think I'm going to die."

Pestergas searched for the source of the smell, and threw the dead skunks out onto the parking lot.

The sight of the two naked adults scampering around was too much for the kids to ignore, so one by one, they rode past the front of the car, smiling and waving at them. Pestergas slowly sank deep into the front seat, while the woman tried desperately to cover all her very ample curves with nothing but her two hands. Sirens were wailing in the distance.

Caroline stopped on her way by, to take the rest of the pictures on her roll of film. She managed to get several angles, including one of Pestergas hanging over the front seat, trying to reach a dead skunk.

After the kids were out of sight again, a man came out of the motel office. He and Pestergas started swearing at each other, while the woman continued to scream and try to cover up.

Three police cars arrived. The chief of police was in the lead car. He turned red when he saw the naked couple, then pulled a long wooden club out of a loop on his belt.

The kids headed for their secret spot in the bushes when Pestergas and the screaming woman were pulled out of the car by two police officers.

"We sure got him good this time," Alex was the first to say when they got there.

"We did for sure," Lester agreed. "What do you think we should do with all those pictures Caroline took? I think she got some good ones."

"Well," Quicker said, "it is against the law for the drugstore to develop pictures with naked people on them."

"That's okay," Caroline said. "I wouldn't ever want Mom to see them. It don't matter, 'cause we got old Hunter better than I ever thought we could."

"What we can do," Alex said, "is hide the roll of film in the manhole, with all of Hunter's keys. We don't have to get it developed, 'cause Hunter knows we took the pictures. I don't think he's going to bother us again anyway. I think the Police Chief was mad."

"I do not believe," Quicker said, "Hunter will be able to go back to the motel with the lady either."

"I just wish Darlene was with us today," Alex said.

They all agreed to that.

Chapter 17

Ralph Bradley came over two days before Dad was going to leave for Korea, with four friends. The smallest friend was bigger than Lester. The biggest friend towered over Alex.

"You chicken babies are gonna get it now," Ralph promised, sounding real tough with his friends along.

"Maybe," Lester said, trying to bluff Ralph, "but it's gonna take all five of you guys. Me and Alex know you ain't tough, Ralph. Even my sister could kick your butt."

"Let's get him first, Guys," Ralph sneered. "He's got a big mouth. I don't like kids what got big mouths."

"You're a chicken, Ralph," Alex sneered back at all of them, when he noticed Ralph's friends were hesitating. "We know you can't fight. All you can do is pick on little girls. Even most of them can beat you. I know I can beat you. I already did it once. I beat you so bad you ran away. I bet you're too scared to fight me now, unless you got all those friends of yours to help."

"Oh boy, are you gonna get it now, you brat."

"From who, Ralph-phee Boy? Not from you. You're too scared to fight me. You're only about twice as big as me. You're chicken, chicken, and more chicken." Alex was scared, but he knew he'd get beaten worse fighting all five of them than he would fighting only Ralph.

"I can beat you with one hand," Ralph said, making no move to fight Alex.

"The hell you can," Alex taunted, moving closer to Ralph. "I beat you when I fought you before, and you ran away on your bike crying. You ran last time you fought Lester too." Alex eased a little closer. "You had to bring your friends along, 'cause you're too chicken to fight me alone. I bet you're even afraid to fight our little sister. You'd need help to fight her too. So how could you fight me?" He moved in next to Ralph and poked him with a finger. "You can't even beat a little girl."

"Did that little kid really beat you in a fight, Ralph?" one of his friends teased.

"He can't beat nobody up," Ralph whined.

"Then let you and me fight," Alex said, pushing Ralph. "I dare you."

"You're too little to fight alone," Ralph argued, getting nervous from Alex's confidence. He and Lester were supposed to be scared and crying and beaten already. Now Ralph didn't know what to do. He was, after all, as stupid as bullies usually are. "We're going to beat the hell out of both of you," he threatened, but his voice squeaked a couple of times.

"Why don't you go ahead and fight him, Ralph?" another friend asked. "You're big enough to take on both of them."

"Ah....come on you guys, let's beat the hell out of these two and get it over with. You've seen what they done to my bike."

"See, Lester," Alex said, flipping his finger under Ralph's chin and closing his mouth, "it's like I told you. He's too scared to fight either one of us. Fatso, pig-face chicken is all he is. Maybe you ought to go in and get Caroline, so she can kick him around some. She's been wanting to fight him."

Ralph's friends were laughing at him now, and he knew he was on his own. Alex put up his fists, but Lester stepped between them.

"Sorry, Alex," he said. "I know you really want to fight him. I'm older though, so I get to fight him first. If there's anything left of him when I get done, you can beat on him some more." He turned to Ralph and smiled. "I'm going to beat you so bad, Ralph, that your friends have to carry you home. I'm going to break your face and knock all your ugly teeth out. I'm going to knock you down and stomp on your stomach until you throw up all over your face. Then I'm gonna make you eat it."

Lester stepped up to Ralph, his fists hanging loose at his sides, and stared into his eyes. Ralph backed away, scared, and totally confused now. His friends laughed even harder.

"Would you look at that," someone said, "big, tough, Ralph Bradley is afraid of a little kid. Come on, Guys, let's get out of here. Ralph gets his ass kicked, I think he's got it coming. He's never been nothing but talk anyway."

The four of them got on their bicycles and rode away. Lester continued to move in on Ralph, actually wanting to fight the bigger kid now.

Ralph panicked and lunged at Lester. Lester didn't move. He simply hit him with his right hand, burying his fist deep into Ralph's soft stomach. He doubled over and Lester hit him again, breaking his nose and sending him reeling backwards. The third blow caught him on the side of the head and he went down hard. Lester stood over him.

"Get up," he told Ralph, "or I'm gonna kick your teeth in."

Ralph wiped a hand across his face. He started crying when he saw the blood gushing from his nose.

"I ain't kidding, Ralph," Lester warned. "Either you get up and fight me, or I'm gonna kick your whole face in."

Ralph got up, but he got up running away.

"I bet," Alex said, a big grin on his face, "that he doesn't ever try to beat you up again, Lester."

Lester's grin was so big it filled his face. "I sure wish I'd fought him before. He ain't even tough."

"Naw," Alex agreed, "he ain't tough at all. He's just a big fat bully. He's afraid of both of us now. From now on, I think me and you should stick together with guys like him. Then pretty soon, no one is gonna try to beat on us."

"Sure, that's a good idea, Alex."

"Of course. That's what brothers are for."

Chapter 18

The day before Dad's National Guard unit was scheduled to leave, he came home with a big grin on his face.

"Are you that anxious to leave?" Mom asked.

"No, Honey," Dad said, "you know I don't want to go."

"Then why the big grin?"

"Because I'm not going. It's been decided that I'm too expensive with four dependents."

Mom hugged him and the kids cheered. They all felt a huge sense of relief and joy.

They were all in for another big surprise a few days later.

"The refrigerator," his dad said to his mom when he got home from work the night of the surprise, "will be delivered tomorrow."

It was a lucky thing for everyone that it was delivered in the morning, because Alex was so excited that he was sure he wouldn't be able to wait until the afternoon for it to come. Everyone around him was equally sure they couldn't stand him that long.

The delivery men brought it in the house, carefully unpacked it, and put it in place in the kitchen. They left it up to Mom and Lester to install the shelves. As Alex watched them put it together, he began to worry.

"I don't think our refrigerator is any good," he said. "It isn't going work."

"What's wrong with it?" Lester asked. "Why won't it work?"

"It won't get cold."

"Why won't it get cold, Alex?"

"It hasn't got any of that white stuff on it."

"What white stuff?!"

"That white stuff around where it makes things freeze."

"It's not supposed to have it."

"It is too, Lester. Every refrigerator I've ever seen has it. So if you can't put it on there, it isn't going to work."

"The white stuff you see on refrigerators," Mom explained, "is only frost. It gets on there from the moisture in the air. It will build up in time, and then I'll have to clean it off."

Alex was quickly bored, just watching them put the shelves in, so he went outside. He was sitting on the back steps, waiting to see if the new refrigerator was going to work, when Quicker came over.

He was wearing a wide brimmed hat, his Sunday suit, and a large pair of glasses without lenses.

"Why are you dressed like that, Quicker?" Alex asked.

"I am a school teacher today."

"Why do you want to be a school teacher?"

"I simply want to. It is fun to be a teacher."

"What's fun about it? What do you do when you're a teacher?"

"I find little kids and be mean to them."

"You can be mean to little kids without being a teacher."

"I know. It is more fun when you are a teacher. Little kids do not get so mad at you when you tell them you are a teacher. They expect you to be mean then."

"I don't want to do that."

"Why not?"

"I'm waiting to see if our refrigerator works."

"Do you have a refrigerator now?"

"Yeah."

"That's good. Do you want to be a teacher today?"

"No. I don't want to be mean to little kids either. Let's wait for the iceman and steal some ice."

"Okay."

When the iceman came, he didn't unload any ice. He just stopped by the steps and asked Alex, "Did your refrigerator come yet?"

"Yes," Alex answered, "my mom's hooking it up now."

"Okay, that's what I stopped to find out. Now I think you kids better hurry up and get your ice out of my truck, because this is the last chance you'll ever have."

"Why?"

"Your icebox was the last one on this block. I won't be coming by here any more."

It wasn't until he finished eating his ice that Alex realized what happened. "You know, Quicker," he said, "I hope that refrigerator of ours doesn't work."

"Why would you not want it to work?"

"Because, if it does we won't be able to steal ice from the iceman ever again. Doing that was more fun than any old refrigerator. I don't think I should have wished for it so much. I guess having stuff isn't as good as doing real things."

"Maybe not."

"You know what else, Quicker? If getting only one regular refrigerator wrecks this much fun, then think what them big, atomic house refrigerators are going to wreck."

"I do not think I want to, Alex. It is very much too terrifying."

"One good thing though, Quicker, my dad doesn't have to go to Korea. That's better than anything I could ever wish for. Except maybe for Darlene to still be alive."

"Yes, Alex, that is a very good thing to wish for. If you got that wish, life would not be as sad."

"You know, Quicker, I've been getting all kinds of things lately I've wished for. But the wish that matters most, can't never happen. Darlene can't be alive again. I think I will miss her, and wish she was alive, for the rest of my life."

He did.

Bud George

I am a high school dropout - expelled weeks before graduation. Married at 18 - it lasted 58 years. There are 4 children, 7 grandchildren, and 4 great-grandchildren. I worked from age 13 - truck farms, grocery stores, roadside produce markets, supermarket produce manager, security guard, computer operator, construction laborer, union carpenter, and state licensed contractor. I enquired about a GED test about 62 years after not graduating. Nope. No paper test - computer only. I am computer illiterate.

Michael Allen George

Michael is a retired carpenter with a varied working background - operated and programmed the old main frame computers, managed a 24/7 service station, managed a dairy farm, owned and operated a furniture building company, worked in various warehouses and food stores, and even picked potatoes with Mexican migrant farm workers. He was married for 55 years, had 5 children with only 3 still living, and has countless grandchildren and great-grandchildren.

David George

In my younger days I worked as a farm laborer, house painter, janitor, and carpenter's helper. I fell in love with theater and worked for many years as an actor and director. That love competed with another: foreign languages and international travel. With many stops and starts I eventually completed my Ph.D. and became a college professor. Though teaching was my true calling, I also published scholarly books and essays, as well as literary translations. In my spare time I wrote short stories, some of which appear in *Stories by Three Brothers*. Now retired, I'm working on my first novel. I've been married for 30+ years and that union produced my pride and joy, a son, whose brilliance keeps the darkness at bay.

www.ingramcontent.com/pod-product-compliance
Lightning Source LLC
Chambersburg PA
CBHW021134310726
48971CB00002B/322